Intiu

ALSO BY STEVE GANNON

STEPPING STONES

GLOW

A SONG FOR THE ASKING

KANE

ALLISON

L.A. SNIPER

KANE: BLOOD MOON

INFIDEL

Steve Gannon

A
KANE
NOVEL

Infidel

Infidel is a work of fiction. Names, characters, places, and incidents are either the product of the author's imagination or are used fictitiously. Any resemblance to actual persons, living or dead, events, or locales is entirely coincidental.

Library of Congress Cataloging-in-Publication Data
Gannon, Steve.
Infidel / Steve Gannon.
p.   cm.
ISBN: 978-0-9979152-3-5

Printed in the United States of America
10 9 8 7 6 5 4 3 2 1

For Susan—muse, kayak coach, and love of my life

And again for Dex, with a final "if only"

"Men never do evil so completely as when they do it with religious conviction."

~ Blaise Pascal

Infidel

Prologue

A rleen, did you order pizza?" Gary Welch called up the staircase.

"What, Gary?" Arleen called down from the second floor of their Bel Air mansion.

Irritated, Gary pressed the entry button, watching on the security monitor as a Wiseguy Pizza van rolled past their wrought-iron gate and started up the driveway. "I asked if you ordered pizza," he answered, thinking his wife seemed to have grown progressively more forgetful since the kids had left for college. "And if so, why? We were going to try that new Italian place in Westwood tonight, remember?"

"Of course I remember," Arleen replied, a slight frost to her tone. "Michelangelo's. I made reservations two days ago. And I *didn't* order pizza."

"Well, somebody did, and it wasn't me. Thank God you're cute, sexy, and smart, babe—because otherwise you're starting to lose it. I hope you at least remembered to get pepperoni on my half."

"Thanks for the compliment, but I didn't order pizza," Arleen insisted, her voice turning from chilly to annoyed.

"Whatever," Gary grumbled as he walked to the front door. After nineteen years of a mostly happy marriage, Gary still loved his wife as much as the day he'd married her. Nevertheless, like anyone else, Arleen occasionally could be irritable, and over the years he had found it was sometimes best to just let things go. Anyway, overlooking one of Arleen's occasional bad moods was worth it, as with the exception of their kids, Gary couldn't think of anyone else with whom he could tolerate spending two straight weeks, let alone nineteen years. With a grin, he decided to cross the kids off the list. Which just left Arleen.

By then the Wiseguy van had topped the driveway and was pulling to a stop beneath the porte-cochère fronting their estate. As Gary opened the door, he noticed a clean-cut young man climbing from the van. He was carrying a thin, flat box wrapped in an insulated covering.

"Hey, Arleen. Know how to get a college grad off your front porch?" Gary called back into the house, deciding to calm the waters. As one of the Westside's top divorce attorneys, Gary knew from years of experience that often the smallest disagreements resulted in the biggest consequences, and an argument over pizza wasn't worth it. Besides, Westwood was generally crowded on Saturday, and he hadn't felt like driving into town anyway.

"How?"

"Pay for the pizza."

"Good one," Arleen laughed. "And so true."

"Good evening, Mr. Welch," said the deliveryman as he topped the stairs to the landing.

"I think there's been a mistake," Gary said with a smile, thinking that the deliveryman really did look like a college student. Absently, he wondered how the young man had known his name. "My wife says we didn't order pizza."

"No, sir, you didn't. But there's no mistake. This weekend Wiseguy is offering complimentary pies to some of our best customers in the area. Is it just yourself and your wife at home tonight, or will we need another pizza?"

"No, it's just the two of us here, but—"

"Excellent," the young man interrupted, turning to wave at the van. "Now, please step back into the house and call your wife."

Puzzled, Gary watched as three additional men began climbing from the delivery vehicle. All three were dressed in black coveralls and had on leather gloves. One appeared to be an older, harder version of the young man at the door. The second, a tall, thin man in his late twenties or early thirties, was carrying a camera and tripod. The third man, short and powerfully built, had a roll of black cloth tucked beneath one arm and what looked like a military rifle slung over the other.

Something was wrong.

"Now, hold on a minute," Gary said, feeling the first tendrils of alarm. "I think we're going to pass on the pizza."

"Too late," said the deliveryman. "You're having pizza, whether you want it or not." Placing a hand on Gary's chest, he pushed. Hard.

Gary stumbled backward. "Hey—"

"Shut up," the deliveryman ordered, pulling an ugly-looking pistol from the back of his belt. "Call your wife."

"Which is it?" Gary demanded. "Shut up, or call my wife? Or maybe I should call the cops," he added, raising his voice in the hope Arleen would hear.

In a motion almost too fast to follow, the deliveryman backhanded Gary with the pistol, a sound suppressor attached to the muzzle opening a gash on Gary's forehead. Gary staggered, blood gushing from the wound.

"Gary, what's going on down—" Arleen froze at the top of the stairs, her eyes widening. She hesitated a split-second, then turned and ran.

By then the men in black coveralls had reached the front door. "Get her," the older one snarled, shoving his fire-plug accomplice toward the staircase.

Thinking that this couldn't be happening, not to them, not in their own home, Gary watched as the shorter man bolted up the stairs. As the one with the camera pushed past into the house, the older man strode to the kitchen and lifted a landline phone from its cradle, punched in several digits, and set the handset on the counter. Then, returning to the entry, he addressed the young deliveryman. "Cuff and bag him," he ordered. "Then move the van."

"You don't have to do this," Gary said, hating himself for the fear he heard in his voice. "We'll give you whatever you want. Just don't hurt us."

"Oh, we'll *take* whatever we want," the young deliveryman said. Keeping his pistol trained on Gary, he reached into his jacket and withdrew a double-cuff, cable-tie restraint. He secured a plastic cuff on Gary's right wrist, then roughly turned him and cuffed the other wrist, fastening Gary's hands behind him. Again reaching into his jacket, the man withdrew a cloth sack and pulled it over Gary's head. Alone in the smothering darkness,

Gary once more thought that this couldn't be happening.

The man forced Gary to his knees. "If you cooperate, you won't be hurt," he promised.

Although Gary wanted to believe him, somehow he didn't. He heard a crashing noise coming from the upper floor, like someone trying to break through a wall. With a sinking feeling, Gary wondered what was happening to Arleen. He prayed she'd had time to call the police.

Upstairs, Arleen cowered in the master bathroom, thankful that during construction she had insisted on installing heavy oak doors throughout the house, even for the bathrooms. Nevertheless, this one wasn't going to hold out much longer against the furious attack from outside. One of the raised oak panels had already cracked, and it was just a matter of time before the intruder got in. If only she had been able to reach the panic button in their bedroom.

Well, it was too late for that.

Frantically, Arleen dialed 911 on her cellphone. Her call didn't go through. Eyes filled with tears of frustration, she disconnected and tried again.

Same result.

Damn! Why isn't it working?

Abruptly, the man punched a fist through the cracked panel. Withdrawing his hand, he glared at Arleen through the hole, his eyes red and angry. Then, reaching in an arm, he groped for the door latch.

Without thinking, Arleen rushed forward. Baring her teeth, she bit down on the man's forearm. The man screamed. He tried to withdraw his arm, but Arleen bit down even harder, drawing blood as her teeth tore into flesh.

Bellowing in pain, the man ripped his arm back through the splintered panel.

Trembling, Arleen readied for another onslaught. If the intruder wanted to come through the door, she vowed she wouldn't make it easy.

Taking another approach, the man began slamming his

shoulder into the door. Seconds later, with an earsplitting crack, the doorjamb gave way. Torn from its hinges, the eight-foot slab of oak toppled into the bathroom, crashing to the tile floor inches from Arleen. The man followed close behind, his arm dripping blood, his eyes filled with rage.

With a scream, Arleen rushed at the intruder—teeth bared, knees and elbows ready, fingernails searching for his eyes.

If I can just make it past him, she thought, *maybe I can get to the stairs and escape. Please, God, please help me get past him.*

With a grunt, the man struck her in the chest with a hamlike fist.

Arleen sank to the floor, unable to breathe.

Take shallow breaths, she told herself, struggling to inhale. *Don't panic. Take shallow breaths. You can get through this . . .*

The man kicked her in the stomach. "That's for bitin' me, bitch," he growled.

Arleen's world became a crucible of pain. Her ribs were on fire. The man kicked her again. Retching, Arleen sensed her vision dimming. She couldn't breathe. Her consciousness fading, she felt the man kick her again, his boot tearing into her side.

For the first time in her life, Arleen thought she was going to die.

As darkness closed in, she wondered whether this would be the end.

Chapter 1

My daughter once told me that she thought the old adage, "What doesn't kill you, makes you stronger," was wrong. She thought that some things make you weaker.

At the time, following a brutal sexual assault, Allison was experiencing an uncharacteristic lack of confidence, as well as suffering the feelings of worthlessness and despair so common to victims of violent attack. Although my wife, Catheryn, and I had found Ali the finest possible counseling and done our best to support her, only the passage of time was able to restore my daughter's belief in herself. And Allison is one of the strongest persons I know.

But did the experience make her weaker? I've had occasion to think about that lately, and I've come to the conclusion that weakening Allison isn't what happened—not exactly, anyway. I don't know the correct description for what happened to my daughter, but one thing is certain. Like so many of the heartrending events that life can bring, Allison's rape forever changed her.

A little over two months ago, in some essential way, I was changed as well. A bullet intended for me took the life of my wife, and nothing has been the same since.

Over the past months I had worked through my anger and guilt, and I'd put aside my "what ifs" and "if onlys" and "why didn't Is," and I had learned to accept all the other self-accusatory regrets that accompanied the death of my wife. Yet one fact remained: Catheryn was gone. And nothing I could do would ever bring her back.

"Deep thoughts, amigo?"

I looked up to find my ex-partner and best friend, Arnie Mercer, regarding me with a look of concern. Years back Arnie had been my training officer when I first graduated from the LAPD police academy. Six years later when I made detective and moved up to homicide, he had become my partner. Arnie and I had been through a lot together, and I knew he was worried about me.

"Deep thoughts? Maybe a few," I answered. I attempted a smile, my hand unconsciously traveling to my shoulder where the bullet that had taken Catheryn had also wounded me.

Noticing this, Arnie asked, "How's the recovery going?"

"Okay," I replied. After the shooting I had taken a six-week injury leave from the department, during which time several reconstructive surgeries and hours of physical therapy had mended my wounds, at least the ones you could see. Nevertheless, I still hadn't returned to active duty, and for the past several weeks instead of rejoining the force, I had been burning through a backlog of accumulated vacation days.

"I saw Banowski and Lieutenant Long on the way in," Arnie continued. "Banowski says everyone at the station is wondering when you're coming back, especially considering the homicides last night in Bel Air. He said they could really use you in West L.A. right now. The murders were, uh . . . particularly disturbing, from what Banowski told me. You hear about them?"

"Nope. Been busy with Ali's wedding. She's getting married today, in case you've forgotten."

"I haven't forgotten, partner," Arnie replied, feigning insult. "Why else would I be here wearing a monkey suit with a present under my arm?"

Instead of responding, I glanced around the Adamson House grounds, pleased with the wedding location that Allison and her fiancée, Mike Cortese, had chosen. The expansive, thirteen-acre site embodied a huge chunk of Malibu history, dating back to the days of the Chumash Indians. Adjacent to the Malibu Pier and the white sands of Surfrider Beach, the Adamson Estate was part of the Malibu Lagoon State Beach Park, and in my opinion, the beautiful, historic spot provided the perfect setting for Ali's wedding. Even the January weather, which could often be foggy, rainy, and cold in Southern California, seemed to be cooperating.

I'd initially had reservations about scheduling the wedding so soon after Catheryn's death. Although Allison and Mike had felt the same way, shortly after Catheryn's memorial Ali had revealed that she was pregnant with Mike's baby, and unless we wanted to wait until after the birth, there would never be a better time. And reluctantly, I had agreed.

"Wedding or not, I don't see how you could've missed *that* kinda news, a multiple homicide on the Westside," Arnie persisted. "Banowski said they could really use your help on the case."

"Yeah, you said that. I'll talk to him at the reception."

When Arnie had retired from the force, I had assumed his position as the D-III supervising detective for the West L.A homicide unit, and I knew that in my absence everyone at the West L.A. station was working overtime to take up the slack.

"So are you going back?" Arnie asked again, not letting it go.

"I'm not sure, Arnie. I still have a lot of thinking to do."

Arnie regarded me for a long moment. "It wasn't your fault, Dan."

I looked away, my gaze traveling the sunny lawns and flowered gardens of the Adamson House grounds. "I wish I could believe that."

"It's the truth. You were just doing your job."

"Yeah, my job," I said, remembering something that Catheryn had once said about my being a cop. We had been discussing my position on the force—arguing, actually—and she had pointed out that my profession was giving me a slanted view on life, contending that it was isolating me from everyone, even my family. "And for what? Do you actually think you're doing any good?" she had demanded. "Arrest one criminal, and two more spring up to take his place."

Angrily, I had replied in kind, certain that I was doing something meaningful.

Now I wasn't so certain.

"You were just doing your job," Arnie repeated.

"If I'd been working a regular job like everyone else, I wouldn't have had some psycho stalking me with a sniper rifle," I countered. "What's worse, that wasn't the first time I had put my family at risk."

"Dan, I'm onboard one hundred percent with whatever you decide to do. I'm not suggesting this, but you could apply for an early-out, take a reduced pension, and come work with me."

After retiring, Arnie had taken a position with a security firm providing policing services to various Westside malls and shopping centers. Since then he'd risen in the corporate structure, and he was now making double what he'd been taking home as a cop—not to mention drawing his LAPD pension as well. But my problem wasn't money.

"Thanks, Arnie," I said. "Actually, I'm thinking about that."

"Anytime, Dan. Just let me know."

"Thanks." I glanced at my watch. 2:15 p.m. The ceremony was scheduled to start in forty-five minutes, and guests had already begun filling the chairs that Ali's wedding coordinator had arranged in a broad, semicircular pattern across the lawn. "Catheryn would have loved this," I said, changing the subject.

"Yeah, she would have," Arnie agreed.

Just then I noticed an older man making his way in from the parking lot, shuffling slowly past one of the lush gardens. Recognizing cellist Arthur West, a former LA Philharmonic associate of Catheryn's, I decided to give him a hand. "I'll see you after the ceremony," I said to Arnie. "You're coming to the reception at the beach house?"

"Wouldn't miss it, amigo. See you there."

I caught up with Arthur West on the far side of the lawn. He was leaning on a cane, which was proving little help on the soft grass. "Let me give you a hand there, Arthur," I said. I placed an arm around the older man's shoulders, surprised at how frail he felt beneath his tuxedo jacket.

"Detective Kane," said Arthur with a brittle smile. "At this point I'd be thankful for any assistance, even from you."

I hadn't seen Arthur since Catheryn's memorial, and I was dismayed at how much he had deteriorated over the intervening months—his cancer seeming to have devoured whatever flesh still remained on his bones, leaving little more than a skeleton. Nevertheless, Arthur had always been a handsome man, and even now he still retained some of his regal bearing.

"Arthur, we haven't always been best of friends, most of which was my fault," I said, guiding him toward one of the lawn chairs in front. "But considering all we've been through, maybe you should call me Dan."

"Fine, Dan," Arthur replied as I helped him to one of the padded white chairs. "And I appreciate your help. I hate being seen in public like this, but I wouldn't have missed Allison's wedding for the world."

"You're welcome, Arthur. And I'm happy you're here," I said, realizing the effort it must have taken him to be present. I hesitated, then sat beside him. There were things I wanted to say to Arthur, and I knew from his appearance that I wouldn't have many more opportunities to do so.

Struck by something in my manner, Arthur regarded me closely. "How are you doing, Dan?"

"I've been better," I admitted.

Arthur smiled. "I know what you mean." Then, glancing around the grounds, "Catheryn would have adored this."

"Yeah. I just told someone the same thing."

"Dan, we didn't get a chance to talk much at the service," Arthur continued. "I want you to know how sorry I am for your loss."

"Thanks. And I know how close you and Catheryn were. I know her death was a terrible loss for you, too. Arthur, we've had our problems in the past, and I want to apologize for—"

"I don't think we need to go into that unfortunate misunderstanding," Arthur interrupted. "Consider the matter closed."

"No, I need to get this off my chest," I said. "For years I was jealous of the bond you and Catheryn had with your music, and when I thought you two were . . . anyway, I said and did things for which I'm ashamed. I'm sorry, Arthur. Truly sorry."

"Well, as we're clearing the air here, I suppose I have a confession of my own," said Arthur. "No offense, Detective, but I always thought that Catheryn could have done so much better than you."

I looked away. "The thought occurred to me, too. More than once."

"And actually, you weren't that far off with your suspicions,"

10

Arthur continued. "I loved Catheryn from the first time I heard her play. The truth is, if I'd been able to, I would have stolen her from you without a second thought."

Surprised by Arthur's admission, I remained silent. For years Catheryn and Arthur had been stand-mates at the LA Philharmonic—Arthur the principal cellist, Catheryn the associate cellist—and over the years I had felt progressively excluded from a pivotal part of Catheryn's life. To my shame, at one point I had even become convinced there was more to their relationship than music.

"But that didn't happen," Arthur went on. "We were close, and we shared a life together in music, but she loved you, only you. You were a lucky man, Dan. I envy you. You had someone who truly loved you."

I nodded. "Sometimes I think it was more than I deserved."

Neither of us said anything for a while. "Will you be coming to the reception at the beach?" I asked at last.

Arthur shook his head. "Unfortunately, no."

Another long silence. Finally I took Arthur's hand. "Thank you for coming," I said. I held his gaze, knowing it would probably be the last time we spoke. In his eyes, I saw that he knew it, too. I held his hand a moment longer, then released it.

"Take care of yourself, Arthur."

"You too, Dan. You, too."

As planned, Allison's wedding commenced promptly at 3:00 p.m., with a string quartet composed of Philharmonic musicians playing a Bach cantata as the processional. By then nearly everyone had arrived, and the chairs on the lawn were filled. Determined to shrug off my depression, I escorted my daughter down a flower-strewn central aisle, trailing behind a smiling young flower girl and an equally young but clearly nervous ring bearer, who were walking together in front of us, side-by-side.

Allison looked movie-star gorgeous, her five-month pregnancy barely showing, if anything making her look even more radiant. She had worn her long auburn hair up for the occasion, and she had on an antique emerald pendant of

Catheryn's. In her full-length white gown, she reminded me so much of her mother. Like Catheryn, Allison could look great without much effort. And when she wanted to, like today, she could look stunning.

Scanning the smiling faces of family and friends as Allison and I proceeded down the aisle, I felt a contradictory mix of pride and regret, recognizing so many of the people who had been pivotal in our family's life, but again wishing that Catheryn could have been present to see them.

All too soon we arrived at an elaborate wedding arch, the place where the ceremony would be performed. Mike, Ali's husband-to-be, stood waiting to the right, looking both elated and nervous as I presented him with Allison's hand. As I did, I caught his eye and gave him a nod that said everything was going to be all right.

Looking tall and handsome in his tux, my older son Travis—who had flown in from New York with his girlfriend and Ali's best friend, McKenzie Wallace—stood with Mike, along with my youngest son, Nate, and Mike's best man, cinematographer Don Sturgess. Bridesmaids McKenzie and Christy White, another close family friend, stood to the left of the matrimonial arch, grinning at Allison as we arrived. Even Nate managed a fleeting smile.

Nate, who would be turning seventeen in June, had shot up several inches in height over the past year. Now at a bit over six feet, he stood nearly as tall as Travis. If he kept growing, I thought absently, he was going to be as big as I am, and the resemblance didn't stop there. Nate was strong, street-smart, and athletically gifted, but he had a dark streak as well. His recent years of adolescence had not been easy, either for him or for the rest of our family. Fiercely loyal, quick to both laughter and anger, his moods as transparent as glass, Nate, God help him, was the most like me.

After leaving Allison at the wedding arbor, I took a front-row seat on the left side of the aisle, settling in beside my mother, Dot, and my sister, Beverly—both of whom had traveled from Texas to attend the wedding. To my right sat Catheryn's mother,

Dorothy. A tall, attractive woman in her early sixties, Dorothy had driven down the coast from her home in Santa Barbara and had been staying at our Malibu beach house to help with Ali's wedding preparations. As I took my seat, Dorothy reached across and grasped my hand, shooting me a smile. I smiled back, not for the first time realizing the source of Catheryn's good looks.

Father Donovan, our parish priest from Our Lady of Malibu Catholic Church, had agreed to perform the ceremony. Years back Father Donovan had married Catheryn and me, and over the following decade he had baptized our four children in turn. Later he had presided over a funeral for our firstborn son, Thomas. And more recently, Father Donovan had presided over a memorial for Catheryn. As such, he had a deep and enduring history with our family, and Allison had been adamant that he perform her wedding ceremony.

There had been a hitch. Because Mike wasn't baptized and couldn't in good conscience agree to be, Allison and Mike had to jump through hoops to get the Catholic Church's blessing for their union. Although a "disparity of cult" dispensation was eventually granted, the wedding ceremony couldn't include a Mass, nor could it take place in a Catholic church, a compromise that would have been a huge disappointment for Catheryn. I stayed out of things, deciding that it was Allison's day and Allison's wedding, so it was her decision to make.

As it was, the compromise actually worked out well, as our family still had painful memories associated with Our Lady of Malibu Church, having attended Catheryn's memorial service there just months earlier. At any rate, I think Catheryn eventually would have approved, and Mike and Ali preferred an outdoor venue, anyway.

Once the ceremony got underway, Father Donovan kept things rolling, and the wedding progressed quickly. There were a few changes to Mike and Allison's nontraditional ceremony, additions they had requested that included the lighting of a unity candle, symbolizing the joining of their lives, and a second departure in which Ali and Mike each poured colored sand into an ornate glass vase, again symbolizing their lives becoming one.

In a surprise inclusion that followed, Father Donovan next asked everyone who approved of Ali and Mike's marriage, family and friends alike, to stand. Then he asked everyone standing, which of course included the entire assembly, to raise a hand and vow to encourage, support, and nurture Mike and Allison's union in every way possible. From the look on my daughter's face, I could tell this wasn't something she had planned. Nevertheless, it was a powerful moment that in a true sense made everyone there an active participant in Mike and Ali's marriage, and I was unexpectedly moved by it.

Before the exchange of rings, the string quartet played again, this time performing the Borodin Nocturne. It was the same piece that Catheryn had arranged to be played at our own wedding, and during the musical interlude I let my mind drift with the music, revisiting memories I hadn't thought about in years.

Not long afterward, following the formal exchange of vows, Father Donovan concluded the ceremony by giving Mike permission to kiss the bride. Then, raising his voice to be heard over an enthusiastic round of whistles and cheers, Father Donovan readdressed the assembly, once again asking everyone to stand. Allison and Mike turned to face us. Placing a hand on each of their shoulders, Father Donovan smiled and said, "It is my great pleasure to ask you to open your hearts and welcome into our midst, now and from this day forward, Mr. and Mrs. Michael Cortese."

Lowering their heads against a showering of rose petals and confetti, Mike and Ali ran hand-in-hand down the center aisle, grinning like school kids.

As if in a dream, I stood with the others and applauded the new couple, pleased by the joy I saw on my daughter's face, yet paradoxically feeling more isolated and alone than ever.

Chapter 2

Jacob Lee Wallace had plenty of reasons to hate Muslims. Topping the list, years back Jacob's older brother, Corporal Benjamin Wallace, had been dragged behind a truck through the streets of Fallujah, dismembered, hung from an Iraqi bridge, and set afire by laughing Muslims chanting anti-American slogans. There were other reasons for Jacob to hate Muslims, almost too many to count, but he kept a mental inventory of them all, adding to it daily. Still, he resisted the temptation to surrender to that hate, for he knew that hate was unacceptable in the eyes of the Lord.

If there was one thing Jacob's minister father had taught him as a boy, it was that you must love your enemies. But Jacob also realized that loving your enemies, even Muslims, didn't mean one had to ignoring the danger their burgeoning numbers posed in our country. With a feeling of pride, Jacob realized he had been chosen as God's instrument to deal with that danger. It was a holy calling, and a calling Jacob fully embraced, certain beyond the slightest doubt that the course upon which he had embarked had always been his one true destiny.

He knew this because God had told him so.

From his airy perch on a tree-covered hillside in Trancas Canyon, concealed beneath the rocky outcrop where God had first spoken to him, Jacob gazed down upon the compound he had built for his followers. He was pleased with what he saw. In the meadow below, at the end of a dirt road accessing Pacific Coast Highway to the south, an expansive headquarters building dominated the commune's central square. The long, cruciform structure served multiple functions—as a venue for daily services, group meetings, and meals; as a fortified food and weapons locker; and as an explosives storehouse that, among its other uses, could be triggered in a cleansing apocalypse should the need ever arise.

Over the years, as the number of Jacob's followers had grown, a number of lesser outbuildings had also been constructed: sleeping dorms for single men and women, larger sleeping structures for couples, a vehicle storage and repair shop, a cookhouse, a generator shack for the community's occasional electrical needs, and a personal sleeping bungalow in which Jacob often entertained willing females from his congregation.

Over the years, Jacob's community had become increasingly self-sufficient, producing most of its own food and other necessities. Although there was no electricity, telephone, or other modern facilities available at their isolated location, those were comforts Jacob considered unnecessary. An occasional visit to the city by a trusted commune member provided what few items they lacked, and Jacob served as a conduit for whatever news he deemed appropriate for his flock.

It was a simple life. Simple, and godly.

As he watched from above, Jacob saw his younger brother, Caleb, leave the men's dorm and start toward the headquarters building. Jacob glanced at his watch. It was almost time for his afternoon service. With a smile, he rose and began making his way down the hillside. He wasn't certain yet what the subject of his sermon would be, but he knew that God would inspire him. He always did.

Moments later Jacob also noticed Rudy Boyle, his sergeant-at-arms, exiting the bunkhouse. Seeing Caleb and Rudy reminded Jacob of their holy mission the previous evening. Caleb, Rudy, and Parker Dillon—another member of their inner circle—had accompanied Jacob to the Bel Air mansion, helping to set in motion events that would eventually expel every Muslim, radical or otherwise, from American soil.

Of that, Jacob was also certain.

For again, God had told him so.

Chapter 3

It's a common misconception that most Malibu residents are either movie stars or millionaires. Or movie-star millionaires. Not that there aren't a few, but there are also plenty of ordinary, hardworking people living in Malibu—people willing to put up with coastal traffic, brushfires, mudslides, floods, and a host of nature's other challenges to reside in an area that's beautiful, close to the city, and relatively smog-free.

Catheryn's mother had grown up spending summers in Malibu at her family's getaway cottage on Las Flores Beach, a structure that at the time had been little more than a shack. Over the years her family's modest bungalow had grown, bit by bootlegged bit, and later when Catheryn and I were married, Dorothy had deeded us the property as a wedding gift. It was there that we had raised our four children, with rooms expanded, a porch walled in, and additional bedrooms tacked on to accommodate our growing family.

Several years back, on a night that had nearly cost us all our lives, our home had burned to the sand, leaving nothing but char and rubble. The value of the original structure had been a mere fraction of the beach lot upon which it sat, and it had been a longstanding family joke that if the termites had moved out and the beach cane and flowering bougainvillea anchoring our shaky structure to the sand were to disappear, our house would have collapsed. Nevertheless, we had all loved it, flaws and all.

Following the fire we had rebuilt on new piers, pilings, and timbers, and our new home was solid, better than ever. Still, it wasn't the same, and we all missed the ramshackle, Gilligan's Island-type dwelling that for so many years had been the linchpin of our lives.

Tonight, upon returning home following what had seemed an interminable round of photos at the wedding venue, I found that with the exception of a single space reserved out front for the new couple, every available parking spot on the street had been taken by partygoers arriving early. Cars lined the shoulders of

Pacific Coast Highway in both directions, and I was forced to leave my Suburban nearly a quarter mile down the beach. Then, upon walking back and descending a side stairway to our redwood deck below, I almost didn't recognize my own home.

Over the years we Kanes had thrown more than a few beach parties, generally rowdy affairs involving hundreds of people, beer kegs, luau pits, bonfires, potluck entrées—occasionally even fireworks. To my amazement, for tonight's reception Ali's wedding coordinator and her catering crew had transformed what was normally our modest, albeit well designed beach home into an elegant venue that would have fit right in on the pages of any of the matrimonial magazines that Ali had been studying for months.

Bordering the sand, white-linened tables with floating candles, table runners, and floral centerpieces ringed our deck, with paper lanterns, balloons, and strings of LED lights hung above, adding a further festive accent. It was low tide, and more tables had been set up on the sand, along with a parquet dance floor near the seawall. To the right, a clutch of bistro tables had been strategically positioned beside a bar serving wine, Champagne, and cocktails. On the left, a DJ was setting up sound equipment, with a jazz guitarist nearby adding his mellow accompaniment to the gathering. Topping things off, appetizer trays of bacon-wrapped scallops, caprese skewers, and mini-crab cakes had started making the rounds, served by smiling young men and women wearing crisp white shirts and black bowties.

Everything looked perfect.

Here and there, clusters of guests had already assembled, each group isolated from the next. Nevertheless, friends from the beach were beginning to flow throughout, their growing presence gradually cementing the entire party into a single, conglomerate mass of celebrants. Even that early, the reception was showing signs of taking on a life of its own.

Keeping the bartenders busy, Lieutenant Long, my commanding officer from the West L.A. division, my ex-partner Arnie, and my current partner, Paul Deluca, had joined Detective John Banowski and several other friends from the force, staking out their territory on the far side of the deck. Fresh drink in hand, Deluca had just stepped from the bar when he spotted me. "Hey, Dan!" he called, heading my way. "Sorry I missed the ceremony," he apologized when he arrived. "Work."

"I heard. Arnie mentioned a multiple homicide."

Deluca's smile faded. He hesitated, seeming at a loss for words. "Yeah," he said, passing a hand across a dark chin-stubble that usually made its appearance on his face by noon, no matter how closely he shaved. "Banowski and I caught the case this morning. At least it was our case at first."

"At first?"

"Snead and his Robbery-Homicide crew showed up about an hour into it, after which they took over. Then the feds thundered in quoting national security issues, and the investigation turned into a Chinese fire drill. Banowski managed to take off, but I had to stick around."

"Well, at least you made it to the party," I said. I knew from Deluca's manner that there was something he wasn't telling me. Being the sensitive person I am, I decided to take the subtle approach. "What aren't you telling me?" I demanded.

Deluca looked away, his face hardening. "I've been working homicide now for, what—twelve years? I thought I'd seen it all, but Jesus, this one . . ." He seemed about to say something more, but stopped, glancing around the party. "This isn't the place to talk about it. C'mon over and have one with the guys. What are you drinking these days—Shirley Temples or Virgin Marys?"

Although curious, I let it go. "Neither. I'm sticking to Coke. And by the way, screw you, pal," I chuckled. I briefly considered heading over to the police enclave, then decided against it. A few years back I'd quit drinking, which in law-enforcement circles naturally became a source of endless ribbing. Not that I minded; I just didn't feel like it at the moment. As for the drinking, sometimes I missed it, mostly I didn't.

"You sure?" said Deluca.

"Yeah. I'll catch up with you and the guys later."

"Okay." Deluca took a long pull on his cocktail. "By the way, is there any chance you'll be coming back to work soon?" he asked, lowering his voice. "We could use some assistance on this Bel Air thing. I mean, if you're ready."

"I don't know what I'm going to do about returning to work yet, Paul."

Deluca sighed. "I understand. Well, anyway . . . see you in a bit."

I watched as Deluca navigated his way back to the cop crowd, then continued scanning the party, making certain everything was proceeding a planned. As I did, I noted a group of Allison's associates from Channel 2 News gathered near the seawall. A few years back Ali had graduated from college with a degree in journalism, and she was now pursuing a career in broadcast news. Recently she had rocketed up the CBS Channel 2 corporate ladder, and I was proud of her. Nevertheless, my daughter's choice of profession had proved a bitter source of conflict between us. The relationship between police officers and reporters usually turned into a no-win situation for the police, and Ali and I were no exception. With mixed feelings, I also noted that the CBS bureau chief, Lauren Van Owen, was present in the group. I had some bad history with Lauren, news reporting and otherwise.

Hoping to avoid the blond, perfectly coiffed Ms. Van Owen, I drifted out onto the crowded deck, on my way skirting a group of Mike's friends from the film industry. I nodded at Mike's best man, Don Sturgess, who was engaged in conversation with Roger Zemo, an award-winning director with whom Don had shot a number of films. A talented documentary filmmaker himself, Mike had served as the second-unit director of photography on one of Zemo's recent films. Mike had subsequently been signed to work on Zemo's upcoming project, a sci-fi thriller, and he was scheduled to start as soon as he and Ali returned from their honeymoon.

As I reached the far side of the deck, I also noticed a number of LA Phil musicians coming down the stairs. In their midst was Adele Washington, one of the musicians who had played at the wedding. Adele, who had brought her children, waved and started toward me, her two young boys in tow.

"How're you doing, handsome?" Adele greeted me when she arrived, kissing me on the cheek.

"Better, now that you're here," I replied. "By the way, you're looking great." One of several black musicians in the Phil's string sections, Adele's maternity leave some years back had provided Catheryn's initial inroad to perform with the Philharmonic, and after that the two had become fast friends.

"Bet you say that to all the women," Adele replied with a grin.

"Only the gorgeous ones. Speaking of which, thanks again for playing at the ceremony. Please thank the rest of the quartet for me, too. The Borodin was lovely. Brought back memories."

Next I turned to the two youngsters standing behind Adele. Both were looking slightly awed by the surroundings. "And who are these two?" I asked. "Are you kids party crashers?"

"No, sir, Detective Kane," laughed the older one, who appeared to be about six. "We came with our mom."

"Is that you, Josh?" I said, pretending to be surprised. "You've grown so much, I hardly recognize you."

"And this is Josh's younger brother William," said Adele, gently pulling the younger boy forward. "I hope you don't mind my bringing them. Pat was unexpectedly called in to work, and we couldn't find a sitter."

"Mind? No way. What's a wedding without kids underfoot?" I bumped fists with Josh, then leaned down and offered my hand to Adele's youngest. "It's a pleasure to meet you, William."

Shyly, William took my hand.

"Now, seeing as how you two are here, could you do me a favor?" I continued. "See that big kid down by the water? Playing with the dog?" I pointed to Nate, who was a hundred yards down the beach. He had just thrown a ball for our family dog, a yellow Labrador retriever named Callie, and was watching as she clawed her way through the surf to retrieve it. Standing with Nate was McKenzie's younger sister and Nate's sometime girlfriend, Nancy. As we watched, Nancy tugged at Nate's sleeve, seeming to be trying to get him to return to the celebration. She finally gave up, yelled something, and began stomping toward us across the sand, not looking back.

"Yes, sir," said Josh. "We see him."

"Could you go tell him that his dad wants him to join us? His sister Allison will be arriving soon, and he should be here to welcome her."

"Yes, sir," said Josh. He started for the beach, his younger brother close behind.

"And try not to drown while you're out there," I called after them. "That kinda thing can ruin a party."

"No, sir, we won't," Josh laughed. "No drowning."

"Great kids," I said to Adele, watching as her children headed out onto the sand. "You and Pat must be doing something right."

"Thanks," Adele replied. "We like them, too. Mostly." Then, as she noticed Lauren Van Owen making her way toward us across the deck, Adele's smile abruptly faded. "I'm going to mingle," she said. "I'll talk to you later, Dan. And congratulations."

Lauren arrived seconds later, the eyes of every nearby male tracking her progress. "Hi," she said, taking my hand. "I hope I didn't chase away your friend."

"Actually, you probably did. I don't think Adele likes you."

"Were she and Catheryn . . ."

"Yeah. Best friends."

"So she knows.

"I would imagine," I sighed.

Lauren was silent for a long moment, then pushed on. "I didn't get a chance to talk with you after Catheryn's memorial," she said. "I'm so sorry for your loss, Dan. And I'm sorry for . . . for what happened between us. I was being selfish, and for that I apologize. The funny thing is, I think that under different circumstances, Catheryn and I might have been friends."

"I'm sorry, too," I said. "And don't go shouldering all the blame. Takes two to tango, as they say."

"Truce?" said Lauren, extending her hand.

"Truce," I agreed—not completely trusting her, but taking her hand anyway.

"Speaking of blame, please don't hold me responsible for

Ali's changing her honeymoon plans. That was her decision, not mine."

I had given Mike and Allison an all-expenses-paid vacation to Costa Rica as a wedding gift, and they were scheduled to leave the following morning. "What change in plans?"

Lauren looked flustered. "You didn't know? Sorry, I shouldn't have said anything. Ali should tell you herself."

"Damn it, Lauren—"

Just then the DJ's amplified voice boomed out over a bank of speakers ringing the dance floor. "May I have your attention, please?" he said. "Those of you on the beach, please join us on the upper deck to welcome the wedding party. They'll be arriving shortly, and you don't want to miss their entrance."

As people began drifting up from the sand, Lauren slipped away, promising that we'd talk soon. Minutes later, members of the wedding party began making their way onto the deck— groomsmen and bridesmaids, ushers, flower girl, and the ring bearer—each being presented by the DJ in turn. As both of Mike's folks had died some years back, I represented the only living parent, and I took my turn in the introduction ceremony as well. Mike and Allison appeared last, grinning at a raucous round of cheers as they were once more formally introduced as Mr. and Mrs. Michael Cortese.

After greeting a number of friends, Mike and Allison headed down to the beach. There, to a classic rendition of *At Last* by Etta James, they took their first turns as a married couple on the dance floor. They looked great together, and it was a lovely moment.

As I watched the newlyweds dance, I sensed a massive presence moving to stand beside me. Turning, I found I'd been joined by my boss, Lieutenant Nelson Long. An African-American whose ascent of LAPD ranks had been based on brains, guts, and solid police work, Lieutenant Long was one of the few members of the brass whom I trusted. I also considered him a friend.

"Congratulations, Dan," he said with a smile. "I'm happy for Ali. She has a good man there."

"Thanks, Lieutenant. I think so, too."

"I know this isn't the best time, but I need to talk with you," Long continued, seeming embarrassed. "Later, in private. Okay?"

"Tonight?"

"Yeah, tonight. Sorry. Can you make that happen?"

"Yes, sir," I said, suspecting from Long's tone that our conversation would entail consequences for the future, and that it wasn't going to be a conversation I liked.

"Good. I'll see you after dinner. And again, congratulations."

The music ended a few minutes later. Smiling, Allison crossed the dance floor toward me, Mike at her side. "Dad, I can't believe how wonderful everything is," she said when she arrived. She gave me a hug, then glanced around the party with obvious pleasure. "It's *way* better than I ever imagined. I'm absolutely stunned."

"Me, too," I said.

"Me, three," Mike joined in. "Really, Mr. Kane, thank you so much for all this."

"You're welcome, Mike. And make it Dan. We're family now."

"Which is something Mike may come to regret," Allison laughed, taking his arm. "Speaking of regret, I love this gown, but I'm ready to slip into something more comfortable." Then, giving Mike a kiss, "I'm going upstairs to change. I'll see you both in a minute."

"Hold on a sec, Ali," I said. "I just had a puzzling conversation with your boss. Lauren mentioned something about your changing the honeymoon plans?"

"Just postponing, Dad. Something important came up at work."

"What's so important that you need to postpone your honeymoon?" I asked, glancing at Mike to see where he stood on the matter. Mike looked away, not meeting my gaze.

"The murders last night in Bel Air," Allison explained. "The FBI took over the case because they think the killings are terrorist-related. Lauren says the story could go national, maybe international."

"Couldn't you and Mike just fly down to Costa Rica and have

a good time?"

"I'm not skipping *this* story," Allison replied, her eyes shining with enthusiasm. "We can take a vacation anytime. Right, Mike?"

"Right," Mike agreed, still avoiding my gaze.

"Anyway, I'm going upstairs to change. I'll be back shortly," said Allison, starting again for the house. "Mike, don't get into any trouble while I'm gone. For that, I want to be present."

"No problem," Mike laughed.

Once Allison had departed, I turned to Mike. "You okay with this?"

"The party? Absolutely. It's wonderful, more than Ali and I could have ever hoped. Thanks again, Mr. Kane . . . uh, Dan."

"I mean postponing your honeymoon."

"Oh." Again, Mike looked away. "It's important to Ali, so I'm all for it. We can go to Costa Rica later. Anyway, it means I'll be able to start work on schedule."

I knew that Mike had gone to considerable trouble to delay starting his DP work on the Zemo film, so from that standpoint, a honeymoon postponement worked out well. Nevertheless, though he tried to hide it, I could tell he was disappointed. "Putting off the trip until later could mean waiting until after the baby comes," I pointed out.

"Yeah, there is that, too," Mike sighed. "What's the old saying? 'Man plans, God laughs.'"

Accompanied by bridesmaids Christy and McKenzie, Ali eventually returned to the reception, now wearing low-heeled shoes and attire better suited for dancing. Minutes later we were all called to dinner. As people found their seats and waiters began serving, Don and McKenzie delivered humorous toasts, each imaginatively skewering the newly married couple. To the delight of everyone, their clever speeches were answered in kind by both Mike and Ali, who had also prepared for the occasion.

Unlike the round of appetizers that had accompanied cocktail hour, I don't remember much of the dinner, except that like most wedding-reception meals it involved a choice of fish or beef, along with rice and some sort of vegetable. Before dessert, the DJ announced that the microphone was now open for anyone who wanted to speak. At that, I noticed Allison's eyes turn toward me.

I had put together a few words for the occasion, and I nodded at Ali and stood. But as I took my place at the microphone, I realized that something other than the speech I'd planned was called for. As the evening had progressed, I'd noticed that many of those present were uncomfortable acknowledging Catheryn's absence, undoubtedly not knowing what to say. It had become the proverbial elephant in the room, and for the sake of Ali and Mike's celebration, it needed to be addressed.

"Good evening, everyone," I began, not certain what I was going to say, but pushing ahead nevertheless. "Those of you who didn't know my daughter Allison when she was younger might be surprised to learn that she was somewhat of a tomboy. And as that tomboy, she often voiced some serious objections to marriage. I'm happy to see those objections seem to have been forgotten."

"Me, too," Mike called from the wedding table.

I paused to let the round of laughter following Mike's comment abate, and then continued. "When Allison joined our family, Catheryn had already given birth to two boys, and until then things had gone pretty smoothly for us as parents. It's a scientific fact that boys are easier to raise. Give 'em a pack of matches to play with and they're happy."

I paused to let another round of laughter subside. "Girls, on the other hand, are a different story," I went on, glancing at Allison. "At the hospital when I first held Allison in my arms, I wasn't certain how things were going to work out. Boys I knew. Raising a girl was another matter. But as the years went by, I'm happy to report that having Ali as a daughter has proved more rewarding than I could have ever imagined. Not that there haven't been a few potholes along the way. I've probably butted heads with Ali more than with all the other kids combined, and some of that head-butting is still going on. It's no secret that Allison is competitive to a fault and as stubborn as they come. By the way, those are traits she definitely didn't inherit from me."

"Yeah, right," Lieutenant Long called from the bar, where most of the LAPD officers had retired after dinner.

"That's my boss weighing in on the subject," I laughed, raising my voice to be heard over the catcalls. "Please consider the source." Then, again turning to Allison, "Seriously, those of you who know my daughter also know that when push comes to shove, Ali is someone you can count on, no matter what. Allison, I'm proud to be your father. And despite our occasional differences, I'm proud of the strong young woman you've become."

Next, turning to Mike, "I'm also delighted that you've found as fine a man as Mike. Mike's father and I went through the police academy together, and it was a great loss when Frank Cortese was killed in the line of duty. I first met Mike at his dad's funeral. Mike was only twelve then, so he probably doesn't remember. I also met Mike's mother, Doris, at the same time, but unfortunately I never saw her again before her death. Nevertheless, I can tell you that Mike comes from a fine, upstanding family, and I'm sure both of his parents would be pleased beyond words if they could see the way their son has turned out. Bottom line, Mike is the kind of man every father wants his daughter to marry. Mike, welcome to the family."

I paused to wait out a round of applause. As I did, I let my gaze travel the deck, deciding it was time to address the elephant. "As you all may know, the Kane family recently suffered a heartbreaking loss with the death of my wife, Catheryn. Our children lost their mother, Grandma Dorothy lost her daughter, and I lost the love of my life. As I look around tonight, I see a lot of familiar faces, faces I just saw a few months ago at Catheryn's memorial, and I want to thank you all for again joining Ali and Mike and our two families to celebrate this wonderful occasion. Like you, I know that if Catheryn were here, she would have loved this . . . all of it."

By now everyone had fallen silent. I took a deep breath and pushed ahead, realizing I had gone too far to back up. "As I look out now upon so many familiar faces, I see more than a few of you who, like those of us in the Kane family, have lost a parent, a husband, a wife, a close friend, or possibly even a child. Life can be beautiful and filled with love, but it can also be unimaginably cruel as well. It's a sad fact that all of us are going to experience tragedy and loss before we exit this world. *All* of us. We are all going to be hurt, and get sick, and feel pain, and lose people we love. But that terrible truth is exactly what makes cherishing moments like this all the more important, because it is moments like this that make our lives truly worth living."

Raising a Coke I'd carried from my table, I concluded. "So with that in mind, I ask you all to lift your drinks now and join me in wishing Allison and Mike—who, by the way is a brave man to be joining the Kane clan—health, joy, long life, and children who make them as proud as they have made their own parents, especially me."

Raising my drink even higher, I said in a voice that I knew would carry to every ear in the assembly, "To Allison and Mike."

The remainder of the evening passed in a blur, hours flying by like minutes, with never enough time to talk with everyone I knew. Following dessert came a final round of toasts from Travis, McKenzie, and a media friend of Mike's. I had hoped that Nate might say a few words as well, but by then he was nowhere to be found. Afterward Allison and I took to the parquet floor, embarking on the traditional father/daughter dance. As we moved to Sinatra's silky-smooth rendition of *The Way You Look Tonight*, I again attempted to question Ali about her decision to postpone her honeymoon. She silenced me with a look that said we could talk about it later, but that her mind was made up.

At the conclusion of our dance, the DJ began playing a selection of more current music, and the dance floor quickly filled with couples who took that as a signal for general dancing to begin. Minutes later the DJ cranked up the volume, and the reception morphed into a boisterous disco celebration, with even the younger kids joining in. Between rounds of dancing came the obligatory cake-cutting, a bouquet and garter toss, and finally Ali and Mike's departure beneath a double row of sparklers held aloft by cheering friends.

By then the sun had long since set over the ocean. With the coming of dark, the lanterns and lights strung over the deck had lent the celebration a magical ambience, bathing the party in soft, multicolored hues. Nevertheless, despite the party atmosphere, following Ali and Mike's departure I again found myself revisited by the sense of isolation that had plagued me throughout the day.

"Great party, Dan."

I turned, recognizing the gravelly voice of Lieutenant Long.

"Evening, Lieutenant," I said, attempting a smile. "And yes, it is. I think Ali and Mike really enjoyed it."

"I know they did."

As Long had told me he had something to discuss, I figured that time had come. And from Long's manner, I again suspected it was going to be something I didn't want to hear. I tried to think of something to say to postpone the moment, but nothing came.

"Dan, I hate to bring this up tonight, but—"

"Whatever it is, can't it wait till tomorrow?"

"Unfortunately, no," Long sighed. "I got a call today from Captain Lincoln," he explained, referring to the West L.A. Division's commanding officer. "It seems Lincoln was contacted by Assistant Chief Owen Strickland. Strickland wants you at headquarters, first thing tomorrow."

I had met Assistant Chief Strickland on several occasions, and I knew him to be a hardheaded, by-the-book, no-nonsense administrator. I also knew from my few encounters with him that for a more complete description, one simply needed to grab a dictionary and look up "asshole." What I didn't know was why he wanted to see me.

"I'm taking some time off, Lieutenant," I said. "What's so important that Strickland can't—"

"It's not Strickland who wants to see you," Long interrupted. "It's Chief Ingram. And it's not a request."

That news caught me completely off guard. I had originally thought that Strickland planned to rake me over the coals for not returning sooner to active duty. But that didn't make sense. Raking me over the coals was Long's job, and so far he hadn't said a word. And now the chief wanted to see me? "What's going on, Lieutenant?" I asked.

Long hesitated. "You didn't hear this from me, okay?"

"Whatever. Just tell me what's going on."

Long hesitated a moment more. Then, seeming to come to a decision, "Okay, here's how it stands. You heard about the murders in Bel Air last night, right?"

I shrugged. "I haven't been following the news, and Deluca didn't want to talk about the case at the party."

Long glanced away. "I'm not surprised," he said, passing a hand across his face. "I haven't run across anything like that since the Callahan murder . . ." He paused, his thoughts seeming a thousand miles away. "Anyway, the investigation is rapidly shaping up to be a political football," he continued. "Elements of the murders indicate there's a terrorist connection. Because of that, the FBI has stepped in."

"And Ingram doesn't want to turn over control to the Bureau?"

"That's part of it, especially as an LAPD task force was already being organized. With the Bureau taking over, our guys will wind up doing most of the legwork and getting none of the credit."

"While the FBI bathes in the spotlight."

Long nodded. "Something like that. There's more. Mayor Fitzpatrick is getting in the act. He called a press conference for tomorrow morning."

"So what does this have to do with me?" I thought a moment, then continued before Long could reply. "This task force you mentioned. Who's heading it?"

Long smiled. "Anyone ever tell you that you have a mind like a steel trap?"

"It's Snead, right?"

"None other. And he wants you on his team again."

I had worked with Lieutenant William Snead on two previous task-force investigations, and I'd sworn there would never be a third. "I should have known Snead was at the bottom of this. Well, I'll go back to working for Snead right after a flock of singing parakeets flies out of my butt."

Long smiled briefly. "A flock of parakeets? Thanks for that disturbing image, Dan." Then, more seriously, "Look, I know you're still recovering from Catheryn's loss, and my heart goes out to you and your family. If things were different, I'd advise you to take all the time you need before returning to work. Or not to come back at all, if that's what you decide. I would hate to see that to happen, as you're one of the best investigators I've ever worked with. But some things are out of my control, and this situation with the chief is one of them. Bottom line, this is important."

"Not to me, it isn't."

"Just hear me out, okay?"

When I didn't respond, Long pushed ahead. "I know you're still working things out, and I knew you wouldn't want to go in. So did Captain Lincoln, and that's what he told Strickland."

"Then there's nothing more to talk about."

"Yeah, there is. I'm sorry, Dan, but here's how Strickland laid things out, without actually saying so. If you want to maintain any possibility of continuing your LAPD career, you need to be in Chief Ingram's office tomorrow morning at ten a.m."

"Well, pass along a message to Strickland from me. Tell him I said to go pound sand."

"Please, Dan. Just go in and hear what Ingram has to say."

Chapter 4

Twenty-seven miles to the west, Jacob Lee Wallace was also engaged in a troubling conversation. It also involved an issue that needed to be addressed, and Jacob knew there was nothing to be gained by postponing the discussion. "No, Rudy, let Brother Caleb speak," he said, raising a hand to signal his muscular sergeant-at-arms back to his seat.

Rudy glared at Caleb, then resumed his place on the couch beside Parker Dillon and Ethan Hess, the other two members of Jacob's inner circle.

Caleb glanced nervously at Rudy, then returned his eyes to Jacob. "I didn't intend any disrespect," he said. "I just think what we did . . . I mean, well, doesn't that make us as bad as they are?"

Jacob sat back and let his gaze travel the interior of his cabin, carefully considering his response. His sermon that afternoon regarding Muslim pedophilia and the Islamic practice of FGM, or female genital mutilation, had gone well. Caleb and his longtime girlfriend, Zoe, had been two of the first in his congregation to recognize the dangers of an expanding Muslim population, and during the service they had been liberal with their "amen" support from the front row. Nevertheless, Caleb was young and impressionable. Several times over the past week Jacob had invited Zoe to spend the night in his cabin, and he knew from their late-night discussions that Caleb was experiencing recurring doubts.

"Let me ask you something, Brother Caleb," Jacob finally replied. "You know that for an act to be sinful, intent is required."

"Yes, but—"

"For example," Jacob interrupted, "if you commit a harmless act but consider it to be evil and do it anyway, it is a sin in the eyes of our Lord. Intent is a necessary component of sin. Agreed?"

Caleb nodded.

"On the other hand," Jacob continued, "if you do something

that would normally be sinful but believe you are doing good, there is no sin. It goes both ways. Motive is a pivotal aspect, Caleb. In and of itself, what we did last night was a sinful act, but it was done for the good of every man, woman, and child living in our country. Our motive was pure, with no sinful intent. Therefore there was no sin."

"Amen," said Rudy.

Jacob glanced at Rudy, troubled that he seemed to have enjoyed the previous evening a bit too much. Jacob suspected that were it not for his presence, Rudy might have done more to their victims than simply kill them, especially the woman. If that trend were to continue, it could present a problem.

Deciding to discuss the issue with Rudy later, Jacob returned his attention to Caleb. "The expanding Muslim population within our borders must be addressed before it becomes unmanageable, and God has given us that task. Radical Muslims are our enemy, and I'm asking you to rededicate yourself to the holy cause of driving them from our borders." Turning to the others, "I'm asking you all. Will you?"

"Absolutely," said Parker. "As long as I don't have to, uh, you know . . . as long as I just operate the camera."

Jacob nodded. "If that is your wish, Brother Parker. You may continue to operate the camera, edit and post our videos, and handle the technical aspects of our operation. If that is all you want to do, that will suffice."

"Count me in for *anything* you need," said Rudy, shooting Parker a barely veiled look of contempt.

"Me, too," Ethan chimed in. "*Especially* if you can get me inside the house for the next one. I want to do more than just drive the damn backup car."

"A backup vehicle is an important safety precaution, Ethan," Jacob pointed out. "I thought you realized that."

Ethan nodded, his greasy ponytail bobbing on his shoulders. "I do. But I want to do more. A lot more."

"Thank you, Ethan. Your time will come," Jacob promised. Then, turning to his brother, "Caleb? Can I count on you as well?"

"Of course," Caleb answered, lowering his gaze. "I know we're doing God's will and it isn't a sin if our motive is pure, like you said. But about our motive, and I know it's not my place to ask, but can you explain one more time why we're . . ."

". . . killing innocents?" Jacob finished.

"It just doesn't seem right."

"It isn't, Caleb. Killing isn't right, not in and of itself. But in our case, the end *does* justify the means. We're fighting a greater evil with a lesser one, following a course that God Himself has set for us. Our actions last night and those in days to come will demonstrate what a growing Muslim presence in our cities will bring, just as it has in Brussels, Madrid, London, Paris, and others. We are demonstrating the horror that militant Islam will bring, sounding the alarm before it's too late. We are giving notice that we must close our borders to Islamists, expel all radical mullahs who preach hate in their mosques, and capture or kill every jihadist planning our destruction."

"So we're going to do it again?" asked Ethan.

"Oh, yes, Brother Ethan. We will do it again. And again. And we will continue to do so until our nation is ablaze with righteous anger. Many Muslims will consider this the beginning of their caliphate revolution, and they will join in the killing. We, too, will expand our operations, with each of you commanding a cell of your own in other cities. And in the end, we will ignite a firestorm of protest that will drive every militant Muslim, every radical mullah, and every Islamic jihadist from our homeland."

"But a lot of Muslims in our country are peace-loving citizens who don't believe in jihad," Caleb objected. "Won't they be caught in the crossfire?"

"What you say is true," Jacob admitted. "But make no mistake, we are at war with radical Islam. Regrettably, in any war there are unintended casualties."

"Besides, I don't see any of your so-called peace-loving Muslims speaking out against their radical brothers," interjected Rudy.

"That also is true," said Jacob. "Our peace-loving Muslims, as Caleb has termed them, have a responsibility to renounce the extremists in their fold. This they have not done. Muslims should cooperate with authorities to purge the jihadists who have hijacked their faith. This, also, they have not done. Last, Muslims must reject all interpretations of the Quran that promote violence. So far, *none* of these things have been done. And for that they must pay."

"I agree," said Rudy, a little too enthusiastically.

Jacob shot a sharp look at his thick-necked assistant. By necessity, the executions of the previous evening had been brutal, as they would have been had they actually been committed by Islamic terrorists. Although Jacob had taken no pleasure in the act, he again sensed that with Rudy, that had not been the case.

"So when's the next one?" asked Ethan.

"Soon," Jacob answered. Then, again addressing Caleb, "Speaking of which, in the future all operations must proceed exactly as planned, with no deviations, including the removal of cellphones or any other property from the houses."

Caleb lowered his eyes. "Yes, Jacob. I apologize. I just thought—"

"*Exactly* as planned," Jacob interrupted. "Is that understood?"

"Yes, Jacob."

Jacob nodded. "Good. Now, as I said earlier, the time will soon come to expand our operations. At present we are the only ones privy to our holy mission, and for the moment it must remain that way. Eventually, however, in order to complete the task God has given us, we will need to add new members to our inner circle. Brothers Caleb, Ethan, Parker, and Rudy, begin considering whom from our congregation you would like to recruit. But consider carefully. Anyone who is asked to join us *must* accept. There can be no exceptions. Do you all understand?"

"Yes, Jacob," said Parker.

"Absolutely," replied Rudy.

"I understand," added Ethan.

Caleb hesitated, then nodded.

"Good," said Jacob. "One final thing. God Himself has set us upon this course, and He will protect us. That is not to say there won't be difficulties. There will be. The authorities will bring every resource to bear against us, and we will need to vary our tactics to achieve our goal. I cannot predict every turn our mission will take, but we will dedicate our lives to it. And, God willing, we will succeed."

Chapter 5

Ali and Mike's reception continued long into the evening, with the final guests straggling out well past midnight. By then even Callie had retired to her dog bed in the kitchen, and most of the party cleanup had been completed. Grandma Dorothy and I were the last ones up, doing a final pickup on the beach and tidying up on the deck before calling it a night.

"Magnificent party, Dan," said Dorothy, drawing the strings on a final bag of trash. "And a gorgeous wedding. Ali and Mike couldn't have been happier."

"And I couldn't be happier for them," I agreed, attempting to turn my thoughts from the troubling conversation I'd had earlier with Lieutenant Long. "Mike's a good man."

"And Ali is a good woman. She'll make a wonderful mother."

"Yes, she will. I'm not too sure how I feel about being a grandfather, though."

"You'll get used to it," Dorothy laughed. "And you'll love it, take it from me. Speaking of my grandchildren, did you hear Trav's news?"

"Don't tell me McKenzie is pregnant," I joked. "I can't afford another wedding right now."

"That's not it, but I do like that girl. She has a lot of spunk. They're talking about renting a place together in New York."

"They are, huh? Is that Trav's news?"

"No, it's about the concert he played with the New York Philharmonic last month. The scheduled soloist was unable to perform, and Gilbert Ashley, the Philharmonic's music director, asked Travis to take his place. Mr. Ashley knows Travis from Juilliard, and he knew that Trav had Beethoven's 'Emperor' Piano Concerto in his repertoire, and when—"

"Yeah, I remember," I broke in. "When the scheduled soloist bailed at the last minute, Travis stepped in and hit a home run."

"He certainly did. Since then he's received offers to perform with several other major symphonies."

"So what's the problem?"

"The problem would involve Trav's continuing his studies at Juilliard. He might have to postpone or even drop out of his master's program to pursue a performance career. It's a wonderful opportunity, but Trav has also shown promise in composition and orchestral conducting, and he thinks those areas might be where his real passion lies."

"Can't he do both?"

"I don't know. Either way, Trav has some career choices to make."

"Not to mention moving in with McKenzie. Well, I'm sure he'll make the right decisions," I said absently, my mind returning to my conversation with Lieutenant Long.

"I noticed you speaking with your police lieutenant earlier," Dorothy continued, seeming to read my thoughts. "Did he say something to upset you?"

"Maybe," I answered, not for the first time wondering how women like Dorothy sensed things so easily.

"Was it about the murders in Bel Air?"

I nodded.

"I saw some coverage on the news. I can't imagine how anyone could do such a thing. Your lieutenant wants you to work on the case, doesn't he?"

"Sort of," I answered. "There's a task force being set up, and I think the chief wants to talk to me about joining it. The chief's lapdog, Assistant Chief Strickland, pretty much indicated that if I'm not at headquarters tomorrow morning, I can forget about resuming my position on the force."

"Can he do that?"

"It's possible. You know how things work."

"So are you going in?"

I didn't answer.

Dorothy set down the trash bag she'd been tying. "Talk to me, Dan."

Instead of responding, I stared out at the ocean. By then the moon had risen over Santa Monica, outlining the waves in glimmers and flashes of soft, silvery light. "I don't know what I'm going to do," I finally admitted. "It seems like my being a cop has caused nothing but trouble for everyone I care about. First the man who attacked us in our home, and then later, Catheryn . . ."

"Those incidents weren't your fault, Dan. You were simply doing your job."

"Right. But if I'd had a different job—"

"Don't do this to yourself," Dorothy interrupted. "Blaming yourself won't change anything."

"I know that. Don't you think I want to pick up the pieces and go back to work? Playing football and being a cop are the only two things I've ever been good at. But I won't go back to police work again at the expense of endangering my family."

"It doesn't have to be that way. What happened to Catheryn was tragic, and it devastated everyone who loved her. But that doesn't mean something like that will ever happen again. It doesn't mean life has to stop. God has a plan for us all, Dan. We just have to have faith that things will work out as they are meant to."

"I'm not too happy with God's plan right now, Dorothy."

"You've taken some hard blows, Dan, and your faith in life has been shaken. I know when you wake up in the morning, Catheryn's death is the first thing you think about. And that's okay. You will never forget Catheryn, or Tommy either. But maybe someday their loss will be the second thing you think about, and that's okay, too. In the meantime, other people are hurting, too. Nate needs you. In case you haven't noticed, the boy is struggling."

"Nate's tough. He'll be fine."

"He's not fine, and I don't see him getting any better. I'm worried about him. He has been through a lot for a sixteen-year-old, so his sadness is understandable on that level, but I'm afraid something more is going on. Maybe he could talk with someone—a counselor or a psychiatrist?"

Having more than once run up against a psychiatrist testifying in court to save some worthless client, I had little faith in the psychiatric community. "A shrink? Nate's not crazy."

"No, I'm not saying that, but—"

"Kate and I took Nate to a counselor last year when he was having trouble at school," I said, cutting her off. "It didn't do any good, and after a couple sessions Nate refused to go back."

"I don't have all the answers, Dan," Dorothy sighed. "I just know that your son needs help."

"What do you want me to do?"

Dorothy took my hand in hers. "Dan, I know you're in pain, but . . ." She hesitated. Then, seeming to come to a decision, she pushed on. "When Catheryn was growing up, there was something I used to tell her when things went wrong, really wrong . . . like when we lost her dad. Now I'm going to tell it to you. It's this: Life can be unimaginably hard, as you said in your toast. That's simply a fact. But if you aren't willing to accept life's sorrows and move through them, you're going to miss out on all the good parts, too."

"Where did you get that, a fortune cookie?" I snapped.

Tears shined Dorothy's eyes, but she didn't look away. "This hasn't been easy for me either, Dan. I loved my daughter more than anything in the world." Dorothy hesitated again, then continued. "It's going to take time, Dan, but things *will* get better. You're going to be okay."

I lowered my head, unable to meet her gaze. "I know," I mumbled.

"No, you don't," Dorothy replied. "But I do."

Chapter 6

At 9:30 a.m. the following morning, thirty minutes before my scheduled appointment with Chief Ingram, I pulled into a parking garage on West First Street, a block down from the Los Angeles Police Administration Building. Colloquially known as PAB, the ten-story, 500,000-square-foot structure of stone and glass had eventually replaced the aging Parker Center, the LAPD's headquarters for decades. Serving as a command center for the department's twenty-one far-flung patrol divisions, the new complex occupied an entire city block and was surrounded by some of the city's most iconic buildings, including Los Angeles City Hall. I knew from experience that PAB's close proximity to the city's seat of power was more than mere coincidence. In the world of modern politics, the administration of the Los Angeles Police Department through the offices of the mayor, the police commission, and the city council had assumed far-reaching implications that no elected official could afford to ignore.

Wondering what the meeting with Chief Ingram would bring, I exited the parking structure and walked to PAB's front entrance, on the way passing a civic plaza, a number of terraces, gardens, a police memorial dedicated to LAPD officers killed in the line of duty, and a large public auditorium that lay outside the building's main footprint. Absently, I realized that these design elements had been included to symbolize the department's new era of openness and connection with the city. I also knew that it would take more than modern architecture to change the department, and when I pushed through the glass doors fronting the building, things would probably be business as usual.

I wasn't disappointed. After threading past a fleet of satellite news vans setting up on the street—undoubtedly preparing for the briefing by the mayor—I entered the lobby, hung my shield on my coat, and fought my way through a snarl of reporters to a reception desk at the rear. After presenting my ID and having my name checked off a typewritten roster, I received a visitor's badge and took an elevator up to Ingram's tenth-floor office. There, as expected, I waited another half hour for the chief to see me.

During the time spent cooling my heels in the chief's reception room, I repeatedly asked myself the same question: Why was I there?

Granted, I'd been ordered to appear, but why had I agreed?

Part of it was curiosity, I suppose. I'd met Chief Ingram on several occasions, and I had found him to be intelligent, engaging, and as forthright as one could expect a high-level administrator to be. We weren't friends, though, not even close— so for Ingram to request my presence that morning was somewhat of a puzzle. Sure, I knew my old departmental enemy, William Snead, had definitely had a hand in things, but that didn't explain everything.

There had to be more.

Another part of my being there, much as I hated to admit it, was because of Assistant Chief Strickland's tacit threat. I hadn't yet decided whether I wanted to return to the department, but whatever my decision, I wanted it to be *my* choice, not someone else's. As I had told Dorothy, I wasn't certain Strickland had the power to freeze me out, but one never knew. If nothing else, Strickland could prove a powerful enemy, and I already had enough of those in the department.

After thirty-five minutes of being ignored in Ingram's outer chamber, I had just about decided to leave and let the chips fall where they may when Strickland poked his head into the room. "We're ready for you," he said, brusquely signaling me through the door with a tilt of his head.

I followed Strickland down a broad hallway, passing several small offices and a large conference area before arriving at Chief Ingram's private suite. As I entered, Ingram looked up from behind an expansive oak desk. Without speaking, Strickland moved to stand behind him. I remained in front, hands clasped behind my back.

"Kane, thanks for coming in," said Ingram, leaning across his desk to offer his hand. "Again, please accept my condolences for the loss of your wife. Catheryn's death was a terrible tragedy, and everyone here shares in your pain."

"Thank you," I replied, shaking Ingram's hand. His grip was firm and dry, and he held my gaze. His concern seemed genuine, but I had seen him use that same father-figure approach in the past, just before sticking in the knife. I also knew that Ingram hadn't asked me there to express his sympathy for Catheryn's death. Despite his friendly manner, Ingram's agenda was going to involve whatever he thought was best for the department, and everything else would be secondary.

"You're probably wondering why you're here," Ingram continued, resuming his seat.

"Yes, sir. You could say that."

Ingram glanced at Strickland. "Owen, you want to fill in Detective Kane on the situation?"

"Of course," said Strickland. "Kane, I'm certain you've heard about the Bel Air murders. That patrol area falls within the West Los Angeles Division's geographical command, correct?"

"It does," I said. "But I haven't been on active duty for some time, so—"

"Nevertheless, you do watch the news," Strickland interrupted. "So you know that Saturday's multiple homicides were among the most sadistic, brutal murders on the Westside in quite some time. What you may not know is that elements of the killings suggest a terrorist connection."

"What elements?" I asked.

"We'll get to that later. For now, all you need to know is that because of the terrorist aspect, media coverage is going through the roof."

"What does this have to do with me?"

"We'll get to that later as well," said Strickland with a scowl. "Hold your questions, Kane. Now, here's the problem. Because of the terrorism link, the FBI has claimed jurisdiction. We will be working with them under the authority of an FBI Joint Terrorism Task Force. We were already in the process of setting up our own task force, but—"

"Led by Lieutenant Snead?"

"That's *Captain* Snead," Strickland corrected, looking increasingly annoyed. "Snead was recently promoted and is now the HSS detectives commanding officer," Strickland continued, referring to the Homicide Special Section of the Robbery-Homicide Division, whose detectives routinely handled high-profile investigations.

"So Snead and his HSS detectives are grousing that their case is being preempted by the Bureau," I said, surprised to hear of Snead's promotion. A rising star in the department sometimes achieved poster-boy status, and for some reason, Snead fit the bill. "If I don't miss my guess, Snead's task force will wind up doing most of the legwork, with the Bureau taking most of the glory," I added.

"There's more to it than that," Ingram broke in. "And there may not be that much glory to go around. This thing is already shaping up to be the kind of political quagmire that ends careers."

"Making matters worse, we now have other bureaus requesting a presence on the case," Strickland added. "The Department of Homeland Security and our own LAPD Counter-Terrorism and Special Operations Bureau, to name a few. By the way, neither of those organizations has a qualified homicide investigator on its staff."

"So CTSOB and Homeland Security both want in, but they can't bring much to the party?"

Strickland nodded. "Unfortunately. And there's more. We have a backlash developing against our Los Angeles Muslim population, with signs that it may spread to other cities as well. Mayor Fitzpatrick is holding a press conference downstairs at eleven. He'll try to get ahead of the curve on this, but as soon as politicians get involved, not to mention our friends in the media, things usually go to hell."

I nodded, deciding that Strickland and I at least agreed on something.

"You see the problem," said Ingram.

"Too many cooks."

"Right," said Ingram. "I want this case closed, and I want it closed quickly, before the whole thing heads south. Despite the

Bureau's taking the lead, we all know that if this is to end well, LAPD will have to do most of the work. It's no secret that the FBI is best suited for handling bank robberies, organized crime, and the like. They have little experience running an actual homicide investigation, which—despite the terrorist connection—is what this case is. Based on his successful leadership of two previous murder task-force investigations, I have appointed Captain Snead to head up this mission."

I groaned, beginning to see where we were heading.

Strickland shot me a look of warning.

"I promised Snead that he would have anything he required to get the job done," Ingram continued, still holding my gaze. "For one, he wants you."

"Not a snowball's chance in hell," I said.

"Damn it, Kane!" said Strickland. "If you ever want to resume—"

"I don't respond to threats, Owen," I said, beginning to lose my temper.

"That's Assistant Chief Strickland to you," Strickland snapped.

"Fine, *Assistant Chief* Strickland. In words even you can understand, under no circumstances will I ever again work for Snead."

Strickland's face darkened. "Kane, you are one insolent son of a bitch. Another word out of you and I'll have your badge."

"Hold on, Owen," Ingram intervened. "Why don't you give us a minute? I want a word with Kane."

"Yes, sir," said Strickland. He headed for the door, still fuming. "But I swear to God, Kane," he added, looking back. "Keep it up and you *will* regret—"

"Just give us a minute, Owen," said Ingram.

After Strickland had closed the door behind him, Ingram rocked back in his chair and regarded me for a long moment. "Dan, I know these past months have been hard on you," he said. "I can't imagine what you must have felt losing your wife like that, and I meant it when I said that everyone here shares your pain."

"Yes, sir."

"I also know you've been taking some time off to deal with things, and your absence is understandable. Under normal circumstances, I would agree that you deserve all the time you need. But these aren't normal circumstances. I'm going to say a few things that I want to stay between us. Agreed?"

I nodded.

"Good," said Ingram, rising to his feet. "Let's step outside."

I followed Ingram through a sliding glass door, stepping out to a large, triangular terrace with an elevated view of the city. When we reached a railing overlooking West First Street and City Hall beyond, Ingram turned to me and asked, "What do you know about the Bel Air case?"

I shrugged. "Not much," I answered, leaning on the railing and staring out over the city. "I do know that the killings were particularly brutal, and on the drive in here this morning I heard on the radio that there was a video posted of the murders."

"Brutal doesn't cover it. Whoever did this is attempting to create as much public outrage as possible, and they are succeeding. The media is already claiming that the police aren't doing enough to protect our citizens, no one is safe in their own homes, and so on."

"Screw the media."

"Unfortunately, that's not an option. And if we don't put a lid on this quickly, it's going to get worse."

"No argument there."

"Now, I know you have some history with Snead," Ingram continued. "To be honest, I don't like the man much myself. I suspect that he's an incompetent ass, but there's more involved here than my personal preferences. The mayor, the police commission, the city council, and every other elected official in Los Angeles are weighing in on the case, and I have to cover myself. Simply put, my hands are tied regarding leadership of the HSS task force."

"That may be—"

Ingram raised a hand to silence me. "I did some research on you, Dan. Among others, I spoke with your detectives' commander, Lieutenant Long. He speaks extremely well of you. In fact, Long says you are one of the few detectives he's ever worked with who is capable of actually detecting anything. Bottom line, you get things done. In the process, you also piss off a lot of people, including Captain Snead. I suppose you can now add Assistant Chief Strickland to the list."

When I didn't respond, Ingram went on. "I also know that Snead's success on his previous task-force investigations were due in large part to your efforts, which is undoubtedly why he requested your presence on this one."

"Not going to happen," I said.

"I know that."

Surprised by this admission, I hesitated, suspecting that we were finally getting to Ingram's real agenda.

"So I'm going to suggest a compromise," said Ingram. "As I noted earlier, the FBI is claiming precedence on the investigation. Nonetheless, even though LAPD will be taking a back seat, we intend to maintain as much autonomy on the case as possible. But in addition to our own investigative efforts, we're going to be tasked with doing a lot of legwork for the Bureau, which pisses off plenty of people at PAB, including me. So here's what I want. I want to know what's going on at FBI headquarters at all times. I need an inside connection, someone who knows how things work, and I want that someone to be you. I want you to act as our liaison with the Bureau."

"Sir, I—"

"Hear me out before you answer," Ingram interrupted. "You would report on a regular basis directly to me, or to someone in my office. You would have only minimal contact with Snead."

"What about Strickland?"

"You would report directly to me," Ingram repeated. He wrote a phone number on the back of a business card and passed it to me. "Written reports weekly; daily updates by phone. I, or someone in my office, will pass along any Bureau requests relayed by you to Snead, and vice-versa. What do you say?"

I pocketed Ingram's card. "Can I think about it?"

Ingram's face closed like a fist. "Not for long. I'll need your answer by the end of today," he said, his friendly manner suddenly evaporating. "I suggest you visit the scene and then talk with FBI Assistant Director Shepherd before coming to a decision."

"Yes, sir."

"Fine," said Ingram. "By the way, I already took the liberty of speaking with Shepherd. He remembers you from your task-force work with Snead. Shepherd signed off on your acting as our liaison, and he's willing to team you with a Bureau agent for the duration of the investigation. He's expecting you in his office this afternoon."

"Shepherd's a good man. I look forward to talking with him, whatever my decision."

"Fine," Ingram repeated, still clearly irritated that I hadn't immediately accepted the liaison position. "I'll require your answer by five o'clock. One more thing. If you do decide to accept the liaison position, and I strongly encourage you to do so, I'll have your back . . . within limits. It's a card worth having, especially for someone like you. Understood?"

"Yes, sir," I replied, realizing from Ingram's tone that if I didn't accept, Strickland's threat would probably be back on the table. Either way, one thing was becoming increasingly apparent. If I wanted to keep my LAPD job options open, I needed to carefully consider Ingram's proposal.

Chapter 7

Sitting at her Channel 2 News desk in Studio City, bureau chief Lauren Van Owen regarded Allison with a look of skepticism. "Are you certain this is what you want?" she asked.

"Heck, yes," Allison replied, her eyes lighting with excitement. "News stories like this don't come along every day. Mike and I can jet off to Costa Rica later. Covering the Bel Air murders is *way* more important than any honeymoon."

"To you, maybe. What about Mike?"

Allison shifted, uncomfortable with the question. "Well, when this story came up, I did sort of decide to postpone things without consulting Mike. He was disappointed . . . but I'm certain he understands."

"Uh huh," said Lauren. "You're certain he understands. Listen, Ali, I'm probably not one to be handing out advice, but you remind me of myself at your age."

"Thanks," said Allison.

"I don't necessarily mean that in a good way," Lauren corrected. "Sure, I admire your drive. It's exactly what someone like you needs to succeed in broadcast news. On the other hand, this business can be tough on relationships. I couldn't figure out how to get my career to work within my own marriage, let alone with my being a mother . . ."

"Don't worry about me," said Allison, a hand absently traveling to her abdomen. Though she was still barely showing, she knew that wouldn't be the case much longer. Fortunately, her expanding middle wouldn't be visible during her on-air reporting from behind the Channel 2 News desk. "Mike understands this could be the chance of a lifetime. We'll be fine, but thanks for your concern."

Lauren shrugged. "Whatever you say."

"So the story is mine?"

"On one condition. I want you to talk with your father and see whether you can get his unofficial cooperation, like before."

"I don't know how comfortable I am doing that," Allison

hedged. "Besides, he's on leave from the department. What makes you think he'll be involved on the case?"

"One of our reporters saw him this morning at PAB. I don't think he was there making a social call."

"Huh," Allison mused. Although encouraged by the prospect of her father's finally returning to work, she wondered why he hadn't mentioned it earlier. "Well, if that's the case, I'll talk to him. No guarantees, but I'll talk to him."

"Fine. Then the story's yours. I want you on it full-time, starting now."

"Yes!" Allison exclaimed, pumping a fist. Then, her smile fading, "What about Network? Are they going to send out one of their big guns to take over when things heat up? Like our old pal, Brent Preston?"

"I can't make any guarantees either, Ali. I can say that I've already talked with Network, and they agreed to leave the story with our Los Angeles Bureau for the time being. Just so you know, Network plans to take the story national tonight on *CBS Evening News*. They're also planning a media blitz if the killings continue, or if the Muslim backlash continues to heat up. If either of those things happen, all bets are off."

"Fair enough," said Allison. "With the caveat that if I do come up with an exclusive, *I* get to report it first, national coverage or not."

"Allison, I can't—"

"That's the deal, Lauren."

Lauren shook her head. "You really do remind me of myself at your age. Okay, depending on what you dig up, I'll see what I can do. Now, you need to get in touch with your dad."

"Yes, ma'am," said Allison, shooting Lauren a sloppy salute.

"One more thing, Ali. I probably shouldn't discuss this with you, but when I talked with Network, they also mentioned that if you continue to do well here in L.A., there might be an on-air spot opening up for you in New York."

"New York? Oh, my God, really?" said Allison, barely able to believe her ears. "That would be a huge step up!"

"For you."

"What do you . . . oh," said Allison, looking away. "You mean, what about Mike?"

Lauren nodded. "And your new baby. Something to think about."

Chapter 8

On my way out of PAB, I decided to stop by the third-floor HSS offices and visit some friends in Robbery-Homicide. As Deluca had been one of the first investigators at the Bel Air crime scene, I knew that he had subsequently been detailed to Snead's HSS task force, and I expected to see him there as well. The one officer I didn't want to run into, namely the recently promoted Captain Snead, was of course the first person I encountered.

"Kane," said Snead upon spotting me, a feral grin splitting his hatchet-thin face. "Welcome back. I knew you couldn't resist working another high-profile case."

"Sorry to disappoint you," I said, "but I turned down your task-force job. In fact, I won't be working for you again—ever. To tell you the truth, I'd rather poke out my eyes with a rusty fork."

Snead's grin froze. "But . . . then, why are you here?"

"I dropped by to visit friends," I answered, glancing into the third-floor conference room. Several detectives were still present, apparently having just completed their initial task-force briefing. "By the way, congratulations on your promotion. You must be so proud."

"Did you talk with Chief Ingram?" Snead demanded, ignoring my sarcasm.

"I did. He suggested that I act as our LAPD/FBI liaison on the investigation."

"Fine. I'll expect daily reports, more if necessary. And your paperwork had better be current at all times. You can start by—"

"That's not the way it's going to work," I broke in. "If I take the liaison position, which I haven't accepted yet, I'll be reporting directly to the chief."

"We'll see about that," Snead snapped, his eyes hardening.

"Yeah, we will," I said, pushing past him into the conference room. "Now, if you'll excuse me . . ."

"Watch yourself, Kane," Snead warned. "If you cross me on

this investigation, even one bit, I'll have you up on charges."

"You'll have to get in line for that, but thanks for the warning," I said over my shoulder, thinking that was the second time I had been threatened since arriving at PAB. The third, actually, if I included Ingram's not-so-friendly insistence that I accept the liaison position.

"Hey, Kane!" Deluca called from across the room as I entered. "What are you doing here?"

"Slumming," I joked. "Actually, I thought I'd drop in to witness firsthand you fine detectives wasting taxpayer money."

"You going to be joining us?" asked Peter Church, a Robbery-Homicide detective with whom I'd worked a previous case.

"Not this time, Pete."

"Won't be the same without you," chimed in Evan Nolan, another detective friend from Robbery-Homicide. "Although things will definitely be a lot more tranquil."

"Tranquility is overrated," I laughed. Then, to Deluca, "Have time to grab a cup of coffee?"

Deluca shook his head. "We're due downstairs in a couple minutes for the Mayor's press conference."

"Been there, done that," I said.

"Yeah," Deluca grumbled. "Fitzpatrick just gave us an abbreviated version of his upcoming press-conference speech. Our task force will have every resource available; the entire city will stand behind us one hundred percent; every detective present is there because he's the best of the best; and so on," Deluca continued, doing a passable imitation of Mayor Fitzpatrick.

"Well, don't let the mayor's speech go to your head," I advised with a smile. "Speaking of which, how's the task force shaping up?"

Deluca glanced around before answering. Then, lowering his voice, "Not good," he sighed. "I swear, with his recent promotion, Snead has turned into even more of an ass than ever. Making matters worse, we now have guys from Homeland Security and CTSOB sitting in the back taking notes. And as usual, Snead thinks the case is going to be closed by establishing organizational protocols, keeping the paperwork straight, and waiting for some magical hotline tip to come in."

"Sorry to hear that."

"Yeah. Me, too."

"You coming, Deluca?" one of the other task-force detectives called from the doorway.

"In a minute," Deluca called back. Then, again lowering his voice, "What are you really doing here, partner?"

"I just had a meeting with the chief," I replied. "He wants me to act as our LAPD/FBI liaison. I'd report directly to him. No contact with Snead."

"Are you going to do it?"

"I don't know. But Strickland made it abundantly clear that if I don't, I won't be coming back to the department . . . ever."

"Screw him."

"My sentiments exactly."

"So what are you going to do?"

"I promised Ingram I'd check out the crime scene and talk with Assistant Director Shepherd before deciding. I have till five p.m. to make up my mind."

"Shepherd is an okay guy, for a feeb," Deluca noted doubtfully.

"Yeah," I agreed. Both Deluca and I had worked with Shepherd on a previous task-force investigation, and like other LAPD officers on the case, we had been impressed by his professionalism. That said, Shepherd was still a member of the FBI, with loyalties and objectives that didn't always coincide with those of the LAPD.

"Still, Bureau guys aren't to be trusted." Deluca hesitated, seeming about to add something else.

"What?" I asked.

"Dan, I would like nothing better than to see you back on the job," Deluca replied. "I also understand why you needed some time off, and maybe you still do. I just hope that if you take the liaison job, you're not getting in over your head."

"I'll be fine."

"I hope so," said Deluca. "This case is already shaping up to be a snake pit, not to mention that Snead is still looking for any excuse to go after your badge. If you decide to get involved, watch your back."

Chapter 9

Though not yet noon, on the drive to Bel Air I encountered more than my share of freeway traffic, and I wound up spending half the commute stuck behind a semi with a bumper sticker that read, "How's my driving? Call 1-800 Eat Shit." Reading that, I smiled, deciding that humor, however coarse, was wherever you found it—even if on the freeway.

Despite efforts to the contrary, on the cross-town journey my thoughts kept returning to Deluca's warning. On the one hand, I was tired of sitting around. I missed being a cop, and I wanted to keep my job options open. On the other hand, I was concerned about returning to work on a high-profile investigation. From what I knew so far, the Bel Air murder case was exactly the type of investigation that had previously caused me trouble. Nevertheless, were I to take the liaison job, serving in that position rather than as an investigator would limit my exposure.

At least in theory.

After hitting the West L.A. interchange and taking the 405 Freeway north, I exited on Sunset and headed east, deciding to wait until I had more information to make a decision. I still had plenty of time before Ingram's 5 p.m. deadline, and by then maybe I would learn something that might make a difference. I had just wheeled onto Bellagio Road and passed beneath the metal arch guarding the estates of Bel Air when my cellphone rang.

"Kane," I said, setting my iPhone to speaker mode and placing it on the dashboard.

"Dad? It's Allison. Do you have a minute?"

"I'm kind of busy, Ali. What's up?"

"This won't take long. Are you going to be working on the Bel Air investigation?"

"Where did you hear that?"

"One of our reporters saw you at police headquarters this morning. So are you?"

"Am I what?"

"C'mon, Dad. Are you going to be working on the case or not?"

"I haven't made a decision on that yet," I answered. "As if I didn't know, why do you ask?"

"Two reasons. First, if you're thinking about going back to work for the department—which would be great, by the way—you should know what you're getting into."

"Everyone has been telling me that lately."

"I'm not surprised. The story is showing signs of turning into a media firestorm, and Lauren says Network is planning a blitz if there are any new killings. Plus there's a growing Muslim backlash, which could become an even bigger story than the murders. In the words of one of our news anchors, this has the makings of a real shitstorm."

"Nice talk, Ali. Thanks for making my day," I added, deciding I now had one more reason not to get involved.

"A murder video was posted on the internet this morning, along with a list of demands," Allison went on.

"Yeah, I heard that."

"Have you watched it?"

"The video? Nope."

"Take my advice. Don't."

"You said you had two reasons for calling?" I said, attempting to change the subject.

"Right," Allison pushed ahead, sounding excited. "If you do get involved, I'm hoping that we could maybe cooperate a little, like before—without crossing ethical lines, of course."

"Of course," I said dryly.

"It's worked for us in the past, Dad. And remember, cooperation can go both ways. It wouldn't be the first time having a friendly ear in the media came in handy for you."

"Ali, I haven't decided yet whether I'm going to get involved, or if I do, to what extent. Can we talk about this later?"

"No problem. See you tonight at dinner?"

"You're coming to the beach?" I asked. By then I had nearly reached the crime scene, and I started looking at street addresses.

"Mike left this morning for the shooting location in

Vancouver. Grandma Dorothy took pity on me and invited me for dinner."

"Okay, I'll see you tonight," I said, feeling a renewed surge of disapproval at Allison's decision to cancel her honeymoon. I still thought she was screwing up, but as Catheryn used to say, at some point you have to let your kids ruin their own lives. "No promises, though," I added. "We've had our problems with this 'cooperation' issue of yours in the past. We can talk, but one more screw-up from you—"

"Don't worry, I'll behave," Allison promised, hanging up before I could change my mind.

As I thumbed off my phone, I noticed a throng of mobile news vans jamming the street a block farther on. Several reporters were outside doing standups in front of a huge mansion, probably enumerating all the things they didn't know and hadn't learned since yesterday. Others had gathered on a sidewalk across the street and were conversing with neighbors. Deciding I no longer needed to verify the crime-scene address, I parked my Suburban and walked the remaining distance to the Welches' estate, hoping to avoid talking with anyone on the way. Moments later, I saw that was not to be.

"Detective Kane!" called one of the reporters "Can you give us a statement?"

"Not right now, Sue," I said, recognizing the woman from a case I'd worked years earlier.

Although seeming surprised that I remembered her name, Sue thrust a microphone in my direction anyway, quickly being joined by other newspersons as well. "Do you have any leads so far?" Sue persisted.

"Is this the work of a terrorist group?" someone else shouted. "Why aren't the police doing anything?"

"Have there been any further developments on the case?" another chimed in.

"No comment," I said, deciding that my best course lay in getting to the other side of a pedestrian gate that flanked a wrought-iron driveway barrier, and doing so as quickly as possible. Unfortunately, the gate was locked. Regarding me with a frosty expression, a slim young woman wearing slacks, a matching jacket, and a cream-colored blouse stood on the other side. Beneath the left shoulder of her jacket, I noticed the bulge of a service weapon.

"FBI?" I said, sizing her up as a low-level agent who had been left to secure the scene.

The woman, who appeared to be in her late twenties or early thirties, nodded without changing expression. She was taller than I had first thought, and a lot more attractive, too.

"A fed, huh?" I continued. "So where are your dark sunglasses?"

"Funny," she said, her tone saying she thought otherwise.

I flipped out my shield, deciding to dispense with the pleasantries. "Detective Kane, LAPD. Open up."

After inspecting my credentials, the woman shook her head, her short blond hair moving in a silky wave, framing a startlingly lovely face. "Someone mentioned there might be an LAPD hotshot showing up," she said. "This is no longer a police investigation, Detective. Sorry."

"You're not going to let me in?"

"No."

"Really?'

"Really. Take a hike."

With a sigh, I pulled out my cellphone. "Fine," I said. "Gimme a second."

The woman regarded me coolly, lifting her shoulders in a casual shrug. "Whatever. But you're not coming in."

Continuing to ignore a barrage of questions from reporters, I stepped away from the gate. I started to dial Lieutenant Long in West L.A., normal protocol in a situation like that—work your way up the chain of command and so on—then changed my mind. Deciding to go right to the top, I fished Chief Ingram's card from my pocket and dialed the number written on the back. After a short conversation, I repocketed my phone and waited.

I didn't have long to wait. Within minutes the blond woman received a phone call of her own. Turning her back, she withdrew a cellphone from a small handbag slung over her shoulder.

Though she lowered her voice, I have excellent hearing, and I could easily make out her end of the conversation.

"Yes, sir," I heard her say. "There *is* someone here named Kane—"

A pause followed, during which she glanced in my direction. "Yes, sir, but—" Another pause. Then, "I apologize, sir. Of course, sir," she said, her face coloring. "Right away, sir."

She seemed about to say something more, probably followed by another "sir," but by then her cellphone connection had apparently been severed. Without speaking, she jammed the phone back into her purse, walked to the pedestrian gate, and flung it open.

Ducking under a ribbon of crime-scene tape, I stepped through and closed the gate behind me, relieved to be escaping the gaggle of reporters. "So," I said, extending my hand. "Want to start over? Daniel Kane, LAPD hotshot."

The woman hesitated, her blue eyes appraising me critically. Then, seeming to come to a decision, she took my hand. "Special Agent Sara Taylor," she said, her grasp surprisingly firm. "Sorry, Detective. Just doing my job."

"No offense taken, Taylor," I replied. Then, starting up a paver driveway toward the Welches' mansion, "And I'm just doing mine."

"Uh, what is that, exactly?" Taylor asked, hurrying to catch up.

"LAPD/Bureau liaison. I'm supposed to take a look at the crime scene," I answered, deciding not to mention that I hadn't officially accepted the position.

"We sealed the residence. You're not going inside?"

"I am. Don't worry, Taylor. I've done this a few times. I promise not to screw anything up."

"I'm supposed to accompany you."

"No problem. Let's take a quick tour of the grounds first. Is there any other way in or out of here besides that gate at the street?"

Taylor shook her head. "Not without climbing the hedges and fencing surrounding the property. There was no sign of anyone entering that way, if that's what you're wondering."

"So the killer or killers probably drove in," I said, taking a look at the perimeter hedge. Although it provided privacy from the street, I also could make out a spine of spiked fencing concealed within the greenery. "I noticed a camera and intercom by the gate. If they came through that way, they either had the gate code, or someone buzzed them in."

"Right. Your LAPD task force is currently canvassing neighbors, maid services, and anyone else with the gate code," Taylor volunteered, anticipating my next question.

"Good," I said, making a mental note to talk with Deluca about that.

Next, with Agent Taylor close behind, I made a circuit of the property, satisfying myself that there was no sign of anyone scaling the hedge. After glancing into a three-car garage fronting the driveway, I circumnavigated the exterior of the house, checking for broken windows, scuff marks, jimmied locks, and so on—finding no sign of forced entry there, either. It seemed that whoever had murdered the Welches had been invited in.

As I crossed a terrace near the rear of the house, I noticed a dark patch of stains on the terracotta tiles beside the Welches' pool. Kneeling, I looked closer. The stains appeared to be oil drips, and they looked fresh. There was no indication—numbered evidence tabs or the like—that the drips had been included in evidence gathered by crime-scene technicians.

After taking several pictures with my iPhone camera, I proceeded to the front of the house. On the way, in a shrubbery planter and on a nearby section of lawn, I could just make out what appeared to be tire tracks.

After taking additional pictures, I turned to Agent Taylor, who during this time had been following me with an air of ill-disguised impatience. "Can you open the garage?" I asked.

"Why?"

"Just do it, Taylor. I need to check something."

Taylor seemed about to argue the point, then changed her mind. Stepping away, she withdrew her phone and dialed a number. After a short conversation, she scribbled something in a notebook.

"Garage door code," she explained, noting my questioning look.

After Taylor had opened one of the garage doors using an exterior keypad, I pulled a pair of latex gloves from my jacket, snapped them on, and stepped into the garage. Three cars were present. Two appeared new—a Mercedes-Benz S-Class and a Porsche Spyder convertible. The third was a late-model Cadillac Escalade. Kneeling, I checked the concrete beneath the engines and drive trains of each vehicle. None leaked oil.

"What are you looking for?" asked Taylor.

I withdrew my phone. "I have to check something," I answered, deflecting her question. Turning my back, I crossed to a bank of storage cabinets and punched in Deluca's cell number.

"Dan," he said, answering almost immediately. "What's up?"

"Just need a little clarification, Paul. You said Snead showed up at the Bel Air crime scene shortly after you did. How shortly?"

"You're asking how far Banowski and I got in processing things before Robbery-Homicide took over?

"Right."

"Not far. Snead and two of his HSS detectives, Church and Nolan, relieved us before we had a chance to do much."

"Who was the criminalist on the case?" I asked, referring to the Special Investigative Division officer who, at the direction of the ranking homicide investigator at the scene—most likely Snead—had been responsible for the procurement and cataloging of trace evidence.

"Frank Tremmel."

"And the coroner's investigator?"

"Art Walters."

"Good," I said. I had investigated cases with both men, and I knew their work was solid.

"Why do you ask?"

"I'm here at the Welches' estate," I explained. "I noticed what look like fresh oil drips on the terrace near the pool. Anyone take samples?"

"There was no mention of that in the crime report. Did we miss something?"

"I'm not sure. It could be nothing, but none of Welches' vehicles leak oil. The drips might have come from a gardener's lawnmower or whatever, but I also noticed what appear to be tire tracks leading back to the terrace. The tracks seem too wide for a lawnmower, and it's unlikely the family would park a car on their back patio."

"You think the killers might have concealed their vehicle back there?"

"Maybe. They had to be in the house for some time murdering Mr. and Mrs. Welch and shooting a video and whatever the hell else they did. Probably took a while, right?"

"Yeah," Deluca agreed. "Damn. The FBI didn't pick up the drips or the tire tracks, either."

"You might want to send SID back out," I suggested. "Have them sample the drips. Maybe even remove the pavers and take them back to the lab. Might come in handy if we locate the murder vehicle. Also get casts of the tire tracks, along with oil samples and reference tire prints from the Welches' vehicles to rule them out as a source."

"I'll talk with Snead. Did you, uh, notice anything else?"

"I haven't finished here yet, but I'll call if I do." As I hung up, I noticed Taylor standing behind me listening.

"We'll be sending our ERT unit back out, too," she informed me stiffly, referring to the Bureau's Evidence Response Team.

"Of course," I said, heading for the front of the house. "It's your case, right?"

"Right."

When we reached the front of the mansion, I found several strips of yellow crime-scene ribbon blocking the entry door. After mounting a short flight of steps, I used a keychain penknife to cut the tape. "The door unlocked?" I asked, glancing at Taylor.

Taylor nodded. "The house was open when investigators arrived. We left it that way."

"Fine," I said, placing a gloved hand on the doorknob. I hesitated a moment. Then, taking a deep breath, I opened the door and crossed the threshold.

Taylor followed me in. We paused in a spacious entry, the large, airy space illuminated by an ornate chandelier and bank of clerestory windows higher up. Dark stains marked the slate floor just inside the door, the treads of several different shoeprints suggesting that there had been more than one intruder. A gigantic living room lay to the left; a hallway led deeper into the house to the right. Straight ahead, a curved staircase ascended to the second floor. I glanced into the living room, struck by the smell of something rotting. Taylor wrinkled her nose, apparently noticing it, too.

"Have you been in here?" I asked, surmising that although the Welches' bodies had been removed by coroner's investigators, the blood cleanup had been left for later. Like a corpse, blood left in a warm, closed environment quickly decays. Like the odor of a decomposing body, it's something you don't soon forget.

Taylor shook her head. "Inside the house? No."

I could tell Taylor was fighting not to show a reaction to the smell. She was almost succeeding.

Over the years I had grown accustomed to the smell of putrefaction, at least accustomed enough to perform my job, but more than once I had seen others lose their lunch at a homicide investigation, adding the nauseating smell of vomit to the crime scene.

"You okay?" I asked.

"I'm fine," Taylor replied. "What, uh, what do you want to see?"

"Everything," I answered. I glanced to the left, concluding from the smell of death emanating from the living room that the murders had taken place there. Deciding to leave that area for last, I headed upstairs. "First I want to get a feel for what happened," I added. "You coming?"

"Yeah, I'm coming."

Accompanied by Agent Taylor, I spent the next twenty minutes inspecting the second floor of the mansion. Turning off my feelings, I concentrated on forensic aspects of the case, noting traps missing from bathroom sinks, shower drains opened, computer leads dangling from an office workstation, numbered tags and stickers designating the location of evidence taken from various places, and a patina of ferric oxide fingerprint powder coating any surface the killers might have touched—especially the smashed paneling of a bathroom door that had apparently been ripped from its frame.

Deciding investigators had done a thorough job of gathering evidence on the upper floor, I descended to the main level of the house. In the kitchen I noted knives missing from a cutting block, a landline phone off the hook, more fingerprint powder and an additional littering of numbered evidence tags, and a second computer missing from a kitchen alcove. A formal dining room, several guest bedrooms, and a number of other areas on the ground floor appeared to have received similar treatment by investigators.

Finally I returned to the living room, having saved the worst for last. Taylor, who until then had trailed several steps behind me, moved a little closer as we entered the room in which the Welches had died. The smell worsened, apparently emanating from a puddle of congealed fluid that had soaked into the carpet. By then I had grown progressively inured to the stench. Fortunately, it seemed Taylor had as well.

Glancing around, I noted more tags and stickers designating areas where fluid, fiber, and other forensic evidence had been gathered. Delineated in white tape, the shapes of two bodies had been outlined, the side-by-side torsos partly immersed in the blood puddle.

Looking closer, I noted what appeared to be several indentations in the carpet. Because a murder video had been shot, I surmised that the marks might have been made by a camera tripod. Both disgusted and angered that the killers had brought a camera to record their act, I noticed something even more chilling. On an adjacent wall, written in a smear of blood, someone had scrawled what looked like an Arabic word.

"Infidel," said Taylor, noticing my gaze.

I stared at the writing, the bloody loops and whorls seeming almost alien on the white plaster wall. "What?"

"We had an expert take a look. It's the Arabic word *kafir*, meaning infidel, or unbeliever," Taylor explained. "We didn't release that detail to the press. Unfortunately, along with their list of demands in the murder video, the killers included a close-up of the bloody writing. So now . . ."

". . . it's worthless as a means of weeding out phony confessions," I concluded. In well publicized crimes, authorities were often swamped with confessions from misguided persons looking for their fifteen minutes of fame, and withholding a descriptor like the bloody writing often proved invaluable as a means of elimination.

Again using my cellphone, I took several pictures of the Arabic writing.

"What now?" asked Taylor, shifting impatiently from foot to foot. "You about done?"

Instead of answering, I began mentally reviewing the investigative elements I'd covered so far, making certain I hadn't overlooked something, and pausing on details that didn't make sense.

For starters, considering the camera equipment and whatever else the killers had brought with them, the intruders had most likely driven into the estate. They had therefore either known the Welshes' gate code, or the Welshes had buzzed them in. And if the latter were the case, why?

Second, the smashed door upstairs indicated that someone—either Mr. or Mrs. Welsh, or possibly both—had taken refuge in the bathroom before eventually being captured. Whatever the case, it must have taken the killers time to break through the heavy door. Why hadn't a 911 call been made in the interim? The kitchen phone off the hook could explain why a landline call hadn't been placed, but everyone has a cellphone. Had the Welshes been surprised by the attack and unable to get to their phones?

I was also curious regarding what sort of killer or killers would bring video equipment to a murder. True, it showed a callous premeditation, but what would motivate posting a video of their act? Was it simply a threat—submit to our demands or further killings will follow—or was there more involved?

I sighed, realizing that although investigators and crime-scene technicians appeared to have done a workmanlike job gathering evidence, it was unlikely that any of it would lead to an arrest. Despite what is shown on TV, forensic evidence rarely solves crimes; it simply comes in handy once you have a suspect. And for that, I knew that the first line of inquiry would be based on the premise that the killers had known the Welshes, at least peripherally. Aside from a close scrutiny of family and friends, the most common way to obtain a suspect or suspects would be via an informant, or as the result of a confession that could be corroborated by physical evidence, and somehow I didn't think either would be forthcoming.

As I was last to arrive on the scene and the bodies had already been removed, I also knew I was getting a skewed version of the crime. Nevertheless, I felt a renewed surge of anger, recalling the murder of my wife at the hands of another killer. Of one thing I was certain: Whoever had butchered the Welshes didn't deserve to be breathing the same air as the rest of us.

"Kane. You done yet?" Taylor repeated. "I'd like to get out of here."

"Why?" I replied, still reviewing the case in my mind. "Late for lunch?"

"No," Taylor replied, frowning. "I just . . . want to get some air. If you're done with your super-sleuthing, that is."

Before I could reply, I heard the front door open. Taylor and I turned toward the sound. A thin, sandy-haired man wearing a dark suit and sunglasses stepped into the entry. He hesitated when he saw us. "What are you doing in here?" he demanded, his gaze traveling from Taylor to me.

"Take it easy, Duffy," said Taylor. "Detective Kane is here from the LAPD. He's our liaison with the locals, and he has permission to inspect the scene. I was instructed to accompany him."

"Jesus, what's that smell?" Duffy mumbled, retching.

"It's what's left of the Welshes," I answered. "Let's take this outside."

His face paling, Duffy nodded and turned for the door, covering his nose and mouth with his palm.

Taylor and I followed him out. Taylor shut the door behind us. "Detective Kane, this is Special Agent Gavin Duffy," she said once we were outside. "Agent Duffy, Detective Kane."

I shook Duffy's hand, noting that although he briefly made eye contact with me, his gaze kept returning to Taylor.

"I . . . I was worried when I arrived and you weren't at your post, Sara . . . I mean Agent Taylor," Duffy stammered. "I came to relieve you and, well, I'm glad you're all right."

Taylor glanced at me, then back at Duffy. "I'm fine," she said. "But thanks for your concern." Then, again to me, "Well, if there's nothing else—"

"There is one more thing, Taylor."

"And that is?"

"I need to talk to your boss."

Chapter 10

As I trailed Taylor's late-model Crown Vic through the streets of Westwood, I felt myself growing more and more disturbed by the Bel Air murders. If what I had learned so far was accurate, the killers had butchered Mr. and Mrs. Welch to make some sort of political statement, even bringing a camera with them to record their act. Although I still hadn't come to a decision regarding Chief Ingram's request, I was angry. I was also becoming increasingly prepared to hear what Director Shepherd had to say.

Fifteen minutes later, after battling stop-and-go Westwood traffic, we reached the Wilshire Federal Building. An architectural example of late modernism, the towering structure that housed FBI headquarters was an aging, seventeen-story monolith with precast concrete fins and a broad white façade, centrally located on twenty-eight landscaped acres of a former golf course. Although its top five floors still housed the FBI's Los Angeles field office, I knew that at one point an effort had been made to construct new FBI headquarters on the current location. Local residents had ultimately blocked that effort, citing traffic congestion, land use concerns, and fears that an expanded FBI presence would paint a terrorist bull's eye on the surrounding community—issues that seemed to be coming true nonetheless.

When we arrived, several hundred anti-Muslim protestors carrying placards lined the sidewalk out front, with a smaller number of pro-Muslim advocates flanking their angry counterparts.

Once past the demonstration, Taylor and I had a short but heated conversation in an exterior parking garage, during which she insisted that I leave my service weapon locked in my car. I had visited Los Angeles FBI headquarters in the past, and I knew that as an active police officer performing my duties, the Law Enforcement Officers Act of 2004 gave me "concealed carry" rights almost everywhere. My LEOSA carry-rights included federal buildings, so I declined. In the end, Taylor decided to see things my way.

After that, any hope of small talk between us seemed to be at an end. Frowning, Taylor walked me to the main entrance and escorted me through building security—an exacting process during which I was eventually issued a temporary visitor's ID. Afterward Taylor accompanied me on a high-speed elevator to the top floor. There, once she had checked me in at the receptionist's desk, she directed me with a wave of her hand toward Assistant Director Shepherd's office down the hall, then started back toward the elevators. "It's been swell, Kane," she said over her shoulder, clearly happy to be rid of me. "Maybe I'll see you around sometime."

"Maybe," I said. From the beginning I had been annoyed by Taylor's attitude, so it was with more than a trace of irritation at myself that I still found myself watching her trim figure as she retreated down the hallway.

When I arrived at Director Shepherd's office, I was told he was out. A sympathetic secretary informed me that he had left a copy of the FBI case file for me, assuring me that Shepherd was expected back soon. Deciding to make the most of my time, I dropped into a chair across from the secretary's desk and spent the next thirty-five minutes perusing the Bureau's report.

Although I occasionally had some difficulty deciphering unfamiliar FBI codes, multi-letter abbreviations, and Bureau-speak, I got through most of it. Toward the end, I began to suspect that the bulk of the file had been lifted directly from an LAPD crime report, then reorganized to conform with FBI protocols.

In brief, here's how the investigation shaped up so far: Early Sunday morning, West L.A. patrol officers Thomas Phelan and Edward Flory had responded to a one-eighty-seven homicide call, arriving at the Bel Air residence of Arleen and Gary Welch at 8:46 a.m. Upon arrival the officers had interviewed Chuck Lohrman, a pool-maintenance worker waiting out front. The pool guy stated that when he had arrived that morning to service the Welches' pool, he had noticed their front door standing open. Twenty minutes later, after adjusting the pool chemicals and performing a surface skim, he had returned to his truck—noting that the Welches' door was still open.

Curious, Mr. Lohrman had mounted the front steps and called into the residence, seeing what appeared to be blood smears in the entry. Alarmed, he had again called into the house. Receiving no answer, he had stepped inside and followed the blood tracks into the living room. Upon finding the bodies of Mr. and Mrs. Welch sprawled in a puddle of blood, he had exited the house, vomited in a shrubbery bed, and called the police.

After questioning Mr. Lohrman regarding his route into and out of the house, as well as asking what items he might have touched or disturbed, Officers Flory and Phelan had entered the residence, determined that a multiple homicide had occurred, and exited, retracing their steps. While Officer Flory established a crime-scene perimeter, Officer Phelan had called West L.A. for backup.

West L.A. homicide detectives Paul Deluca and John Banowski had arrived at 9:27 a.m. After talking with Mr. Lohrman and completing an initial assessment of the scene, Deluca had placed a call to the LAPD Special Investigative Division, whose criminalist and crime-scene unit would be responsible for the procurement and cataloguing of all trace evidence taken from the site. Deluca had also made a call to the Los Angeles County Coroner's Office, as the presence of a coroner's investigator was required during any examination and moving of the Welches' bodies.

The SID crime-scene unit—whose members included a latent-prints technician, an officer from the photo section, and criminalist Ron Tremmel—arrived forty minutes later. Art Walters, an investigator from the coroner's office, arrived shortly after that. Also arriving around that time was Captain William Snead, accompanied by two Robbery-Homicide investigators from the LAPD's HSS unit, Detectives Peter Church and Evan Nolan. Captain Snead subsequently informed Deluca and Banowski that Robbery-Homicide was taking responsibility for the investigation and ordered them to stand down.

With Banowski and Deluca now relegated to the sidelines,

Officers Snead, Church, and Nolan proceeded with the investigation. Latent prints were lifted, blood samples and other forensic evidence collected, and photos and videos taken from various angles throughout the residence.

Several hours later, as Captain Snead and coroner's investigator Art Walters were examining the bodies, an FBI unit arrived at the Welch residence. The Bureau's five-man team of special agents was led by Special Agent in Charge Aaron Gibbs, and was accompanied by a fifty-three-foot mobile forensic van and an FBI Evidence Response Team. Citing national security issues that superseded LAPD authority, Gibbs ordered Snead to relinquish control of the scene. Following a spate of angry phone calls, responsibility for the case again changed hands, with the FBI now taking control.

I paused, recalling my comment to Chief Ingram about too many cooks. From what I had read so far, it looked like I'd been right on target, which didn't make for a good beginning on a case like this. With a sigh, I read on.

The significant investigative elements in the FBI file—some probably taken from the LAPD's SID investigation, some from the FBI's ERT results—were as follows: Unmatched latent prints had been lifted (no computer hits), and a number of unidentified hairs not matching those of Mr. or Mrs. Welch had been recovered. Unexplained type AB-negative blood not matching the Welches had been found in an upstairs bathroom. DNA testing was currently being performed on the unexplained blood. The autopsy results were still out, as were the toxicology and other lab results, but given the circumstance, I didn't expect those findings to change things much. Last, a hard-drive recording from the Welches' onsite security system had been removed, presumably by the killers.

The eight-by-ten crime scene photos were particularly chilling, and though I'd seen almost everything over the course of my career, I had a hard time looking at them. As I flipped through, I understood why Deluca hadn't wanted to discuss details of the case at Ali's reception.

Also included in the Bureau file was an inventory of items

that investigators had removed from the Welch residence—computers, phone records, daily calendars, bills, letters, personal correspondence, bank statements, and so on. These items were currently being examined to determine whether the killers might have had any connection, however tenuous, with the Welch family. Also removed by investigators were a number of knives, scissors, and other cutting instruments that were being tested for the presence of blood. As I finished scanning the impound list, I had a feeling I was missing something. Unable to pin it down, I pushed on, deciding to return to the impound list when I had a chance.

Three things rounded out what I considered a "probably useless" category in the Bureau file: A search of the NCIC (National Crime Index Computer) databank had been completed, with no hits; a VICAP (Violent Criminal Apprehension Program) report was currently underway; and an FBI psychological profile was being procured.

Bottom line, unless investigators got lucky with the DNA analysis of blood found in the bathroom, I saw nothing of significance in the forensic evidence that could prove useful, much less lead to the arrest of a suspect or suspects. Worse, I knew from experience that most murder cases were closed quickly, or not at all. After the first twenty-four hours evidence evaporated, witnesses' memories grew cloudy, and the killers' trail cooled. The clock was running, and I didn't like how things were shaping up.

As I was completing my perusal of the file, I heard the door click open behind me. Glancing up, I saw Assistant Director Shepherd entering the room. As always, I was struck by Shepherd's youthful appearance, although I knew he was considerably older than he looked. Shepherd was accompanied by a lean, weathered-looking man whose close-cropped hair and granite-hard eyes spoke of a military background.

"Kane, good to see you again," said Shepherd, shaking my hand as I rose to greet him. "This is Special Agent in Charge, Aaron Gibbs," he added, indicating the stern-looking man beside him. "Gibbs is heading up our investigative team on the Welch murders. SAC Gibbs, Detective Kane."

I shook Gibbs's hand next, deciding I had been right. Definitely military—been there, done that, and come back for more.

"Detective Kane," said Gibbs with a brief nod.

"Dan, I again would like to extend my condolence for your loss," Shepherd continued.

"Thank you," I said. Although I appreciated Shepherd's sympathy, I didn't know what else to say.

Seeming to sense my discomfort, Shepherd changed the subject. "Did you have a chance to review the file?" he asked, glancing at the paperwork in my hand.

I passed him the file. "I did."

"And?"

"Not much to go on. Might get lucky with the DNA."

"Let's head back to my office," Shepherd suggested. "There's something you should see, if you haven't already."

Curious, I followed Shepherd and Gibbs to an office down the hall. Shepherd held the door open, then closed it behind us as we entered. Next he walked to a desk and swiveled a computer monitor to face us. Without speaking, he brought up a video program and clicked an icon to make the image fill the screen.

"What are we watching?" I asked.

"Wait," Gibbs said grimly.

A moment later a video began, displaying the images of three men. All were wearing black polo shirts, dark pants, and leather gloves. Balaclavas and sunglasses hid their faces. One man stood to the left, holding what appeared to be an AK-47 automatic weapon. The other two, who had just entered the frame when the video began, were shoving a couple before them whom I assumed to be Mr. and Mrs. Welch. Both captives had sacks over their heads. Their hands were bound behind their backs with what looked like plastic handcuff restraints. As the couple stumbled into view, one of the men kicked the back of the man's legs, forcing him to his knees. The other man pushed the woman to her knees as well.

Shepherd froze the image.

Much as I dreaded it, I had known the time would come when I would have to watch the murder video, as it might contain information that could prove helpful. It seemed that time was now. "I'm guessing that's Mr. and Mrs. Welch," I said.

"Correct," said Shepherd. "See that black flag behind them?"

Behind the two men, a rectangular piece of fabric had been hung from a frame, forming a backdrop for the video. What appeared to be a scrawl of Arabic letters ran across the top, with an irregular white oval and more indecipherable writing in the center.

"What is that?" I asked.

"It's called the Black Standard," answered Gibbs. "Its origins go way back, but lately it has been used by Al-Qaeda in the Arabian Peninsula and Al-Shabaab in Somalia, among others. More recently, ISIS members have been co-opting it for their own use."

"These guys are ISIS?"

"Maybe," said Gibbs. "Or ISIL, or whatever the hell they're calling themselves these days."

"What does the writing mean?"

Shepherd spoke up. "The top line, known as the *shadada*, translates as 'There is no god but God. Muhammad is the messenger of God.' The circular symbol lower down represents the 'Seal of Muhammad,' allegedly used by Muhammad on several ancient communications. The *shadada* and the Prophet's seal are something all Muslims share, so by hijacking words and symbols that in themselves have nothing to do with jihad, ISIS is attempting to broaden its ideological reach."

"Where did they get it?" I asked.

"Get what?" asked Gibbs.

"The flag. It doesn't look like something you just buy on Amazon. Did they have it made, and if so, where? Is the source of the flag something you're checking into?"

Shepherd looked doubtful. "Gibbs?"

Gibbs shook his head. "Not so far, sir. I'll look into it."

"Do that," said Shepherd. Then, with a reluctant sigh, he restarted the video. Grimly, we watched as the murder of Mr. and

Mrs. Welch resumed.

Head lowered, Mr. Welch appeared to be weeping, his sobs clearly audible. Mrs. Welch was angry, first ordering her captors to take whatever they wanted and get out, then threatening that if she or her husband were harmed in any way, they would regret it.

None of the hooded men responded. Instead, the video faded to black and lines of writing began scrolling across the screen.

"America, be God's curse on you," the killers' scripted message began. "We call on your president, the dog of Rome, to witness our acts. Now hear our words. Today we are slaughtering your people in their homes, as our soldiers are slaughtering your soldiers in our holy lands. With Allah's permission, we will break your last crusade, until the final hour when the words, 'There is no god but God shall be heard in every corner of the world.'

"America, now hear our demands. You will remove all U.S. troops from our holy lands. You will establish shariah law in all Muslim communities throughout your country. You will release all Muslim prisoners now held in Guantanamo and other American jails, and in the jails of your proxy puppets. You will establish laws throughout your land forbidding blasphemy of any kind against Allah and the Prophet Muhammad.

"We say to you, in Allah's name we make these demands. Allah willing, we will slaughter your people in their homes until our demands are met, for we are hungry lions whose drink is blood and play is carnage. All praise be to Allah, and peace and blessings be upon his Prophet Muhammad."

The writing faded to black. A moment later the screen again displayed the images of Mr. and Mrs. Welch, kneeling before their captors. Without speaking, the man with the assault rifle stepped out of frame. Moments later he returned with a metal vessel containing two dark-handled knives. The video cut to a shot of the men behind the Welches as they each withdrew a knife. The blades were serrated near the hilt and gleamed as they cleared the metal vessel.

Next, knives held in gloved hands, the terrorists yanked the sacks from their captives' heads. Then the men each curled a forearm around his victim's face, trapping Mr. and Mrs.

Welches' heads in the crooks of their left arms. Mrs. Welch stiffened and began struggling. Mr. Welch continued sobbing, pleading for his life. The man behind Mr. Welch leaned closer and appeared to whisper something.

At this Mr. Welch began struggling in earnest.

Until then I had avoided thinking about how the murders would be accomplished. I knew from viewing the crime-scene photos what the final, horrific result would be, but I suppose I'd preferred to think that the hideous dismemberments had been accomplished with one clean stroke. With a chill, I suddenly realized that the killings weren't going to be clean at all.

The men forced back their captives' heads, exposing their necks.

And a moment later it began.

Although I wanted to look away, I forced myself to watch. Brutally, the men began sawing their blades through the Welches' necks, like clumsy butchers hacking through thick slabs of meat. As blood began spurting, the man murdering Mr. Welch leaned forward, using his weight to topple his victim to the carpet, trapping him beneath his torso. The man savaging Mrs. Welch did the same.

I sat frozen in horror, watching with a mix of shock and disbelief. At one point the short, muscular man paused to stare directly into the camera, his hooded face and dark sunglasses lending him a look of pure, unadulterated evil. Deliberately, he tipped back Mr. Welch's partly severed head, exposing the gushing neck-stump. Then, with animal ferocity, he returned to his task.

Although the Welches were undoubtedly dead before the final cuts were made, it took what seemed forever for the men to complete their murders. Then the men rose together and stood over their victims, each holding a dripping head by the hair, displaying it for the camera. Still brandishing their bloodstained knives, they then placed their hideous trophies on each victim's back, balancing the severed heads between the bodies' bound arms.

The camera held on the grisly scene for several seconds. Next the shot panned down to a close-up of blood still flowing from the Welches' severed necks. Then the video cut to the Arabic word for "infidel" painted in blood on the wall, finally concluding with a close-up of the ISIS flag before fading to black.

I was trembling. I swallowed hard, feeling as if I'd been punched. I forced myself to breathe, realizing I'd been holding my breath.

Over the course of my career I had witnessed more than my share of the unthinkable things people can do to one another. I had also investigated more murders than I cared to remember, but this was the first time I had actually witnessed one taking place. It was something I will never forget.

Shepherd, who had been sitting on the edge of his desk, stood and shut off the monitor.

"*That* was posted on the internet?" I asked, struggling to get a hold of my emotions.

Shepherd nodded.

"Any chance of tracing the IP address?"

"We're still working on that," Gibbs answered. "The video was uploaded to a Russian social network called VK, using an IP masking service called the Tor Project. Since then the video has been posted on sites all over the world, including YouTube. Google took it down almost immediately, but it keeps popping up elsewhere. There's no stopping it now."

"Tor?"

"Tor stands for 'The Onion Router," Gibbs explained. "Tor is a hidden-service-protocol network that lets someone post a video in, say, Los Angeles, and have their traffic show up as originating from someplace else—Berlin or Rome, for instance—with a different IP address. With help from our friends at NSA, we were able to trace the original upload to a Starbucks in Santa Monica. From there we hit a brick wall. We're currently watching that particular café and others like it in the area, hoping the killers come back."

"Was there any video surveillance at the Starbucks site?"

Gibbs shook his head. "Unfortunately, no."

"Do you have any impressions on the video, Kane?" Shepherd broke in.

"A few," I said. I took a deep breath, attempting to set aside my feelings by concentrating on forensic aspects of the investigation. "First, anyone with basic computer skills could have produced that video," I continued. "Second, they were clearly going for maximum shock value, and they succeeded."

"That's putting it mildly," noted Gibbs.

"There were three men involved, possibly four," I went on. "The video mostly consisted of straight cuts between edits, so they could have locked down the camera and removed any unnecessary footage later—in which case they wouldn't have needed a fourth man to operate the camera. There *was* a shot at the end during which the camera panned down to the blood puddle. That would have required someone moving the camera, but it could have been the guy with the assault rifle. We never saw him after he delivered the knives."

"That's what we figured, too," said Shepherd. "Anything else?"

I thought for a moment. "There were a couple of things that struck me as odd," I said. "For one, what's with the sunglasses? Wearing balaclavas and gloves I can understand, but sunglasses? Seems like overkill. And not one word being spoken by the killers. Were they just being cautious, or is something else going on?"

"We're assuming cautious," said Gibbs.

"The presence of the AK-47 also seemed strange," I continued. "Sure, an AK is the terrorist rifle of choice in the Middle East, but this is West Los Angeles. A bit theatrical, don't you think? And where did they get the weapon?"

"We have ATF looking into that," Shepherd answered, referring to the Department of Justice's Bureau of Alcohol, Tobacco, Firearms and Explosives. "No results yet. Anything else?"

I paused again to collect my thoughts. "What about the stilted text?" I asked, taking a shot in the dark. "It reads like something from a bad movie."

"Actually, much of it was lifted from a speech given by the British terrorist, Jihadi John, just before he and other ISIS members engaged in a mass beheading of Syrian military personnel," Gibbs explained. "A video of those murders was shot in the desert outside Dabiq, and that bit about hungry lions was the clincher. It was a direct translation of a quote from ISIS leader Abu Bakr al-Baghdadi, a quote that was included in the same video."

"So are we dealing with foreign nationals or home-grown terrorists?"

Gibbs shrugged. "We're concluding from an analysis of the text—grammar, syntax, and so on—that foreign terrorists are involved. But we're not ruling out the presence of a domestic faction, either."

"Either way, they can't actually believe their demands will be met."

Again, Gibbs shrugged.

"I talked with Agent Taylor on my way in," Shepherd noted, glancing at me as he moved to sit behind his desk. "She was impressed with your discovery of the oil drips and tire tracks, which might be from the unsubs' vehicle," he added, referring in Bureau-speak to the unknown subjects of the investigation. "Good work on that."

I hesitated, surprised to hear that Taylor had anything positive to say about me. "With two investigative agencies vying for authority, it's easy to overlook something like that," I granted, wondering what else might have been missed.

"I also spoke with Chief Ingram this morning, Detective Kane," Shepherd continued. "I know you have concerns about returning to work so soon after your wife's death, and I understand that. But as I'm certain Chief Ingram mentioned, these are extraordinary circumstances. The Bureau will be requesting LAPD assistance at various points in the investigation, and we need a liaison to facilitate cooperation between our two agencies. Simply put, we need to find the people responsible for those murders, and you can help. Are you in?"

In retrospect, I knew that I had been kidding myself by

thinking there could be any response on my part but one, especially after viewing the murder video. On one level, I had hoped returning to work might help take my mind off Catheryn. On another, I was concerned that my job would again prove dangerous to my family, as it had in the past. I was prepared to say no, despite any consequences to my career. Granted, working as a liaison would keep me on the periphery of the investigation, and I was a long way from being ready to retire. Were I to refuse, I had no doubt what the outcome would be.

What tipped the scales for me, however, was the look of unalloyed evil I had seen in the man who had stared into the camera and exposed Mr. Welch's neck-stump, just before finishing his horrific decapitation.

"Are you in?" Shepherd asked again.

I hesitated a moment more. Then, although uncertain where my decision would lead, I nodded.

"I'm in."

Chapter 11

Still profoundly disturbed by the terrorists' video, I spent an additional forty-five minutes at Bureau headquarters being issued a parking pass and a Federal Building ID. Afterward, I returned to my Suburban and headed home. Partway down San Vicente Boulevard, however, I decided to stop at the West L.A. station to check in with Lieutenant Long. I also wanted to give myself some time to get my emotions under control before returning to the beach. A short detour on surface streets took me to Butler Avenue, where I parked in a mostly empty visitors' lot outside the West Los Angeles County Courthouse.

After shutting off my ignition, I made two quick calls. The first was to Chief Ingram, well before his 5:00 p.m. deadline, leaving a message with his secretary that I was officially onboard. The second was to Gavin Chan, a friend in SID's Questioned Documents Division. Following a brief conversation, I emailed Chan a photo of the Arabic word that had been smeared in blood on the Welches' wall.

Calls completed, I walked a half-block down Butler to the West L.A. station. With a nod to a patrol officer manning the lobby desk, I headed upstairs to the detectives' squad room. There, gathered around a table in the back, I found Deluca, Banowski, and Lieutenant Long sifting through a stack of files. All three looked up as I entered.

"Kane," said Deluca with a grin. "Twice in one day. We're going to have to stop meeting like this, *paisano*. People might talk."

"Hey, Dan," said Banowski, surprising me by rising from the desk and giving me a brief, bearlike hug. "Good to see you back. We could use some help around here."

"Sorry to disappoint you, John," I said. "I *am* back on the payroll, but for the moment I'm working for Chief Ingram, acting as a liaison with our Bureau friends."

"The Bel Air murders?" asked Long.

I nodded.

Long's brow furrowed. "I'm happy to see you back at work. It could be the best thing for you. But the last time we talked, you seemed pretty adamant on the subject. What changed your mind?"

"The murder video. Not that Assistant Chief Strickland didn't threaten my career if I declined."

"Screw Strickland," said Banowski. "He can't do that."

"Maybe not. But once I saw that video, Strickland's threat didn't matter much any more," I said. "I want those guys taken down, and if I have to work with the feds to see that happen, then that's what I'll do."

"I hear you," said Deluca. "That video was . . . I've never seen anything like it."

"Me, neither," said Banowski. "And I've seen a lot."

We all fell silent.

"LAPD/FBI liaison, huh? At least that should keep your name out of the papers," said Long, changing the subject. "You really okay chumming with the feds?"

I shrugged. "Better than working for Snead."

"Tell me about it," Deluca grumbled. Then, brightening, "Do you know the three most overrated things in the world?"

"Yep," I said, having heard it before. "Champagne, caviar, and the FBI."

"Some truth there," laughed Banowski. "The Bureau guys *are* good at some things, though. Like taking credit when things go well, and shifting the blame when they don't."

Like many police investigators, both Deluca and Banowski had been stung in the past when dealing with the FBI, and I knew that Banowski had a point. To be fair, I also knew that there were plenty of capable men and women in the Bureau, and despite the FBI's habit of bulldozing into any investigation it considered its turf—often without the ability to investigate the case—it wasn't reasonable to dismiss the entire agency. For that matter, there were a few mutts in the LAPD as well, and it was still a first-class organization. At the thought of mutts, my thoughts turned to Snead. "So how are things going on the task force?" I asked.

Deluca's expression darkened. "About as well as could be expected," he answered. "Considering that we're going to be running errands for the feds, taking orders from Snead, and following up on useless hotline tips, things are just swell. Snead gave us the day to reassign all our ongoing cases," he added, glancing at the files on Long's desk. "By the way, Snead wasn't too happy about your visit this morning. He ordered every detective on the task force to avoid you like an STD. Needless to say, I'll give you a heads-up if anything develops."

"Thanks, Paul."

"No problem. Just watch yourself around Snead."

"I'm reporting directly to Ingram, not Snead. Besides, I can handle Snead."

"Yeah, you said that. Just be careful."

"Speaking of being careful, how did you guys miss the oil drips?" I asked.

"Sorry about that," said Deluca, looking embarrassed. "Like I said, Snead showed up before we had a chance to do much, and Banowski and I wound up sitting on the sidelines."

"And then the feds barged in," added Banowski. "With everyone claiming a piece of the turf, the oil drips got overlooked."

"Sounds about right," I said, once more wondering what else might have slipped through the cracks. "Along those lines, where did the killers get their black flag? You might check into that."

"Good idea," said Deluca.

"They probably brought the cloth sacks and handcuff ties with them. It's a long shot, but trying to locate the source of those items should also be on the list," I suggested. "Try tracing the source of the sunglasses they were wearing, too. They looked identical, and maybe they were bought locally."

Deluca nodded. "I'll propose that to Snead."

"Make it your idea. Don't say it came from me."

"Right."

"I thought a moment. "You guys are checking everyone with a gate code, right? You might expand that search to include looking for a work vehicle or delivery van seen in the area. If the killers didn't have the gate code, maybe the Welches buzzed them in."

"I'll suggest that, too."

"So are you coming back to work here once the Bel Air case is over?" Banowski broke in, glancing at the files on Long's desk.

With Deluca detailed to the HSS task force, I realized that my former D-III duties would now fall on Banowski. "One step at a time, John," I answered. "Don't worry, I'm sure you can handle the added responsibility. It'll look good on your resume."

"Yeah, right," Banowski grumbled.

I glanced at my watch, realizing that if I wanted to avoid rush-hour traffic, I needed to hit the road. "Well, if there's nothing else . . ."

"There *is* one more thing, Dan," said Long. "Two things, actually. First, like I said, I'm glad you're back, even if it is on an organizational mess like the Bel Air case. If there's anything I can do to help, let me know."

"Thanks, Lieutenant. I appreciate that. What's the other thing?"

"Some advice, whether you want to hear it or not."

"And that is?"

"Don't trust the feds."

Chapter 12

"Make no mistake, we are at war with radical Islam," said Jacob, sweeping his gaze across his congregation as he began his evening service. "And we are losing that war," he added softly. "We are losing."

Jacob paused to let his words sink in. Then, again raising his voice, "In view of the terrorist murders that were recently reported in the news—brutal, gruesome killings committed by Muslims in our own country—we must turn our hearts and minds to this important issue, for our very survival is at stake."

"Amen, Brother Jacob," came a call from the back.

"Amen, indeed," said Jacob. "The time has come to tell the truth about our enemy," he continued. "Our government, and in particular our president and our state department, has lied to us. Our leaders aren't even willing to name our enemy, labeling them 'terrorist groups,' or 'violent extremists,' or some other misleading term. I want to clarify the issue. In plain English, our enemy is radical Islam, whose Muslim members want to impose their religion on us by force, and who will cut off our heads if we don't comply.

"Everywhere we look, radical Islam is on the march. Its goal is to dominate the world. It may take different names in different places—Al-Shabaab in Somalia; Al-Qaeda in Yemen, Libya, and India; Hezbollah in Lebanon; the Islamic State and the Levant in Iraq and Syria. Some Islamists are Shi'ites; others are Sunnis. Some want to restore a medieval caliphate from the seventh century; others want the apocalyptic return of a ninth-century imam. But *all* militant Islamists share one thing in common. They all want to establish a world order in which Christians are subjugated, freedom and tolerance are things of the past, and 'infidels' like you and me are given but one, single choice: Convert or die."

Again, Jacob paused for emphasis. Then, pushing on, "Consider the statement of Iran's founding ruler, Ayatollah Khomeini: 'We will export our revolution to the entire world, until the cry, "There is no god but God" will echo throughout the world.' These are the words of our declared enemy, and we must not take them lightly. Radical Muslims considered Osama bin Laden a holy warrior. They cheered when thousands of our citizens were murdered on 9/11.They hate our culture, our religion, our way of life."

Once more Jacob swept his gaze over his followers. "We must not take their threats lightly," he repeated. "I know that many of you think a Muslim takeover couldn't happen here in our country. You are wrong. It is already happening, as it has in many countries around the world, and this is how it proceeds: To begin, Muslims begin infiltrating a non-Muslim host country like ours, portraying Islam as a peaceful religion and Muslims as victims of racism and misunderstanding. As their population grows, increasing numbers of mosques are built to further spread Islam, along with fostering hate for the host country.

"Sound familiar?" asked Jacob. "Of course it does. And we're not alone. Nearly every nation on earth is suffering an Islamic infiltration. Worse, the Muslim Brotherhood openly states that their goal is to dissolve each nation's sovereignty, replacing it with shariah law. To that end, an Islamic consolidation of power follows next, with Muslim immigrants and converts demanding special treatment in regard to social services, education, employment, and even how they're treated in the courts," Jacob continued. "During this phase there is a marked increase in jihadist cells, along with Muslim propaganda and a demand for the adoption of shariah law. The nations of France, where Muslim youths regularly set the countryside ablaze, and the Netherlands, where a filmmaker was murdered for insulting Islam, are currently in this second consolidation stage. And we are not far behind.

"During the third phase, we see open violence used to impose shariah law. Much of the Middle East is in this chaotic stage. Opposition is silenced by intimidation, barbarity, and executions, with the ethnic cleansing of even moderate Muslims who don't support radical Islam. There is a widespread destruction of synagogues, churches, and other non-Muslim buildings, along with bombings, assassinations, and mass executions of non-Muslims. Consider recent events in London, France, Spain, Belgium, and the Netherlands, not to mention the attacks on our own Pentagon and the twin towers of New York's World Trade Center."

By now the congregation had fallen silent, every eye focused on Jacob. "The last stage of a Muslim takeover is the most chilling," he concluded. "It ends with the establishment of a totalitarian Islamic theocracy, a government in which Islam becomes an all-encompassing religious, judicial, political, and cultural ideology. Shariah becomes the 'law of the land,' with all non-Islamic rights cancelled. Under shariah law, barbaric practices like female genital mutilation, amputation, stoning, execution of apostates and homosexuals, and military rape become commonplace. All other religions are outlawed, free speech and freedom of the press are rescinded, and non-Muslim populations are either enslaved or eliminated."

Jacob raised his arms, his voice ringing with conviction. "This is happening right now in the Middle East, with states disintegrating and Islamists rushing in to fill the void. I believe that Iran, which is well on its way to possessing a nuclear weapon, is close to joining other nations already enslaved by militant Islam. When it does, it will become the newest member of the House of Islam, *Dar al-Islam*, whose citizens live under the yoke of shariah law."

Jacob glanced at Caleb, who was sitting beside Zoe in the front row. "I believe that Armageddon is militant Islam's endgame, with a worldwide caliphate rising from the ashes of nuclear holocaust," he declared, bringing the sermon to a close. "The scale of this problem is global, but first we must confront it here at home. When our government fails us, as it is now doing, we have an obligation to take up the fight ourselves. Radical Islam is a cancer, and it is spreading. Before it is too late, we must remove this cancer from our midst. It will be too late when we have jihadi attacks in the hearts of our cities. It will be too late when we have suicide bombers targeting our citizens. It will be too late when we have militants with automatic weapons slaughtering our children. We must act now, and we must act decisively. Never forget, we have a God-given right to do *whatever* is necessary to preserve our Christian way of life."

"Amen, Brother Jacob," another follower shouted, his call quickly taken up by others.

"When someone tells us that we can either convert to Islam or they will cut off our heads, we should take them at their word," Jacob concluded, holding Caleb in his gaze. "Some of you have already dedicated yourselves to this fight. I commend you, for you are doing God's work."

With a nod toward his brother, Jacob lifted his gaze and readdressed the congregation, his eyes burning with passion. "God has spoken to me. He has made this *my* cause. He has made this *our* cause. In the future, some of you may be asked to join in this battle. I am confident that with God's help, you will be prepared to accept His call."

Then, bowing his head, "Let us pray . . ."

Chapter 13

W hat's for dinner?" I called into the house, somehow having managed to miss most of the evening traffic on my drive home from West L.A. Leaning down, I rubbed Callie's head, smiling at the customarily enthusiastic welcome being extended to me by the four-legged member of our family.

"Hello to you, too, Dan," Dorothy answered from the kitchen. "And yes, my day went well. Thank you for asking."

"Hey, Pop," Allison responded from the kitchen as well. "My day was great, too. And to answer your question, we're having Grandma's split pea soup. Trav and McKenzie are joining us."

"Hi, Dad," said Travis as I made my way into the kitchen, followed by Callie. "Good to see you again, Mr. Kane," added McKenzie, who was standing at the counter helping Allison assemble a salad.

Following Catheryn's death, all of us in the Kane family had been struggling to maintain a false sense of cheer, a strained equilibrium that had replaced our household's typical give-and-take, rough-and-tumble exchanges. Thanksgiving, weeks after the funeral, had been a dismal affair, and Christmas had proved even worse. Allison's recent wedding had provided a welcome respite, with everyone briefly caught up in the joy of the moment. With the letdown following Ali's celebration, however, I sensed that polite conversation and cautious smiles were again the order of the day.

"Hey, kids," I said, forcing a smile. Then, crossing to the stove where Dorothy was stirring a large pot of soup, "Smells great. When do we eat?"

"As soon as Ali finishes making the salad," Dorothy answered. "If you want to speed things along, you can help Travis set the table."

"I'll help Trav," McKenzie offered. "Are we eating outside or up here?"

"Up here," said Dorothy. "Too cold outside. Besides, it'll be dark before long."

"Yes, ma'am," said McKenzie. "Up here it is."

Disappointed not to be eating at the picnic table outside, I walked to the window and gazed down at the beach. The tide was receding, and a littering of driftwood and kelp had marked the water's retreat, piled in random piles and clumps to the water's edge. To the west, past a small raft I had anchored offshore some years back, the sun was descending into a low-lying bank of fog. Creeping shoreward, the gray mist was slowly making its way onto the sand, tendrils of gray just beginning to envelop our lower deck. Illuminated in our deck lights, I could still see remnants of Ali's reception, the lanterns, ribbons, and decorations of the previous evening now seeming misplaced, a universe away from the harsh reality I had encountered that afternoon.

"Trav, are you and McKenzie still flying back to New York tomorrow morning?" I asked, attempting to turn my mind from darker thoughts.

"Yep. Seven a.m.," answered Travis.

"Need a ride? I can drop you off."

Travis shook his head. "We have to return our rental car at LAX anyway, so we're good. But thanks for the offer," he added with a smile.

"Looking forward to getting back to school?"

Travis's smile faltered. "I guess so."

"You don't sound too certain."

"He isn't," McKenzie broke in. "Trav is considering accepting some of the concert performances he's been offered. It's a great opportunity, but he has to give them an answer soon."

I thought a moment. "And that would mean dropping out of Juilliard?"

Travis nodded. "Probably. As soon as we get back, I'm meeting with my program advisor. Maybe we can make some adjustments to my course schedule. If that's not possible, I'm not sure what I'm going to do."

"Big decisions, eh? Well, I'm behind you one hundred percent, Trav. Whatever you decide."

"Thanks, Dad."

"We're thinking of getting a place together when we get back," McKenzie broke in again, watching me closely.

"Dorothy told me," I said. "That's great, Mac, although I'm not certain Kate would have approved. God knows, she had a fit when Ali moved in with Mike before they were married. But as we know, that situation turned out fine," I added. "Proving Kate wasn't right *all* the time."

"New York apartments are a lot more affordable for two people than one," McKenzie pointed out, moving to a cabinet and withdrawing a stack of plates. "Plus I'm working now, so I can help with expenses."

"McKenzie has been hired as an agent at one of New York's top literary agencies," said Allison.

"I'm still learning the ropes," Mac explained, beginning to set the table. "But I've already landed a big client," she added, glancing at Allison. "I wish Ali would let me represent her new book, assuming she ever finishes it."

"You working on something new, Ali?" I asked. My daughter had published a novel several years back—a fictionalized account of our family and the events preceding her brother Tom's death. In it, I had been depicted as a less-than-sympathetic character, which, to be fair, I deserved. "I'm not in your new one, am I?" I asked suspiciously.

Allison placed the salad she had been making on the kitchen table. "Uh, maybe a little. It's about the Sharon French case," she explained, referring to the murder of a Hollywood starlet that I had investigated. Allison had been an intern at Channel 2 News at the time, and her position at the TV station had led to considerable strife in the Kane household, not to mention almost getting me fired. "You were the lead investigator, so you have to be in it," she added.

"But it's also about the influential role that the news media play in today's world," McKenzie jumped in. "It's an inside account of how TV reporting really works, and it's not pretty. It could blow the top off the news business."

"It could also blow any chance I have of moving up at CBS," Allison noted.

"It doesn't have to," said McKenzie. "All you would need to do is—"

"Let's talk about this later, Mac."

"Sure, Ali. I just think—"

"Later, Mac."

"Fine," McKenzie sighed. "As long as you promise to consider it." Then, turning to Dorothy, "Are you planning to return to Santa Barbara soon, Mrs. Erickson?"

Dorothy looked up from the stove. "Mac, please call me Dorothy," she said. "And yes, I thought I'd head home soon. But I'd like to stay a few more days, if it's okay with Dan," she added, glancing at me. "It's not often that I get to spend time with my grandchildren."

"Of course. Please stay as long as you want," I said. "Actually, I started back to work today," I added. "I'm probably going to be gone a lot over the next few weeks, and I was hoping you could stick around and help with Nate."

"I'd be happy to. Speaking of Nate, dinner is almost ready. Why don't you go find your wayward son and tell him it's time to eat?"

"You started back to work?" Allison broke in. "I knew it! Are you going to be working on the Bel Air Beheadings?"

Irritated that the news media had already crafted a catchphrase for the investigation, I called to Nate's bedroom, ignoring Allison's question. "Hey, Nate! Chow time!"

When Nate didn't answer, I started toward his room, with Allison following close behind. "Are you really going to be working the Bel Air case?" she persisted.

Again ignoring Ali's question, I knocked on Nate's door. When no one responded, I peered inside. Normally Nate kept his room neat and clean—clothes hung, toys put away, books and schoolwork organized on his desk, bed made. Now his room looked like it had been turned upside down and shaken.

"Wow, what a mess," observed Allison, peering over my shoulder. "And I thought Nate was bordering on OCD. Looks like he finally got over his compulsive neatness."

"That's an understatement," I agreed, puzzled. "Where is

he?"

"I saw him heading out to the beach earlier. He's not back yet, so let's talk about the Bel Air story until he returns."

"The Bel Air story?" I said, deciding I couldn't dodge her questions any longer. "So now you're calling murder a *story*? I take it that instead of going on your honeymoon, you'll be reporting on this . . . *story*?"

Allison nodded.

"And Mike is okay with that?"

"Mike realizes that this is a big opportunity for me. He's okay with postponing the honeymoon."

"Don't be too sure."

"Mike is fine with it," Allison insisted, folding her arms across her chest. "Besides, because of the honeymoon, he was going to be late for the film he's shooting. Now he's on location, right on time."

"So this so-called story is that important to you?"

"It is, Dad. Lauren put me on it full-time. She said Channel 2 will be handling the story locally, with no Network honchos coming out to take over. Not yet, anyway."

"Honchos like your pal Brent Preston?"

"Among others. And he's not my pal. Anyway, the story is already going through the roof. I need to talk with you about it."

"Ali, I told you earlier—"

"Before you say anything, just hear me out," Allison pleaded. "Like I said, this is huge. Lauren hinted that if I handle things right, which includes maybe getting your cooperation a little, there might be a network spot opening up for me in New York. I know we've had problems in the past with your being a police detective and my being a news reporter, and—"

"Problems? That's putting it mildly."

"—and I regret some of the things I did," Allison continued, ignoring my interruption. "It won't happen again, I promise. Anything you might be able to pass on to me, without an ethical conflict, of course, will be held in strictest confidence. Nothing will come out until I have your permission to use it. And I won't pry."

"Ali, even if I wanted to help, which I don't, I'm only going to be acting as a Bureau liaison. I won't be involved in the actual investigation, so you'll have to get your information like everyone else. Snead will communicate with the press for the LAPD, and I'm sure the Bureau will have its own spokesperson as well."

"But you'll be on the inside, Dad. That counts for a lot. I'm just asking you to stay open to the idea that maybe we can cooperate, as long as we don't cross any lines. I think we might even be able to help each other, too. You never know."

"Help each other, huh?"

"That's right. And from talking with Lauren, I know that's happened in the past."

"What exactly did Lauren tell you?"

"Nothing much. Look, I'm simply saying it might come in handy for you to have a friendly ear in the media. Please, Dad. Just think about it."

I hesitated. This was the second time Allison had mentioned having a friendly ear in the media, and I wondered how much Lauren had told her. If truth be told, I had used the press for my own reasons in the past, and more than once. Unfortunately, on one such occasion Lauren had paid the price, and it had almost cost me my career. "Fine, Ali," I said. "I'll think about it. No promises, but I'll think about it. I'm warning you, though. No screw-ups. Now go help Mac set the table. I'm going to go find Nate."

After locking my service weapon in the handgun safe in my bedroom, I pulled on a jacket and stepped out to the redwood deck. Callie, who was always ready for a walk on the beach no matter how lousy the weather, joined me. By then the fog had thickened, bringing in the dank, musky smells of the ocean. The sun had set minutes earlier, and in the failing light I could barely see a dozen yards. Peering into the mist, I cupped my hands to my mouth and called, "Nate!"

No answer.

Wondering where he'd gone, I sat on the seawall, removed

my shoes and socks, and headed out onto the sand. As I did, I noticed a set of fresh footprints leading down toward the water. Turning up my collar against the cold night air, I followed the tracks to the ocean, where I lost them in the surge of the up-rushing waves. I hesitated, wondering whether to go right or left. Again, I called for Nate.

Again, nothing.

Deciding I had a fifty-fifty chance of being correct, I headed left, keeping to the firm sand near the water's edge, Callie leading the way. Several minutes later, just as I had about decided to turn around and try the other direction, a shadowy figure appeared in the mist.

Nate.

My son was walking slowly toward me, hands thrust deep in his pockets. He was wearing a pair of oversized stereo headphones, and at first he didn't notice me. I stopped and waited for him to arrive. Callie stayed back with me until she caught Nate's scent, then bounded ahead to greet him.

"Hey, Nate," I said when he reached me.

Nate looked up, seeming surprised. "Uh, hi, Dad," he said, removing his headphones. "What are you doing out here?"

"I came looking for you. Dinner's almost ready. Everyone's waiting."

"Sorry. I felt like getting some air," Nate explained, again starting down the beach. "Anyway, I'm not hungry."

I turned and walked beside Nate, heading back toward the house. "Not hungry? Are you sick?"

Nate shrugged.

"Something bothering you?"

"Not really. Why does everyone keep asking that?"

"Because you seem . . . *different* lately. And because everyone knows you're hurting. Grandma Dorothy is worried. She thinks maybe you should see a shrink."

"I'm not crazy."

"That's what I told her. But if you're sad, sometimes it helps to talk with someone. Maybe a counselor?"

"I don't think so. Can we drop this?"

"C'mon, Nate. Things have been tough for the entire Kane clan, and we're all trying to get through each day. But you haven't seemed yourself in quite a while. If something's bugging you, I want to know."

"Okay, how about this?" Nate snapped, his mood abruptly shifting. "I heard from Ali that you're thinking about going back to work for the police department. Is that right?"

"Yes, Nate, it is. I had a talk with the chief today. He wants me to act as an LAPD liaison with the FBI on a case that just came up."

"The Bel Air murder story that Ali's covering?"

I nodded. "I won't be investigating—just relaying Bureau requests and keeping the departmental wheels greased. I said yes."

"So now you're going to be working on another big investigation, just like your sniper case."

I saw where Nate was going. "I'll only be peripherally involved, Nate. The FBI will be handling the case. My work won't endanger our family in any way."

Nate stopped walking. "How can you know that?" he demanded.

I hesitated. "Nate, I—"

"How can you know that?" Nate repeated angrily. "How do you know that your job won't make something bad happen again, like . . ."

". . . like what happened to Mom?" I finished.

"That's right," Nate shot back, tears starting in his eyes. "Like what happened to Mom."

I knew that on some level Nate held me responsible for Catheryn's death, but until then I hadn't heard him voice it so openly. Not that I blamed him. I held myself responsible, too. "I'm sorry, Nate," I said. "I . . . I should have talked with you and Ali and Trav before accepting the job. I'm sorry."

"So now you're going back to work like nothing happened," Nate continued as if he hadn't heard. Furiously palming his eyes, he started again down the beach.

I caught up in two quick steps, stung by my son's bitterness.

Placing a hand on his shoulder, I gently turned him, searching his eyes with mine. "Nate, I know you're angry, but I swear I would never do anything to put our family in danger again. If that means quitting the force, then that's what I'll do."

"Yeah, sure."

"I mean it. I'll find another way to pay the bills. In the meantime, this liaison position will give me time to make some decisions. And because I'll be on the sidelines—"

"Sure you will."

"Nate, nothing bad is going to happen."

Nate started to say something, then stopped, his anger suddenly seeming to deflate. "Anyway, it doesn't matter anymore," he said, once more heading toward the house.

I caught up again, adjusting my pace to walk beside him. "It doesn't matter? What's that supposed to mean?"

"Nothing. It's just . . . I miss Mom."

As the youngest in the Kane clan, Nate had always been the one to see the brighter side of life. Given a Christmas present of road apples, he'd start looking for the pony. That had changed. Once again I wished Catheryn were present. She would have known what to do.

"I miss her, too," I said. "More than I can say."

By then we had nearly made it back to the house. Emerging like sentinels in the fog, I could make out the thick stands of palm and beach cane flanking our home, seeming to anchor it to the sand. Placing an arm around Nate's shoulders, I headed toward the glow of the windows above our upper deck. In one of them I noticed Dorothy peering out. Spotting us, she waved. I waved back.

With a sigh, I decided there would be time enough to think about things later. Until then, a hot meal might help put things in perspective. I tightened my grip around Nate's shoulders. The temperature had dropped even more, and beneath his thin jacket I could feel him shivering.

"C'mon, kid," I said. "Let's go eat."

Chapter 14

The following morning, if I'd had any expectation of receiving a warm, fuzzy reception at my initial FBI briefing, that misconception was quickly dispelled. As soon as I entered the Bureau's Command and Tactical Operations Center, I saw how things were going to be. Although my welcome there was both respectful and polite, it was immediately clear to me that I would be treated as an outsider . . . not that I much cared.

I had checked with Chief Ingram's office and placed a call to Deluca on the drive from Malibu to West L.A., arriving early at the Federal Building for the FBI briefing. As directed, I had then made my way to the FBI's Command and Tactical Operations Center on the sixteenth floor.

CTOC turned out to be a windowless, brightly lit suite of interconnected rooms that included two command centers, a control room, and a large conference area. The command centers, marked OPS1 and OPS2, both contained long, curving banks of computer workstations, most of which were already manned. Past the control room, the CTOC conference area was filled with unsmiling men and somber women. From the number of agents already present, it looked like everyone else had arrived early as well.

As I stepped inside, Special Agent in Charge Gibbs, whom I had met the previous afternoon, pushed through a throng of agents to greet me. "Good morning, Kane. Good to see you again," he said, shaking my hand. Once more his grip felt firm, and his eyes never left mine. Again, I thought military.

"Likewise," I said.

Gibbs glanced at his watch. "We should just have time for me to introduce you to the rest of the Command Group before we get started. Let's head over there by the monitors," he suggested, inclining his head toward the far side of the room.

I followed Gibbs to a wall covered with TV screens, a world map, and clocks displaying the time in various cities. On the way over I spotted Agent Taylor talking with her friend, Agent Duffy.

Taylor nodded at me without smiling, then returned to her conversation. Duffy noticed her glance. Following her gaze, he spotted me and frowned.

Trailing Gibbs across the crowded room, I felt the eyes of many others upon me as well, most of them about as friendly as Duffy's. It had been a long time since I'd been "the new guy." But again, I didn't much care.

A group assembled near the TV monitors looked up at our approach. "Detective Kane, this is Assistant Special Agent in Charge Mason Vaughn," Gibbs said when we arrived, indicating a tall man with dark, slicked back hair. "ASAC Vaughn is currently coordinating our efforts with the LAPD under the umbrella of the FBI's Los Angeles Joint Terrorism Task Force, or JTTF. Mason, Detective Kane."

Vaughn nodded without offering his hand. I nodded back. Despite Vaughn's whip-thin frame and aristocratic, almost feminine bearing, I sensed a glimmer of something as hard as steel behind his eyes.

"ASAC Vaughn will be your designated contact with the Bureau. He will keep you apprised of investigative areas best suited for the LAPD task force to pursue," Gibbs continued. "Along with working with LAPD investigators, the JTTF will also bring to bear the expertise of forty-five local, state, and federal agencies currently investigating terrorist activities, as well as interfacing with other satellite Joint Terrorism Task Forces in Orange County, Long Beach, and the Inland Empire. Needless to say, JTTF will also be staying in close contact with the National Counterterrorism Center in McLean, Virginia."

"Needless to say," I said, again thinking too many cooks.

"Special Agent Luis Garcia, Detective Kane," Gibbs continued, indicating a thick-set Hispanic who had a hint of sweat glistening on his forehead, even though the room seemed cool to me. "Garcia heads up our Field Intelligence Group, which interfaces with the FBI's multi-agency Joint Regional Intelligence Center, providing agent and analyst support to our law enforcement and intelligence partners in all of California."

"Good to meet you," said Garcia, wiping his palm on a pant

leg before offering to shake.

"Likewise," I said, taking his hand, which still felt damp.

"The Los Angeles Joint Terrorism Task Force headed by Vaughn also coordinates with Garcia's Field Intelligence Group in a collaboration known as TITAN," Gibbs went on. "TITAN is an intelligence initiative that collects and shares information on terrorist operations with law enforcement and critical asset partners nationwide. The Bureau is currently investigating over 900 active cases in the United States involving Islamic State sympathizers and Muslim terrorist cells. Our present Los Angeles terrorist investigation will be linked with all open cases now being pursued by FBI field divisions across the country."

"With that many agents working the case, you should have things wrapped up in no time," I observed, mentally attempting to calculate the number of people involved. I decided that whatever that number was, it was huge. Nevertheless, as I had learned more than once, throwing men and money at a problem didn't necessarily bring results.

Ignoring my comment, Gibbs turned to the final member of the Command Group, a muscular man with crew-cut hair and a noticeably flattened nose. "This is Special Agent Brody Young," said Gibbs. "Young heads our Counterintelligence Domain Program, bringing together the FBI and our counterintelligence partners with members of private industry, academia, and other government agencies to protect the special interests of our country."

"Special interests like not having someone cut off your head?" I noted, offering my hand to Young.

Brody Young was a large man, almost as big as I am, and I could tell from his expression that he didn't like my previous comment. He also didn't like looking up to meet someone's gaze. "Exactly," said Young, taking my hand and squeezing just a bit too hard, something men occasionally do when confronted by someone bigger than they are.

Two could play that game. I smiled and squeezed back, increasing the force of my handshake to match Young's escalating effort. Seconds later Young's enthusiasm for our impromptu competition turned to surprise, and then shock as his grip suddenly collapsed, his knuckles grinding audibly. Grimacing, he tried to retrieve his hand. I held on a moment longer, then released it.

"That's a good grip you've got there, Agent Young," I noted. "I've always hated a flabby handshake myself," I added, quoting from one of my favorite John Wayne films—a reference apparently lost on Young.

"Me, too," Young agreed sheepishly.

Gibbs, who had witnessed our puerile contest, regarded us both with impatience. "Brody, if there's time following the briefing, I'd like you to introduce Kane to the rest of our field agents working the case," he said. "That is, if you're done screwing around."

"Uh, yes, sir," said Young, massaging his hand to restore the flow of blood. "I'm done."

"Good."

Gibbs seemed about to say something else, but stopped abruptly as he noticed Assistant Director Shepherd entering the room. Gibbs turned and nodded to Vaughn, who moved to the front and raised a hand for attention.

"Everyone find a seat," Vaughn ordered as the room began to settle. "I know many of you have been here all night, so let's get the briefing underway. Special Agent in Charge Gibbs will bring us up-to-date, after which we'll move on to assignments. SAC Gibbs, you want to take it from here?"

I glanced at Shepherd, who had moved to a spot near the computer screens, seeming content to let Gibbs handle the proceedings. Meeting my gaze, Shepherd looked back and nodded briefly, then returned his attention to Gibbs.

"Thanks, Mason," said Gibbs, stepping to the front. "Since yesterday there have been several new developments in the investigation, which has been code-named 'Infidel.' First, Detective Daniel Kane is present from the LAPD and will be acting as our Joint Terrorism Task Force liaison. Kane will keep us apprised and updated on all areas of the LAPD's 'Infidel' inquiry, as well as bringing the JTTF/LAPD task force up-to-date on Bureau progress."

Heads turned in my direction. Several agents nodded. Most simply stared.

"Second, there are several new areas of investigation underway," Gibbs continued. "Fresh oil drips and a tire track imprint, both possibly from the murder vehicle, were discovered at the Bel Air scene. Oil samples and tire prints from the Welches' vehicles and a gardener's ride-on-top mower have ruled them out as the source. Our lab is currently analyzing the oil drips, which, along with the imprint casts, may be useful when we locate the murder vehicle."

"LAPD already has the oil-drip analysis," I interjected.

"Oh?" said Gibbs.

"Yes, sir. The oil was a mix of five-thirty Chevron Supreme and forty-weight Havoline. SID sent a sample over to the Standard Oil refining lab in El Segundo, so we'll have a more detailed breakdown shortly."

"Thank you, Detective," said Gibbs. "Actually, this might be as good a time as any for you to bring us current on any ancillary investigative areas that the LAPD is pursuing."

"Yes, sir." I paused to revisit my conversation that morning with Deluca, then continued without referring to notes. "To start, LAPD looked hard at Chuck Lohrman, the pool guy who reported the murders. He's been ruled out as having any connection with the homicides. Unfortunately, a canvass of the Bel Air neighborhood has been unable to turn up any witnesses to date. We're still reviewing footage from a number of neighborhood security cameras that might have caught a shot of the murder vehicle. Nothing there yet. And working on the assumption that the killers knew the Welches' gate code, we're interviewing anyone who had the code—friends, neighbors, landscape service, the cleaning woman, and so on. Nothing there yet, either."

"How about the tip line?" asked Garcia.

I knew from talking with Deluca that a host of FBI personnel had been detailed to assist in manning the LAPD's twenty-four-hour hot line. Although Bureau agents were working side-by-side with a team of Snead's investigators, most of the legwork generated by the tip line would be done by Snead's detectives.

"Nothing useful has developed so far," I answered. "Not that there haven't been a flood of calls, all of which have to be checked out, seriously impacting LAPD man-hours. In my opinion, if you're expecting anything worthwhile to come in on the so-called hot line, don't hold your breath."

Several agents nodded in agreement.

"We're also trying to run down the source of the ISIS flag on the video," I continued. "We've determined that the Arabic letters on the flag are an exact copy of an image currently posted on the internet."

"How does that help?" asked an agent near the front.

"Because of the size of the flag, we think the killers had it custom made—silkscreened, not embroidered, as it's an *exact* copy—and they used the internet image as a pattern," I explained. "We're checking print shops, silkscreen facilities, and online services, trying to locate the source. It's a long shot, but we're also checking for the source of the cloth sacks and plastic handcuff ties, which we think the killers brought with them."

"Keep us updated on those investigations," said Vaughn.

"Yes, sir," I said. "One more thing. We had our lab blow up several of the video images. We think the killers were all wearing identical Maui Jim sunglasses. They're expensive, so we're hoping if they were bought locally, someone might have a record of the purchase. It's another long shot, but we don't have a lot to go on."

"Keep us updated on that as well," Vaughn ordered, seeming impatient to proceed. "Anything else?"

I shrugged. "That's about it on the LAPD side, except for an analysis of the fingerprint, blood, and other forensic material that was taken at the scene. I'm sure your lab will come up with the same results we do."

"Thanks for that update, Detective Kane," said Gibbs. Then, turning back to Vaughn, "Mason, you want to bring us current on our investigative efforts since yesterday?"

"Yes, sir," said Vaughn, opening a file he'd carried tucked

under an arm. "I'll make this brief so we can get to our assignments. Several intersecting lines of inquiry are underway, the most important of which is locating the source of the murder video. Whoever posted it used an IP masking service called the Tor Project. With help from NSA, our Computer Analysis Response Team unit was able to trace the original upload to a Starbucks in Santa Monica. From there we hit a brick wall. CART is still working on breaking into the Tor network. We also have surveillance on the Starbucks in question, along with several other coffee shops in the area. If the killers do it again and upload another video, we'll have them on tape."

An uneasy rustling travelled the room as everyone considered the possibility of more killings.

"At present none of the unmatched prints found at the scene has turned up in the system," Vaughn continued. "Forensic analysis of materials recovered from the Welch residence has also proved unproductive. The murder knives seen in the video were not found in the house, so we're assuming they were retained by the killers. None of the kitchen knives or other cutting instruments in the home showed the presence of blood, but we're running them for prints just to be certain. DNA analysis of the blood of unknown origin discovered in the master bathroom— blood we think might belong to one of the unsubs—came back from the lab this morning. No matches have been located in the system."

Vaughn paused to refer to his file, then continued. "On a positive note, earlier this morning our CART unit was able to break into the Welches' personal computers. CART is currently downloading all files, email messages, and other correspondence from the Welches' hard drives. Along with an examination of the family's checkbooks and bank statements, this material may lead to a connection with the killers. Garcia, your team is working that angle, correct?"

"Yes, sir," said Garcia, using a handkerchief to wipe his brow. "Nothing has turned up so far, but getting a look at the Welches' computer files will help."

"Good," said Vaughn, looking satisfied. "We sent an

Emergency Disclosure Request to Verizon, so we should have the Welches' phone records later today. We'll see whether anything helpful shows up there, especially on the night of the murders."

"Yes, sir," said Garcia.

"Okay, two more items, both of which may be promising," Vaughn pushed on. "Young, your team is working the gun angle with ATF. What have you learned so far?"

Appearing uncomfortable under the combined gaze of everyone present, Agent Young stood. "Uh, we have made some progress locating the source of the AK-47," he began, referring to a notebook. "It's a Chinese knockoff known as a Norinco or Chicom Type 56. Among other things, the Chicom Type 56 differs from a Russian AK-47 in having a fully enclosed front sight and a folding bayonet mount attached to the barrel just aft of the muzzle. ATF is reviewing registration logs, checking for ownership of this type of weapon. If there's a record of that rifle being purchased or transferred, I'm confident we'll find it."

"Not to rain on your parade, Brody, but what if it was purchased at a private sale?" asked Taylor. A number of heads turned in her direction. "Like at a gun show?" she continued stubbornly, ignoring looks of impatience from several in the room.

It was a good question. I'd been thinking the same thing, and upon hearing Taylor ask it, my estimation of her ascended several notches. I knew from working other cases that tracing a firearm could sometimes be an impossible task. Although federal law required anyone engaged in the business of selling guns to have a Federal Firearm License and keep a record of their FFL sales, the rule didn't apply to anyone selling rifles or handguns from a private collection—say at a gun show. Hence the so-called "gun-show loophole." A few states like California had passed laws requiring background checks on all gun-show firearm sales, but most states had done nothing to close the loophole. And two of those states were right across the California border.

"We've asked ATF to look into that angle, too," replied Young. "California has strict laws regarding the transfer of assault weapons like an AK, but other states aren't as stringent.

So, yeah, it's a problem."

"Let's move on," Vaughn suggested. "Notwithstanding other areas of inquiry, and because of the terrorist aspect of the crime, the main thrust of our investigation will focus on reaching out to our contacts and operational partners in the Muslim world. Someone in the Islamic community knows who did this. Using the resources of our Los Angeles Joint Terrorism Task Force, our Joint Regional Intelligence Center, TITAN's Field Intelligence Group, and working with our multi-agency colleagues across public and private sectors—both here in California and in other states as well—we *will* find them. Following the briefing, each of you meet with your Command Group leader and pick up your assignments." Vaughn glanced at his watch. "Any final questions?"

I had a few, but as I had no investigative position on the case, I decided to keep my mouth shut.

"So we're assuming this was done by Muslim extremists, and we're looking for a source or informant in the Muslim community?" asked an agent near the rear. "If that's the case, how do you explain the Welches' inviting a team of Islamic terrorists into their living room? It doesn't make sense."

In my opinion, his question was right on target. Why had the Welches' allowed the killers past their gate? From the beginning, I'd thought there had to be something more. Against my better judgment, I decided to weigh in. "As I mentioned earlier, LAPD is checking everyone with the Welches' gate code," I said. "I could suggest to our guys that they widen their search. Maybe somebody saw a suspicious work vehicle or trade van cruising the area," I added, deciding not to mention I had already suggested that line of inquiry to Deluca.

Gibbs spoke up. "Good idea, Kane."

"Yes, sir. Another thing," I continued, unable to stay silent. "Am I the only one here who thinks something stinks about that murder video?"

Again, Vaughn glanced at his watch. "We appreciate your input, Detective Kane, but please remember you're here as a liaison, not as an investigator. Now, if there are—"

"Let's hear what Kane has to say," interrupted Director Shepherd, speaking for the first time. "An outside opinion might prove useful."

"Yes, sir," said Vaughn. Then, turning to me with an ill-disguised look of irritation, "What impressions on the murder video would you like to share, Kane?"

"I just think something's . . . off about it," I said. "Sure, they were going for shock value, and they succeeded. But what's with the sunglasses, and completely covering their features with hoods and gloves? And the AK-47, or Chicom Type 56, or whatever it was. Just a little too theatrical, in my opinion. Plus those demands they made . . . they can't possibly think they'll be met. It doesn't add up. I have a hunch something more is going on."

"Hunches are fine, as long as they're discarded once evidence has proved them wrong," said Vaughn, closing his file. "Facts will determine our conclusions on this investigation, and the facts indicate that these murders were committed by members of an unknown extremist cell. As such, until the facts prove otherwise, we will proceed accordingly. Now, if there are no other questions, let's—"

"I do have one more question," I broke in again. Since reviewing the impound list of items taken from the Welches' residence, I had been plagued by the feeling I was missing something. I'd been chewing on it since yesterday, and during the drive to the briefing that morning I had finally realized what it was. An examination of any crime scene should consider not only what is present, but what is *not* present as well. It wasn't something that *I* was missing. It was something that was missing from the impound list.

"Yes?" said Vaughn, finally seeming out of patience.

"Where are the Welches' cellphones?"

"Excuse me?"

"I asked, where are the Welches' cellphones? Everyone has a cellphone. I checked the list of items taken from their house. Cellphones weren't on it."

"Are you certain?"

I have a good memory. Maybe better than good. At times it

wasn't something I valued, especially lately when I couldn't get thoughts of Catheryn out of my mind. But at other times, like now, it was. I took a moment to rerun the impound list in my mind, reviewing each item as plainly as if I were reading the original file. "I'm certain," I said.

"Even if it's true, I don't see how—"

"I think Kane is suggesting that the killers might have taken the Welches' cellphones with them," Gibbs jumped in. "And if that's the case, we might have a chance of locating them."

The room fell silent.

"Damn," said an agent sitting near Taylor. "It's a long shot, but if those phones are still turned on and the batteries aren't dead yet . . ."

"Mason, we need that authorization from Verizon ASAP," said Gibbs. "We might just have a chance of winding this up sooner than later. And check with legal about getting a warrant for a cellphone-location trace. Verizon may ask for it, and we don't want to screw things up on a technicality. In the meantime, all agents pick up your assignments and hit the streets."

Next, Gibbs turned in my direction. "Kane, I need to talk with you after the briefing," he said. "Taylor, after you pick up your assignment, I'll need to talk with you, too."

Chapter 15

"What did you want to see me about, sir?" asked Taylor, addressing SAC Gibbs. I was standing nearby, also having sought out Gibbs after the briefing. Duffy had followed Taylor over as well, seeming as puzzled as the rest of us by Gibbs's request.

"Change of assignment, Agent Taylor," said Gibbs. "I'm teaming you with Detective Kane for the next few days, assuming the case continues that long."

"But, sir, why do I have to babysit—"

"This isn't a request, Taylor."

Taylor scowled. "Yes, sir. May I ask why?"

"No, you may not."

Duffy, who had initially looked more upset about the change in assignment than Taylor, seemed to have been about to object as well. At this he closed his mouth.

"Taylor, you will complete today's field assignment with Kane accompanying you as an observer," Gibbs continued. "Duffy, you are being detailed to ASAC Vaughn's unit and will assist in locating the Welches' cellphones."

"Yes, sir," said Duffy, visibly brightening.

"Well? Why are you all still standing here? Get to work."

"Yes, sir. Thank you, sir," said Duffy. With a guilty glance at Taylor, he turned and headed across the room toward Vaughn, who already had several enthusiastic agents gathered around him.

"What do you say, Taylor?" I asked, part of me surprised by Gibbs's pairing me with Taylor, another part perversely enjoying her irritation. "Ready to hit the streets?"

Taylor's face darkened. Without replying, she started for the door.

"Hey, Taylor, wait up. I have a question," I called, taking long strides to catch up.

"You're just full of questions, aren't you?" Taylor grumbled without slowing her pace.

"This is an easy one. Where's the Computer Analysis

Response Team that Vaughn mentioned? CART? They have the Welches' computers, right? Are they here in the building?"

"Our CART lab is on the fourteenth floor. Why?"

"Fourteenth floor? Okay, I just thought of something I want to check, so I need to make a quick stop there on the way out. You coming?"

"No, I'm not going to the CART lab. And neither are you. I have my assignment, and you're going to accompany me on it, whether I like it or not."

"What's the assignment? Hitting some downtown mosque and interviewing an uncooperative mullah who probably doesn't know anything and wouldn't tell you if he did?"

Taylor looked away. "We're interviewing a Bureau asset at the King Fahad Mosque."

"Sorry, Taylor. You and I both know it'll be a waste of time, but I'll go with you. But first I'm going to talk with your CART unit. If you don't want to join me, I'll meet you in the parking garage." By then we had reached the elevators. "Either that, or you can leave on your assignment and explain later to Gibbs why you didn't bring me along."

"Damn it, Kane . . ."

"Come on, Taylor. I have an idea I want to check out. It'll just take a minute," I coaxed, stepping into a waiting elevator and punching the button for the fourteenth floor.

"What idea?"

"You'll see."

By then the elevator door had started to close. Taylor hesitated. Then, with a look of irritation, she held the door and stepped inside. "This had better be quick," she warned.

"What's your problem, Taylor?"

"I don't have a problem, Kane. I just love babysitting our LAPD liaison while my partner actually gets to work the case."

I knew that Taylor had a point, and I remained silent as we descended to the fourteenth floor, thinking that the built-in bias against women in law enforcement, justified or not, was probably the same in the Bureau as it was at the LAPD.

The CART facility turned out to be a large, well-lit room

down the hall from the elevators. Several men looked up from a workbench as we entered, clearly surprised by our visit. "Can I help you guys?" one of the technicians asked.

"I'm hoping you can," I said before Taylor could answer. "In the briefing upstairs just now, ASAC Vaughn said you guys were able to break into the Welches' computers. Good work."

"Thanks," the technician replied, pleased at the compliment. "Actually, it wasn't as difficult as you'd think. Both of them were using the same password, which helped. We've downloaded most of the pertinent files, but Mr. Welch's machine also has an encrypted partition that we weren't able to decode. We're sending both computers over to our RFCL lab in Orange County to see what they can do."

"RFCL?"

"Regional Forensic Computer Laboratory," the man explained.

"Are the Welches' computers still here, or have you already sent them to Orange County?"

The technician called to a man at another workbench. "Hey, Arturo, have those computers gone out yet?"

"They're still in the back," Arturo replied. "All boxed up and ready to go."

"Can I take a look?" I asked.

"Sure," the first man answered. "We're done with them. Don't see how it could hurt."

"What are you doing, Kane?" Taylor demanded.

"Just give me a minute," I said, watching as Arturo retrieved a large cardboard box, slit open a strip of packing tape, and withdrew two Mac computers—a laptop and an iMac desktop model—along with a wireless keyboard and mouse.

"Can you fire them up?" I asked, pleased to see that the Welches had been Mac users. I had been an Apple customer for years and was familiar with most of the Mac features, including the seamless syncing of all their products. As such, I knew there was a good chance that the Welches had owned iPhones as well.

Arturo carried the iMac to a nearby counter, plugged it in, and hit the power button. As the desktop machine began booting up, he opened the laptop and turned it on as well.

The iMac screen came up first, displaying a password panel in the center. I glanced at Arturo.

"DivorceInc1," he said. "Initial caps on the 'D' and 'I.' Same for both machines."

Using the wireless keyboard, I tapped in the password. An instant later a desktop screen appeared, with a number of icons superimposed on an outdoor scene. From the file names below several of the icons, it was clear that the machine had belonged to Mr. Welch.

Taylor stared at the computer screen. "Kane, what the hell—"

"Trust me, Taylor," I said, moving the cursor to the bottom of the screen and clicking a Safari icon. When the internet browser display appeared, I typed "icloud.com" into the address bar. A moment later another screen appeared, this one with a further assortment of icons. One of them—a green circle resembling a radar screen—had the words "Find my iPhone" written beneath it. Clicking on that, I got an Apple sign-in request. Hoping Mr. Welch had used the same password for his iCloud account, I mentally crossed my fingers and typed in "DivorceInc1."

No luck.

Before Taylor could object, I switched to the laptop and repeated the procedure.

This time it worked.

Following the brief image of a compass, a map of Santa Monica appeared. A gray marker was pulsing on Second Street between Broadway and Colorado Avenue, a few blocks from the Santa Monica pier. I clicked on the marker. It read "Arleen's iPhone." Accompanying the location marker, whose gray color indicated it had been sent when Mrs. Welch's cellphone charge became critically low, was the transmission time of the final signal.

Arleen's cellphone battery had died early Monday morning, approximately twenty-nine hours after her murder.

"Cool," said Arturo, who had been watching over my shoulder. "We didn't know the Welches' cellphones were missing, or we would have done that search ourselves," he added, seeming embarrassed.

I made a mental note of Arleen's cellphone location and shut off both computers. "Don't beat yourself up. We just recently figured out the phones were missing," I said, adding, "Thanks for your help, guys."

"No problem," said Arturo.

"C'mon, Taylor," I said, heading for the door. "Let's take a ride."

"Take a ride?" Taylor said incredulously once we were outside. "That was good work, Kane, but you have to be kidding. I need to report this."

"Why? So Vaughn and your boyfriend Duffy can take over?"

Taylor's face darkened. "Screw you, Kane," she snapped. "Duffy isn't my boyfriend."

"Maybe you should let him know that," I advised. "At any rate, this is a chance for you to get in on the investigation, instead of sitting on the sidelines babysitting me, as you put it. Unless I'm reading you wrong, that's what you want, right?"

Taylor hesitated. "Yes, but we—"

"Listen to me for a minute," I interrupted. "Mrs. Welch's cellphone being in Santa Monica can mean one of three things. Scenario one: The killers still have it, in which case we proceed to the location, make sure they don't leave, and call for backup. Scenario two: Mrs. Welch's cellphone is down there in Santa Monica somewhere, maybe in a trashcan. While your guys upstairs are dicking around with Verizon—getting a location warrant and organizing an Evidence Response Team search—that phone could be picked up and on its way to a landfill. Scenario three: Mrs. Welch's cellphone has already been moved, in which case we'd both look like idiots calling in the mighty resources of the FBI without first checking things out. Whatever the case, we need to move, Taylor. And we need to move now."

"You heard Gibbs, Kane. Without a warrant, the case could be compromised."

"I know the law, Taylor. The Welches' cellphones were stolen, so the killers can't claim any expectation of privacy. And under the circumstances, I don't think the Welches will object to our trampling their Fourth Amendment rights."

Taylor still looked unconvinced.

"I'm heading to Santa Monica," I said. "If there's trouble about this later, blame it on me. Come with me or not, Taylor, I don't care. But I'm going."

In the end Taylor decided to accompany me, as I was going with or without her. She also agreed to postpone calling Gibbs, at least until after we had determined the situation in Santa Monica.

We rode in my car. Taking surface streets, we arrived at an industrial section in Santa Monica twenty minutes later. The Second Street neighborhood was zoned for restaurants, shops, and the like—no residential structures.

Which left looking for a dump site.

Following a brief search, we located a dumpster behind a local McDonald's, close to the spot I had noted on the "Find my iPhone" screen. As luck would have it, we arrived minutes ahead of a scheduled garbage pickup. Glancing at Taylor, I flashed my badge and waved off the trash truck. Then, after removing my jacket, I donned a pair of latex gloves and started looking. After a moment's deliberation, Taylor opened her handbag, pulled out a pair of gloves of her own, and joined me.

Within minutes, our dumpster-diving paid off. We discovered Mrs. Welch's cellphone in a black plastic trash bag, buried beneath paper waste, spoiling garbage including McDonald's fare and a partially eaten pizza, and a broken wicker chair. The trash bag containing Mrs. Welch's cellphone also held a second phone, presumably Mr. Welch's, along with towels and a wadded mass of black clothing—all of which appeared to be stained with dried blood.

"Damn, Kane," said Taylor, staring at the cellphones. "I . . . I need to report this."

"Right," I agreed. "It's time to call in the cavalry. You might suggest they keep their response low-key, however. If the killers aren't aware that we've found their dump site, they might try to use it again."

Looking both apprehensive and excited, Taylor withdrew her

cellphone. She hesitated, again glancing at the phones and stained clothing, which we'd piled on the hood of my Suburban.

"Like I said, if there's any fallout for not reporting this immediately, you can blame it on me," I offered.

Taylor began punching numbers into her phone. "I don't need your help, Kane," she said. "We sure as hell didn't follow protocol, but there were extenuating circumstances. If Gibbs or Vaughn want to write me up on this, I'll take the heat."

Chapter 16

Jacob had long been troubled by the source of the voices. It had only been over the course of the past year, as he had gradually come to realize that it was the voice of God speaking to him, that things had started to make sense.

And God had spoken to him again.

From his rocky outcrop high above the compound, Jacob felt a surge of regret. It was unfortunate that more innocents would have to die. Nevertheless, in the words of Mr. Spock, a *Star Trek* character portrayed by Leonard Nimoy, the needs of the many outweighed the needs of the few. And although they were the words of an imaginary character in a science-fiction series, they were true nevertheless. Jacob sighed, steeling himself for what was to come.

For God had spoken to him once more, and God had given him a message.

It was time to do it again.

And the more horrendous the killings . . . the more effective would they be.

Chapter 17

The next morning, as I sat in the Bureau conference room waiting for the FBI briefing to begin, I sensed that the cautious mood of the previous day had been replaced by a guarded feeling of optimism. Without it being said, everyone there was thinking the same thing.

The killers had made mistakes.

And those mistakes might just give investigators an opening.

After our discovery of the Welches' cellphones, Taylor's call to FBI headquarters had summoned the full force of the Bureau's Evidence Response Team. Ignoring my suggestion that they keep their investigation low-key, the Bureau's ERT unit, assisted by an army of agents including ASAC Vaughn, Agent Duffy, and others, had cordoned off an entire block on Second Avenue before taking custody of the cellphones and bloodstained clothing. The ERT unit had then painstakingly recovered, recorded, and taken into evidence every other item in the dumpster—paper trash, spoiled food, even the smashed wicker chair.

While awaiting the FBI's arrival, I had made a call to Chief Ingram's office, relaying an update on the dumpster development. Upon hearing the news, the chief himself had come on the line to give me an enthusiastic "attaboy."

ASAC Vaughn's reaction upon arriving, however, had been the opposite. With a disapproving scowl, Vaughn had reminded me, not so patiently on this occasion, that I was present on the Bureau task force as a liaison, not as an investigator. I didn't respond, figuring I would let the facts speak for themselves. Irritated by my silence, Vaughn proceeded to giving Taylor a thorough chewing-out as well.

Taylor, I'll concede, did a respectable job of standing her ground—pointing out that were it not for our immediate action, the Welches' cellphones would now be buried beneath tons of garbage in a landfill somewhere. Although Vaughn had no response for that, I knew from experience how office politics worked, and I that Taylor's attitude hadn't done her career much good.

On the upside, at the meeting that morning there seemed to be a shift in the way other agents were regarding Taylor. I think I might have even gained a little "dumpster credibility" myself. But again, my priority wasn't earning Bureau approval. The clock was ticking, and as far as I was concerned, the FBI's investigation, with its dependence on critical asset partners, multiagency task forces, and intelligence networks with acronyms like TITAN or JTTF, wasn't getting the job done. They needed investigators hitting the streets doing solid, methodical police work, and I didn't see that happening. Unfortunately, considering that Snead was running the LAPD's side of things, I suspected that progress wasn't being made over there, either.

"Everyone quiet down," Vaughn ordered at precisely 8:00 a.m. Then, referring to an index card, "There are several new developments. First, the Welches' cellphones turned up yesterday in a Santa Monica dumpster, along with bloodstained towels and several articles of clothing. No prints other than those of Mr. and Mrs. Welch were found on the phones. We've determined that the blood types present on the towels and clothing are consistent with those of the murdered victims."

Vaughn referred to his notes and continued. "The recovered clothing appears similar to that seen worn by the terrorists in the murder video. DNA analysis is underway on materials recovered from both the clothing and the towels. When available, we'll run those results through the system, as well as comparing the blood analysis to the unknown DNA found in the Welches' bathroom."

"Did anyone see the killers dumping the phones and clothing?" someone asked.

Vaughn glanced in my direction. "LAPD has been canvassing the neighborhood for witnesses. Any results on that, Kane?"

"None," I answered. "Not yet, anyway. Because the dumpster is located in a business area, the feeling on the task force is that if the phones and clothes were discarded at night, it's unlikely anyone was around."

"Keep us apprised," Vaughn ordered.

"Right. Speaking of which, you might think about putting some surveillance on the dumpster, in case they do it again," I suggested. "A hidden webcam or whatever, like you're doing at Starbucks. Maybe put some coverage on other nearby dumpsters as well. The killers might not realize we found the phones and clothes, and they might use the site again. Although considering the parade of agents you had down there yesterday, that's probably a long shot."

Vaughn glanced at Gibbs, who nodded. Without commenting on my suggestion, Vaughn scribbled something in his notebook and continued. "On another front, we received the Welches' telephone records from Verizon. Some of you will be detailed to run down their contacts, checking for a possible connection with their murderers. Also, you'll note that the call log on Mrs. Welch's phone shows a nine-second 911 outgoing call followed by another four-second 911 call having been attempted around the time we estimate the terrorist attack began. Her calls were never completed, so they aren't listed on the Verizon records. Kane, your LAPD task force is checking into that, correct?"

I nodded. "All 911 calls originating in Los Angeles arrive at one of two central Public Safety Answering Points—Valley Dispatch Center and Metropolitan Dispatch Center," I explained. "There are over 500 Police Service Responder operators on staff, but the number on duty at any given time is less, maybe a quarter to a third of that. LAPD is contacting all PSR operators who were working that night. So far no one has any record of receiving a call made from Mrs. Welch's cellphone."

"Keep us updated."

"Yes, sir." I thought a moment. "It's my understanding that Mrs. Welch's cellphone showed a "cancelled call" status on her 911 attempts. Maybe the killers used a tactical jammer? You know, like our SWAT teams use to block cellphone reception at an active crime scene?"

"That's getting us a little far afield," said Vaughn. "It's more reasonable to think that Mrs. Welch simply panicked and hung up before a phone connection was made."

"That may be, but the LAPD task force is still canvassing the

Welches' neighborhood," I persisted. "While they're at it, how about if we ask them to check for anyone who might have lost cellphone reception that evening?"

"Fine," said Vaughn with a dismissive nod. Again he paused to check his index card. "Okay, two final items before you pick up your assignments. First, summary sheets with copies of the Welches' phone records, a listing of clothing and other items recovered from the dumpster, and updates on current and ongoing lab tests will be available after the briefing. Second, Dr. Jonathan Schwartz, who consults with the Bureau on Islamic affairs, has flown in from Quantico to give us his impressions on the case. Listen up, as anything he has to say might be helpful." Turning to a short, bearded man standing behind him, "Dr. Schwartz?"

"Thank you, Agent Vaughn," said Dr. Schwartz, stepping to the front. "I'm not certain I can help, but you never know, so I'll try. First I want to briefly go over some background on militant Islam that might help put your case in perspective. Following that, I'll talk about the beheading issue."

At the mention of beheading, a number of agents leaned forward in their seats.

"To start, first let me make the point that we're not engaged in a 'war on terror,' as has been reported in the press," Dr. Schwartz began. "Terrorism is a tactic, not an enemy. Simply put, our enemy is radical Islam, and to give you an idea of the scope of the problem, consider this: There are over a billion Muslims globally, of which it's estimated that ten to fifteen percent fall into the 'militant' category. That's 100 to 150 million militant Muslims worldwide. Radical Islam has already established strongholds in Egypt, Somalia, Syria, Algeria, Saudi Arabia, the Palestinian territories, Jordan, Lebanon, Pakistan, Malaysia, the Philippines, Nigeria, and a host of other countries. And America is on their radar."

Schwartz paused for emphasis, then continued. "In the United States, no one knows exactly how many Muslims there are, but their number is clearly in the millions. As far as a demographic breakdown, our Muslim population consists of immigrants and converts, with immigrants from South Asia, Iran, and Arabic-speaking countries outnumbering a primarily African-American convert population by two- or three-to-one. The ratio of militant to moderate Muslims is approximately the same as it is worldwide—ten to fifteen percent—meaning that by conservative estimate there are several hundred thousand militant Muslims now within our borders."

At that statement, I sensed an uncomfortable shifting in the room as ten to fifteen percent or not, the scope of the problem became apparent.

"Integrationist or moderate Muslims, who constitute the majority of Muslims residing in our country, believe that our American values are compatible with Islamic beliefs," Dr. Schwartz continued. "They accept that the United States is not and never will be a Muslim country. Rather than seeking to promote shariah law, they give their allegiance to our non-Muslim government and work to integrate themselves into our culture, accepting our framework of constitutional principles.

"On the other hand, there are Muslims in our country who expound the Islamist view that our American way of life is godless and profane, and that it should be replaced by a new paradigm modeled on strict, Islamic lines. They consider our culture anathema and will never integrate into our society, never accept the American order—believing it to be against the ordainments of Allah. As such, they promote Islam as the solution to our moral and social ills. More important, they believe that over time the United States will become a Muslim country ruled by shariah law.

"The main debate within this latter group centers not on the desirability of transforming the U.S. into a Muslim nation, but on how to achieve that goal, however outlandish it may seem to us. One faction believes in a gradual, peaceful transformation through conversion to Islam. Another believes in the swifter route of violence. Granted, members of this final contingent constitute a much smaller faction, but events have shown that this faction cannot be ignored. Clearly, it is members of this last group with whom you are dealing."

"These guys think that beheading people is going to make us

change our government?" someone asked. "Seems to me it would have the opposite effect."

From the looks of many in the room, a majority of agents appeared to agree.

"It's not quite that simple," said Schwartz. "You have to understand some history here. Beheading is not new in the Muslim community. Although psychological warfare is an essential element in radical Islam's current strategy, beheading as a means of inspiring terror dates back to the days of the Prophet. The earliest biographer of Muhammad, for example, reported that the Prophet ordered the beheading of 700 men of the Jewish *Banu Qurayza* tribe for allegedly plotting against him. More recently, the Ottoman Empire used decapitation to execute hundreds of British soldiers captured in Egypt. In more modern times, our friends the Saudis, acting under the authority of shariah law, executed 345 prisoners over a three-year period, all by public beheading. And lately there have been the numerous cases of journalists, construction contractors, and Western businessmen being decapitated by ISIS. Examples are countless, but the point is that beheading has always played an important role in the Muslim religion."

"If that's so, why are we seeing more of it now?" asked Agent Young.

"It's simple if you think about it," said Schwartz. "The purpose of terrorism is to strike fear in the hearts of your enemies, right? In the seventies and eighties, terrorists grabbed headlines by hijacking airliners. In the eighties and nineties car bombs took center stage, followed by suicide bombings and the like. But the Western world grew calloused, and what once garnered headlines eventually only received a paragraph on page two. Terrorists crave attention, and in order to maintain the shock value of their acts, they have revisited earlier methods. In an odd return to the past, decapitation has now become the latest fashion. That said, I want to stress that beheading has a long history in Islamic theology, as I mentioned earlier," Schwartz concluded. "Speaking of which, although I haven't seen the murder video, I understand that the Arabic word *kafir* was written on the victims' wall?"

"They wrote something," muttered someone at the back of the room. "Looked like chicken scratching to me."

"That's correct, Dr. Schwartz," said Gibbs, ignoring the comment from the rear. "I was told the word means 'one who does not believe in Allah,' or 'infidel.'"

"Close enough," said Schwartz. "According to the interpretation of most militant Muslims, the meaning of *kafir* has been extended to include anyone who doesn't believe in the Qur'an, or in the prophetic status of Muhammad. Whatever the case, many Muslims also believe that a famous passage of the Qur'an at Sura 47:4, 'When you meet the unbelievers, smite at their necks,' should be interpreted literally."

"They believe the Qur'an gives them the right to behead anyone who isn't a Muslim?" someone else spoke up. "That can't be right."

"It is. And it involves more than that," said Schwartz. "Many militants believe their holy book not only gives them the right to kill infidels, but that it also conveys an *obligation* to do so. They believe the beheading of a *harbi kafir*, or non-Muslim infidel, is a blessed act for which they will be rewarded in paradise. To peaceful Muslims worldwide, beheadings in the name of Allah are a defilement of their religion. But to a fanatical Islamic minority intent on *jihad*, beheadings are exactly what Allah ordered."

No one said anything for several moments. "So our killers think they're doing the will of Allah," noted Gibbs, breaking the silence. "Does that mean they'll do it again?"

Schwartz paused, looking thoughtful. "The killers seem to be taking great care not to be caught, so I don't think these attacks are motivated by the prospect of martyrdom."

"Meaning?"

"Meaning I hope I'm wrong," said Schwartz. "But unless something changes, I think they're going to keep killing until they're caught."

Chapter 18

"Mmm, this is delicious," said Taylor, digging into a steaming bowl of *shrimp pho*, a Vietnamese noodle soup garnished with jalapeño, onion, bean sprouts, lime, and cilantro.

Following an unproductive morning accompanying Taylor on several Bureau assignments—interviewing a truculent mullah and talking with FBI informants at an Islamic community center—we had decided to grab lunch at a popular, hole-in-the-wall restaurant on North Broadway.

"How did you ever find this place?" Taylor asked, taking a sip of the white wine she had ordered with her meal. Noticing something in my expression, she shrugged. "It's just one glass, Kane. No big deal."

"Whatever you say, Taylor."

"So how'd you find this place?" she asked again.

"Been eating here for years, coming in whenever I had to be downtown for court appearances," I answered. "Great food, and the price is right," I added, starting in on my order of *bun thit nuong cho gio*—grilled pork atop a bed of rice vermicelli, accompanied by veggies, fresh herbs, and spring rolls with dipping sauce.

"Well, this place definitely gets *my* vote," Taylor declared, taking another sip of wine. Then, glancing at the wedding ring on my left hand, "So what's your story, Kane? Married, huh?"

"Used to be."

"Divorced? No surprise there. Why are you still wearing the ring?"

"Habit," I answered, deciding to let Taylor's divorce assumption slide.

"Kids?"

"Three." I didn't feel like mentioning Tommy, either.

"Boys or girls?"

"Two boys, one girl."

"Jeez, Kane. This is like pulling teeth. Your kids live with you or your wife?"

"My oldest son Travis is doing graduate work at Juilliard," I answered, again sidestepping the issue of Catheryn's death. "My youngest son Nate is living with me and doing everything he can to give me ulcers. My daughter Allison is married and works as a newscaster for Channel 2, so more ulcers there. All three of them adore me."

"I'll bet," Taylor chuckled. Then, her eyes lighting with recognition, "Allison Kane? She's your daughter? I've been following her career since she reported on the Sharon French abduction. She's one of the rising stars at Channel 2, right?"

"I suppose so," I sighed. "Unfortunately, Ali's job hasn't made life any easier for me."

"Veteran LAPD homicide investigator versus ambitious, news-reporter daughter. Sounds like a movie premise. Or at least a TV series."

"Glad you think so."

"Well, in case you haven't noticed, your daughter has been reporting nonstop on our Infidel investigation, and I can't say as I like how things are shaping up in the media. Everyone is looking for a scapegoat, and it's a tossup as to who's their first choice—the Bureau or the LAPD."

I *had* noticed recent developments in the media, and it wasn't a topic I wanted to discuss. Since I had last talked with Allison, her prediction of a media blitz had materialized with a vengeance, with every TV station, newspaper, and supermarket rag devoting more and more attention to the investigation. Worse, thanks to inflamed media coverage, a Muslim backlash was flaring up across the country. Mosques had been burned in Texas, Alabama, and Philadelphia, with a number of related deaths reported nationwide as well.

"Scapegoats, eh? Well, that's why we're getting the big bucks," I said, trying to divert the conversation.

"How are your LAPD task-force pals holding up?" Taylor asked, ignoring my attempt at humor.

I shrugged. "About as well as can be expected. LAPD investigators don't like doing Bureau legwork instead of handling the case on their own."

"You sure you're not talking about yourself?"

"Maybe," I admitted. "But I'm just a Bureau liaison, so I have no cause to complain. What about you, Taylor?" I asked, again attempting to steer the conversation in another direction. "As long as we're sharing here, what's your story? How'd you find your way into the Bureau?"

"Just lucky, I guess."

"Just lucky? That's your idea of sharing?"

Taylor lifted her shoulders and concentrated on her soup.

"Jeez, Taylor. Like someone said, this is like pulling teeth. I thought women were supposed to be the talkative gender."

"Fine," said Taylor, taking a final spoonful of *pho* and pushing away her empty bowl. "I grew up in Salmon, Idaho. Got married at eighteen, right out of high school," she added, unable to hide a trace of bitterness in her voice. "I worked as a secretary to put my husband Mark through college and law school. Later I went back to school myself, earned my undergraduate degree, and attended Chapman Law. After graduation I joined Mark at a law firm in Burbank. When our marriage imploded, I took some time off, did some thinking, and decided I needed a change. I applied to the FBI and was accepted. After graduating from the FBI Academy in Quantico, I paid my dues as an FOA in a five-man RA back east. I spent my time there on a fugitive squad with another FOA rookie and a seasoned SA chasing down Class Forty-two deserters. On my next office assignment I moved up to major crimes, and later I wound up in L.A."

I smiled, again thinking that Bureau agents seemed genetically unable to complete two declarative sentences without resorting to abbreviations. Nevertheless, I nodded as if I had understood Taylor's alphabet explanation, which I did . . . mostly.

Taylor paused, working on a thumbnail with her teeth. "Let's see, what else? No children, one living parent, my mom. I also have a sister, Jeannie, who is married with two kids and living in Detroit. I drive a Jeep Renegade and my take-home bucar, the Crown Vic. I own a two-bedroom condo in Santa Monica and live with my cat, Chuck. In my spare time I surf, ski, and do a little whitewater kayaking. Last but not least, my therapist thinks I have abandonment issues and feelings of inadequacy. That about cover it?"

"Inadequacy and abandonment issues," I mused, rubbing my chin in an attempt to strike an analytical pose. "And how do *you* feel about that?"

Taylor grinned. "Actually, I think I'm perfect, and I wish my therapist would leave me alone."

"Good answer," I laughed. Then, changing gears, "How do you like working at the Bureau?"

Taylor stopped chewing her nail and looked away. "It's just peachy."

"Having trouble breaking into the boys' club?"

"None of your business," she snapped. Then, catching herself, "Sorry. Didn't mean to take it out on you."

When I remained silent, Taylor squared her shoulders and continued. "To answer your question, women in the FBI have every opportunity the Bureau offers their male counterparts, at least on paper. In practice it's another matter."

"Probably the same in a lot of professions, especially law enforcement," I said, knowing that advancement for women at many police agencies, including the LAPD, was often problematic.

By then our lunch bill had arrived. Taylor glanced at her watch, pulled a wallet from her purse, and tossed a credit card onto the tray. "Let's split this and get moving. We have three more interviews to do today, and it's already one o'clock."

"Cash-only service here," I said, sliding her card back across the table.

Taylor looked embarrassed. "I, uh, don't usually carry much money—"

"I've got it," I said.

"Thanks. I'll pay you back tomorrow."

"Don't worry about it."

"I'll pay you back," Taylor repeated firmly.

"How about this?" I suggested. "You get the next one. We'll

go someplace really, really expensive."

"Whatever," Taylor replied, clearly impatient to get back to work.

"About those interviews," I went on, placing enough money on the table to cover the meal and leave a good tip. "We're in the area, and there's a quick stop I want to make."

"Not this time. We have things to do."

"I'm driving, remember?"

"Damn it, Kane—"

"Don't worry, Taylor. My stop is nearby in East L.A., and it won't take long. Plus, it may turn out to be important. Trust me."

Taylor smiled thinly. "Trust you? Gee, where have I heard that before?"

After retrieving my Suburban from the parking lot behind the restaurant, we took the I-10 Freeway east and arrived at the Los Angeles Cal State University campus a few minutes later. The Hertzberg-Davis Forensic Science Center, a state-of-the-art regional forensic laboratory that housed both the LAPD's and the Los Angeles Sheriff's Department's crime labs, was situated on a triangular section of campus on the southeast corner of the university. As I pulled into a visitor's slot and killed the engine, Taylor, who on the drive had repeatedly demanded to know where we were going, regarded the immense, five-story forensic science center suspiciously.

"What are we doing here?" she asked.

"I told you, there's something I want to check," I said, stepping from the Suburban. "It'll only take a few minutes, after which we can resume our very important Bureau assignments1."

With a sigh, Taylor followed me into the building. Navigating a broad corridor past a series of California Forensic Science Institute offices, we eventually arrived at the LAPD's Scientific Investigation Division crime lab. After registering with an officer manning the SID reception desk, I guided Taylor to a bank of elevators deeper in the building. From there we took an elevator one floor up and proceeded to an office down the hall, along the way passing labs marked "Trace Analysis" and "Serology/DNA."

The plate on the door at the end of the hall read, "Questioned Documents."

I knocked. Receiving no answer, I opened the door and stuck my head inside. Several technicians looked up from their work. One, a thin Asian man wearing dark slacks and a blue shirt with the sleeves rolled up, rose from his desk and smiled. "Kane. I was going to call," he said apologetically, crossing the room to greet us.

"No problem, Gavin," I replied, shaking his hand. "I was in the area and thought I would swing by. This is Special Agent Taylor," I added, noticing my analyst friend's admiring glance at my companion. "Agent Taylor, Gavin Chan."

"Pleased," said Chan, taking Taylor's hand.

"Likewise," said Taylor.

"Any progress on the photo?" I asked.

"The shot of that Arabic word? Yes, I took a look," said Chan, reluctantly releasing Taylor's hand. "It's impossible to do a thorough analysis based on a photograph, but—"

"Just give me what you've got," I suggested, ignoring a curious look from Taylor.

"Well, it's the Arabic word *kafir*, meaning 'infidel,' as I'm sure you already know. Let's go over to my desk. I made a blow-up print of your photo. There *is* one thing that stood out."

We followed Chan to a workspace at the back of the room. Upon arriving, my friend shuffled through several files before finding what he wanted. "Ah, here's the photo," he said, laying an eight-by-ten print of the bloody writing atop his desk.

"Graphology is a pseudoscience based on how you dot your i's and cross your t's, right?" Taylor noted with a frown, staring down at the photo. "Assuming it even works, how could you possibly perform any meaningful analysis on something written in a foreign language?"

"Graphology does take into account certain letter formations, in particular that of a number of upper- and lowercase letters," Chan agreed. "But it also considers writing pressure, slanting, letter size, word spacing, and so on. As far as it being a pseudoscience, most people classify graphology as a credible social science that falls in the same category as psychology. You'd be surprised what a skilled analyst, using either the 'Trait Stroke' method or the 'Gestalt' approach, can learn from an examination of your handwriting."

"What about a foreign language?" Taylor persisted.

"Depends on the alphabet," said Gavin, warming to the subject. "For example, the strokes of Latin-based languages like English, Italian, Spanish, and French are all similar and well researched. Analysis of non-Latin languages like Arabic requires a completely different technique."

"So you don't do Arabic graphology."

"Actually, in Questioned Documents we don't do *any* graphology," Gavin sniffed. "I just wanted you to realize the issues involved."

"So what *do* you do?" asked Taylor, still clearly irritated by our unscheduled visit to the forensic center.

"Why don't we just let him tell us?" I suggested.

Taylor folded her arms. "I'm all ears," she said, her posture indicating otherwise.

"Most of our work here involves examining documents to determine various facts about their preparation and subsequent treatment," explained Gavin, appearing disappointed by Taylor's attitude. "Checking for possible alterations by someone using computer or photocopier manipulation, for instance. We also do handwriting comparison, document dating, and ink analysis— details that routinely wind up in court."

"You said there was something that stood out on the photo I sent?" I prodded, attempting to get my friend back on track.

"There was," said Gavin, picking up the photo. "First, the writing on the wall appears to have been done with a finely bristled lettering brush, similar to one you can purchase at any artists' supply house. Look here, and here," he continued, pointing to several areas on the photo.

"Uh, what are we looking at?" I asked.

"See how the brushstrokes start out thick in the body of each letter, then feather to the right, trailing off so you can make out the individual bristles of the brush?"

"Yeah," I said. "So?"

"Arabic script, which includes twenty-eight letters, is written cursive-style from right-to-left," Chan explained.

I was beginning to understand. "And whoever wrote the Arabic word for 'infidel' on the Welches' wall—"

"—wrote it left-to-right," Chan finished. "It was *copied* onto the wall . . . and not by someone familiar with the Arabic language."

"And you're sure about this left-to-right thing?" asked Taylor.

"Absolutely positive," said Chan. "Brushstroke analysis may not be accurate on everything, but on this issue, there's no doubt."

"It still could have been done by a foreign national," Taylor pointed out. "The illiteracy rate in Arab countries is huge."

"Any Arabic-speaking national, illiterate or not, knows that Arabic is written right-to-left," Chan countered. "Whoever copied that word wasn't from an Arabic-speaking nation. Of that I'm certain."

I thought a moment, considering the implications of Chan's discovery. "Gavin, you're going to get a call later today from an LAPD investigator asking you to do the same analysis for him that you just did for me. Don't mention we talked, okay?"

Chan shrugged. "What analysis?"

"Thanks, Gavin," I said. "I owe you one."

Once we had left the building, I called Deluca and filled him in. Next I suggested that he call Gavin Chan in Questioned Documents, ask Chan's opinion of the Arabic writing, and then bring his "discovery" to Snead.

As soon as I had hung up, Taylor asked, "What's going on?"

"You mean my giving the backward-writing thing to Deluca? Simple. After our dumpster incident, we can't afford to have it look like we're running our own investigation here. Not a second time, anyway."

"Not we, Kane. *You.* And as a matter of fact, isn't that exactly what you're doing?"

"I'm simply doing what you Bureau guys should have done in the first place. To be fair, LAPD should have done it, too. Either way, I'm just a liaison, remember?"

"I remember," Taylor said with a smile. Then, her brow furrowing, "So how does this handwriting issue affect the investigation? What difference does it make whether or not the Arabic word was written by a non-Arab? We never ruled out the possibility that our terrorists could have a homegrown element."

"Taylor, no one at the Welches' residence that night was a foreign national. If anyone there had spoken Arabic, they would have been the one to write that word on the wall. And copied or not, the word would have been written right-to-left."

"You're probably correct, but—"

"And if that's the case," I went on, "we're wasting our time beating the bushes of our immigrant population for Muslim terrorists. We should be checking the ranks of our *homegrown* converts, investigating websites and prisons where they're recruited and radicalized, for instance."

Taylor started to object, then stopped.

"There's something else," I said. "It's been bothering me since I first watched that beheading video."

"What?"

"The stilted language in their text. 'Be God's curse on you,' and so on."

"I don't see what you're getting at."

"Look, we just learned that whoever killed the Welches didn't know the first thing about Arabic. They're *not* foreign terrorists, Muslim or otherwise."

"So?"

"So why are they trying so hard to make us think they are?"

Chapter 19

From his seat in the front of the van, Jacob watched as a procession of Sunset Boulevard estates rolled past his window. Steeling himself for what was to come, he mentally reviewed his preparations for the evening.

First, on the off-chance their van was recorded on some random security camera, the license plates on their vehicle had been pilfered that morning at a Westwood mall, with a second set replacing the stolen plates so the owner wouldn't immediately notice their loss. The same precaution had been taken for their backup vehicle, which was now being driven by Ethan.

Second, on their way into Beverly Hills that evening they had picked up several pizzas in Santa Monica. The pies were now in the back, staying warm in insulated vinyl delivery bags . . . not that their temperature would matter, except possibly to Rudy.

And third, all equipment for tonight's venture had been stowed in the van and covered with a tarp—camera gear, assault rifle, pistols and sound suppressors, balaclavas and gloves, knives, hoods, handcuff cable-ties, magnetic signs, clean clothes, and trash bags.

Everything was ready.

Jacob glanced at Caleb, who was driving. As instructed, his younger brother was concentrating on the road and keeping their speed within the posted limit. "Do you know our escape routes, Caleb?" Jacob asked.

Caleb nodded, not taking his eyes from the road. "Of course. Mapleton to Beverly Glen, or north on Mapleton to Sunset. From there we either head toward Westwood or Beverly Hills."

"Alternate sites, in case something isn't right?" Jacob continued his query, even though he knew it was unlikely that the Holmby Hills residence they had chosen for tonight's killings would need to be changed. They had studied Noah and Emma Davenport's gated estate over a period of weeks, and they knew the family's schedule well. They knew when Mr. Davenport, the CEO of an internet security company, departed for work in the morning and when he arrived home at night, and that housewife Emma, who routinely visited a health club on weekdays and sometimes had lunch with friends in Westwood, was always present for Noah's return. The Davenports had no children, and during the time they had been observed, never had friends visited during the week. Last, neighboring homes were far enough away as to not present a problem. No, the Davenports' residence was perfect—quiet, secluded, and private . . . once they got past the gate.

"Alternate sites for tonight," Caleb replied, referring to additional residences that had been chosen months earlier. "South Hudson in Hancock Park, and Rivas Canyon in the Palisades."

"Escape routes for the alternate sites?"

"Hancock Park: West Third Street to Western, then south to the Santa Monica Freeway. In the Palisades we take Rivas Canyon to Sunset, then east or west.

"Backup vehicle locations?"

"Tonight Ethan is parking one block over on Sunset. In Hancock Park, the backup vehicle will park across the golf course on Rimpau. In the Palisades, our second car will wait on a side street near Will Rogers State Park. There's only one way out of Rivas Canyon, and we don't want to get bottled up back in there."

"We're not going to need alternate sites, escape routes, or backup cars," Rudy noted from the rear of the van.

"It doesn't hurt to prepare for contingences," Jacob pointed out. "Or do you think otherwise?"

"No," Rudy backtracked. "You know best, Jacob."

Jacob thought he detected a trace of sarcasm in Rudy's response. Maybe it was time for his sergeant-at-arms to sit out a mission. Ethan was eager to increase his involvement, and Ethan could certainly assume Rudy's responsibilities on the next outing. "Caleb, Parker, Rudy—you all know your duties for tonight?" he asked, deciding to postpone a decision on increasing Ethan's involvement.

"I get us past the gate, make certain it's only the Mr. and Mrs. at home, disable the security system, and cuff and hood the

Davenports," Caleb replied without hesitation.

"I disable the landline, secure the residence, and set up the black flag," said Rudy, his response as automatic as Caleb's.

Parker, sitting beside Rudy in the back, spoke last. "I'm setting up the lighting, positioning the tripod and camera, and recording the, uh, event."

Jacob nodded. "And I'll take care of the rest," he concluded, confident their operation would proceed with military precision, just as it had the last time. Well, not *exactly* like the last time. There had been minor missteps on that one, like Caleb removing the cellphones from the residence, but those errors would not be repeated. They had practiced thoroughly for tonight's mission, and practice led to perfection, with nothing left to chance.

In addition to the rehearsals, Jacob had familiarized himself with Parker's camera equipment, as well as with his untraceable means of posting their videos. The murder videos were an essential element of their plan, and relying on one individual for something that important was unwise.

Earlier that afternoon Jacob had also retested their cellphone jammer—another of Parker's contributions. The small but powerful unit had worked perfectly. Jacob's hand traveled to his waist, where the compact device was clipped to his belt beside his silenced pistol. As he had on their first expedition, Jacob decided to wait until later to attach the jammer's flexible antennas, activating the blocking unit only when they had reached the residence.

Forcing his mind back to the present, Jacob checked his watch. "Time to put out the signs," he said. "Pull over on that street up ahead, Caleb."

As before, in case they were stopped, Jacob had postponed attaching the fake magnetic signs until they had neared their destination. Being observed attaching the signs could present a problem, but it was an acceptable risk.

Caleb turned off Sunset onto a side street. After proceeding several hundred yards, he pulled to a stop beneath an overhanging sycamore and killed the headlights, leaving the engine running. Satisfied they weren't being observed, Jacob nodded to Rudy. Reaching into the back of the van, Rudy pulled a lighted roof cap and two magnetic door signs from under the tarp. Signs and cap in hand, he stepped from the vehicle.

As he waited for Rudy to complete his task, Jacob placed a call to Ethan.

"In position," said Ethan, answering almost immediately.

"Good," Jacob replied. "Five minutes."

Within thirty seconds of exiting the van, Rudy had the door signs and illuminated roof cap installed. Task completed, he climbed back into the vehicle and quietly closed the door behind him. "Let's do this," he said. "It's showtime."

*****

"Noah, come take a look at this."

"I'd rather not, Emma," Noah Davenport replied from the kitchen. "You know how I feel about watching the news. It's usually depressing, and there's nothing one can do about it. How about watching a movie on Netflix?"

"Later, Noah. You need to see this. The Muslim-backlash thing is getting worse. Another mosque was bombed today, this time in D.C. Several people were killed, some of them children."

With a sigh, Noah joined his wife in the den, finding Emma curled up on the couch watching *CBS Evening News*. The newscaster, a rising network star named Brent Preston, was delivering what Noah considered to be an overly dramatic summation of the day's events.

". . . sparked by the terrorist beheadings last week in Los Angeles," the handsome reporter was saying as Noah settled in beside his wife. "Since then," the newscaster continued, "a total of thirteen mosques and Islamic centers, including the one bombed today in our nation's capital, have been destroyed in cities across the country."

At that moment their gate buzzer sounded.

"Who could that be?" asked Emma, still concentrating on the newscast. "Are you expecting anyone?"

"No. Maybe they'll go away."

By then Brent Preston's face had been replaced with the image of a large, burning structure and the words "Omar As-Sunnah Islamic Center, Washington, D.C." superimposed at the bottom. "Fatalities attributed to the Muslim backlash have now reached sixty-seven, with that number expected to rise in days to come," the newscaster's voice continued over the shot.

Next, the broadcast returned to Brent Preston in the news studio. "A spokesperson for the FBI declined to comment on the investigation, saying only that they hope to have a suspect or suspects in custody shortly," Brent concluded, turning to a second camera angle. "In other news . . ."

The gate buzzer sounded again.

"I'll go see who it is," said Noah, rising from the couch.

Thankful to be leaving Brent Preston's annoying newscast behind, Noah made his way to the front door. Curious, he glanced out the window. A Wiseguy Pizza van was at the gate, sitting at the end of their long driveway. "Yes?" he said, pressing the intercom button.

"Pizza," a voice replied.

"Hold on," said Noah. Calling back into the house, "Emma, did we order pizza?"

"I didn't," Emma's voice came back. "But I am hungry. Maybe we *should* have, although pizza doesn't exactly fit into your new gluten-free diet."

"We didn't order pizza," said Noah, speaking into the intercom. "Must be a mistake."

"No mistake, Mr. Davenport," said the voice. "We're sponsoring a free giveaway this week. Maybe you've seen our ads on TV? 'We'll make you a pizza you can't refuse?' And that commercial where a guy wakes up with a Wiseguy pizza on the pillow next to him? Anyway, a number of Holmby Hills residents were chosen to receive a complimentary pie as part of our promo, and you're one of them. We've been delivering pizzas all evening, so we're running a little low, but we still have several to choose from."

Noah hesitated, surprised that the delivery man had known

his name, but reassured that this wasn't a scam. "Do you have any pepperoni?" he asked, feeling a bit guilty. Sure, he'd lost weight over the past weeks by avoiding gluten, which meant avoiding a lot of grease and sugar as well. But life was short, and one didn't have to be good *all* the time . . .

"Yes, sir. Pepperoni and cheese," the voice came back. "And another with pepperoni, mushrooms, and roasted garlic. We also have one last pie topped with barbequed chicken, red pepper, and sun-dried tomatoes. If you're not hungry now, our pizzas keep great in the fridge. A lot of people prefer our pies cold, along with a beer or a soft drink or whatever.

"No, we like them hot," said Noah. "And actually, that barbequed chicken sounds pretty good."

"Yes, sir. It's still hot, and it's free. You want it?"

Noah hesitated a moment more. Then, giving in to temptation, he pressed the gate release.

Only live once, he thought, deciding he could resume his diet in the morning.

Chapter 20

M oving to the front of the conference chamber, Agent Vaughn cleared his throat for attention. "Everyone quiet down. SAC Gibbs has something to say before we start."

I glanced around the room. The mood there that morning was bleak, with a lot of anger and frustration thrown in as well. I had talked with Deluca on the drive in from Malibu, and I knew that Snead's task-force detectives were taking the murder of a second family hard as well.

From talking with Deluca, I also knew that although LAPD investigators had been swamped with hot line tips, they still had nothing to show for their efforts. Locating the source of the ISIS flag, finding the Maui Jim sunglasses retailer, and checking friends, neighbors, and workers who knew the Welches' gate code had also stalled out. A canvass of the Bel Air neighborhood had come up empty as well. It had been four days since the first murders, and with this second round of killings, it was clear that the clock was ticking. As such, investigators working the case were growing increasingly desperate to come up with a lead, a viable suspect, *anything* that could move the investigation forward. So far that wasn't happening.

And everyone knew it.

With a nod to Vaughn, Gibbs stepped forward. He looked tired. "As I'm certain you all know, there was a second incident last night in Holmby Hills," he began. "Two more individuals were killed. A video of their murder turned up this morning on the internet."

"Same guys?" someone asked.

"Same guys," said Gibbs. "Responding to an anonymous call, LAPD detectives arrived at the Holmby Hills residence around midnight, then called us. Our ERT unit is still processing the scene. So far we've recovered more oil drips, several bloody shoe-tread impressions, a number of unmatched prints, blood and hair from the drains, and so on."

"How about witnesses?" asked Garcia.

"LAPD is canvassing the neighborhood. At this point, it appears that nobody saw or heard anything."

"911 calls?" asked someone else.

"The residence landline was disabled, like last time, with a phone in the kitchen left off the hook. The victims' cellphones were still present in the house. No incoming or outgoing calls were logged on either of them that evening." Gibbs glanced at me. "911 or otherwise."

"How about security cameras? Anything show up there?" asked Taylor.

Gibbs shook his head. "We're still checking."

An uneasy silence descended over the room. The Bureau's strategy of reaching out to "critical asset partners" in the intelligence and Muslim communities hadn't paid off, and the realization that a forensic breakthrough wasn't going to close the case was beginning to sink in as well. The Bureau's best chance to come up with a suspect or suspects had been the analysis of the AB-negative blood found in the Welches' master bathroom. Yesterday the DNA results had come back from the lab. Matching the unexplained blood to someone in the system had been unsuccessful.

"Okay, at this time ASAC Vaughn will bring us current on the investigation," said Gibbs.

Vaughn again stepped to the front. "First some updates, then on to new business," he said, opening a file he'd carried with him. "VICAP failed to turn up a match to similar crimes," he began, referring to a search of the FBI's Violent Criminal Apprehension Program. "Nothing has shown up in the Welches' correspondence or computers that might prove helpful. The Welch autopsy results were also unremarkable. Both victims died of exsanguination following decapitation. Their toxicology screens were negative. Prints, negative. DNA matching, negative. Copies of these reports will be available at the end of the briefing."

Vaughn checked his notes, then pushed on. "LAPD is currently canvassing the Holmby Hills neighborhood, along with checking security cameras in the area and talking with anyone who knows the Davenports' gate code. Speaking of which, the Davenports' home-security system has an upload link to offsite storage, but as the Davenports were home at the time, their system wasn't active. The killers took the onsite unit with them."

"Damn, is there *any* good news?" someone grumbled.

"A little," said Vaughn. "Blood typing of the clothes and towels found in the Santa Monica dumpster corresponds with that of Mr. and Mrs. Welch—AB and O. One of the towels in the dumpster also shows a blood typing consistent with blood found in the Welches' master bath, type AB-negative, which we're assuming came from one of the killers. Comparison of the bloody shoeprints at both murder locations was a match as well."

Not much, I thought. Again, forensic results were important once you had a suspect, but nothing Vaughn had said brought us any closer to that.

"This is the second residence that's had a security gate," Garcia noted. "Is there a significance there?"

"Possibly," Vaughn replied. "Anyone have an idea on that?"

"Maybe the killers are picking homes that provide the privacy and time they need to do whatever they want," suggested Young. "Once past the gate, they don't have to worry about visitors."

"They could be sending a message as well," added Taylor. "No one's safe in their own homes, even behind a security gate."

"I suppose we'll know more if it happens again," said Vaughn. Then, addressing Agent Young, "Anything on the Chinese AK-47?"

"No, sir. AFT is interviewing owners in the Los Angeles area. They plan to move farther out next."

Vaughn glanced around the room. "Anyone?"

"This is on a different subject," said an older agent near the front. "We impounded the Davenports' checkbooks, computers, phone records, and so on—just like at the Welch residence. The two families lived fairly close to each other. How about looking for a correlation between them? Common country clubs, maid services, gardeners, pool guys—like that. Maybe we can figure out how the victims were chosen."

"Good idea," said Vaughn, making a note in his file.

"Anything show up on the dumpster surveillance?" someone else asked.

Vaughn shook his head. "No. Nor at the Starbucks site, either. By the way, this time the terrorists' video was uploaded at a coffee shop in Venice. They used the Tor masking service again, along with the same Russian social-media platform. Our tech guys are trying to run a trace, but they're not hopeful."

I spoke up. "There have been a couple new developments on LAPD's end."

"What do you have, Kane?"

"LAPD checked every one of the 217 Police Service Responder operators who were on duty the night of the Welches' murders," I replied. "None of the PSR operators has a record of anything coming in from Mrs. Welch."

"No surprise there," said Vaughn. "Her phone log listed those attempts as cancelled calls."

By then I had studied the briefing notes from yesterday's meeting. The briefing summary was a four-page document that contained copies of the Welches' Verizon records, their cellphone data usage, and a list of clothing and other items recovered from the Santa Monica dumpster. "That's correct," I said. "But Mrs. Welch's initial 911 call lasted *nine seconds* before she disconnected. Her next call was considerably shorter, but I still think there might be a—"

"I see where you're going on this," Vaughn interrupted. "Your cellphone-jammer theory again, right?"

"Yes, sir."

"Do you know the average pickup time for an emergency call in Los Angeles, Kane?"

"Not exactly," I admitted.

"In Los Angeles, the current *goal* for 911 pickups is for them to be answered in fewer than ten seconds," said Vaughn. "Depending on the call volume and the number of operators on duty at any given time, that ten-second wait could be considerably more. Rather than theorizing about the use of an illegal, hard-to-acquire piece of equipment like a cellphone jammer, isn't it more reasonable to think that Mrs. Welch simply got tired of waiting on a busy signal, panicked, and hung up?"

"Maybe, but—"

Again, Vaughn cut me off. "During the Bel Air canvass, did investigators turn up *anyone* who had experienced a loss of cellphone service on the night of the Welch murders?"

"No, sir. But jammers are only good for a limited distance."

"Limited distance or not, I think we're wasting time here." Vaughn glanced at Gibbs, who nodded in agreement. "Let's move on. You said there were several LAPD developments?"

Reluctantly, I continued. "Just one more. LAPD ran the bloody word painted on the Welches' wall through our Questioned Documents unit. Turns out the Arabic script was written left-to-right, European style—not right-to-left, as would have been done by a foreign national."

Vaughn looked confused. "I don't see what difference that makes."

Director Shepherd, who to date had attended every briefing but had rarely spoken, broke in. "I think I do," he said. "We've been working on the assumption that our terrorists are foreign nationals, or at least that some of them are. But if that were the case, the Arabic word would have been written correctly from right-to-left, not left-to-right by someone with no knowledge of Arabic."

"So now our terrorists are homegrown?" someone asked.

"Looks that way," Taylor spoke up. "Which begs the question, what's with the stilted language they used on their video?"

"What do you mean?" asked Duffy.

"If our terrorists aren't foreign nationals, why are they working so hard to make us think they are?" Taylor replied.

"Good point, Taylor," Vaughn noted.

"Actually, Kane came up with it,' said Taylor.

"Well, in any case, this changes things," said Vaughn, frowning. "I'm not certain how, but we'll need to factor that parameter into the investigation."

At this I sensed a shift in the room, the mood changing from frustration to one of guarded hope. At least now there was something new to chew on.

Vaughn thought a moment. "Garcia, have your Field Intelligence Group increase their focus on areas where homegrown Muslims are being recruited and radicalized— prisons, social media sites, and so on. Reach out to the Bureau's TITAN partners, too. Someone out there knows these guys. We just need to find them."

"Yes, sir," said Garcia.

"Kane, this could be an area in which your task force might be able to help," Vaughn suggested. "You know, get the word out on the street."

"I'll pass it on," I said.

"Anyone else have an idea on this?" asked Vaughn.

When no one responded, Vaughn made a final entry in his file, checked his watch, and glanced at Gibbs. "That's it for this morning," he said. "There are briefing sheets in the back. Pick them up on your way out. But before you leave on your assignments, SAC Gibbs would like a final word."

Once more Gibbs moved to the front. "What you're about to see will be hard for many of you," he warned, waving several agents back to their seats. "Probably for all of you, in fact, so I apologize in advance for what you're about to experience. That being said, and in an effort to understand the type of terrorists with whom we're dealing, I want you to view their latest video. No exceptions."

A chill ran through the room. I knew from talking with Taylor that a number of agents had watched the first murder video, but probably just as many had elected not to. Now they weren't being given a choice.

Gibbs motioned to an agent at one of the workstations. The overhead lights flickered off, darkening the room, and a monitor on the wall behind Gibbs came to life.

A moment later the video began.

I didn't want to watch. But like everyone else, I did.

Similar to their first production, the terrorists' new video began with three dark-clothed men standing in front of an ISIS flag. All three were wearing balaclavas, leather gloves, and sunglasses. No one spoke. The man on the left appeared to be holding the same automatic weapon I'd seen in the earlier video. The other two were positioned behind a man and a woman, who both had sacks covering their heads. Although I couldn't be certain, the terrorists looked similar to the ones I'd seen in the first video—the tallest holding the rifle, the second man short and muscular, the third slim and a bit taller. From a glare illuminating the scene, it appeared that spotlights had been now added behind the camera.

The couple, whom I assumed to be Emma and Noah Davenport, were kneeling in the foreground, hands fastened behind their backs. Mrs. Davenport sounded like she was weeping, her soft sobs muffled by the cloth sack. Otherwise, silence.

There was silence in the conference room as well.

The video faded to black, and lines of script began scrolling across the screen. "America, be God's curse on you," the writing began, as it had before. The terrorists' message, an exact duplicate of the one I'd seen earlier, took several minutes to cycle past. During this time I felt a grim tension building in the room, as palpable as an electric current.

We all knew what was coming.

All too soon the video returned to the images of Mr. and Mrs. Davenport, kneeling before their captors. As before, the rifle-carrying terrorist stepped out of frame, returning with a metal vessel containing two dark-handled knives. The video then cut to a medium shot of the men behind the Davenports. Each withdrew a knife from the metal container. Next they tore the cloth sacks from the heads of their captives.

The video cut to a close shot of the Davenports. The hapless couple blinked in the harsh light. Mr. Davenport looked angry. Mrs. Davenport was crying. Tears had run her mascara, smearing her cheeks in sad, dark rivulets.

"We have money," begged Mr. Davenport. "We'll pay whatever you want. Just . . . let us go."

Neither of the hooded men responded. Instead, they encircled each captive's head with a forearm. In unison, they forced back

Mr. and Mrs. Davenport's chins. Knives held in gloved hands, they placed their blades to their victims' throats. The Davenports began struggling. Screaming, Mrs. Davenport vainly tried to bite her captor's hand. In what seemed an almost intimate gesture, the short, muscular killer placed his mouth near Mr. Davenport's ear and said something. At this Mr. Davenport stiffened and redoubled his efforts to break free.

And then it began.

More than anything, I wanted to look away. I didn't. Heart pounding, I watched in horror as the men began sawing their blades through the Davenports' necks. A wave of shock coursed through the room. Several agents gasped, looking away as blood began to flow.

As before, the muscular man murdering Noah Davenport leaned forward and used his weight to topple his captive to the floor. Lying atop his struggling victim, the killer continued his grisly work. The man executing Mrs. Davenport remained standing, seeming able to control his smaller victim without taking her down.

Like others in the room, I sat frozen, sickened by the violence. At one point the muscular killer stared directly into the camera, as he had in the first video. Again he tipped back his victim's partially severed head, exposing the gushing neck-stump. By then Mr. Davenport was probably dead. Mrs. Davenport had gone limp seconds earlier, and at that point she was most likely dead as well.

Blood was everywhere.

Although the killers completed their hideous decapitations shortly afterward, the executions seemed to go on forever. The final severing, as the terrorists hacked through the vertebrae at the back of each victim's neck, took the longest.

Finally it was over.

Covered in gore, the killers stood over the bodies of Mr. and Mrs. Davenport. Grasping the severed heads by the hair, the men held aloft their gruesome trophies, displaying them for the camera. Then, in a ritualistic act that seemed almost surreal in its cruelty, they placed the severed heads on the backs of the headless corpses, balancing them between Mr. and Mrs. Davenport's pinioned arms.

The camera held on the horrific scene for several seconds, then moved in for a close shot of the severed heads. Seeing this, I concluded that the camera was now probably being operated by the third terrorist. Next the video cut to the Arabic word for "infidel," smeared in blood on a nearby wall. Finally the camera panned left for a close-up of the ISIS flag. The video held on the flag, then faded to black.

Moments later the overhead lights in the room came back on.

Once again I found myself trembling, shaken by the violence I had witnessed. I glanced around the room. An agent near the front was quietly sobbing, a hand to her mouth. I saw tears in the eyes of other agents as well, many of them men. As my gaze traveled the room, Taylor caught my eye. Her face was pale. It was clear that like everyone present, she had been shocked by the video. She also looked angry.

"Damn," someone said softly.

"That was uploaded to the web early this morning," said Gibbs, again addressing the room. "Since then it has been reposted just about everywhere, including a number of Islamic sites worldwide."

"Any chance of shutting it down?" asked Vaughn.

Gibbs shook his head. "There's no putting that one back in the bottle."

"Is the media onto it yet?" asked someone else.

Gibbs nodded. "Coverage is ramping up."

"And it's probably going to get worse," added Vaughn. "A lot worse."

Chapter 21

As usual, I placed a call to Chief Ingram's office following the briefing. After bringing the chief up to date on the current "homegrown Muslim" theory, I relayed the Bureau's request that Snead's task force begin looking into sources of domestic Muslim recruitment and radicalization. I also mentioned that I planned to visit the Holmby Hills crime scene a soon as possible.

Upon hanging up, I noticed Taylor standing nearby. "Ready to hit the streets?" she asked.

"Hang on," I replied. "I need a moment with Gibbs."

Gibbs was engaged in conversation with Director Shepherd and Agent Vaughn. Ignoring a questioning look from Taylor, I waited for a chance to break in. While waiting, I scanned the briefing sheets I had picked up after the meeting. Among other things, the briefing summary contained a copy of the Welch autopsy protocols. Vaughn had been correct in his assessment that they contained nothing unusual. Both of the Bel Air victims had died of exsanguination subsequent to the severing of their carotid arteries. Toxicology showed that Mrs. Welch had been taking a tricyclic antidepressant called Elavil. Mr. Welch was being treated with a cholesterol-lowering statin. Otherwise, the autopsy results were unremarkable.

"You have a question, Kane?" said Gibbs, finally noticing me waiting.

"Yes, sir," I said. "A request, actually. I'd like to visit the Holmby Hills crime scene."

Vaughn scowled. "Once again, Kane, need I remind you that your liaison position doesn't—"

"What could it hurt?" Gibbs interrupted. "You know, a fresh pair of eyes."

"I'm inclined to agree," Shepherd weighed in. "Do we need to clear this with Chief Ingram, Detective?"

"I already did. Ingram's onboard," I said, stretching the truth a bit. "Thank you, Director," I added, turning on my heel before anyone could change his mind.

*****

When Taylor and I arrived in Holmby Hills, we found the Davenports' security gate standing open at the street. Someone had angled an LAPD black-and-white across the entrance, blocking the driveway. I flashed my shield and identified myself to a young patrolman stationed nearby. The patrolman logged my name and badge number into his notebook, adding Agent Taylor's name and her Bureau ID to the record as well. That done, he backed up his vehicle and allowed us to proceed down the driveway. As we approached the Davenports' rambling, one-story home, I noted that several other LAPD patrolman were still onsite. I smiled, happy to see that even though the Bureau had taken priority, LAPD was maintaining a presence.

"What?" asked Taylor.

"Nothing." I said, pulling to a stop in front of the Davenports' three-car garage. "Let's get to work," I added, shutting off the engine and stepping from the car.

As at the Welch crime scene, I first made a complete circuit of the grounds, finding no evidence that the killers had gained access to the Davenports' home other than via the security gate.

Again, I wondered how.

Inside the residence, a number of FBI agents were still at work. From their manner, I concluded that they were members of the Bureau's Evidence Response Team. "LAPD," I said to an older investigator who seemed to be in charge, again flipping out my ID.

The man glanced at my shield, then at Taylor, who flashed her Bureau creds as well. "Don't see why not," he said with a shrug. "We're about done here. Just don't move anything."

"I won't." I thought a moment. "Were the Davenport's cellphones found onsite?"

The investigator nodded.

"You check the phone logs?"

"After dusting for prints. No outgoing or incoming calls on either phone since yesterday."

"What about the residence landline? Or is there one?"

"There's a landline hookup through AT&T. According to a phone bill we found in the den, that line was used mostly for their security system—which is missing, by the way."

"What are you getting at, Kane?" asked Taylor.

"I'm not certain," I admitted, "but I still think we're overlooking something. Like how the killers are getting past the gates, for one."

"That's the sixty-four-thousand-dollar question, isn't it?" said the investigator.

"It is," I agreed, checking my watch. "How much longer are you going to be here?"

"Maybe twenty minutes."

"Could you let me know before you take off? I might have another question or two."

"Sure," the investigator replied. He looked at me carefully. "Kane, right?"

I nodded.

"I heard about your visit to the Welch scene. I, uh, wouldn't mind a heads-up if you think we missed something," he said quietly.

"No problem."

"Thanks. In that case, I'll stick around till you're done."

Taylor trailed me through the house as I inspected each room, starting with the entry. As at the Welch residence, forensic investigators appeared to have done a thorough job of gathering evidence—sink and shower traps removed, numbered tags marking the location of recovered material, ferric oxide darkening any surface the killers might have touched. I noted bloody shoe prints in the entry. In the kitchen, I thought I detected the faint smell of vomit, concluding that someone had been sick at the scene, like the pool guy at the Welches' estate.

As before, I saved the murder room for last.

Like the Welches, the Davenports had died in their living room. Two taped body outlines and a large, congealing puddle of blood marked the location where the killers had executed Noah and Emma Davenport. On a wall to the left, painted in blood, was the Arabic word for infidel, apparently written by the same hand that had scrawled the twisting cursive at the Welches' mansion. Now that I knew what to look for, I could tell that the word had been written incorrectly, left-to-right.

Same guys.

Across from the blood puddle, delineated by a numbered tag, indentations in the carpet marked an area where the killers had set up their camera tripod. Also indicated with numbered tags, I noted several other carpet depressions behind the body outlines, marks that had probably been made by a frame displaying the black flag. With a sick, hollow feeling, I glanced around the murder site, trying to imagine Mr. and Mrs. Davenport's final moments.

"You find anything?" asked the ERT tech, who had followed me into the living room.

I fought to bring my feelings under control. "Your team seems to have done a thorough job," I replied. "I wish I had something to add. Unfortunately, I don't. Sorry."

"Yeah, me too," said the investigator. "Maybe they'll make a mistake next time."

"Maybe," I said, not wanting to consider that this might happen again. "Who got sick in the kitchen?" I asked, changing the subject. "Not that I blame him."

"Nobody got sick," the investigator replied, looking puzzled. "Why do you ask?"

"I thought I smelled something in there," I said. "Maybe it wasn't vomit."

With Taylor and the ERT technician following, I returned to the kitchen. "There," I said, sniffing the room. "Smell that?"

"I don't smell anything," said the technician.

"I do," said Taylor. "Pizza."

I sniffed again. "Yeah, I think you're right." I checked under the sink, looking for a pizza wrapping. A plastic bin there was empty.

"We took everything from the residence trash cans, but there wasn't much," said the technician. "No pizza box or frozen pizza wrappings, if that's what you're looking for."

"Napkins or plates with pizza stains?"

The technician thought a moment. "No."

"Anything in the cans by the garage?" I asked, referring to several trash containers I had noticed on the drive in.

"Empty. But trash pickup was yesterday morning. I checked. Some neighbors still have their cans on the street."

"Maybe the Davenports reheated leftovers," Taylor suggested.

I crossed to a built-in microwave near the fridge. Tripping the door latch, I opened the microwave and sniffed. The smell inside the microwave was stronger. Definitely pizza. "Were there any dirty plates, leftovers, or anything to indicate that the Davenports had pizza for dinner?" I asked the technician.

The investigator shook his head. "The dishwasher was empty, too."

"What are you getting at, Kane?" asked Taylor. "So we smell pizza. So what?"

"I'm not sure," I answered. "But think for a minute. The killers have been choosing gated estates for their killings. Why?"

"So they can set up their camera, complete their killings, and film the murders without being interrupted, like Agent Young suggested," Taylor replied. "And maybe to demonstrate that no one is safe, even behind a locked gate."

"Right. But the big question has always been, 'How are they getting in?'"

"You think the terrorists are delivering pizzas?" Taylor scoffed.

"I know it's a long shot, but *someone* here ate pizza. It's unlikely the smell would last more than a day, so it was probably yesterday. And if it *was* the Davenports who ate pizza, where's the box, or frozen pizza wrapper, or dinner plates?"

"There could be several explanations for that," Taylor said doubtfully.

"Maybe. But there's a way to find out."

"How?"

"Remember when we were digging through the dumpster in Santa Monica?"

"Yes, but—"

"What did we find right on top of the bag containing the Welches' cellphones?"

"How am I supposed to remember every piece of trash—"

"Think, Taylor."

Taylor's eyes widened. "A pizza box. Wiseguy Pizza."

"And there were several partially eaten pieces inside, remember? Pieces that probably have saliva on them."

The ERT technician broke in. "We took the entire contents of the dumpster to the lab. We haven't finished processing all of it yet, so most of that stuff's still there. We can test the pizza remnants for blood type and DNA," he added, pulling out his cellphone. "It's been a few days, which is usually the limit for testing saliva DNA, but most of the perishable items have been stored in our cold room," he added, punching numbers into his phone. "Maybe we're still good," he mumbled, at that point seeming to be talking to himself.

"Dust the pizza box for prints, too," I suggested.

"Right," the technician agreed distractedly, stepping away as he began speaking on his phone.

Taylor regarded me with a look I couldn't quite fathom. "Kane, if you're right about this . . ."

". . . maybe we just got lucky," I finished. "And make that, 'If *we're* right about this.' You identified the pizza smell, remember?"

"Yeah, but—"

"Call it in, Taylor. And leave me out of it."

"You want me to take credit? Why?"

"For one, I think the idea will go down better coming from you." I glanced into the living room, recalling the video I had watched that morning. "For another, I don't need recognition from Vaughn or Gibbs or anyone else for doing something that needs doing."

"And what's that?"

"Taking the guys who did this off the street. Permanently."

Chapter 22

An emergency Bureau meeting was convened later that afternoon. Present from the Command Group were Agents Gibbs, Vaughn, Young, and Garcia. Also in attendance was Assistant Director Shepherd, along with several dozen field agents including Taylor and Duffy. And me.

By then an initial testing of the dumpster pizza had been completed. Whoever had discarded the partially eaten pizza had been a "secretor," a person who secretes ABO blood-group antigens in bodily fluids like sweat, tears, and saliva. Saliva on the pizza showed type AB-negative blood antigens, which matched the ABO typing of blood found in the Welches' master bath. Although analysis was still underway to compare the saliva DNA with material recovered from the inside of the killers' bloody clothing, for the moment—because AB-negative was a relatively rare blood type—confidence was high that we had a positive match.

Along those same lines, because no pizza had been found in either of the Welches' stomachs at autopsy, it was further assumed that the pizza had been brought to the Welch residence by the killers. In fact, adopting a theory suggested by Agent Taylor, pizza delivery was now considered as a possible means by which the terrorists were gaining access to their victims' homes. Granted, the latter conclusion was based on the smell of pizza *supposedly* being present at the second murder site, a subjective finding at best. The pizza-delivery theory was further brought into question by the fact that neither the Welches' nor the Davenports' telephone records showed any recent calls to pizza establishments, Wiseguy or otherwise.

Despite the ABO blood-type match, in the opinion of several agents, the pizza-delivery theory was simply that. A theory. As such, ASAC Vaughn argued that the FBI's main investigative effort should still focus on finding a connection in the Muslim community. Nevertheless, Bureau investigators were desperate for a new lead—*any* new lead—and a discussion subsequently ensued regarding what direction the Bureau investigation could take from there. Although it would be days before a saliva DNA confirmation was possible, a positive result was expected. Working on the assumption that the terrorists were using a pizza-delivery deception of some kind, several courses of action were proposed.

Garcia suggested a frontal attack: We could drag in every Wiseguy Pizza employee on the Westside and interrogate them until something shook loose. Unfortunately, a number of Wiseguy franchises lay within an easy drive of the murder sites, each franchise with its own owners, employees, dispatch operators, and delivery vans. In addition, because the pizza connection could present a viable opportunity to locate the killers, it was felt that investigators should proceed cautiously. Using Garcia's sledgehammer approach would undoubtedly draw the attention of the media, forfeiting any chance of keeping this new development quiet. Ultimately a decision was made to keep the pizza aspect of the investigation undercover, at least for the moment. But the problem of how to proceed still remained.

According to the victims' phone records, neither family had actually *ordered* pizza on the nights in question. Nevertheless, it was proposed that discreet inquiries be made to determine whether any of the Wiseguy parlors in the area had a record of pizza being delivered to the victims. That proposal was also rejected. If someone at one of the parlors had actually been involved—a dispatch operator or a delivery man, for example—it was likely they would have covered their tracks by now. And again, an inquiry would tip the Bureau's hand.

In the end a third strategy was proposed, one that was eventually adopted. At the request of the Bureau, agents of the U.S. Citizen and Immigration Services would contact owners at each Wiseguy franchise and request a complete list of employees, supposedly to check their resident status. Bureau investigators would then run background checks and establish twenty-four-hour surveillance on every Wiseguy employee, concentrating on anyone with ties to the Muslim community. To cover all bases, each Wiseguy franchise would also be placed under surveillance, along with every other pizza establishment in the area. I shook my head at this, awed by the amount of manpower that approach would require. But as I was learning, Bureau manpower was never in short supply.

Later, a fourth and final tactic was also suggested: We could attempt to match the oil drips and tire-tread impressions found at the Welches' residence to a Wiseguy delivery van, or to a vehicle owned by a Wiseguy employee. This strategy was problematic, considering the lack of a search warrant. Nor, with the evidence in hand so far, would a warrant be forthcoming. This approach was about to be abandoned when I decided to speak.

"I can't believe this," I said. "People are getting beheaded, and you're worried about procuring a warrant for some lousy oil drips?"

Vaughn, who had been leading the discussion, turned in my direction. "We don't run things the way LAPD does, Kane," he said with exaggerated patience. "Without a warrant, any evidence collected would be inadmissible in court, and our unsubs would walk. So unless you have a better idea . . ."

I thought a moment. "Set up a sting."

"Excuse me?" said Vaughn.

"Set up a sting operation," I repeated. "In fact, set up several stings, however many you need. Rent some Westside residences with security gates, order pizzas, and sample any oil drips left by delivery vans on those nice, recently cleaned mansion driveways out front. That way you don't need a warrant for the drips. And if you do it right, you could get tire-track imprints at the same time."

Vaughn glanced at Gibbs, who glanced at Shepherd. "That might just work, Kane," said Shepherd thoughtfully. "We would have to clear it with legal at DOJ . . . but your idea might just work."

"And we might run into the killers while we're at it," one of the field agents suggested. "Assuming this pizza thing is for real."

"It's possible," another agent spoke up. "We should make sure our teams are ready for that, just in case."

"I hate to say this, but I wouldn't get too excited just yet," I pointed out. "The pizza-delivery approach is still a long shot."

"It was *your* idea," said Vaughn. "Yours and Taylor's. Now you're saying you don't believe it?"

"No, I believe it. But the killers have been careful so far. Seems to me they would realize that if any of them had an actual connection to Wiseguy Pizza—say, if one of them was a dispatch operator—we'd figure it out."

"So what are you suggesting?"

"I'm not discounting the pizza connection," I explained. "I just think we should widen the net. Check manufacturers for someone who ordered Wiseguy Pizza signs, for instance. I've seen phony magnetic door panels used this way before."

"Good idea," said Young.

"Along those lines, it's obvious from the presence of security gates at both homes that the killers have been choosing their killing grounds ahead of time," I reasoned. "Which means they've spent time in those neighborhoods. We're already checking neighbors in Bel Air to see whether anyone remembers a suspicious vehicle cruising the area on the day of the murders. We could extend that to checking both neighborhoods for vehicles cruising the area days or even weeks *prior* to the murders, especially cars or vans with trade markings, including Wiseguy Pizza."

Gibbs spoke up. "Both are excellent lines of inquiry, Kane, areas that I think would be appropriate for Captain Snead's task force to handle. Please forward our request to LAPD that they work those aspects of the case."

I nodded, making a mental note to call Ingram's office as soon as the Bureau meeting concluded. Still puzzling over Arleen Welch's unanswered 911 calls, I considered requesting that LAPD investigators look into cellphone jammers as well, despite Vaughn's orders to the contrary. In the end I decided against it, figuring I had already rocked enough boats.

"Anyone have other suggestions?" asked Gibbs.

I felt a number of eyes turn in my direction, but by then I was fresh out of ideas.

"No?" said Gibbs. "In that case, let's get to work."

Chapter 23

"Y ou promised that Network would let us handle the story," Allison complained. "Now you're telling me they're sending out Brent Preston? That's not fair, Lauren."

Lauren glanced up from her desk, regarding the angry young newscaster standing in her doorway. "Ali, I said I couldn't make any guarantees," she said. "Network agreed to leave the story with the Los Angeles Bureau, but with the caveat that if the terrorist murders continued, all bets were off. Following this second set of murders in Holmby Hills, not to mention the escalating Muslim backlash, they want a Network presence out here."

"Yes, but—"

"Ali, this has become national news," Lauren interrupted. "Actually, it's gone international. Yesterday another mosque and two more Islamic centers were bombed, as you know. Making matters worse, there was a copycat beheading in Portland, anti-Muslim protests are being organized nationwide, and mass demonstrations have spread to Europe, with ISIS taking credit for several recent murders there as well."

"I know all that, Lauren. But why should—"

"Ali, people are angry," Lauren interrupted. "Speaking from the White House, even the president has weighed in, and every bureaucrat in Washington is getting in on the act now, too. Bottom line, this has become a polarizing issue for our country. Like it or not, Network is sending out Brent. Period. Just strap yourself in and get ready for the ride."

"Fine," Allison grumbled. "When is he arriving?"

"Brent is flying in tonight, so he'll be here tomorrow. When he arrives, I want you to put aside your differences with him and act like the professional you are."

"Okay," Allison sighed. "One thing, though. You promised that if I came up with an exclusive, I would get to report it first, national coverage or not."

"I did. Network may not agree, but I'll do my best to stand by my word. Speaking of which, have you talked with your father yet?"

"You mean have I managed to worm any info out of my dad? That's not how it works, Lauren."

"I didn't mean to suggest that it did."

"In that case, no. I haven't spoken to my dad in several days. I've left messages, but he hasn't called back. I imagine he's been busy."

"Yes, I would imagine so. Well, let me know when you do talk with him. In the meantime, word coming down from Network is that they're happy with your coverage of the story so far. That position I mentioned for you in New York may be opening up soon."

"Great," said Allison, wondering how Mike would react to that possibility. Although she had talked with him every night since he'd arrived in Vancouver, she had yet to mention the possibility of their moving to New York.

Guiltily, Allison decided she needed to talk with Mike about it soon . . . before it became a problem.

Chapter 24

L ater that evening, following a solitary dinner of leftovers
that Dorothy had kept warm for me in the oven, I retired
to the swing on our redwood deck. I had been sitting in the
darkness for several minutes, staring out at the ocean and mulling
over elements of the case, when I heard the outside door creak
open behind me. A moment later Dorothy stepped out to the
deck, followed by our family dog, Callie. As Dorothy joined me
on the swing, Callie found a place nearby, circled, and settled
into a full curl, thumping the deck several times with her tail.

Settling back against the cushions, Dorothy gave the swing a
push with her foot, setting us in motion. "I've always envied how
comfortable dogs seem to be able make themselves in just about
any situation," Dorothy noted, glancing at Callie.

"As long as their owner's around, they're happy to be just
about anywhere," I agreed.

After a relaxed silence, Dorothy asked, "Have you talked
with Ali recently? I miss that girl."

"I got a call from her on the drive home tonight," I answered.
"She said she's been talking with Mike every day, and things are
going well for him in Vancouver. Shooting on the film is ahead
of schedule. She says he might even be able to come home for a
long weekend soon."

"She told me that, too. By the way, I invited your daughter to
join us for dinner anytime she wants, but she said she usually gets
home too late. She's really wrapped up in that job of hers."

"Yes, she is," I sighed.

"She's good at it, too. Ali has matured so much in the past
few years. Have you watched any of her newscasts lately?"

"Nope. Haven't had time." I knew that Allison was reporting
daily on the beheading investigations. I also knew she would
have loved for me to give her something to use on-air, as she had
broached the subject again during our phone conversation that
evening. It was something I decided not to mention to Dorothy,
as it was a continuing sore point between Allison and me.

"How's the case going?"

"I can't talk about that, Dorothy."

"Sorry. I wasn't asking for details, I just . . . well, I suppose I can tell from your face what I need to know. Things could be better."

"You could say that," I agreed.

The Bureau was in the process of setting up a number of "pizza sting" sites in Bel Air, Beverly Hills, Westwood, and North Hollywood. Starting the following day, each of the gated residences they'd rented would be occupied by a six-person surveillance team. The plan was to have the teams order pizza from each of the Wiseguy franchises currently under surveillance, as well as from several other Westside pizza parlors. If present, oil drips from the delivery vehicles would be collected and sampled, hoping for a match to the drips discovered at the Welch residence. Provisions were also being made to record tire-tread imprints as well.

Although the "pizza sting" approach had been my suggestion, I didn't have much faith in it. Nevertheless, considering the lack of progress elsewhere, it was worth a shot. As such, I had requested to be included on one of the stakeout teams, and after a short discussion with Director Shepherd, Gibbs had agreed.

"I hope you catch whoever is doing it," Dorothy continued. "Those horrible murders can't go on. I can't believe what I'm seeing on the news. Our country is coming apart at the seams."

"No one wants those guys off the street more than I do, Dorothy. And believe me, I'll do whatever it takes to see that happen."

"I know you will, Dan. You always do."

"Speaking of which, thanks for sticking around to help with Nate. Actually, I was hoping you could stay until the investigation is closed."

"Of course. I love having the chance to spend time with family. It's I who should be thanking you."

"Well, in that case, you're more than welcome," I laughed. "Although I wouldn't call hanging out with a teenager like Nate something that requires thanks. By the way, I didn't see him when I got home. Actually, I haven't seen much of him all week. How's he doing?"

"He's been keeping to himself a lot," Dorothy answered. "He said he wasn't hungry again tonight, and he just had a bowl of cereal in his room."

"Not hungry? That doesn't sound like Nate. He's not sick, is he?"

"No. I don't think there's anything wrong with him physically."

"You're not suggesting that Nate get counseling again, are you? I know he's been through a lot. We all have, but the kid will be fine. Plus he doesn't want that kind of help."

Dorothy paused thoughtfully. "Let me ask you something, Dan. Do you remember the toast you made at Allison and Mike's reception?"

"Sure."

"What did you say?"

Although puzzled by her question, I thought back to the night of the party, easily recalling my toast. "I said life could be beautiful and filled with love, but that it could also be unimaginably cruel. I reminded everyone that we were all going to experience heartbreak and loss before we left this world, and that we all were going to be hurt, and get sick, and experience pain, and lose people we loved. And that was exactly what made cherishing moments like Ali and Mike's wedding all the more important."

"Sounds almost verbatim," said Dorothy. "I keep forgetting that memory of yours."

I shrugged.

"Do you believe what you said?"

"In my toast to Ali and Mike? Of course. How can you ask that?"

"I ask because I know you, Dan. And I know what you're doing."

"And what's that?"

"You're throwing yourself into this terrorist investigation so you don't have to deal with other things in your life, things that hurt more than anyone should have to endure," Dorothy said gently. "Please don't misunderstand, Dan. I'm happy that you're back at work, but . . . ."

"But what?"

Again, Dorothy paused before answering. "I know you, Dan. And I know how deeply Catheryn's loss wounded you. You've withdrawn, wrapped yourself in a shell so nothing and no one can reach you. And I don't blame you. I understand, I really do. But now that you have an investigation to focus on, this protective wall you've built has grown even higher. And I understand that, too. But you need to realize that your withdrawal is hurting people who need you, people you love. You have to let them back in. For one, you need to reconnect with Nate, and you need to do it now."

When I didn't reply, Dorothy took a deep breath and continued. "At the risk of repeating myself, I'm going to give you some more advice, whether you want it or not. I told you this on the night of the reception, and I'm going to tell you again. Life can be hard, Dan. Unimaginably hard, as you said in your toast. But if you're not willing to accept life's sorrows, you're going to miss out on the good parts, too."

*****

"Nate? You awake?" I called, hesitating outside my son's bedroom door. Although it was past midnight, light was filtering from beneath a crack at the bottom of his door.

"Yeah, Dad. I'm still up," Nate's voice came back.

"Good. We need to talk." I opened the door and stepped inside. Nate's bedside light was on, and he was sitting at his desk writing on a yellow pad of paper.

I looked around the room, again thinking that it looked like a tornado had just passed through. "Jeez, what's with the mess?"

Nate glanced around, seeming surprised by the condition of his bedroom. "I'll . . . I'll clean it up tomorrow."

"See that you do."

"Yes, sir."

"What were you writing?"

Nate turned the yellow pad facedown on his desk. "Nothing. Just homework."

This wasn't going the way I wanted. After my conversation with Dorothy, I had remained on the swing after she'd gone to bed, thinking about what she had said. I still rejected the idea that something was wrong with Nate. Like every member of our family, he had been through some hard times, and his sadness was understandable. On the other hand, I had learned not to discount Dorothy's opinion. Although I didn't understand how, Dorothy, like Catheryn, often simply knew things. And she thought Nate was in trouble.

"Can't sleep, huh?" I said.

Nate shook his head. "Actually, I haven't been sleeping much lately. Sleep is overrated. Do you know that lots of people get by on just a couple hours of sleep each day?"

"Is that so? Is this something you're trying to do? Get by on less sleep?"

"Maybe," Nate answered. "I just finished reading a book on Ubersleep. The book talks about polyphasic sleep systems—forty-five minute naps several times a day and you're good to go. A number of famous people like Leonardo da Vinci, Napoleon, and Tesla were polyphasic sleepers."

"I always try to get eight hours myself," I said doubtfully. "I'm not sure functioning on a couple hours of sleep is a good idea, Nate."

Nate shrugged, not meeting my gaze. "Whatever."

For some reason, Nate seemed agitated. He had been bouncing his left leg as we talked, his nervous movement vibrating items on his desk.

"Do you have to go to the bathroom?" I asked, glancing at his leg.

"Huh?" Nate replied. Then, catching on, "Oh. Burns off energy. It's a good way to get exercise."

"Can you stop, please?"

Again, Nate shrugged. He stopped briefly, then started up

again, seemingly unaware of what he was doing. "What did you want to talk about, Dad?" he asked.

"You okay?"

"Why do you ask?"

"Because Grandma Dorothy thinks something is wrong with you. We talked about this before, but—"

"Nothing's wrong with me," Nate interrupted, suddenly angry. "Why does everyone keep asking that?"

"Everyone? Who else?"

"Those morons at Samohigh, for instance," Nate shot back. "By the way, I quit the baseball team. You'll be hearing about that soon enough, I imagine."

"You quit the Vikings? Why?"

"Because nobody over there likes me. Besides, it's a stupid game, and I was never any good at it anyway."

"You *were* good at it, Nate. And you still are. Where did you get the idea that you weren't? You were the Viking's starting pitcher last season. I thought you liked playing ball."

"Not anymore."

"I can't believe that. How's about next weekend you and I toss the ball around on the beach? Maybe you'll—"

"I gave away my glove, Dad," Nate broke in again. "Look, baseball isn't important to me anymore. A lot of things aren't important anymore."

"I'm sorry to hear that," I said, surprised by Nate's sudden anger.

"I'm sorry, too, Dad. I know you're disappointed," Nate went on, his anger suddenly deflating. "And I'm sorry that you're worried about me. I know most of the problems around here are my fault. I don't want to make things worse for you, or for anyone else."

"You're not making things worse, Nate. I'm just concerned. And so is Grandma Dorothy. You seem so sad sometimes. I understand, I really do. Your mother's death was—"

"I don't want to talk about mom."

I hesitated, then pushed on. "I know we discussed this before, but if you ever want to get some counseling—"

"I don't. And don't worry about me. Things will get better soon, I promise."

"Okay," I sighed, unsure of where to go from there. "It's getting late. Why don't we try to get some sleep, and not the polyphasic kind, either," I added with a smile. "And if you ever want to talk . . ."

Although Nate smiled back, his eyes were hollow and empty. "You know I love you, Dad," he said.

"I know that, Nate," I replied, now more confused than ever. "I love you, too."

Chapter 25

"Hey, Kane. What's the difference between pizza and an award-winning foreign film?"

Along with Taylor and four other Bureau agents, I had been on stakeout in Westwood for the past week, detailed to one of the FBI's pizza-sting operations. Like me, everyone there was tired, bored, and more than a little sick of pizza. Nevertheless, it was better than interviewing uncooperative mullahs and running down questionable hot-line tips. "I give up, Jenkins," I said, turning from a second-story window to regard the agent who'd asked. "What's the difference?"

Jenkins looked up from a game of solitaire he had spread across a nearby desk. "Simple," he laughed. "Pizzas are good."

"After eating pizza for seven straight days, one could argue that," Taylor noted from her station at a window across the room. "Speaking of which, whose idea was this pizza sting, anyway?"

"Kane's," grumbled Frank Gillespie, another stakeout agent. "I swear, if I eat one more slice of pepperoni, I'm gonna puke."

"No one's forcing that pizza down your throat, Frank," I pointed out.

Gillespie grinned. "What can I say? It calls to me."

I smiled and resumed staring out at the street, waiting for our next pizza delivery. Not every delivery vehicle leaked oil, but from the ones that did we were getting clean samples. So far none of the collected oil had matched the drips found at the Welch residence, but the comparison process took twenty-four hours, and we still hadn't received the results from material gathered the previous day. Nevertheless, after a week of ordering pizza, things didn't look good. And this was assuming the terrorists hadn't gone in for an oil change in the meantime.

None of the tire-tread impressions recovered from sections of cardboard laid across our pizza-sting driveways had matched the casts from the Welches' estate, either. Nor had a murder squad shown up at any of the sting locations. The general feeling was that if our operation were going to draw out the killers, it would have done so by now.

On the upside, a DNA comparison of saliva on the dumpster pizza had proved a positive match with blood found in the Welches' master bathroom, as well as with DNA present on the inside of bloodstained clothing discovered in the dumpster. Not much, but something. Also on the plus side, there had been no further terrorist attacks.

"Hey, get down here," Duffy called from the living room. "You guys have to see this. I swear to God, you're not going to believe it."

Curious, I followed Taylor, Jenkins, and Gillespie down a flight of stairs to the living room, where we joined Duffy and a long-haired Asian named Beverly Choi, the final two members of our surveillance team. Duffy and Choi were staring at a television across the room. Filling most of the TV screen was the tanned, perfectly symmetrical face of a reporter I knew all too well: Brent Preston. I groaned, expecting the worst.

". . . *CBS Evening News* regarding the recent beheading murders in Los Angeles," Brent was saying, delivering his lines directly to camera. "Sources close to the FBI/LAPD Joint Terrorism Task Force have confirmed that investigators now believe the killers responsible for last week's execution-style murders may have gained entrance to gated estates in Bel Air and Holmby Hills via a pizza-delivery vehicle. Authorities are searching for a van or other delivery vehicle that might have been used in the murders. Anyone with information please call the number shown at the bottom of the screen."

Disgusted, Duffy thumbed a remote control, sending the TV screen to darkness. "Damn," he said.

"Pretty much blows our sting operation," Gillespie noted. "Not that it was going anywhere anyway."

"Yeah. I heard they were gonna pull the plug tomorrow," added Jenkins.

"Nonetheless, it was the best lead we've had," Taylor pointed out. "I wonder who leaked."

"Probably some hump at LAPD," said Gillespie. Then, glancing at me, "No offense, Kane."

"None taken," I said, thinking he might have been right. I had been reporting daily to Chief Ingram. And Ingram, or someone in his office, had been relaying that information directly to Snead's task force, the district attorney's office, and numerous ancillary departments at PAB. All were a potential source of leaks. But if I had been forced to guess, I would have bet the leak came from Snead or someone close to him, making me wonder whether sharing information with Ingram had been in the best interests of the investigation. On the other hand, LAPD was paying my salary, not the Bureau.

"Look at the bright side, Gillespie," suggested Taylor.

"What bright side?" Gillespie grumbled.

"After tonight, you won't have to choke down any more pepperoni."

Although I smiled at Taylor's gibe, I wasn't feeling the humor. The pizza connection had been the only real lead we'd had so far, and we'd blown it. Which left waiting for the killers to do it again . . . and hoping they made a mistake.

*****

"Hey, Tammy," Dr. Oliver Clark called from the entry. "I thought we were having dinner at your brother's."

"We are, Ollie," answered Tammy Sanders, Dr. Clark's surgical assistant and sometimes girlfriend.

"So why the pizza?" asked Dr. Clark, pressing the gate release button. "Oh, I get it," he continued, watching from an entry window as a Wiseguy Pizza van headed up the driveway. "We're bringing pizza to your brother's, just in case. He really isn't much of a cook."

"I didn't order pizza," Tammy replied from the kitchen, her voice filled with alarm, "Ollie, I just saw a news report on those terrorists who are beheading people. It said they're using a pizza van to get in."

"Sweetheart, don't worry about it. What are the odds? Besides, it's pizza, for God's sake."

"I'm calling the cops, Ollie."

"You're overreacting, babe. Let's just—"

"Ollie, I'm calling the cops."

* * * * *

Twenty minutes later my cellphone buzzed. And with that call, everything changed. I pulled my phone from my pocket and checked the number. Deluca. "What's up, Paul?" I asked, stepping away from my surveillance position at the window.

"Plenty," said Deluca. "Or maybe nothing. Either way, I thought I'd let you know."

Sensing something in Deluca's tone, I glanced across the room. Taylor was stationed at another window nearby, watching the street. Jenkins was back to cheating through his game of solitaire. Gillespie had drifted downstairs, saying he wanted something to eat. "Let me know what?" I asked, lowering my voice.

"A 911 call just came in from some lady in the Palisades. She reported a pizza van in their driveway, supposedly delivering food they didn't order. She just saw your pal Brent Preston's news report, and—"

"Are you guys rolling on it?"

"Yep. It could be nothing, like I said, but Snead is taking it seriously. He called a SWAT unit to the location and told them to wait for his arrival. We're on our way."

"I don't suppose Snead notified the Bureau."

"You've gotta be kidding. Snead?"

"What's the address?"

"1102 Rivas Canyon Road. Off Sunset near Will Rogers State Park."

"I'm a couple minutes away. I'll meet you there."

"Kane . . ."

"What?"

"Never mind. I'll see you there. Just . . . stay clear of Snead."

"I told you before. I can handle Snead."

"Just be careful."

As I hung up, I noticed Taylor regarding me curiously. "Who was that?" she asked.

"Nobody," I answered. Then, with a casual glance out the window, "Look, as nothing's happening around here, especially after that newscast, I'm taking off. See you tomorrow."

"I don't think so," said Taylor. "I've been around you long enough to know when something's up. What is it?"

I shrugged. "Probably nothing," I answered, irritated that Taylor had read me so easily.

"What's going on, Kane?" she demanded, not letting it go.

"A 911 call in the Palisades. Something about a pizza delivery."

"I'm going with you."

"Like hell you are."

"It's either me, or we can invite the whole stakeout team to join us."

I glanced at Gillespie. He was still concentrating on his cards, oblivious of our conversation. "Okay," I sighed, again lowering my voice. "Just you. But this is LAPD business, so when we get there, stay out of my way."

"Excuse me? Stay out of your way?" said Taylor. "Gosh, Detective Kane, I'll be sure to do that."

Chapter 26

When Taylor and I arrived in Rivas Canyon, we found an LAPD black-and-white already onsite. The police vehicle was stationed in front of a rambling, two-story home set far back off the narrow street, most of the house hidden behind a gigantic hedge of oleander. I pulled to a stop behind the police car and killed my engine, noting that the responding officers had positioned their vehicle so it wouldn't be visible from the residence. As Taylor and I climbed from my Suburban, two uniformed officers exited their car to meet us.

"Kane, LAPD," I said, flipping out my ID. Taylor did the same.

The older of the two officers, whose plate read "Fagen," checked my credentials, glanced at Taylor's, and turned back to me. "Are the feds involved in this?" he asked.

"Not at the moment," I answered. Then, ignoring a curious look from Officer Fagen, I walked to a security gate at the end of the driveway, careful to stay out of sight of the house. I noted a keypad and intercom mounted beside the gate. No camera. A mailbox there displayed the name "Clark."

Still keeping out of sight, I checked the residence. It lay at the end of a broad driveway, nestled in a grove of eucalyptus and fir. At the front of the house, parked beneath an overhanging porte-cochère, was a Wiseguy Pizza van.

"Damn, this could be it," whispered Taylor, who had followed me over.

I didn't reply. Instead, I returned to the police cruiser. "Have you tried contacting anyone in the house?" I asked Officer Fagen.

"No, sir," he replied. "We were ordered to keep out of sight and wait for SWAT. Captain Snead and a Robbery-Homicide team will be arriving shortly."

"How long have you been onsite?"

"Nine, ten minutes. Haven't seen any action from the house since we got here. You think it might be the terrorists in there?"

"Doesn't take ten minutes to deliver a pizza," I noted.

"I need to call this in," said Taylor.

"Do what you have to." I thought a moment, deciding that if the Clarks were being visited by a pizza-delivering murder squad, the arrival of a SWAT unit would quickly escalate things into a hostage situation, assuming the residents were still alive by then. Either way, with SWAT and Snead on the scene, the killers would have nothing to lose, and surrender was unlikely.

Coming to a decision, I started toward an adjacent residence that we had passed on the way in. Like the Clark house, the neighboring home had a long, curving driveway. Unlike the Clark residence, it didn't have a security gate.

I hadn't gone more than two steps when Taylor caught up and grabbed my arm. "Kane, what are you doing?" she demanded. "Didn't you hear the officer? We need to wait for backup."

At that point Fagen also weighed in, looking concerned. "Detective, our orders were to wait for SWAT. Captain Snead made it crystal clear that nothing is supposed to happen until he arrives."

"I don't take orders from Snead," I said, freeing my arm from Taylor's grasp. "Listen, both of you. If it *is* our terrorist friends in there, by the time SWAT arrives it may be too late. We need to do something, and we need to do it now. Otherwise we're going to have a lot of dead people on our hands."

Taylor looked doubtful. "But—"

"Make your call to the Bureau," I said, cutting her off. "Then phone me on my cell." I scribbled my number on the back of one of my cards and passed it to her, then withdrew my cellphone and set the ringer to vibrate. "If things go south, we can at least stay in contact."

Next I addressed Patrolman Fagen. "Listen up, Fagen. This is important. When SWAT arrives, tell them there's an officer inside. I can be their eyes and ears."

"You're going in?"

I nodded. "Tell them that. I want to make sure I don't wind up in some SWAT sharpshooter's crosshairs. You understand me?"

"Yes, sir."

"Good." I removed my jacket and laid it on the hood of my Suburban. Hoping Fagen did as I'd asked, I withdrew my service weapon, a Glock.45 ACP model 21. With my index finger paralleling the trigger guard, I "press checked" the pistol by easing the slide slightly rearward, confirming the presence of a chambered cartridge. There were thirteen more just like it in the Glock's staggered-stack magazine, and I had a pair of fully loaded spares in my holster's magazine carrier. Satisfied, I returned the weapon to my shoulder rig and started again for the neighboring home.

"Damn it, Kane, " Taylor called after me.

"Make your calls," I said over my shoulder, not looking back.

A jog up the neighbor's driveway and a short trek across a landscaped yard brought me abreast of the Clark residence. Staying to the shadows, I squeezed through a wall of shrubbery and vaulted a wrought-iron fence. Once on the other side, I headed for a terrace in the Clarks' backyard.

Moments later I arrived at a patio adjacent to a large swimming pool and several tennis courts. Beneath a latticed pergola to the left, a sliding glass door led into the house. Approaching cautiously, I looked inside. The room beyond was dark. Holding my breath, I tried the door handle.

Locked.

As I was gauging my chances of scaling the pergola to a second-story deck twenty feet up, my phone vibrated. I checked the screen. "Taylor?" I whispered, not recognizing the number.

"Kane," Taylor's voice came back. "Where are you?"

"In the backyard. I'll be inside shortly."

"I notified Gibbs," said Taylor, sounding nervous. "A Bureau team is on the way. Your Captain Snead called, too. SWAT is still ten minutes out. Snead's ETA is about the same. He was none too pleased to hear you were present. He ordered you to stand down."

"Like I said, I don't take orders from Snead. Besides, in ten minutes we could be too late, with the residents already dead. Stay on the phone and keep the line open."

Time was running out for the Clarks. I muted my cellphone,

repocketed it, and assessed my situation. With the ground-floor door locked, my best chance of entering the house undetected now lay in climbing to the second-story deck over the pergola, and hoping the door there wasn't locked as well.

I eased out from the shadows. Silently, I moved to a nearby pergola support, a six-by-six post that helped carry the weight of the lattice structure above. Placing one foot against the post and another against the house, and then doing the same with my hands, I bridged the distance with my body. Slowly, I began moving upward, alternately inching up my hands and feet as I progressed. Several minutes of strenuous effort brought me to the lattice structure atop the column. Grabbing a support beam in both hands, I swung over a leg and manteled onto the framework.

Breathing hard, I stopped and listened.

Nothing.

Careful not to make a sound, I crossed the lattice and stepped over a railing to the second-story deck. A glass-paneled door led into a darkened bedroom beyond. I peered through the glass.

Again, nothing.

Mentally crossing my fingers, I withdrew my Glock and tried the doorknob.

The door was unlocked.

I slipped inside. From somewhere deeper in the house came the sound of voices. I withdrew my cellphone, intending to let Taylor know I was in. The phone's status bar read "No Service." Puzzled, I returned the phone to my pocket, hoping that when SWAT arrived, Patrolman Fagen remembered to inform them of my presence.

Deciding it was too late to worry about that now, I crossed the bedroom and eased open the door to a second-floor hallway.

Again, I listened.

No sound came from the upper floor. But from downstairs, the voices had grown louder. I still couldn't make out the words, but they sounded angry.

Palms slippery with sweat, Glock held before me in a two-handed grip, I edged out into the hall.

*****

Jacob scowled, angrily regarding the scene in the living room. Not for the first time, he wondered whether assigning Rudy to escape-vehicle duty that night had been a mistake. Ethan, Rudy's replacement for the evening, simply couldn't follow directions. Despite Rudy's insubordination and the perverse enjoyment he seemed to take in the killings, at least he could follow orders.

"Okay, let's try the knife shot one more time," suggested Parker.

"This isn't rocket science, Ethan," added Caleb. "Just take the knife from the jar and hold it in front of you. It's not that complicated, bro."

"Screw you, Caleb," said Ethan. "I did it right the first time."

"Just do it again," said Parker.

Bound and hooded, Dr. Clark and his young girlfriend were kneeling in the glare of the floodlights. The girlfriend was sobbing. Dr. Clark had initially put up some resistance, but that hadn't lasted long. Blood seeping through his hood bore testament to a beating from Ethan that had brought Dr. Clark into line. For a fleeting moment Jacob felt a pang of sympathy, knowing what was to come. Resolutely, he pushed away his misgivings, reminding himself that this was God's will. The couple on their knees were dying for the greater good of all.

Suddenly Jacob heard a noise.

He froze.

Someone upstairs?

Concealed in the shadow of a curving staircase, Jacob gazed up to the second floor. Ethan had already checked the house. No one else was home. Yet against all reason, at the top of the stairs Jacob saw the shadow of a man move across a wall. The man had a gun.

"How's about we just forget the knife shot, Parker?" Ethan said angrily. "I'm doin' this guy now. If you don't like it, tough. Start recording."

With a surge of alarm, Jacob glanced across the room to

where the AK-47 was propped against a wall where he'd left it.

Too far.

"Not yet, Ethan, God damn it!" Parker yelled, losing patience. "I've gotta refocus."

Keeping his back to the stairs, Jacob retreated to the kitchen. Earlier he'd noticed a door leading to the backyard. Maybe it wasn't too late . . .

"Too bad," Ethan snarled, ripping the hood from Dr. Clark's head. "Like Rudy says, it's showtime!"

Fighting panic, Jacob crept to the door at the rear of the kitchen. With trembling hands, he tried the knob. The door was locked. He twisted a thumb latch and tried again. The door swung open.

Jacob glanced back into the living room, wondering how things could have gone so wrong. Despite Parker's instructions, Ethan had started his work with the knife, and blood was beginning to flow.

"Police! Freeze!" someone shouted.

*****

The voices grew louder as I neared the top of a circular staircase. Now I could make out what the men below were saying. "Not yet, Ethan, God damn it!" one of them yelled. "I've gotta refocus."

If I'd had any doubts about what was happening, one glance into the living room dispelled them. Hands bound with plastic ties, sacks covering their heads, a man and a woman were kneeling in front of a camera. Floodlights were attached to either side of a tripod supporting the camera. Blood stained the side of the man's hood. It sounded like the woman was sobbing.

A tall man with dark hair and a prominent nose stood behind the camera. An AK-47 rifle lay propped against a nearby wall. Two other men, both wearing balaclavas, were positioned behind the couple. Both men were holding long, serrated knives. They were knives I had seen before.

"Too bad, Parker," one of the men laughed, yanking the hood from his captive's head. "Like Rudy says, it's showtime!"

I watched in horror as the masked terrorist placed his blade to the man's throat and began sawing.

"Police! Freeze!" I yelled.

I was too late. Left forearm circling his captive's head, the terrorist sawed his blade across the man's throat, opening a mortal gash. Blood spurted, gushing down the man's shirt.

I routinely scored in the top percentage of shooters at the LAPD handgun range. During a tactical situation, something clicked and I shot even better. Although his victim's body shielded most of his own, the killer's head was exposed. When he ignored my warning, I put a bullet through his forehead.

He dropped like a stone.

At the deafening concussion of my shot, time seemed to slow. I saw the man behind the camera start toward the AK-47. The other man released his female captive. Screaming, the woman fell forward. The hooded killer drew a pistol from the small of his back.

I knew the man with the pistol would get off the first shot, but the man with the rifle presented a far greater danger.

Which one?

The man with the pistol made my decision for me. Dropping to one knee, he put a round into a hallway mirror behind me. The mirror exploded, sending glass shards flying. Blood bathed the side of my face. Ignoring my injury, I double-tapped two into the man's chest.

By then the third man had reached the rifle. An AK-47 assault weapon has been described as a "bullet hose"—having questionable accuracy at distance, but deadly at close range. The barrel swung toward me. An instant later it began spraying rounds.

Without hesitation, I dropped the third man as well.

*****

After easing shut the door behind him, Jacob ran as he'd never run before. Reeling from the horror of witnessing his brother's death, he raced through the Dr. Clark's backyard, hoping against hope to escape the trap that someone had set.

How had they known?

Upon reaching the rear of the property, Jacob vaulted a wrought-iron fence and continued on. Racing through the darkness, he followed a dirt footpath across a wooded section of parkland and then crossed another backyard, finally spotting their emergency vehicle on Villa Woods Drive.

At Jacob's approach, Rudy sat straighter behind the wheel, his eyes widening in alarm.

Closing the final yards to the vehicle, Jacob once more asked himself how things could have gone so wrong. They had prepared for every circumstance, practiced for every contingency. Yet somehow disaster had struck. Parker was gone. And Ethan. And Caleb, whose loss was immeasurable.

How could God have allowed this to happen?

Panting, Jacob threw open the passenger's door. "Go!" he yelled, climbing inside. "Get us out of here."

"Wha . . . what happened?" Rudy stammered.

"Just shut up and drive," Jacob ordered, still fighting not to panic.

Seconds later, they slowed briefly at a stop sign on Sunset. From there they headed west, skirting a police barricade blocking the mouth of Rivas Canyon, the lights atop a swarm of police vehicles there illuminating the intersection in staccato flashes of red and blue. Heart still hammering in his chest, Jacob was again thankful that he'd taken the precaution of having an escape car present.

Several minutes of steady driving brought them to the 405 Freeway. From there it was a straight shot to the San Fernando Valley. And from there, the Trancas Canyon compound, and home. As Rudy merged onto the freeway, Jacob's heart finally began to slow. Still not believing he had escaped, he stared out the window, stunned that everything had so unexpectedly fallen apart.

Nevertheless, he refused to believe that Caleb's death had been a part of God's plan.

Something else must have been at play. Something evil. *Someone* evil.

Tears of rage streaming down his cheeks, Jacob lowered his head and made a silent vow—both to himself, and to his God. It was a promise he intended to keep.

*****

I felt my phone vibrate. Ignoring it, I rushed downstairs, taking the treads three at a time.

After kicking away the terrorists' weapons in turn, I confirmed that all three were dead. The male resident whose throat had been cut was unconscious. Lying nearby, the woman was still crying. She screamed when I removed her hood.

"Police," I said. "I'm not going to hurt you."

"That's what *they* said," the woman sobbed, staring at my face in shock. Curious, I touched my cheek. My hand came away red.

"Cut me loose," the woman pleaded. Then, noticing the man beside her, "Oh, God, Ollie. What did they do to you?"

Using one of the terrorist's knives, I severed the handcuff ties binding the woman. Once freed, she stripped off her sweater, wadded it, and began applying pressure to the man's neck, attempting to stem the flow of blood.

Leaving her, I made a quick circuit of the ground floor to make certain no one else was present. As I was heading upstairs to check the second level, I felt my phone vibrate again. I checked the screen. Recognizing Taylor's number, I answered.

"Kane, we heard shots. What's going on?" Taylor's voice demanded.

"One of the residents is injured," I replied. "Get an ambulance here ASAP."

I heard Taylor speak to someone, then come back to me. "Are you okay?

"I'm fine. But the guys who broke in here aren't."

"Please tell me you left one of them alive to interrogate."

"Sorry. Judgment call. Stay on the line, Taylor. There's something I have to do."

After checking the upstairs and finding no one, I returned to the living room. The young woman was still applying pressure to her friend's throat. The bleeding seemed to have stopped. Probably not a good sign, I thought. From the size of the blood puddle, it looked like he had already bled out.

I moved to the bodies of the two masked terrorists. Leaning down, I pulled off their balaclavas. One was blond, maybe in his early twenties. The other had red hair and appeared a bit older than his partner. Like the third man who had been operating the camera, both looked like clean-cut American youths. Young men you might see on the street every day. Definitely not foreign Muslims.

I raised my phone. "Has SWAT arrived?" I asked Taylor, who was still on the line.

"Their van just pulled up," Taylor's voice came back. "Captain Snead and his team are here, too."

"Good," I sighed, suddenly feeling exhausted. "Tell them I'm coming out. Ask them not to shoot me."

Again I heard Taylor speak to someone. Then, again back to me, "Holster your weapon and exit the front door with your hands raised," she instructed. "SWAT will stand down. As for Snead . . . that I can't guarantee."

Chapter 27

A ll incidents involving the use of deadly force by an LAPD officer are investigated by the department's Force Investigation Division. Following my exit from the Clark residence, I was ordered to proceed downtown, where I was round-robin interviewed by several teams of FID detectives. Simply put, the purpose of their investigation was to determine whether, under the circumstances, my use of deadly force had been objectively reasonable.

The bulk of the interview, which took the remainder of the evening, was conducted by a pair of seasoned FID investigators, Detectives John Madison and Emily Logan. Two hours into it, Snead stormed into the room.

Ignoring surprised looks from both Madison and Logan, Snead placed his fists on the table and leaned over, bringing his face within inches of mine. "You screwed the pooch this time, hotshot," he said with a sneer.

"Damn, Snead," I said. "Ever hear of breath mints?"

"With all due respect, Captain Snead, you can't be here," Madison intervened. "Someone will be taking your statement later."

"Fine," said Snead. He took a step back, raising his hands in concession. "I just want to make it absolutely clear that Detective Kane disobeyed my direct orders when he entered the Clark residence."

"I was serving as a Bureau liaison and not under your command," I countered.

"I was the senior investigative officer at the scene, which *gave* me command," Snead snapped.

"You weren't on the scene, Bill. I was. And as it looked like a developing hostage situation, that put *me* in command."

"That's *Captain* Snead, you insubordinate bastard," Snead shot back, his face mottled with rage.

"Okay," I replied. "Let's call a spade a spade here, *Captain* Snead. If we had waited for your arrival, there would have been even more dead bodies inside than there already were."

"You can't be certain of that," Snead spat. "Speaking of which, how did you know to be there? Who tipped you off? It was Deluca, wasn't it?"

"Deluca isn't my only friend on the force," I replied, dodging his question.

"You don't get it, do you?" Snead continued. "As of now, your career is over, hotshot. I knew if I waited long enough, I'd see the day. Well, that day has come. You'll be lucky if you don't wind up serving time."

"What are you talking about?"

"Who gave you the right to execute those suspects? You didn't even give them a warning, did you? Just blew them away, right?"

"That's not how it happened."

"Captain, if Detective Kane was responding to aggressive actions by the suspects, either toward him or the residents, a verbal warning wouldn't have been necessary," Logan pointed out. "Now, if you'll let us get back to our job . . ."

"Ask him why he turned off his cellphone," said Snead.

"What?" asked Madison, looking puzzled.

"Before Kane entered the Clark residence, he agreed to remain in cellphone contact with Special Agent Taylor," Snead explained. "As soon as he entered the house, Kane broke the connection. Why? Simple. He disconnected so no one could monitor his actions."

"I lost cell service when I got inside," I said.

"Bull," Snead snapped. "And after the shooting, your service was miraculously restored? That's just a little too *convenient*, don't you think?"

"A cellphone jammer could have—"

"I heard about your bogus jammer theory," Snead cut me off. "No cellphone blocker of any kind was found in the house. So I'll ask you again. If you didn't hang up, how do you explain losing contact with Taylor?"

I couldn't.

"And now, with no corroboration, you expect us to simply

take your word for what happened in there?" Snead snorted. "No way, Kane."

Detective Madison stood. "We'll be taking your statement later, Captain," he repeated. "With all due respect, you have to leave. Now. We'll take it from here."

"Fine," Snead repeated, turning on his heel. "See that you do."

After Snead had slammed out the door, the interview continued for several more hours, with Detectives Madison and Logan repeatedly going over my version of events—establishing a timeline, asking and re-asking questions, and nailing down every detail of my statement. The sun had risen by the time the interview was over.

I knew that FID's investigative results would be reviewed by Chief Ingram, the Office of the Inspector General, and finally the Los Angeles County District Attorney's Justice System Integrity Division, which would conduct a final review of all facts in evidence. And ultimately, at the end of an involved, painstaking process that often took months, the investigative conclusions would be reviewed, adjudicated, and published by the Los Angeles Board of Police Commissioners.

What I didn't know was how much Snead's statements would count. I was also troubled to learn that prior to going to Chief Ingram, the FID's findings would be forwarded to Assistant Chief Strickland for comment. Nevertheless, at issue was whether my use of deadly force had been objectively reasonable. Given the circumstances, I felt confident there was no question of that. Unfortunately, I also knew there could be more involved.

Hours later I learned that I wasn't being relieved of duty, either via administrative leave or by disciplinary suspension—at least for the time being. I took this to be a good sign. Still, on the return drive to West Los Angeles for the FBI briefing, I placed a call to my Police Protective League representative and put her on notice. I had seen situations like this blow up more than once, with careers ruined in the process.

*****

No one at the FBI briefing that morning appeared to have had much sleep, including me. I hadn't had time to return home following my FID interview, although at one point during my interrogation I had cleaned up some in a restroom down the hall. Still, I knew I looked like hell. And I felt like it, too. The head injury I had received at the Clark residence, which turned out to be a deep, mirror-shard slice near my hairline, had finally stopped bleeding, but my collar and the front of my shirt were covered with blood. My jacket hid some of it, but not all. Wearily, I dropped into a chair at the back of the room. To my surprise, Taylor settled in beside me.

"How did the shooting investigation go?" she asked.

"Not as well as I would have hoped," I answered. "Snead is trying to make an issue of my supposedly severing phone contact with you after I entered the residence. "

"I'm sorry about that, Kane."

I knew that Taylor had been interviewed by LAPD detectives at the scene. "Don't worry about it," I said. "You told the truth. I'll be fine."

"I hope so. What is it with you and Snead, anyway?"

"Long story. Maybe I'll tell you sometime."

"Okay, I look forward to hearing it. In the meantime, if there's anything I can do . . ."

"If there is, I'll let you know," I replied, lowering my voice as Vaughn stepped to the front of the assembly. "And thanks."

Vaughn raised his hands for silence. "I'll make this quick," he said. "Last evening at approximately seven-thirty p.m., a terrorist team entered the Pacific Palisades home of Dr. Oliver Clark. Dr. Clark was present at the time, along with a friend, Ms. Tammy Sanders. Ms. Sanders had recently watched a CBS news report detailing the pizza-delivery connection with the terrorist murders. When a Wiseguy van unexpectedly showed up at the Clark residence, Ms. Sanders called 911."

"How did CBS get that information, anyway?" Duffy broke in. "The leak sure as hell didn't come from us," he added, glancing in my direction.

Although I ignored Duffy's tacit accusation, I decided to quiz Allison about the leak. I knew she couldn't give specifics, but I hoped she might be able to point me in the right direction. And I suspected that the direction would lead to Snead.

"We're checking into that," said Vaughn, also glancing at me. "Rest assured, we'll know soon enough."

An uncomfortable silence settled over the room. Finally Vaughn continued. "The M.O. of the Rivas Canyon intruders matches that of the terrorists in Bel Air and Holmby Hills, including the presence of video equipment and an AK-47 rifle."

"Same guys," someone muttered.

Vaughn nodded. "During the attack, Dr. Clark was wounded and died on route to UCLA Medical Center. Ms. Sanders sustained minor injuries and was released from the hospital early this morning. All three terrorists died at the scene from gunshot wounds inflicted by Detective Kane."

At this, more heads turned in my direction. I ignored them, saddened but not surprised to learn that Dr. Clark hadn't survived.

"Kane, we'll discuss your unauthorized actions at the Clark residence in a moment," Vaughn went on. "But before that, can you explain how you happened to be there in the first place?"

"I got a tip," I replied.

"And after receiving this . . . *tip*, you and Taylor abandoned your Bureau stakeout and proceeded to the Clark residence. Is that correct?"

"It was a judgment call," I said for the second time in twelve hours.

"And when you were making this judgment call of yours, did it ever occur to you that it might have been useful to have at least one intruder left alive to interrogate?"

"With respect, ASAC Vaughn, we should be kissing Kane's butt right now," Taylor broke in.

At this, eyes in the room shifted in surprise to Taylor. Stubbornly, she glared back.

"Nice talk, Taylor," said an agent nearby.

"Screw you, Dave," Taylor shot back. "You know I'm right."

"You approve of Kane's actions?" demanded Vaughn.

"Not entirely," Taylor replied. "But if Kane hadn't gone in, both residents would be dead right now, and we still wouldn't have anyone left to interrogate. Those guys weren't going to surrender."

"That may be, Taylor, but it doesn't excuse—"

"I think we're getting off-subject here, Mason," interrupted Gibbs, who was standing at a workstation near Director Shepherd. "Let's move on."

"Yes, sir," said Vaughn. He referred to an index card, then pushed ahead. "It's now clear that the terrorists were not foreign nationals, as we first suspected."

"Do we have IDs on any of them?" someone asked.

"One of the three," Vaughn replied. "Ethan James Hess— arrested for car theft when he was twenty. He got probation, then dropped off the grid about four years ago. No current address, phone record, driver's license, tax payments, utility bills, known-associates, and so on. The other two suspects' prints aren't in our IAFIS database, so we don't have anything on them yet."

"Any connection with the pizza parlor?" asked Young.

"We're checking Wiseguy franchises," Vaughn answered, again referring to his notes. "Other pizza establishments, too. At this point, aside from establishing that the killers purchased a Wiseguy pepperoni pizza found in the house, we've come up cold. We're fairly certain that the terrorists had their phony magnetic signs custom made, probably online. LAPD is running down the source of those signs."

"Did we get a statement from Ms. Sanders?" someone else asked.

"She was understandably distraught at the scene," Vaughn replied. "Later at the hospital she stated that after forcing their way into the house, the killers bound her hands and placed a hood over her head. Dr. Clark resisted and they beat him into submission. After that Ms. Sanders doesn't remember much, except that she was terrified."

"What about the killers' van?" asked Garcia, for once not looking like he had just stepped from a sauna.

"The van was stolen from an LAX parking lot two years ago," Vaughn replied. "The plates on it didn't match the vehicle registration. The plates belong on a Chevy Camaro. When we checked the Camaro's owner—a housewife in Playa del Rey—she hadn't noticed that her plates had been switched. We're checking the plates on her vehicle for prints, as well as examining the terrorists' van for blood, hair and fibers, prints, and so on. On a positive note, we were able to match the tire-track impressions from the Bel Air crime scene to the van. We're also analyzing oil from the van, and we're confident that the oil drips will prove a match, too."

"So it's the same vehicle used in the murders of Arleen and Gary Welch?" asked an agent near the front.

"No doubt about it," answered Vaughn. "We'll be reviewing footage from the terrorists' camera for any additional information that might prove useful, but we're tentatively concluding that the terrorist attacks have ended with the deaths of the individuals killed last night. Nevertheless, they may have had help from associates, and in days to come we will vigorously investigate that possibility."

I shifted in my seat, suspecting from Vaughn's manner that the final bit of his speech had been lifted from an official Bureau statement scheduled for later.

"To that effect, we will be making a news announcement later this morning," Vaughn concluded, confirming my suspicions. "In the meantime, thank you all for your excellent work. That being said, we still have things to mop up, and there's plenty left to do. Please pick up your assignments after the briefing."

A few minutes later, following a further address by Gibbs, the meeting concluded. With a sigh, I turned to Taylor. "Thanks for sticking up for me," I said. "But take my advice and make that the last time. I have a feeling you didn't help your career much just now."

Taylor shrugged. "It needed to be said."

"Anyway, it's been interesting." I extended my hand.

Puzzled, Taylor shook my hand. "You going somewhere?"

she asked.

I nodded. "I have a feeling I'm not going to be around much longer."

"Well, if that's the case . . . stay in touch."

"Sure."

"Kane," Gibbs called from across the room. "Director Shepherd wants a word."

"Be right there," I called back. Then, to Taylor, "Take care of yourself."

"You, too, Kane."

I crossed the room without looking back. I nodded at Gibbs upon arriving, then addressed Director Shepherd. "You wanted to see me, sir?" I asked, already suspecting what was coming.

"Dan, I'd be lying if I said I wasn't upset about the leak," Shepherd replied. "We know it didn't come from us, which leaves the LAPD and Captain Snead's task force as a possible source."

"Don't forget the DA's office," I advised. "Wouldn't be the first time they sprung a leak over there."

"I'm also disappointed that Captain Snead didn't see fit to notify us of the developing situation in Rivas Canyon," Shepherd continued, ignoring my interruption. "If it hadn't been for a call from Agent Taylor, the Bureau would have been completely left out of the loop. That's not the way this was supposed to go down."

"No, sir. Unfortunately, I'm not in a position to explain the actions of Captain Snead."

"No, I don't suppose you are. Anyway, I spoke with Chief Ingram earlier this morning. Now that the case is over, he wants you detailed back to LAPD, effective immediately."

"Yeah, I figured," I said, still not certain whether I wanted to return to my job on the force.

When Shepherd didn't continue, I asked, "Is there something else?"

Shepherd hesitated. "There is one more thing," he finally replied, lowering his voice. "Dan, I didn't request your presence on our investigation merely as a liaison. I wanted you here because I needed a fresh perspective from someone who could think outside the box. I had seen your work on previous task-force investigations, and despite your methods, I knew you got results. You didn't disappoint me on either count."

"Uh, thanks . . . I think."

"No, thank you," said Shepherd, shaking my hand. "If for some reason you ever find yourself looking for a job, give me a call."

"If I'm ever looking for a job? Is there something I should know?"

Shepherd laughed. "Nothing I've heard, at least on my end. I'm just saying."

I smiled. "Then I appreciate the offer. Who knows? I might take you up on it."

Gibbs, who had remained silent during our conversation, shook my hand as well. "See you around, Kane," he said. "Good luck."

At that moment my cellphone vibrated. Realizing I hadn't changed the ringer setting since the previous evening, I pulled my phone from my pocket and checked the caller.

It was Chief Ingram's number.

"Thanks, Gibbs," I sighed, suspecting that the chief wasn't going to be as understanding as Director Shepherd. "I may need it," I added, stepping away to answer the call.

"Detective Kane?" said a voice I recognized as belonging to Assistant Chief Strickland.

"That depends," I replied, at that moment wanting nothing more than to head home, grab a shower, and sleep for the next twelve hours. "What did he do?"

"This is no time for jokes, Kane."

"Right. What's up, Assistant Chief Strickland?"

"You need to get your ass down here to headquarters. Now."

"Why?" I asked, already certain of the answer.

"The chief wants to see you."

"Now?"

"That's what I said, Kane. Right now."

Chapter 28

On my cross-town drive to PAB, I received a call from Allison. "An LAPD task-force officer killed the terrorists," she said as soon as I picked up. "But I suppose you already knew that," she added, clearly fishing for details.

"A task-force member killed the terrorists, huh? That's what you're reporting?"

"Is that wrong? Was the FBI involved?"

"Where are you getting your information, Ali?"

"Just rumors so far," Allison admitted. "I was at the scene last night, but after giving us the bare bones, no one was saying much."

As I had been leaving the Clark residence the previous evening, I had noticed my daughter arriving, joining a throng of reporters and a fleet of mobile news vans already present. She hadn't noticed me there, and I wanted to keep things that way.

"The FBI/LAPD Joint Terrorism Task Force has scheduled a press conference for later this morning," Allison continued. "I thought I'd get a jump on things. Anything you can tell me?"

I hesitated. "Maybe. But before we get to that, I have a question for you."

"Shoot."

"Who leaked the pizza connection?"

"Dad . . ."

"That was Brent Preston's exclusive, right? Where'd he get it?"

"Brent was quoting a confidential source. Even if I knew who it was, which I don't, I couldn't say anything."

"I'm not asking for names, Ali. Just point me in the right direction."

Allison paused before replying. "Almost all of Brent's sources are on the force," she said at last. "I heard him complaining yesterday about not having any leverage with the Bureau. If he got a tip from someone, my guess is that it came from one of yours. Probably someone high up."

"That's what I thought."

"Your turn now, Dad. Quid pro quo. Give me something."

I considered a moment, deciding I could reveal a few details to Allison without compromising the case. Besides, most of what I was about to say would be revealed in the upcoming press briefing, so I was simply giving Allison a head start, like she said. "Don't quote me on any of this," I warned.

"Right. Sources close to the investigation it is. Talk."

As I battled my way through freeway traffic, I gave Allison a brief rundown of the previous evening's events, avoiding any mention of my involvement. I also avoided disclosing the name of the terrorist who had been identified, in case the Bureau planned to withhold that information pending further investigation. I did confirm that three terrorists had been killed at the scene, and that none of them appeared to be of Arabic descent.

When I'd finished, Allison remained silent for several seconds. "So Brent's report on the pizza-delivery connection actually saved that woman's life?"

"I suppose you could look at it that way," I grumbled.

"And now this appears to be a case of domestic terrorism, not the work of ISIS or ISIL or some other radical Muslim organization?"

"A foreign connection hasn't been ruled out. That aspect is still up in the air."

"Who was the officer who went inside?"

"His name won't be available until a departmental risk assessment and an officer use-of-force determination has been made."

"C'mon, Dad. It's me. People will want to know who the hero was last night."

"Hero, eh? You mean *another* hero besides Brent Preston, who leaked confidential information that saved a woman's life?"

"Yeah, besides Brent," Allison laughed. "Who was it?"

"Let it go, Ali."

"Okay, we'll go with 'Unnamed Police Officer' for now. Or maybe 'Mystery Hero." Which do you like better, Dad?"

"Neither."

*****

This time when I arrived at Chief Ingram's office, I wasn't kept waiting. Within seconds of pushing through his tenth-floor office door, I was summarily ushered into the chief's private suite. Ingram was again sitting at his desk. And again, he looked irritated. Assistant Chief Strickland was once more standing nearby, hands clasped behind his back. I also noticed Captain Snead across the room, slouched against a wall.

"Kane, thank you for coming in," said Ingram.

"Didn't know I had a choice."

"You damn well didn't," said Strickland. "What the hell were you thinking last night?"

"I'm assuming you're referring to my entering the Clark residence," I replied, quickly assessing where things were headed, and not liking the direction.

"Against my direct orders," Snead chimed in, stepping toward me with clenched fists. "I'm bringing you up on charges, you smug bastard."

"As I said earlier, Captain Snead . . . I don't take orders from you."

Snead scowled. "As ranking officer at the scene, I—"

"You weren't at the scene. *I* was. It was my call."

"We're getting off-track," Ingram interjected. "We have a press conference in twenty minutes, and we need to decide what we're going to say."

"Yes, sir," said Snead. "But when this is over . . ."

"When this is over, we'll discuss what's going to happen next," said Ingram. Then, to me, "Much of that will depend on you, Kane. Do you understand?"

I nodded, deciding that Ingram's promise to "have my back" was no longer in play.

"So here's the situation in which we find ourselves," Ingram continued, folding his hands on his desktop. "First, we have an active, officer-involved shooting investigation. At present, the facts surrounding this incident are cloudy. We have an LAPD detective who putatively disobeyed orders and entered a crime scene. Instead of maintaining cellphone contact with officers outside, this detective disconnected his phone and proceeded into the residence. Next, with no one to corroborate his account of events, he shot and killed three suspects. Are you following me so far, Kane?"

"Perfectly," I said, understanding Ingram's not-so-veiled FID threat, and having a hard time controlling my temper.

"Excellent," said Ingram. "Second, and here we get to the interesting part. We have a high-profile case in which the department has been taking a backseat to the Bureau, as well as doing most of their work. Worse, every time the media has searched for someone to blame, the LAPD has been served up as a scapegoat. Now we have a chance to change things."

"I'm not certain I follow," I said.

"Then I'll suggest a scenario you can follow, something I think we can all live with," said Ingram. "Last night in Rivas Canyon, the unnamed LAPD officer was actually a member of our LAPD task force. Working under the direction of Captain Snead, this unnamed officer entered the Clark residence and at great personal risk, he saved the life of one of the residents, sustaining significant injuries himself in the process. Unfortunately, during the rescue he was forced to shoot and kill all three terrorists."

"I can't condone this," Snead objected. "Kane was—"

"Bill, you'll condone whatever the hell I tell you to condone," Ingram warned.

Snead looked away. "Yes, sir."

Ingram turned back to me. "Kane?"

"Let me make certain I'm following you, Chief," I said. "Last night I was actually working for Snead. I entered the Clark residence acting under LAPD task-force orders. Everything else follows from there. The department gets credit for closing the case, the FBI winds things up, and everyone's happy."

"Correct."

"Will the Bureau go along?"

Ingram nodded. "Already done. Director Shepherd wants to avoid further notoriety concerning the Bureau's role in this. As it is, considering the organizational mess at the first murder scene and the pizza-connection leak after that, we're *all* looking bad enough without attracting additional attention from the media."

I thought a moment. "I can live with your scenario," I said, deciding I didn't have much choice. "On one condition."

"God damn it, Kane," Strickland jumped in. "You are in no position to make demands."

"That may be, but it's still something I want. And it's non-negotiable."

"And that is?" said Ingram, also seeming about to lose his temper.

"I want my name kept out of things. You mentioned an 'unnamed officer' in your version of what happened. Let's leave it at that."

Ingram rocked back in his chair. "Who knows so far?"

I thought a moment. "Two LAPD patrol officers at the scene—uh, Officer Fagen was one. I didn't get his partner's name. The responding SWAT guys know, too—as they politely refrained from shooting me. And Snead's task-force detectives. No one in the press."

"What about the FBI?"

"Special Agent Taylor was present. She called her supervisor, ASAC Gibbs, who mentioned my name at this morning's briefing. I'm not certain how far up and down the chain it went from there."

"A lot of people," Ingram mused. "But it might be possible to keep a lid on things." Then, addressing Strickland, "Owen?"

"I think we can swing it," said Strickland. "At least for the foreseeable future. We could cite the risk of a terrorist retaliation as the reason for withholding Kane's identity. State law prohibits divulging the names of police officers in public documents, so the FID report won't be a problem, either. It might fly."

"Then we're in agreement," said Ingram. Turning to me, he regarded my bloody shirt, seeming to notice my appearance for the first time. "You were seriously injured last night."

"No big deal," I said, my hand traveling to the scabbed-over wound on my forehead. "Flying glass."

"That wasn't a question, Kane. You sustained significant injuries during your efforts at the Clark residence. As of now, consider yourself on injury leave, with full pay and benefits. I'm certain you will need several weeks to recuperate, at minimum. I trust you'll keep your head down during that time."

"Yes, sir."

"Then all's well that ends well." Ingram paused, then turned to Strickland. "Owen, please give Kane and me a minute. I'll meet you and Captain Snead downstairs."

"Yes, sir," said Strickland.

After Strickland and Snead had exited, Ingram regarded me for a long moment. "Dan, I can tell from your expression that you don't like how things are going down," he said. "You're also probably wondering what happened to my promise to have your back."

Although the chief was right, I didn't reply.

"No one is questioning your decision last night to remove those guys from the gene pool," Ingram continued. "Not one person in the department has a problem with that, including me. At issue is how you did it."

"Chief, I—"

"Don't say anything," Ingram interrupted. "I don't know what happened in that house last night, and I don't want to know. A lot of things have gone sideways on this case, including the fiasco in Rivas Canyon. Given the circumstances, I came up with the best solution I could craft for all parties involved, including you. Bottom line, I *do* have your back. Maybe more than you realize."

"Yes, sir," I mumbled.

Ingram rose and shook my hand, signaling an end to the meeting. "I'm going downstairs now to talk with the media," he said. "As you and I are in agreement on what happened in Rivas Canyon, I don't expect to hear anything to the contrary."

I shrugged. Even though I was disgusted that Snead would once again be taking credit for something he didn't deserve, there was nothing to be gained by objecting. "Not from me," I said. "I was working for Captain Snead."

Ingram nodded. "Despite what people think, you *can* be a team player, and I appreciate that. After the dust settles, we'll speak further regarding your future in the department."

Chapter 29

That evening found Jacob and Rudy sitting in Neptune's Locker, a local seaside restaurant and bar at the mouth of Trancas Canyon. Although Jacob's compound lay a mere six miles up a winding road from the popular establishment, compared with the commune's atmosphere of prayer and seclusion, Neptune's Locker could well have been on another planet.

Jacob was sitting at the bar sipping a diet soda. Rudy sat beside him, drinking Wild Turkey. Across the lacquered bar top, a television mounted above a rack of liquor bottles was tuned to *CBS Evening News*. Jacob and Rudy turned their attention to the newscast as it began. After a lead-in from Dan Fairly, the network's New York anchor, the news broadcast switched to Los Angeles for the evening's lead story. Reporting from Los Angeles was correspondent Brent Preston.

"Turn up the sound," Rudy ordered the bartender, a muscular, thick-necked biker-type with a shaved scalp and blurry tattoos festooning both arms.

The bartender looked up from a blender, where he was mixing a round of drinks for a rowdy group of women in the back. Scowling, he flipped off the blender and grabbed a TV remote control. Pointing it toward the TV, he turned up the volume.

". . . Preston reporting from Studio City, Los Angeles," the blond reporter was saying. "Responding to a 911 call, authorities arrived at the Pacific Palisades home of Dr. Oliver Clark. Here, with an on-the-scene report from earlier last evening, is CBS correspondent Allison Kane."

The scene switched to a darkened street, where a thicket of police cars jammed the road in front of a two-story residence. Near the police barricade, bracketed by a fleet of mobile news vans, stood a tall woman reporter, microphone in hand.

"This evening at approximately nine p.m., a van displaying counterfeit pizza-restaurant markings arrived at the Pacific

Palisades home of Dr. Oliver Clark," the female reporter began, turning briefly to glance at the gated estate behind her. "Ms. Tammy Sanders, a friend visiting Dr. Clark at the time, grew suspicious, having recently viewed a CBS News report detailing a pizza-delivery connection with the Los Angeles beheading murders. Alarmed, Ms. Sanders dialed 911. Unfortunately for Dr. Clark, she was too late."

Earlier, Jacob had learned of his mistake. In many respects, the lack of electricity, telephone reception, and internet services at his remote compound had proved a blessing, fostering a more godly existence for his followers. Nevertheless, it had been foolish of him not to have maintained up-to-the-minute intelligence on what the authorities knew, as well as what they might be planning. With a sense of shame, Jacob realized that his hubris had led to the previous evening's disaster. Had he kept up on current developments, he would have known that their pizza-delivery ruse had been discovered. As a result, his overconfidence had nearly cost them everything.

It was a mistake he would not repeat.

"Members of the FBI/LAPD Joint Terrorism Task Force arrived at the scene, accompanied by an LAPD SWAT unit," the female reporter continued. "At that point, acting under the direction of Captain William Snead, an unnamed LAPD officer entered the Clark residence.

"In a gun battle that followed, all three terrorists were killed. At this time, the intruders' identities still remain unknown. Dr. Oliver Clark later died of wounds inflicted by one of the terrorists. The unnamed LAPD officer, who is credited with saving the life of Ms. Sanders, sustained injuries in the shootout and is currently receiving medical treatment. At present, the identity of this 'mystery hero' remains unknown. Reporting for CBS News, this is Allison Kane, Los Angeles."

The report switched back to the news studio, with Brent Preston's face again filling the screen. "That was CBS correspondent Allison Kane with an on-the-scene report from last evening. At eleven a.m. this morning, authorities held a press conference at LAPD headquarters. This is what we learned."

The telecast switched to a large auditorium, where Mayor Fitzpatrick, LAPD Chief Ingram, and FBI Assistant Director Shepherd were standing shoulder-to-shoulder in front of a bank of microphones.

Ignoring shouted questions, Mayor Fitzpatrick spoke first, raising his hands for silence. "Welcome. I am happy to report that the terrorist threat endangering our city has been brought to an end. Last night, under the direction of my office and working hand-in-hand with the FBI's Joint Terrorism Task Force, the U.S. Department of Homeland Security, and LAPD's Counter-Terrorism and Special Operations Bureau, a Los Angeles Police Department task force led by Captain William Snead brought the terrorist investigation to a successful conclusion. Although the case is still ongoing, with the deaths of the three men responsible for the Westside beheading murders, we are confident that the danger to our citizens has now passed."

Mayor Fitzpatrick turned to Director Shepherd and Chief Ingram. "I want to thank each of you for your efforts," he said, grasping their hands in turn, prolonging each handshake to give photographers time to capture the moment. Then, turning back to the roomful of reporters, "That said, this might be as good a time as any to throw open the briefing for questions."

"Have you identified the killers?" came a question from the front.

Chief Ingram stepped back, deferring to Director Shepherd.

"All of the deceased terrorists were Caucasian males," Shepherd replied. "At present we have identified one of the intruders as Ethan James Hess, a natural born American citizen. We still don't know the identity of the other suspects killed at the scene."

"An American citizen. So is this a case of domestic terrorism, not an ISIS plot?" asked another reporter.

"At this time we are not ruling out a foreign connection," Shepherd cautioned. "As Mayor Fitzpatrick indicated, we still consider the case to be ongoing. There are a number of questions left unanswered, including how these men came to be radicalized as Islamic terrorists. In an effort to determine whether others are involved, the FBI will continue to work with its critical asset partners across the country, as well as with members of the LAPD and the U.S. Department of Homeland Security. We intend to leave no stone unturned in our effort to bring to justice those responsible for these murders."

"Why isn't the name of the 'mystery hero' being released?" someone called from the back.

Chief Ingram stepped forward. "For security reasons, and pending the results of an LAPD use-of-force review, we are currently withholding the identity of the officer who saved the life of Ms. Sanders."

At that point the newscast switched back to Brent Preston. "The identity of the LAPD officer involved in the deadly shootout still remains a mystery," he said. "Meanwhile, as our country's leaders call for an end to the violence, a nationwide Muslim backlash continues, with hundreds of deaths and dozens of Islamic centers being destroyed over the past weeks. Muslims, both foreign and domestic, are now in the crosshairs of an angry, frightened population, with no end in sight. This is Brent Preston, CBS News, Los Angeles. Now back to Dan Fairly in New York. Dan?"

"Thanks, Brent," said the network anchor as the broadcast returned to the CBS studios in New York. "That was Brent Preston and Allison Kane, reporting from Los Angeles. In a related story, earlier today in a televised address from the National Counterterrorism Center in McLean, Virginia, the president again called for an end to the violence targeting our nation's Muslim population. Amid renewed fears of terrorism, the president promised that by being strong and smart, resilient and relentless, we will overcome any and all terrorist threats we may face, both foreign and domestic, now and in the future. In his remarks the president also stated that although the FBI currently has no evidence that the Los Angeles execution-style murders were directed by extremists overseas, he cautioned that terrorism seems to have evolved into a new phase, with attacks being hatched at home as a result of foreign fanatics poisoning the minds of killers already on U.S. soil. Here, with more from our nation's capital, is CBS News correspondent Manuel Gallegos . . ."

"What now?" asked Rudy, turning his attention from the television.

"You heard the news report," said Jacob, "A cleansing Muslim backlash is sweeping our nation, with a decisive blow being struck against radical Islam. We knew there would be setbacks," he added, lowering his voice. "Nevertheless, we dedicated ourselves to our cause, and we will proceed."

"When?"

"Soon."

"We'll need new members for the kill squad," said Rudy, also lowering his voice.

"That won't be a problem," Jacob replied, already considering several candidates who might fit the bill. Possibly even Sister Zoe, if he decided to add a woman to the team. He thought a moment, deciding that replacing their lost equipment wouldn't be a problem, either.

"What about the cop who killed Caleb and Ethan and Parker?"

"All in good time. The authorities can't keep the identity of their 'mystery hero' a secret forever. Sooner or later, we'll find out who he is."

Chapter 30

Ispent the next few days keeping my head down at home, as ordered by Chief Ingram. Allison dropped by the beach house several times after work, joining Grandma Dorothy and me for dinner. Nate continued to remain reclusive. He missed school several times, saying he had a stomachache, and he skipped dinner each evening, staying in his room.

During that time I learned from Allison that the media, as usual demonstrating an insatiable desire to uncover anything that was considered secret, had risen to the challenge of identifying the LAPD's "mystery hero."

With a lack of other developments, Lauren had tasked Allison with discovering the identity of the officer who had entered the Clark residence. Allison had objected, pointing out that revealing the officer's name could put him in jeopardy, but Lauren had remained firm, stating that it wasn't their call to make. So far no one had talked. Nevertheless, a lot of people knew what had taken place in Rivas Canyon, and although I suspected it was just a matter of time before my name was leaked, I hadn't decided how to handle things when that happened.

As for the investigation, I'd had no further contact with the Bureau, but I knew from watching TV that FBI agents had interviewed a number of persons-of-interest connected with Ethan Hess, the only identified terrorist to date. So far nothing had shaken loose, at least nothing the Bureau was sharing with the media.

Because the two remaining terrorists' prints weren't in the system, I wasn't surprised to learn that they still hadn't been identified. Television crime series routinely show someone feeding a fingerprint into a computer, and seconds later out pops the suspect's name, date of birth, employer, his most recent address, and what the guy ate for breakfast.

In real life, print comparisons rarely happen that quickly. For one, not all tenprint cards are stored in IAFIS, the FBI's Integrated Automated Fingerprint Identifying System. For another, although millions of individuals have been fingerprinted for government positions, military service, and security clearances—not to mention people employed in civil occupations that require fingerprinting—there are countless tenprint cards gathering dust in files somewhere that have never been scanned into IAFIS. Bottom line, if someone has never been arrested, there's no guarantee that his or her prints are in the system.

Facial recognition was another modern technology that worked best on TV. Other means of identification—dental record comparisons or finding a DNA match, for example—require someplace to start, something against which to compare your subject. In this case, investigators had nothing. Stymied, the Bureau had eventually released photos of the dead terrorists, requesting the public's assistance in identifying them. I knew from talking with Deluca that hundreds of calls had come in, but as yet nothing had panned out. A number of calls threatening the "mystery hero" had also come in, all of which were being discounted as being from misguided individuals trying for their fifteen minutes of fame.

On the upside, I had learned from Deluca that Snead's task force, which was still wrapping up the case, had finally located the source of the counterfeit magnetic signs. The fake Wiseguy Pizza door panels and illuminated roof cap had been ordered online and shipped to a private postal delivery service in Flagstaff, Arizona. The Flagstaff postal account, a Mail Box Plus box rented under the name of a Mr. David Miller, had been closed for more than a year, but the delivery service still had Mr. Miller's registration materials on file. A comparison of fingerprints present on the signature card matched those of the tall intruder at the Clark residence. Unfortunately, the trail had ended with a check of the credit card linked to the Mail Box Plus account.

Not surprisingly, David Miller didn't exist.

Using false ID probably attained online, the killer had opened a local bank account in Flagstaff, deposited several thousand dollars, and applied for a credit card. The card had subsequently been used to make automatic payments on the postal box. Bank records showed that the credit card had also been used to purchase the Wiseguy Pizza signs. With the exception of monthly payments to the Mail Box Plus account, only three other purchases had been made on the card. One involved a custom silkscreen payment, which turned out to be for the ISIS flag. The second payment was for a second set of magnetic signs and an illuminated roof-cap for a company called "United Delivery Service," whose UDS logo closely resembled the United Parcel Service insignia. The final charge was for a third set of magnetic signs, this time for a company called "Onkin," whose logo looked suspiciously like that of a national pest-control company. Learning this, LAPD had issued a be-on-the-lookout to all divisions, avoiding giving a reason for the BOLO but advising all units to exercise extreme caution when approaching any vehicles with those markings.

Not much, but something.

Later that week, after insisting that Nate resume attendance at school, upset stomach or not, I decided to drive to Orange County to visit a psychiatrist friend, Dr. Sidney Berns. Actually, my decision to visit Dr. Berns was inspired by a repeated encouragement from Dorothy, who was still worried about Nate and insisted that I at least confer with a psychiatrist about his depression. Although I didn't agree with Dorothy that something was seriously wrong with my youngest son, I had learned long ago that it was easier to go along with Dorothy than to argue. And anyway, I had time on my hands, and I felt like getting out of the house.

Dr. Berns was a forensic psychiatrist employed at the Department of Psychiatry and Human Behavior at the California College of Medicine. Dr. Berns also regularly served as an expert witness for the Orange County District Attorney's office. Like most police officers, I held a long-standing mistrust for the psychiatric profession. That being said, I had met Dr. Berns in the course of working several earlier cases, and I had grudgingly come to trust his opinion.

Following several hours of battling afternoon traffic, I pulled up in front of the Orange County UCI Neuropsychiatric Center.

Leaving my car in a lot across the street, I entered the white, three-story building and proceeded down a hallway to the right. Upon arriving at an outpatient waiting room, I approached the reception desk and tapped on a glass partition, signaling a nurse on the other side.

The woman slid open the window. "Dan Kane to see Dr. Berns," I said. "I called earlier."

The woman checked her schedule. "Yes, Detective Kane," she said. "Dr. Berns is expecting you."

Minutes later Dr. Sidney Berns, a tall, lean man with penetrating pale eyes and a gray-streaked ponytail, stepped into the waiting room. "Dan, it's good to see you," he said, shaking my hand. "I was so sorry to hear about Catheryn," he added quietly. "If there is ever anything I can do . . ."

"Thanks, Sid," I said. "Anyway, I know you're busy, and I appreciate your seeing me on short notice."

"Anytime," said Berns. "Come on back. We can talk in my office."

I followed Berns through a residents' lounge to a dismal, eight-by-twelve cubicle with a single window opening out onto a cement patio. Sliding in behind a desk littered with files, photos, and an ashtray overflowing with cigarette butts, Berns signaled me to a chair opposite his desk.

"I see you haven't kicked the habit," I noted, glancing at the ashtray.

"Not yet," said Berns.

"I read somewhere that thousands of people quit every day, Sid," I said. "By dying."

"Funny," said Berns. "You sound like my wife."

"Sorry. I'm just saying . . ."

"Yeah, I hear you." Then, pointedly changing the subject, "What have you been up to?"

"I took some time off after Catheryn's memorial," I answered, welcoming the opportunity to delay discussing the reason for my visit. "Recently I returned to work, kind of on a temporary basis."

In true psychiatrist fashion, Berns raised an eyebrow but

didn't comment.

"Until a few days ago, I was acting as an LAPD liaison with the FBI on the Westside terrorism case," I continued, filling the gap in our conversation.

"Interesting situation, that," mused Berns.

"Interesting?" I said, thinking of the loss and suffering the terrorists had caused. "Kind of a callous way of looking at things, Sid."

"Sorry. Maybe *unusual* would be a better word," Berns conceded. "For one, most instances of mass murder involve the use of a gun. That the killers have been executing victims by beheading them, actually *sawing* off their heads with a knife, is particularly uncommon."

"No argument there."

"For another, although over the past fifteen years there have been more than 160 mass-murder incidents in our country, almost all of them have involved a lone killer, most often someone mentally unstable and consumed with rage. The percentage of mass murders involving two killers acting in concert is extremely small. And a killing team of three is even more unlikely. In this case, three terrorists were involved, correct?"

I nodded, wondering where Berns was headed.

"There *are* notable cases of multiple killers working together, however," Berns continued. "Charles Manson and his cult family, for instance. The Hillside Stranglers, Angelo Buono, Jr. and Kenneth Bianchi, were another killing team, as were Leonard Lake and Charles Ng. More recently, the Beltway Snipers—John Allen Muhammad and Lee Malvo—constitute a fourth. There are other examples of two or more individuals hunting together for victims, but they all share one underlying similarity."

"And that is?"

Berns leaned forward. "The common thread in *all* cases of multiple murderers working in tandem, including your terrorist beheadings, is that there is always one dominant individual calling the shots. The other members of the team, or in your case the terrorist cell, are followers—accomplices who wouldn't be involved in the killings were it not for the leader-follower relationship."

I remained silent, wondering which of the three men I'd killed in the Clark residence was their leader.

Berns paused, regarding me thoughtfully. "But you're not here because of your terrorist investigation, are you?"

"No, this isn't about work," I admitted, surprised that Berns had been able to read me so easily. "I . . . I came to talk about something else."

Again Berns didn't reply, letting the silence grow.

"Catheryn's mother, Dorothy, has been staying at the house," I finally continued. "She's worried about my youngest son, Nate. I guess I'm a little worried, too. The kid's having a tough time dealing with the loss of his mom. We all are, but . . ."

"How old is Nate?" asked Berns.

"Sixteen."

"What's going on with him?"

"I don't know, Sid. He's taking Catheryn's death really hard, which is understandable. Our whole family was devastated, but Nate . . . I don't know. He doesn't seem the same."

"Can you be more specific?"

I shrugged. "There's no one particular thing, but he seems changed. Like he doesn't care about anything anymore. He doesn't sleep, doesn't eat, doesn't even want to get out of bed in the morning to go to school. Recently he quit the high school baseball team without discussing it with anyone. He seems so . . . sad. He had a few problems last year in school—fighting, lousy grades, and so on—but this is different. I don't know what to do."

"Is Nate drinking or using drugs? Pot, cocaine, mollies, acid—anything like that?"

"Not that I know of. Nate and a friend got in an alcohol-related scrape last year, and Nate's pal had weed on him at the time. But I don't think that's it."

"I hope not. Pot and some of the other so-called recreational drugs out there aren't as harmless as many people think, especially for a young person who might have a developing mental illness."

"I don't think that's it," I repeated, disturbed by Berns's

mention of mental illness.

"Good. Although I would advise drug testing your son to make certain." Berns regarded me thoughtfully. "Dan, I can't tell much without actually talking with Nate, but I don't like what I'm hearing. Let me ask you something. What do you know about depression?"

"You think the kid's depressed?" I snapped, unable to hide my irritation. "Hell, that didn't take much figuring. Sid. Nate's mother was murdered. Everyone in our family is depressed."

"Not that kind of depression," Berns said patiently. "I'm talking about a medical condition called clinical depression, or MDD—major depressive disorder."

"Sorry. I'm kind of stressed out about this," I apologized. "But Nate isn't crazy. He's just . . ."

"I know the idea that someone you love might have a mental illness is difficult to accept, Dan. Our society places a heavy burden of stigma and shame on mental illness, but—"

"I told you, Nate's not crazy," I interrupted.

"All right, Nate's not crazy," Berns agreed, raising his hands in surrender. "Although there's a standing joke in the psychiatric community that it's difficult to distinguish between mental illness and normal teenage behavior. Look, I'd like to give you some background on clinical depression anyway. I don't want to be an alarmist, but MDD is a serious condition, and I want to make certain you understand what might be involved."

"Go ahead. But I just talked with Nate. Mental illness is not the problem."

"Fine. Let's go over a few things anyway. Never hurts to err on the side of caution," said Berns. "First, there are orders of magnitude between what we normally think of as depression and MDD. Anyone can develop MDD, including children, teens, and adults. In the United States, one out of five people will be diagnosed with severe depression at some point during his or her life."

"One out of five?" I said, surprised. "That many?"

Berns nodded. "Making matters worse, depression isn't visible, and there's the idea out there that it isn't really a disease.

Depressed people should simply cheer up, try harder, and snap out of it. Because of that, people with depression are often ashamed and don't talk about it. As a society, we don't talk about it, either. In many ways, depression is stigmatized more than mental illnesses like bipolar disease, obsessive-compulsive disorder, and even schizophrenia.

"We don't really know the cause," Berns continued. "We do know that clinical depression is a mood disorder believed to be triggered by chemical changes in the brain, changes that result in feelings of sadness, frustration, loss, and anger. MDD can be genetic and run in families, or it can be brought on by a stressful event. Often it's a combination of both."

Berns paused to light a cigarette. Then, exhaling a cloud of smoke toward the window, "I've had clinically depressed patients describe their symptoms like this: Imagine you wake up every morning, if you have been able to sleep at all, with a feeling that something horrible is about to happen, but you aren't sure what it is. Or maybe you are. Maybe you do have specific fears, and they constantly torment you. Or this: Imagine there's a glass wall between you and the rest of the world, and even on sunny days everything is dark and miserable and filled with doom. Your life is worthless, and so are you. Imagine your saddest day and multiply it by ten, a hundred, a thousand. Imagine you're drowning in a bottomless pit, trapped and suffocating, with no hope of escape . . . ever. And this goes on day after day, with no end in sight, until sometimes even death seems a welcome alternative."

Listening to Berns's description, I sensed a hollow feeling building inside. Though I didn't want to admit it, I recognized myself in his words, as surely as if I'd been looking into a mirror. I'd had those same feelings, and more than once.

But Nate?

"And you're saying this . . . mood disorder can be genetic?" I asked numbly.

"Sometimes," said Berns. "And sometimes, following a trigger event of some sort, it just happens."

I hesitated. Like all LAPD employees, I had completed the

department's Behavioral Science Services' suicide prevention program, which included recognizing the risk factors, signs, and symptoms involved with depression. Thinking about my son's behavior over the past months, I wondered whether Berns might be right. I also wondered whether Dorothy had been correct in her assessment that rather than paying attention to important matters in my life, I had found it easier to bury myself in work and ignore problems that were staring me in the face.

Like Nate.

"I've heard there are treatments," I ventured. "Counseling, pills, and whatnot. Are any of them effective?"

"Sometimes, sometimes not—depending on the severity of the illness. Has your son ever talked about hurting himself?"

"Hell, no," I answered, shocked by the suggestion. "Nate would never do anything like that."

"You need to make absolutely certain, Dan. Talk with him about it. If you're sincere when you ask, most people will open up about such feelings."

"I . . . I will," I said. "I'll talk with him. But I'm sure Nate wouldn't do anything to hurt himself. Or anyone else, for that matter."

"I'm glad to hear that. But as I pointed out, there's nothing wrong with erring on the side of caution. Again, I'm going out on a limb discussing Nate's condition without actually talking with him. Nevertheless, whatever Nate's problem is, there are warning signs you should watch out for. I'm concerned that Nate isn't sleeping. Not eating is another symptom of depression, as are unexplained mood swings and behaving recklessly. I would be especially concerned if Nate begins saying things like he feels he's a burden to others, or that he has no reason to live."

"I'll talk with him," I repeated.

"And get him professional help. I can't stress that enough."

"Catheryn and I tried to do that when Nate was having problems at school. After a couple sessions, he wouldn't return. Recently I suggested going back. Nate refused, but I'll . . . I'll try again," I promised.

"If you want me to talk with him, I'm available anytime."

"I appreciate that, Sid. I'll see what I can do and let you know. And . . . thanks."

On the ride back to Los Angeles, I pondered what I had learned from Berns. My friend had cautioned that he couldn't tell what was going on in Nate's head without actually talking with him, and Berns's description of clinical depression had simply been cautionary. Yet somehow his words had rung true. Guiltily, I wondered whether I had been ignoring a growing problem in my family, as Dorothy had suggested. And if so, why? Was it the shame and stigma associated with mental illness that Berns had mentioned?

Whatever the case, I was concerned about Nate, and I had to do something. But hours later, by the time I had turned onto the Santa Monica Freeway and headed for the beach, I still hadn't decided what.

Unfortunately, by then I had a more immediate concern.

I was being followed.

Chapter 31

When driving, I often found myself sweeping my eyes over passing vehicles, streets, and alleys—looking for anything out of the ordinary. Scanning my surroundings was a habit I'd developed years back while riding patrol, and it was one I'd never been able to shake. Shortly after leaving the UCI California College of Medicine, I had noticed a dark SUV climbing the freeway ramp behind me. I saw it several more times on the return drive to the city. Eventually, an alarm began sounding in my mind.

The SUV followed me all the way to Santa Monica, matching my speed and taking every interchange I did—hanging several cars back but staying in whatever lane I happened to be in. Although I couldn't get a look at who was driving, there appeared to be two men sitting in the front.

Before returning to the beach, I decided to find out who was riding my tail. As the Westside was my home turf, I knew exactly how to do that. Ignoring a bad feeling about what I was about to do, I exited the freeway in Santa Monica, taking the 4th Street off-ramp. As I merged into exiting traffic, I glanced into my rearview mirror.

The SUV was still following.

Upon reaching 4th Street, I stopped in the center of the single-lane off-ramp, completely obstructing the lane. The driver behind me slammed on his brakes and leaned on his horn. The car behind him did the same. Three cars back, the SUV slowed to a stop and was immediately blocked from behind by a growing line of traffic.

Ignoring a digital salute from the irate driver behind me, I withdrew my service weapon and stepped from my car, leaving the engine running. With my pistol held loosely against my right thigh, I walked back toward the trapped SUV. As I advanced, I kept a close watch on the vehicle's occupants. So far neither had made any suspicious movements. If they did, I planned to be ready.

With nowhere to go, the SUV's driver watched impassively as I approached. Undoubtedly having spotted my weapon, he kept his hands visible, resting them on the steering wheel. The man riding shotgun placed his hands on the dashboard, keeping them visible as well.

When I arrived, the driver rolled down his window and grinned.

"Duffy?" I said. "What the hell—"

"Easy, Kane," said Duffy. "You can stand down now. We're all on the same side here."

"I'm not so sure about that," I said, holstering my weapon. "Talk, Duffy. What's going on?"

"I can't tell you anything," said Duffy. With the disappearance of my pistol, the man riding shotgun withdrew a cellphone and began punching in numbers.

"Bull," I said. "You've been tailing me for a reason, which means someone at the Bureau is keeping tabs on me. Why?"

"I told you, I can't say anything," Duffy repeated. "I'm just doing my job. If you want information, you'll have to talk with someone a lot higher on the food chain."

By then traffic had jammed up all the way back to the freeway. Occasionally glancing at me, Duffy's partner was speaking quietly on his phone.

"Are you going to keep us here all afternoon?" asked Duffy.

Deciding I wasn't going to get anything from Duffy, I turned and started back to my vehicle. "This isn't over," I said over my shoulder.

"Whatever you say, Detective."

Puzzled, I returned to my car, wondering what was going on. As it turned out, I didn't have to wait long to find out. Shortly after I had slid behind the wheel of my Suburban, my cellphone rang.

As I pulled forward to unplug the traffic jam, I glanced at the phone display. It was Taylor. "Kane," I said, answering.

"Kane, it's Taylor."

"Yeah, I know. Nice to hear from you, Taylor. By the way, I just ran into your boyfriend. For some reason he's been tailing me."

"Yes, I heard. And he's not my boyfriend. Listen, we need to talk. Is there somewhere we can meet?"

"Gee, I'm flattered. But why?"

"It's important. Just take my word for it, okay? There's something you need to know."

Chapter 32

After calling Dorothy to let her know I wouldn't be home for dinner, I met Taylor in West Los Angeles at one of my former watering holes, the Scotch 'n' Sirloin Restaurant. A holdover from earlier days of deep-red carpets, sailboat photos, and navigational charts laminated onto tabletops, the Scotch had prospered for as long as I could remember by offering reasonably priced chops, steaks, and seafood to hungry diners, as well as by serving an honest drink to any thirsty customer who happened to wander in.

I arrived early, taking a seat near the rear of the bar. Glancing around, I saw no one I recognized, although I knew that a few LAPD personnel would probably show up later. When a waitress approached, I ordered a Coke and nursed it for the next few minutes, waiting for Taylor to arrive. By the time I had finished my drink, chewed the ice, and checked my watch, I saw Taylor entering the room.

She had apparently changed clothes after work. Instead of her Bureau-approved slacks and suit coat, Taylor now had on a short wool jacket, mid-height heels, and a tight black skirt that showed off her legs. She had also applied a touch of makeup to her eyes and lips, something I'd noticed she avoided when on the job.

Taylor paused at the hostess station, peering into the dimly lit room. I waited until her eyes swept my way, then raised a hand to get her attention. She smiled and started over, leaving a host of male patrons appreciatively following her progress as she made her way to my table.

"Thanks for meeting me," said Taylor as she slipped into a seat across from me. "Haven't been in here before," she added, glancing around the room. "Seems nice."

By then the bar had begun filling with people having after-dinner drinks, along with a sizable nightclub crowd that had come to listen to a jazz combo setting up in the back.

"It is," I agreed. "I used to drop by here a lot. Excellent food if you like steaks and seafood. The music is great, too," I added, noticing Taylor eyeing my empty glass. "Want something to drink?"

"What are you having?"

"Coke."

"I think I'll need something stronger."

"No problem. You're in the right place," I said, signaling the waitress.

"You're not a drinker, Kane?"

"Used to be."

"What happened?"

"Decided I was better off without it."

"Huh," Taylor said with a noncommittal shrug, her eyes making another circuit of the room.

"Some people consider this a cop hangout, but I've never noticed anyone here from the Bureau, if that's what you're worried about."

"Good," said Taylor, seeming relieved.

When our waitress arrived, Taylor ordered a margarita—double shot of tequila, shaken, no salt. I ordered another Coke. Although curious regarding why Taylor had called our meeting, I decided to wait until our drinks had arrived to broach the subject. By then the jazz combo was embarking on its first set, a tribute to pianist Thelonious Monk, and Taylor and I listened for a few minutes without speaking. After our waitress had delivered our order and departed, I finally asked, "So what was it you needed to tell me?"

Taylor took a sip of her margarita. "Good," she said, nodding appreciatively. "Not too much triple sec, just enough lime."

"Glad you're happy. So what's up?"

Taylor regarded me for a long moment. "First, I need to know something."

"And that is?"

"Word on the street is that you executed those men in the Clark house," she said. "Not that they didn't deserve it, but is that true?"

"Damn, Taylor. Are you asking whether I murdered those guys?

"I guess I am. I have reason to believe that you didn't, but I want to hear it from you. I remember your saying that you wanted to take the killers off the street—permanently. Is that what you did?"

"No. I gave warning. They didn't comply. What happened afterward was on them."

"Pretty good shooting considering it was three-against-one, not to mention the presence of an automatic weapon and two civilian vics at the scene."

I shrugged.

"What about turning off your cellphone once you were inside?"

"I didn't. I lost service. I can't explain it, but that's what happened."

"Okay, I believe you. Probably no one else does, but I can usually tell when someone's lying, and I don't think you are."

"Thanks," I said, wondering whether the FID shooting-investigation officers had believed me, too.

Taylor drained her margarita and signaled our waitress. "Another one of these, please," she called. Then, to me, "Any idea who leaked the pizza connection?"

"What's that have to do with anything?"

"Believe me, it does. It was someone on Snead's task force, right?"

"Probably. What are you getting at?"

Taylor hesitated a moment more, then seemed to come to a decision. "What I'm about to tell you could get me fired," she said. "I'm asking you to keep quiet regarding what I'm about to say. Agreed?"

"That depends. You can't expect me to—"

"You can't tell anyone what I'm about to say, Kane. Otherwise, no deal."

"Fine. I'll keep whatever you say in confidence. What is it?"

"It's not over."

"The terrorist case? Those guys are dead."

"Listen to me, Kane. It's not over. We received a credible tip threatening the life of the 'mystery hero' and his family, meaning others are involved."

"LAPD got the same tip. In fact, they got lots of tips like that, undoubtedly from misguided idiots looking for notoriety."

"That may be, but the Bureau knows something the LAPD doesn't."

Curious, I remained silent.

"We examined the footage on the killers' camera," Taylor continued, lowering her voice. "It showed that there were *four* terrorists in the house that night."

A chill ran up my spine. "But—"

"The fourth man escaped," Taylor interrupted, anticipating my question. "Probably out the back door that you claim was locked, but that we found *unlocked*. So there is still at least one more terrorist out there, and possibly others. And you're in their crosshairs."

We both fell silent as our waitress delivered Taylor's second drink.

"Agent Duffy and his friend were riding my tail to *protect* me?" I said when our waitress had once more departed.

"Not exactly. Actually, the Bureau thinks this might present an opportunity to capture any remaining cell members."

"By using me as bait."

"It was a high-level decision, and it was only supposed to be temporary. A few days at most. Considering the pizza-connection leak, the Bureau thought that if Snead's task force got involved, the case might spring another leak and we would forfeit any chance of wrapping things up. Although your name hasn't been revealed in the media, Vaughn thinks it's only a matter of time. We wanted our agents present when that happens."

"Kind of jumping the gun, don't you think? How about having your guys back off until it becomes a problem."

"Already done."

"Good. By the way, this sucks."

"I agree. And so does Gibbs and most of the other SAs working the case. That's why I'm here."

"Gibbs knows you're talking to me?"

"Not officially. If any of this comes out, he's covered his ass.

But when I talked with him, he gave me tacit approval to let you know that you might become a target, with the understanding you won't share this information with LAPD—at least not until we've had a chance to locate any remaining terrorists. If your name *is* revealed in the press, we'll immediately bring LAPD into the loop so they can have surveillance teams covering your back."

"How reassuring."

Ignoring my sarcasm, Taylor opened her purse and rummaged inside. "What Gibbs doesn't know is that I'm giving you this," she said, finding what she wanted. She withdrew a USB thumb drive and slid the small device across the table.

"What's on it?"

"The video from the killers' camera," Taylor replied. "It could come in handy, depending on how your FID investigation goes. The footage is choppy, but the audio track proves you gave verbal warning before any shooting began. It could mean my job if that's traced back to me," she added.

There were no guarantees that I would be exonerated by the FID inquiry, and it felt good to have a little insurance, even if I couldn't deliver a copy of it to my Police Protective League representative just yet. "I'll keep the source of this quiet," I promised, pocketing the flash-drive device. "And I appreciate your help."

"No problem." Taylor sipped her drink, regarding me across the rim of her glass. "You know, before I came here tonight, I talked with some people about another case you worked on. The Candlelight Killer investigation. You were a member of a task force led by Captain Snead back then, right?"

I nodded, wondering where she was going. "It was Lieutenant Snead at the time, but yeah."

"After hearing about your, um . . . *association* with the CBS News bureau chief, what's her name—Lauren something?

"Lauren van Owen."

"Anyway, after doing the addition about what went down on the Candlelight Case, including your nearly being brought up on charges for your relationship with Lauren, I thought you might have been the one who leaked the pizza connection."

"Wasn't me."

"I know that now," said Taylor, regarding me pensively. "Kane, for a smart guy, you sure manage to get into a lot of trouble."

"No argument on that. What about you? Have things been going any better for you at the Bureau now that I'm gone?"

Taylor shrugged. "I was having issues at the Bureau long before you showed up."

"How so?"

"Knowing you, I doubt you'd understand," said Taylor, taking another sip of margarita.

Although women, for the most part, have always been a mystery to me, one thing I had learned about them long ago was that if you really wanted to know something, just be open and ask. "Try me," I said.

"Okay, it's simple," said Taylor. "As we discussed at lunch the other day, the Bureau is still a boys' club, regardless of what they say in their glossy recruitment brochures."

"Yeah, your glass-ceiling problem."

"For a woman in the Bureau, it's more like a *labyrinth*, with obstacles at every turn," Taylor noted. "Don't get me wrong. I love what I'm doing, but there *are* problems. When I was growing up, my dad always told me I could be anything I wanted to be in life. Later I found out how things really work."

"And how is that?"

"For one, as a woman I'm routinely judged by my appearance and what I happen to be wearing, rather than by my ability, and the FBI is no exception. It's demeaning to be called a 'split-tail,' or a 'skirt,' or my particular Bureau favorite, a 'breast-fed.' It makes me feel like a fraud, posing at being competent. Well, screw that. When I was younger I tried to please everyone. I'm working hard to get over that."

"Judging from what went on at a few of the Bureau briefings, I'd say you're making headway there," I joked. Then, noticing Taylor's expression, "Sorry, Taylor. Just kidding."

"You may be, but I'm not. I'd love to swap places with you for a day and see how you like being judged on your looks, not by what you do."

"Judged on my looks? If that were the case, I'd be in big trouble," I said, trying to lighten the conversation.

"Oh, I don't know," said Taylor. "You definitely have your charms, in a tough sort of way."

"Thanks . . . I think."

"Seriously, Kane, the only thing in my life for which I've been rated on ability rather than appearance is whitewater kayaking. How pathetic is that?"

"You mentioned kayaking at lunch. What, you compete or something?"

"Occasionally," Taylor admitted, suddenly seeming embarrassed. She drained her drink and signaled for another. Noticing my questioning glance, she added, "Don't worry, I'll be taking a cab home. I may occasionally overindulge, but I'm not stupid." Then, with a grin, "Enough about me. Let's talk about you. So . . . what do you think of *me*?"

I laughed. "I think you're funny, when you're not angry. And despite the FBI being a boys' club, I think the Bureau is lucky to have you."

Taylor smiled. "Thanks. What's your ex-wife like, Kane?"

"Why do you ask?" I stalled, taken off-guard by her question.

"I don't know. I suppose I'm wondering what kind of woman would put up with you. Why did you get divorced, for instance? Was it your affair with that newswoman?"

"Taylor, I . . . I don't want to talk about my wife."

"Too personal? No fair, Kane. You ask me to open up, then tell me you don't want to talk about yourself?"

I nodded. "Exactly. For the first time in quite a while, I'm enjoying being out for the evening, and I don't want to spoil things. And believe it or not, I'm also enjoying your company— mostly."

"Imagine that," said Taylor. "Well, I'm having an okay time, too. Maybe better than okay. I'm not used to being out with someone who isn't always . . ."

". . . trying to get into your pants?" I finished.

"I was going to say, 'impress me,'" Taylor laughed. "But

there is that."

By then the jazz combo was well into its opening set, and several couples had taken to the dance floor. "So how about this," I suggested. "Let's forget about work, put aside our differences, and listen to some music."

And for the next hour, we did just that. During that time Taylor ordered another margarita. I stuck with Coke, despite Taylor's repeated suggestion that I join her for "just one."

After the musicians had announced a break following their second set, I glanced at my watch. "I'm going to hit the road." I said, having quietly settled our tab a few minutes earlier. "Are you staying, or do you want me to call you a cab?"

"Which way are you headed?"

"Malibu."

Taylor downed the last of her current margarita and gathered her purse. "I'm in Santa Monica. It's on your way. Can you give your ex-partner a ride?"

"No problem," I said, deciding to make certain she wouldn't change her mind and try to drive. "You can pick up your car tomorrow. It'll be fine right here in the lot outside."

"Great," said Taylor, following me out. "You can meet my cat."

"Chuck," I said.

"How'd you know that?" Taylor asked, looking at me in amazement.

"You told me at lunch a couple weeks back. I have a good memory."

"You do, huh? Okay, what else did I say?"

"At lunch?"

"Yeah," Taylor laughed. "Demonstrate this good memory of yours."

I thought back, recalling our conversation. "You said that you grew up in Salmon, Idaho, and got married at eighteen, right out of high school. After that you worked as a secretary to put your husband Mark through college and law school. Later you went back to school yourself, earned your undergraduate degree, and attended Chapman Law. After graduation you joined Mark at a law firm in Burbank."

Taylor stared in amazement.

"Want me to go on?

"No, that's enough. You're a strange guy, Kane."

"So I've been told."

Fifteen minutes later we pulled to a stop in front of Taylor's Santa Monica condo, an attractive, two-story residence a few blocks off the beach. Taylor slid out of the Suburban and circled to my side of the car. As I opened my window to say goodnight, she leaned in and twisted off the ignition. "C'mon in for a sec," she said, slightly slurring her words. "I was serious when I said I wanted you to meet my kitty, and I meant that in a strictly feline sense," she added, giggling. "At least walk me to the door."

"Okay, if only to make certain you don't fall down on the way," I joked, thinking that Taylor's margaritas were definitely catching up with her.

After climbing from the Suburban, I accompanied Taylor to her front entry. Mounted beside the door, I noticed a mailbox that read "Blackadar."

"Taylor was my married name," said Taylor, noting my glance at the mailbox. "I still use Taylor at work, but otherwise I go by my family name. Come on in and meet Chuck."

"Thanks, Taylor, but I've gotta be going."

"Jeez, Kane. It'll just take a minute," Taylor insisted, fishing a set of keys from her purse.

"Fine," I sighed. "Let's go meet Chuck."

Inside, Taylor's condo was neat and tidy, with the exception of several colorful kayaks and a clutch of double-bladed paddles stacked against a far wall. I paused in the entry, inspecting a photo of a kayaker punching through an impossibly huge wave— paddle digging for purchase, whitewater flying everywhere. "You?" I asked.

Taylor nodded. "My dad taught me to paddle when I was a kid. My granddad, who was a pioneer in the sport, taught him. You could say class-five whitewater runs in our blood."

Curious, I picked up an odd metal gauntlet propped in the

corner. The strange sculpture resembled a hand with outspread fingers, the digits curling downward as if grasping an invisible grapefruit. Engraved at the base were the words:

North Fork Championship VII
Elite Division: Second Place
Sara Blackadar

"What's this thing?" I asked.

"The brown claw?" Taylor laughed, rolling her eyes. "Don't ask. It's a kayaker thing." Then, bending over, she scooped up a huge orange cat that had ambled over to greet us. "Here, meet Chuck."

"Hey, Chuck," I said, stroking the soft fur beneath the cat's chin. "You sure are a big boy."

"He's a Maine Coon, one of the largest of the domesticated breeds. He's a lover, too," Taylor said affectionately, returning Chuck to the floor.

Standing in the condo's small entry, I suddenly grew conscious of Taylor's nearness. As Chuck strolled off into the living room, Taylor moved even closer. "I'd offer you something to drink, but you don't drink," she said shyly.

"Yeah, well—"

Taylor placed a finger to my lips. Then, circling me with her arms, she moved closer still. I felt her thighs touching mine, her breasts lightly pressing against my chest. "It's nice being with someone taller than I am," she said.

I could smell the sweet scent of her hair, a fragrance reminiscent of cinnamon. "Taylor . . ."

"Shhh," she whispered, bringing her lips to mine. Caught off guard yet making no effort to resist, I felt myself beginning to respond. With a shiver of desire, Taylor parted her lips and kissed me again, her mouth soft and warm on mine. Gradually at first, and then with increasing intimacy, she began moving against me, her hands exploring as she felt my need growing to match hers.

A rush of blood pounding in my ears, I surrendered to the sweetness of Taylor's embrace. Raking her fingers across my back, she again found my mouth with hers. She felt smooth and sleek in my arms, and this time I returned her kiss, wanting more. Nevertheless, though desire flowed through me like molten iron, I knew I wasn't ready. The long months since Catheryn's death, months of heartache and isolation, had left me unprepared for something new, something like this with Taylor. She deserved more than I was able to offer, and I knew that.

As for me . . . it was just too soon. And I knew that, too.

"I can't do this," I said, gently pushing her away.

"Why not? What did I do?"

"It's not you. There's something I haven't told you—"

"Of course it's me," Taylor said angrily. "It's always me. Actually, I'm getting used to rejection. This isn't the first time it's happened, and it probably won't be the last."

"Taylor, it's not that. Since I lost Catheryn—"

"That would be Catheryn, your long-suffering wife?" Taylor interrupted, her tone turning resentful. "The one you loved so much that you cheated on her with newscaster Lauren what's-her-name? And now you don't want to have anything to do with me because of feelings you still have for your poor, deserted wife? Don't bullshit me, Kane. What's the real reason? You don't drink and I got tipsy tonight. Is that it?"

"Catheryn and I weren't divorced, Taylor."

"But I thought . . ." Taylor hesitated. Then, her tone hardening, "You told me you *used* to be married, but of course you lied about that, too. You're still married, aren't you? Damn you, Kane. You're just like every other—"

"Catheryn was murdered."

"What?"

"She was struck by a bullet meant for me."

Taylor paled. "Oh, my God," she said, bringing a hand to her mouth. "I remember now. The L.A. Sniper case. That was *you*?"

I nodded.

"Oh, Jesus. I . . . I'm sorry," said Taylor, tears starting in her eyes. "I didn't know. I didn't mean what I said about your wife. I'm so sorry, Kane. I drink too much when I get nervous, like tonight. I'm such an ass—"

"Stop, Taylor," I said gently. "This wasn't your fault. I should have told you."

"Yes, but—"

"I should have told you. I just didn't want to talk about it."

"I understand," Taylor mumbled. "Who would? I can't imagine losing someone like that. I'm so sorry about shooting off my mouth, Kane. I was embarrassed and . . . and ashamed of throwing myself at you. In case you haven't noticed, I don't take rejection very well. But that's no excuse," she added bitterly, her tears now flowing.

"It's okay. You didn't know."

She shook her head. "No, it's not okay," she said, fighting to get herself under control. "God, I'm a mess."

I hesitated, unprepared for Taylor's emotional meltdown. Nevertheless, I understood that her previous rancor had been at least partially inspired by the margaritas, and her apology seemed heartfelt. Once again revising my opinion of Agent Taylor, I clumsily took her in my arms and held her until her shoulders stopped shaking.

"It's okay, Taylor," I repeated.

After a long moment she pulled away. "Can I ask you a favor?"

"What?"

"I'd like to start over, if that's possible," she said, attempting to palm away her tears. "Can we forget this happened?"

I nodded. "Already done. And Taylor?"

"Yes?"

"Thanks for going out on a limb for me with the Bureau. I owe you."

"You're welcome," she said. Then, with a sad smile, "Maybe I can collect on that someday."

Chapter 33

'F reudian slip, eh?' the guy says to his buddy. 'Hmm. So what *exactly* did you say to your wife?'" Nate smiled, enjoying his own joke to a degree routinely unwarranted by his teenaged material. Nevertheless, everyone at the dinner table, including me, waited for the punch line.

"Looking embarrassed, the guy's buddy shrugs and says, 'Well, I meant to ask Martha to pass the peas,'" Nate continued, beginning to giggle. "'Instead what came out was, 'You rotten bitch, you ruined my life!'"

I busted up. So did Allison, nearly choking on a mouthful of Grandma Dorothy's chili. Dorothy, who didn't approve of rough language, especially at the dinner table, tried not to join in, her frown of censure making it all the more difficult for the rest of us not to laugh.

"It's not nice calling a woman a bitch, Nate," Dorothy admonished, having trouble maintaining a serious expression herself.

Nate grinned. "So why is everyone laughing?"

Of course Dorothy had no answer for that, after which she surrendered to the moment and joined the rest of us in Nate's light-hearted humor.

"Good one, kid," I chuckled. "It's great to see you happy again."

"Amen to that," said Allison.

"Thanks," said Nate. "I *am* feeling better. Must be Grandma's chili. You should get the recipe, Dad."

It had been several days since I had visited Dr. Berns. Since then I'd tried to find an appropriate time to talk with Nate about the issues Berns had raised, but the opportunity had never presented itself. With a sense of relief, I realized that maybe that particular conversation would no longer be necessary.

"I'd be happy to write down the recipe for you, Dan," Dorothy offered. "Appropriately enough, I call it, 'Grandma Dorothy's Famous Chili.'"

"You know that 'Grandma Dorothy's Famous Chili' will become 'Dan Kane's Famous Chili' as soon as he's cooked it a few times, right?" Nate pointed out.

"Yes, but *we'll* know, won't we?" Dorothy replied with a smile. "Would you like some more, Nate?"

"Thanks, I'm stuffed."

"Me, too," said Allison.

"Seriously, though," Nate continued. "I know that everyone has been worried about me, and I'm really sorry about that. Things are going to be better, I promise. Dad, I'm going to see about getting back on the Vikings baseball team, and I plan to start hitting the books at school again, too. The SAT college exams are coming up, and I plan to ace them."

"Excellent," I said, relieved to see the old Nate back once more. "While you're at it, how about straightening up your room?"

"It's on the list, Dad."

"Hey, I have some news," Allison jumped in, sending our freewheeling conversation spinning in another direction. "Mike is getting a few days off from work. He's coming home tomorrow."

"That's great, Ali," I said. "How's the shoot going?"

"Couldn't be better," Allison replied. "They're several days ahead of schedule, which is unusual on a big project like that. By the way, Mike said that Tom Grant, who's starring in the film, asked how you were and sends his best." Allison regarded me curiously. "How do you happen to know an Academy Award-winning movie star?"

"I know everyone in this town worth knowing."

"Seriously, how did you meet Tom Grant?"

I shrugged. "We have something in common. I'll tell you about it sometime."

"I have some news, too," Dorothy announced. "Travis called today. He says he's going to accept a few of the concert dates he was offered. Trav met with his program advisor at Juilliard, and as long as Trav maintains his grades and his current course schedule, he can still perform. He's going to be playing with the Chicago Symphony Orchestra in May. Maybe we could attend?"

"Maybe," I replied.

"May doesn't work for me," said Allison, placing a hand on her abdomen. "I have an important event scheduled for then myself."

"Of course," said Dorothy. Then, glancing at me, "Now that your terrorist case is over, I'll be returning to Santa Barbara soon, but would it be all right if I came back in May for the birthing?"

"Absolutely," I said. "You know you're welcome here anytime, Dorothy. And I'm sure Ali could use your help."

"Thank you, Dan."

"Speaking of the terrorist case," Allison jumped in, "anything new on that, Dad?"

"Nope."

"With the investigation all wrapped up, the only thing left now is to discover the identity of the LAPD's 'mystery hero,'" Allison persisted. "You wouldn't know anything about that, would you?"

"Nope," I repeated.

"Well, Brent says it's just a matter of time." Allison regarded me closely. "There's something you're not saying. What?"

I shrugged. "Does every female on this planet think she knows what's going on in my head?"

"You're not that complicated," Allison laughed. "C'mon, give."

"Okay, there is one thing, but don't quote me on this," I conceded. "You might want to rethink the case being all wrapped up, as you put it. If I were you, I'd hold off on popping the Champagne."

"Duly noted," said Allison. "So what about the 'mystery hero?' Anything you can give me on that?"

"Allison, please stop," Dorothy intervened. "The dinner table isn't the place to discuss a murder investigation." Then, pointedly changing the subject, "Trav also told me that the apartment he and McKenzie are sharing is working out well. Maybe we'll see grandchildren coming from that direction as well. I certainly hope so. I like that girl."

"Me, too, Grandma," Allison agreed. "Mac was my friend

first, before Trav stole her away. As for babies . . . I wouldn't get ahead of yourself on that."

"This talk of babies is my cue to say goodnight," said Nate.

"No dessert?" coaxed Dorothy. "We're having peach cobbler and ice cream."

"None for me," Nate replied, rising from the table. "Like I said, I'm stuffed."

"Actually, I should get going myself," said Allison, also standing. "Early day tomorrow."

I pushed back from the table as well. "Great meal, Dorothy. We'll have the cobbler tomorrow. Thanks for cooking."

"Yeah, thanks, Grandma," said Nate, giving her a hug. Then, moving to Allison, he embraced her as well. "'Night, Ali."

"Goodnight, Nate," said Allison, unable to conceal her surprise. "I haven't had one of those from you in quite a while. Feels good."

"Yeah, it does, sis."

Finally Nate moved to me. With an odd smile, he circled me with his arms and gave me a hug that seemed to last just a moment too long. "You know I love you, Dad," he said quietly.

"I know that, Nate," I replied, recalling that he had said those same words to me several weeks back. "I've always known that. I love you, too."

*****

Twenty-five miles to the east, in a residential enclave in Hancock Park, the Nichols family was also finishing dinner. "Do you have anything on your schedule tomorrow, Blake?" asked Julie Nichols, regarding her screenwriter husband across the table. "If not, I was hoping you could join me for Max's parent-teacher conferences at Harvard-Westlake."

"It's that time *again*?" said Blake. "I swear, between holidays, field trips, and parent-teacher conferences, do our children ever attend class? It seems like the more we pay to send them to expensive schools, the less time they actually spend going."

"Seems like plenty of time to me," grumbled Max, their seventeen-year-old son.

Ignoring Max's comment, Julie continued. "Megan's grades are fine, as always," she said, smiling across the table at her daughter and thinking that although Megan was a year younger than Max, she had always seemed so much more mature. "But I'm worried about you, Mister," Julie went on, her smile morphing to a frown as she focused her attention on Max. "I plan on talking with *all* your teachers this time. Your counselor, too. If possible, I'd like you to be there with me, Blake."

"Sorry," said Blake. "I'm getting together with Brad tomorrow at Paramount. And I have a follow-up meeting later with Donna at Universal."

"Why are you pitching your screenplay to Brad?" asked Julie. "I thought Donna was going to green-light it."

"Things aren't that easy anymore," Blake replied. "Relationships and promises still count, but nowadays the numbers trump all, and Universal's accountants are still poring over projections for the home entertainment market. Despite any promises from Donna, things won't actually get done until the numbers are crunched. Can't hurt to talk with Paramount in the meantime."

"Marlborough's parent-teacher conferences are next week," Megan jumped in. "Think you can make it to those, Dad?"

"Maybe," Blake answered.

"I hope so. I'd like you to meet my teachers," said Megan. "Now if I may be excused, I'll clear the table and do the dishes."

"Really? Thanks, honey," said Julie, regarding her daughter with surprise.

"What is it you want, Megan?" Blake asked suspiciously.

Just then the gate buzzer sounded.

"I'll check that," said Max, rising from the table.

"Can't I offer to help around here without having some dark, ulterior motive?" asked Megan, feigning insult.

"Not really," said Julie.

"Absolutely not," added Blake.

"I'm hurt," laughed Megan. Then, "Um, actually . . . I was wondering whether I could spend the night at Chiloe's tomorrow. She's having a sleepover."

"No boys at Chiloe's, right?" said Blake.

"Of course not, Dad."

"We'll discuss it later," said Julie. Then, rising to help clear the table, "Who was at the gate, Max?"

"UPS delivery," Max replied, calling from the entry. "I buzzed them in."

Chapter 34

D"*an, there's more to life than being a police officer," said Catheryn, carefully setting down her fork.*

I hesitated before answering, not for the first time thinking that my wife looked more beautiful than any woman I'd ever known—even when she was angry. We were having dinner at Patina, a street-level Los Angeles restaurant situated in a corner of the Walt Disney Concert Hall. Around us, amid an atmosphere of muted pastels and understated elegance, an evening-gowned and dinner-jacketed crowd had gradually filled Patina's interior as we dined, with theatergoers like us arriving early to enjoy an intimate meal before the evening's performance.

"I could say the same to you, Kate," I replied, unable to hide my irritation. We had tilled this ground in the past, and more than once. "There's more to life than being a musician, too. With your added responsibilities at the Philharmonic, you're gone from home now as much as I am. Maybe more."

"That's not true, and you know it. The truth is, you spend more time chasing criminals than you do with your own children. And even when you are home, you're thinking about your job."

"I'm a cop. That's what I do. You knew that when you married me."

"I knew. I just didn't know all the things it would do to you. And for what? Arrest one criminal, and two more spring up to take his place."

"I just take 'em one at a time, Kate. As for the job affecting me—that's what happens when you're on the street."

"Exactly. You're developing a slanted view of life, and it's affecting everyone you love. Every time you go to work, you shut down a part of yourself to get the job done. Granted, someone has to do police work . . ."

"And that someone is me. Sure, it affects me some. Maybe a lot, but—"

"You need to make time for your children, Dan. Especially Nate."

"Nate's tough. He'll be fine."

"Are you that oblivious? Nate is not fine, and he's not getting any better. Let me put this another way. I know how you feel about our children, Dan. You love them more than you can say."

I nodded. "We have the finest kids any parent could wish for, and that's the God's truth."

"And you want the very best for them."

"Absolutely."

"They all think you're some kind of hero, Dan. It's almost painful to see how much they want to please you. You may be a cop, but you're also a father, and they need something from you that I can't give—not anymore."

"I can't always be there holding their hands."

Leaning forward, Catheryn reached across the table. Grabbing my arms in frustration, she shook me. "Wake up, Dan! Your children need you."

"Kate—"

Catheryn shook me again, harder this time. "Your children need you, Dan. Wake up!"

"Dan! Wake up!"

I sat up in bed. "Huh?"

"Something's happened," said Dorothy, still gripping my arms.

Instantly, I was fully awake. "What?"

"Nate's gone."

I turned on a bedside lamp. "What do you mean, *gone?*"

"I heard him get up earlier and take a shower. I fell back asleep. Then I woke up again when I heard someone going out the front door. I checked to see who it was. I got there just in time to see Nate driving off in Catheryn's Volvo."

Puzzled, I glanced at the clock. 12:37 a.m. "Where the hell would Nate be going at this time of night?"

"I don't know, Dan. But I'm worried." Dorothy handed me a sheet of paper. "This was on the kitchen table, next to his cellphone."

I looked at the paper she'd handed me. On it, in Nate's

printed scrawl, were the words, "I love you all."

"I'm sure he's okay," I said, suddenly not certain of anything. "He probably just—"

I glanced across the room, a sinking feeling in the pit of my stomach.

The door to my handgun safe stood open. Even in the dim light, I could see inside.

My service weapon was missing.

Chapter 35

After hurriedly throwing on some clothes, I raced outside and jumped into my Suburban, leaving Dorothy at the house in case Nate returned.

Which way? I wondered, realizing I didn't have time to make a mistake.

East, toward Santa Monica?

No. He wouldn't drive into the city. He would want to be alone . . .

The other way. And quickly . . .

Close to panic, I started the Suburban, slammed it into gear, and swerved out onto Pacific Coast Highway. Fortunately, there was little traffic at that time of night. Cranking the wheel, I pulled an illegal U-turn and headed west.

Where is he? Oh, God . . .

Battling a growing premonition of disaster, I frantically scanned both sides of the highway, searching for Catheryn's Volvo. When I reached the light at Las Flores Canyon, I considered turning right and driving up into the hills, then decided against it. Time was running out. Hunting for Nate in the mountains behind our house would take forever. Besides, by then I thought I knew where he was going.

Ignoring the speed limit, I blasted through a string of red lights on the deserted highway, reaching the Malibu Pier in minutes. Without slowing, I glanced into the Surfrider Beach parking lot.

No Volvo.

After racing past the Adamson House and the California State Park grounds where Allison had been married, I blew across the bridge spanning Malibu Lagoon. As I shot by the Malibu Country Mart and started up the hill toward Pepperdine University, I realized it had only been weeks since my daughter's wedding.

How could things have gone so wrong since then?

I ran another red light at Malibu Canyon and turned left into the Malibu Bluffs Park, a six-acre facility overlooking the

Pacific. The park had two baseball diamonds, and Nate had played ball there when he was younger.

Please, God, please let him be here . . .

The parking lot was empty.

I skidded to a stop. With a sick, hollow feeling, I tried to decide what to do next.

Head back and search Las Flores Canyon?

Again, I rejected that. Not enough time.

Think! Malibu Colony Road? Nate has friends there—

Suddenly I had another idea. Stomping the accelerator, I exited the park and turned west on PCH. A quarter mile down the highway was a geologically unstable bluff that lay between the highway and the beach below, an area that had long been zoned unsuitable for building. Years back I had driven there every morning at dawn to train our family's first dog, a black Labrador retriever named Sam. Later, after Sammy had died, it was there that I'd brought Nate one morning for a serious, father-son talk. Our conversation had been intended as a discussion regarding the role Nate would play in our family's next dog, but it had wound up covering considerably more ground than that.

As a result, the abandoned parcel of land there had become a place that held a strong emotional attachment for both of us, and I knew it was a place that Nate would always remember. Considering what had happened between us that morning, it was a place I would always remember as well.

I slowed, scanning the roadside.

Catheryn's Volvo was there.

I skidded into another U-turn and screeched to a stop behind the Volvo.

The Volvo was empty.

Leaving my engine running, I slammed open the door and vaulted from the Suburban. As I did, I heard a gunshot.

My heart fell.

Too late? Oh, God, am I too late?

"Nate!" I screamed.

Please, God, don't let me be too late . . .

A second shot echoed across the field. This time, outlined

against the moonlit landscape, I saw a muzzle flash.

"Nate, wait!" I screamed again. From years on the job, I knew that test shots were often fired by someone determined to end his life with a gun. Praying I had arrived in time, I raced across the field. Scrub and sage tearing at my clothes, I sprinted toward a small hill overlooking the ocean—the area from which I'd seen the muzzle flash.

"Nate!" I yelled, stumbling through knee-high chaparral as I neared the knoll.

No answer.

"Nate!"

Oh, Jesus. Please, please don't let him be . . .

I stopped. Atop the knoll, staring out at the ocean, sat a small, lonely figure.

Nate.

"I know you can hear me," I said, approaching cautiously. "Don't do anything yet. Please wait, okay? Please, please just let me talk to you."

As I neared, I saw that Nate was crying. "Go away," he sobbed.

"I can't do that, son," I said. In the moonlight, I could also see that he was holding my pistol in his lap. "Let me talk to you," I begged. "I promise I won't . . . do anything. Just let me talk, okay?"

Tears streaming down his cheeks, Nate lowered his head and shrugged.

Moving slowly, I closed the distance between us and eased down beside him on the knoll, sitting several feet away. More than anything I wanted to put my arm around my son and tell him everything was going to be all right. But I didn't. Nate still had the pistol, and I didn't want to do anything that might force his hand. Although I needed to remove the weapon from him as soon as possible, I also knew there was now more at stake than simply wrestling away the gun. There was tomorrow to consider . . . and all the tomorrows after that.

Keeping a careful watch, ready to move if Nate raised the pistol, I sat for several seconds without speaking, wondering what to say to my sweet, hopeless, confused, despairing son. Above all, whatever I said, I knew I had to speak from my heart, and I had to speak the truth.

But what was that?

Wishing I had paid more attention to the department's suicide-prevention program, I considered telling Nate that things would get better, but I knew saying those words wouldn't solve anything. Worse, after talking with Berns, I knew that those words might not even be true. I considered telling Nate that I loved him with all my heart, for that was certainly true, but telling him I loved him wasn't going to solve anything, either. I considered telling him that his death, especially if he were to die in this manner, would forever shatter the lives of everyone who loved him. This was true as well, but I knew from Nate's sobs that he was far beyond considering the effect his death would have on others.

And in the end, as I sat with my son staring out over the endless Pacific, it was he who finally broke the silence between us. "I'm sorry, Dad," he said, struggling to bring his tears under control. "Since Mom died . . . I just don't want to be here anymore."

"I understand, Nate. Believe me, I do. And it's not your fault. You have nothing to be sorry for."

"Yes, I do," Nate said, wiping his nose on his sleeve. "With Mom gone, things have been hard on everyone, especially you, without having to worry about me."

I tensed at Nate's arm movement, but the pistol remained in his lap.

"Remember the first time I brought you here?" I asked, deciding to approach things from a different direction.

"Why?"

"Do you remember?"

Though puzzled, Nate shrugged. "I . . . I guess so," he sniffed. "It was when Callie was a puppy. We brought her here, and . . . and you gave her to me. You said that Tommy would be going away to college, and Travis and Ali weren't far behind. So before long it was just going to be you, and me, and Mom. You said that if our family was going to have another dog, she was going to have to be mine."

"You were so angry at me that morning. Do you remember why?"

"You killed Sammy."

"It was her time," I replied. "I should have given you the opportunity to say goodbye, but I didn't. I felt so bad about putting her down, and I was trying to spare you and the rest of our family that pain. But I was wrong. I don't know whether I ever apologized for that, but I'm sorry, Nate. I truly am."

"It doesn't matter now."

"Yes, it does. Remember what I said when I gave you Callie?"

Nate thought a moment. "You told me she would become my best friend in the world, and that I would love her more than anything—maybe even as much as I had loved Sammy."

"What else?"

"You promised to help me train her."

I smiled. "And I did. For the next year we got up early every morning and brought her up here for lessons, remember? And by the end of that year she was marking multiple falls, making water retrieves, accepting hand and whistle commands, and handling like a field-trial champion. We turned her into just about the finest gun dog anyone could ever ask for. What's more, she loved it. And she formed a bond with you that will last her entire life. You know that, right?"

Nate nodded.

"But when I gave you Callie, I also told you there were some strings attached. Do you remember what they were?"

Nate's expression darkened. "You said that I would be responsible for feeding her, and taking her to the vet, and giving her pills when she need them, and . . ."

"And?"

". . . and when her time came to go, it would be my job to help her to do that, too," Nate finished, tears starting again in his eyes. "Like you did with Sammy."

"That's right. I told you that having a dog was one of life's greatest joys, but there were hard parts to it too. And unless you were willing to accept the hard parts, you were going to miss out on all the good parts as well." I hesitated, realizing that over the past weeks Dorothy had been telling me the same thing.

"I remember," said Nate.

"You have so many wonderful things ahead for you in life, Nate," I continued. "Things like growing up, and falling in love, and having a family of your own. But along the way you're going to discover that some of the best things in life, the ones you treasure the most, often come with a heavy price. But unless you're willing to pay that price, you're going to miss out."

"Like losing Mom," said Nate, staring at the gun in his lap.

"Like losing Mom, and Tommy, and all the other hurtful things that our family has gone through," I said. "Losing your mother the way we did is more than anyone your age should have to bear, and I'm so, so sorry for the part I played in her death. But that isn't the answer," I added, glancing at the pistol. Nate's index finger still lay outside the trigger guard, and I decided to delay taking the weapon from him for just a little longer.

"You may think having kids of your own is a long way off," I continued. "Take it from me, the years will fly by and it will happen sooner than you think. And when it does, it will be an experience that will change your life, and I mean that in the very best way. You'll love your children so much that you'll find yourself trying to protect them from all the things that could hurt them. But in the end, you'll discover that you can't. I wish I could take your pain, Nate, but that's not possible. Which brings us to where we are right now, sitting here in this field trying to decide what to do."

I paused, wondering how to proceed. Finally I continued with a confession that had been a long time coming. "I see myself in you, Nate. And I'm proud to be your father, more than I can say. I see a lot of Catheryn in you as well, but of all my children, you're the most like me. This may be hard for you to believe, but I know exactly what you're feeling right now, because I've felt that way, too."

At this, Nate looked up.

"When we lost your mom, I didn't want to go on either," I said quietly. "Every day at work, I carry that weapon you're holding. And every day after your mother died, and on more than one occasion before that when I was still drinking, I thought about turning it on myself."

"But you didn't."

"No. I didn't."

"Why not?"

"I don't know," I answered. "I could say that I didn't want to hurt the people who love me. I could say that I knew life would get better and it was foolish to use a permanent solution to fix a temporary problem. I could say that I wasn't certain whether the place I went afterward, if I went anywhere at all, wouldn't be worse than it is here. And all those explanations would be true, at least to a point. But I think the real reason I'm still here is because I didn't want to disappoint your mom."

"And now Mom is gone."

"I know. And I still want to honor her memory."

"I . . . I want that, too," said Nate. "But . . ."

". . . you're afraid you aren't strong enough."

"Maybe. I don't know what to think."

"Nate, do you trust me?"

Nate didn't answer.

"Do you trust me?"

Nate took a deep breath, then let it out. Finally he nodded.

"That's good, Nate. I promise I won't ever betray your trust. Not ever. I know you're confused right now about a lot of things, including whether you want to go on living, but please believe me when I say that ending your life isn't the way. I don't know what tomorrow may bring, and to be honest, I don't know if anyone is strong enough to survive your kind of pain. I'm not even sure about myself, but I'm going to try. And I want you to try with me. People get through tragedies, so maybe we can, too. I promise I'll be with you every step of the way, and there are others who will help. Our whole family will stand with you— Trav, and Ali, and Grandma Dorothy—no matter what. Will you give it a try?"

Nate thought a long time. At last he nodded.

"Good," I said, realizing that although Nate's journey was just beginning, this was a hopeful first step. Then, once more glancing at the pistol, "I believe that belongs to me?"

With a look of embarrassment, Nate passed me the weapon, carefully keeping his finger off the trigger.

Pointing the Glock toward the sky, I ejected the magazine and dropped it into my pocket. Next, racking the slide, I cleared a final cartridge from the chamber. As I shoved the pistol into my belt, I asked, "How did you open my handgun safe?"

"Guessing the combo wasn't hard, Dad. Your badge number?"

"I'll be changing that combination," I said, disturbed that Nate had so easily accessed my service weapon. All my children had taken gun-safety training, but I realized with dismay that even safety training and the best security in the world provided no guarantee that a gun in the house couldn't fall into the wrong hands.

Leaning down, I retrieved the final cartridge I'd ejected. Holding it in my palm, I stared at the .45 caliber round that had nearly taken the life of my son. Extending my hand, I offered the bullet to Nate.

Nate hesitated, making no move to accept it.

"Take it," I said. "And for the rest of your life, never forget the strength you showed getting through this night."

With trembling fingers, Nate took the cartridge, closing his fist around it tightly. Unexpectedly, he again began to cry. "God, I'm a mess," he mumbled, fighting to stem his tears. "Jeez, look at me . . ."

"I am looking at you, Nate," I said. Moving closer, I put my arm around his shoulders. "And I'll tell you what I see. I see someone I love. I see someone who's confused and in pain, but I also see someone who is going to recover. I see a young man who has his entire life ahead of him, a life filled with wonderful things he can't yet imagine. I see someone who has just taken a big step toward becoming a man. I see you, Nate. I see you."

"Thanks for . . . for being here, Dad," Nate said quietly, his face wet with tears.

I nodded, struck by the thought that as parents, Catheryn and I had often worried about what life might do to our children. It had never occurred to us to consider what *we* might do to them, or what they might do to themselves.

Giving Nate's shoulders a final squeeze, I stood. "I'm sure Grandma Dorothy is still waiting up for us," I sighed. "Let's go home."

I didn't sleep again that night. Instead, I remained in my son's room, watching over him as he slept. Along with a profound sense of relief that things had turned out as they had, I felt a crushing burden of guilt, realizing that Dorothy had been right all long. Immersed in my own despair following Catheryn's death, I had let my emotional withdrawal isolate me from the very people who needed me most. And that withdrawal, and my refusal to recognize its effect on those I loved, had nearly cost the life of my son.

As I sat in darkness listening to the soft sounds of Nate's breathing, I searched deep within myself, exploring a place I rarely visited. And as I took a long, hard look at myself, I didn't like what I saw. Though it was difficult to accept, I knew that over the years, in one way or another, I had brought disaster to my family. First Tommy, lost because of my failure to consider any perspective other than my own. And the night our house had burned to the sand, almost taking our family with it, had also been because of me. And Catheryn, who had died in my arms, killed by a bullet meant for me.

And now Nate.

I knew, beyond a doubt, that had the sniper's bullet ended my life instead of Catheryn's, my son's suicide attempt would never have happened. Catheryn wouldn't have allowed it.

But *I* had.

It was the longest night of my life. And as the sun rose the following morning, I knew that nothing could ever again be the same.

Chapter 36

L ater that morning while Nate still slept, I asked Dorothy to spell me in his room. After leaving her with Nate and taking a quick shower, I made a pot of coffee. Then, determined to get my son the best treatment possible, I called Dr. Berns.

Berns had just arrived at work when I reached him. Upon hearing what had happened, he advised me to first make certain that Nate didn't have access to any items with which he could harm himself. Also, under no circumstances were we to leave him alone. Berns then instructed me to take Nate to the Saperstein Emergency Department at Ronald Reagan UCLA Medical Center—adding that he would call an associate there to let her know we were coming.

Before leaving for UCLA, I also called Allison.

"Dad?" she said, picking up on the second ring. "I'm at work, so I just have a minute. You're calling about last night's murders, right? It looks like the terrorists *aren't* dead, at least not all of them. It's all over the news, and the video they released this morning is worse than ever, if that's possible."

"There's been another terrorist murder? I hadn't heard," I replied, shaken by the news. "But that's not why I called—"

"Turn on your TV," Allison broke in. "This time an entire family in Hancock Park was executed."

"I'm sorry to hear that, Ali. But that's not why I called." Quickly, I told my daughter what had happened. There was a long silence when I finished.

Finally Allison spoke. "Oh, my God," she said softly. "This is my fault. I knew Nate was having problems. I should have seen this coming. I should have talked with him."

"If anyone's to blame, it's me," I said. "We're leaving for the UCLA Med Center right now. I don't know what's going to happen, but getting Nate some help is the first step."

"I'll meet you there."

"That's not necessary, Ali, but—"

"I'll see you there. And . . . and tell Nate I love him."

"I will," I promised. "I'll tell him we all love him. Unfortunately, right now I don't think that's going to help."

Minutes later Dorothy, Nate, and I piled into the Suburban, Dorothy sliding into the passenger seat in front, Nate sitting silently in the rear. As I started the car, I noticed that Catheryn's Volvo was parked several spaces back. On our return drive the previous evening, I had called Brian Safire—a friend at the Malibu Sheriff's Department—and asked him to retrieve Catheryn's car, having left the keys for him inside the vehicle. As I pulled onto PCH and merged into rush-hour traffic, I made a mental note to thank Brian for his help.

Although on the ride to Westwood Dorothy tried to engage Nate in conversation, his answers were brief and perfunctory. Eventually she gave up, after which no one spoke. Twenty minutes later, as I passed through the McClure Tunnel and joined traffic on the Santa Monica Freeway, my cellphone rang. Thinking it was Allison, I answered without checking the number.

"We're still a few minutes out, Ali," I said. "Where are you?"

"This isn't Ali," said a deep voice belonging to Assistant Chief Strickland.

Strickland was the last person I wanted to hear from, and I considered hanging up. Instead I said, "Assistant Chief Strickland, this isn't a good time. Can I call you back—"

"No, you may not," Strickland interrupted. "In case you haven't heard, there's been a new development on the terrorist case."

"I heard," I said, waiting for the other shoe to drop.

"The chief wants you in his office."

"I'm on injury leave."

"I don't care if you're in a body cast. Get down here."

"No can do, Assistant Chief Strickland," I said, glancing at Nate in the review mirror. "Something has come up—"

"Let me make myself perfectly clear, Kane. You will either be in Chief Ingram's office within the hour, or you can consider your LAPD career at an end."

"In that case, let me make *myself* perfectly clear, Assistant

Chief Strickland," I said. "I'm in the middle of a family emergency. I will see Chief Ingram in his office as soon as I'm able. If that's not good enough, tough."

Allison met us outside the UCLA Medical Center Emergency reception room. On the verge of tears, she gave Nate a hug, then hugged Dorothy and me as well. Leaving Allison and Dorothy in the reception area, Nate and I spent the next twenty minutes with an admissions and registration counselor. After that, while Dorothy and Allison remained in the reception area, a triage nurse escorted Nate and me to a treatment room down the hall.

For the next half hour, as I sat in a chair to one side, the nurse examined Nate and took a brief medical history, purportedly to determine the severity of his condition. Although Nate answered her questions truthfully, admitting that he had intended to end his life the previous night, he seemed strangely remote, as if he no longer cared what happened to him. When asked by the nurse whether he still wanted to die, he looked away and shrugged.

Next an emergency department physician, accompanied by a second doctor who introduced himself as an attending psychiatry resident from the UCLA Neuropsychiatric Institute, entered the room. At that point the triage nurse and I stepped out.

While Nate's examination continued, the triage nurse and a social worker from the hospital met with Allison, Dorothy, and me in a corner of the reception area. We were all interviewed at length regarding Nate's suicide attempt, as well as being asked our opinion of his current mental state. Although many questions were posed, it seemed the most important ones regarded Nate's ongoing depression, his access to and willingness to use lethal methods to harm himself, and the strength of his family and support groups.

During that time Dr. Maggie Freimer, the professional associate that Dr. Berns had mentioned calling on Nate's behalf, sought me out in the reception area. Dr. Freimer, a short, middle-aged woman with a direct, no-nonsense manner, was the director of UCLA's Semel Institute for Neuroscience and Human Behavior. She explained that although she was not a clinician,

Infidel

she knew that as things progressed we would have questions regarding Nate's treatment, and that she would be happy to help in any way she could—including checking on Nate from time to time if inpatient treatment was indicated.

Later Arnie, Deluca, and Lieutenant Long arrived. When I looked at them questioningly, Arnie shrugged and said, "Allison called."

"We're so sorry, Dan," said Lieutenant Long. "If there's anything we can do, just name it."

"I will. And thanks for being here. It means a lot," I said, not trusting myself to say more.

After what seemed forever, the emergency physician and the attending psych resident came out to speak with us. Neither was smiling. Allison, Dorothy, and I stood as they approached. The psychiatric resident, whose nameplate read "Dr. James Rota," spoke first. "I'm sure you have a lot of questions, so I'll be direct," he said. "We need to keep Nate here for inpatient treatment. He'll have to stay for several days, possibly more. We won't know how long until we've had time to further assess his condition."

"Whatever is necessary," I said. "And whatever the cost. We want the best possible treatment."

Dr. Rota nodded. "Sometimes families want to take their loved ones home with them immediately. That is *not* an option for Nate. Adolescents who have attempted suicide are considered high-risk patients, and Nate falls into that category. As such, I'm directing that your son be admitted to the Resnick Neuropsychiatric Hospital here in the medical center. Our immediate focus will be Nate's safety. He will be initially placed on a twenty-four-hour watch to ensure there are no further attempts at self-harm. During this time we will complete a psychological assessment for a possible mental disorder—in Nate's case the most likely being a condition known as major depressive disorder."

"Can we visit him?" asked Allison.

"Yes. There are visiting hours, depending on each patient's situation," Dr. Rota replied. "I strongly encourage you all to visit

251

Nate as much as possible. I can't stress enough the importance of continued family contact during this initial period."

"We'll visit every day," Allison promised, glancing at me. "Right?"

"Right," I said.

"Absolutely," added Dorothy.

"That will make a big difference," said Dr. Rota. "I realize families often have responsibilities including work, but—"

"This is more important than work," I said. "We'll be here."

"Every day," added Allison.

Dr. Rota nodded again, seeming satisfied.

"How long will Nate have to be hospitalized?" asked Dorothy.

"A minimum of seventy-two hours will be required for his initial evaluation," the doctor answered, glancing at me. "Additional time may be necessary, again depending on the situation. Please understand that because of the risk of self-harm, Nate will *not* be allowed to leave against medical advice. To that end, there will be some papers you'll need to sign."

"Of course," I agreed, feeling as if I were stumbling through a dark, unspeakable nightmare.

"Fine," said the doctor. "Once we know more, we can talk about a possible treatment plan for your son. In the meantime, the ER staff is preparing to move him to the Resnick Hospital wing. This might be a good time for you all to say goodbye."

Dorothy, Allison, and I spent a final few minutes with Nate, who for the most part seemed indifferent to our presence. Later, on our way back to the reception area, Allison pulled me aside, telling Dorothy that we'd catch up in a moment.

Once Dorothy had proceeded on, Allison turned to face me. "There's something I have to tell you," she said, her expression informing me that whatever it was, it wasn't good.

"More bad news?"

"You could say that. Brent discovered the identity of the LAPD's 'mystery hero.' CBS notified the LAPD that we would be releasing the officer's name later this morning. It was you,

Dad."

"Damn," I said. Although I'd realized my name would come out sooner or later, I had hoped it would be later.

"Before long, a gazillion people are going to recognize your face, Dad."

"A gazillion? Swell."

"I'm certain Brent got his information from the same source as his pizza-connection tip," Allison continued, regarding me with a look I couldn't quite decipher. "You saved that woman's life, Dad. I'm proud of you."

"I did what I had to," I replied. "But in doing that, I've put our family at risk again," I added, coming to a decision. "I'm sorry, Ali, but you have to leave. You need to get somewhere far away from here, and you need to do that immediately. So does Dorothy."

"Why?"

"Because there are more of those guys out there, and they're still killing people. According to an FBI friend, the Bureau received a credible threat that as soon as my name was made public, I would be in the terrorists' crosshairs—along with anyone who's close to me, including my family."

"I'm not worried. And I'm not going anywhere."

"Ali, I know you're all wrapped up in this news story, but your safety is more important than any job."

"This isn't about my job. This is about Nate. You heard what the doctor said. Nate needs us."

"Ali—"

"I called Travis, too," Allison cut me off. "He's flying back tonight. Mike will be home by then, too."

"Damn it, Allison. You don't understand what's involved here."

"I do, Dad. I understand exactly what's involved, and I promise I'll cooperate in every way possible to make certain that nothing bad happens. But I'm not leaving. Nate needs us, and I'm staying. I'm positive Travis and Dorothy will feel the same. Mike, too. I'd think that you, of all people, would understand. Or have you forgotten?"

"Forgotten what?"

"It's something you've been drilling into us our whole lives, starting when we were kids," Allison replied.

"And that is?"

"Kanes stand together . . . no matter what."

Chapter 37

"Would you like me to call Nate's school?" Dorothy asked on the drive to LAPD headquarters. "Someone should probably explain his absence."

I'd offered to drop Dorothy at the beach house before proceeding to PAB. Insisting that making an extra trip was unnecessary, she had joined me on the ride downtown. "Yes, I agree," I said. "I hadn't thought about that, but you're right."

"What do you want me to tell them?"

My initial reaction was simply to tell school authorities that Nate was sick. As I was about to reply, I hesitated, recalling Berns's words regarding the unfair shame and stigma our society placed on mental illness. "Tell them that Nate is dealing with depression following his mother's death," I said instead, deciding that curtailing the cycle of shame had to start somewhere. Nate's depression wasn't his fault, any more than if he had broken his arm. "Tell them he's having a hard time, and we're getting him some treatment."

"Are you sure?"

"I'm sure."

Twenty minutes later, after leaving the Suburban in the parking structure on First Street, Dorothy and I walked the remaining distance to PAB. Leaving Dorothy to wait for me in a nearby café, I proceeded to the main entrance alone.

Once again, an armada of news vans jammed the street out front. Not surprised by their presence, I hung my shield on my coat and pushed through PAB's glass doors into the lobby. Once inside, I bulled my way through a further logjam of journalists, ignoring shouted questions from nearly every reporter there— every one of them referring to me by name.

Apparently the word was out.

Upon arriving at the tenth floor, I was immediately ushered into Chief Ingram's private office. "It's about time you showed up," said Assistant Chief Strickland as I entered. "I ordered you here three hours ago."

Snead was present as well. Ignoring both Strickland and Snead, I addressed Chief Ingram. "I had a family emergency, as I explained to Assistant Chief Strickland. This was the soonest I could get here, and I'm here now. So what's this about?"

"Before we go any further, I suggest you adjust your attitude, Kane," warned Snead. "In case you've forgotten, you're still the subject of an FID use-of-force inquiry. That investigation could go either way."

I turned to Snead. "Bill, as I've told you repeatedly, I don't respond well to threats."

Snead's face darkened. "I swear to God, you're going to regret your insubordination. I'll make certain of it."

"I agree," Strickland jumped in. "You can't just waltz in here and—"

"Let's cut the bull," I interrupted, struggling not to lose my temper. "The FID investigation will exonerate me. If there were ever any question of that, the video from the terrorists' camera will clear me." Noticing something in Strickland's eyes, I added, "But you already knew that, didn't you?"

"What I know or don't know is none of your concern," Strickland snapped, avoiding my gaze.

"What's Kane talking about?" asked Snead.

"I'm talking about a video clip from the terrorists' camera that proves I acted properly in my use of force," I answered. "By the way, I'm certain I can get a copy of that, should the need arise," I added, deciding not to reveal that I had already done just that.

Chief Ingram spoke up. "Let's tone things down a bit," he suggested. "No one is threatening you, Detective Kane. I'm sure Captain Snead didn't mean to suggest that the outcome of the FID investigation was dependent on anything other than the facts. Isn't that right, Bill?"

"Uh, yes, sir," Snead mumbled.

"Sorry, Bill, I didn't quite hear that," I said.

"Don't push it, Kane," Snead warned.

Ingram frowned. "We all need to get on the same page here. Kane, I'm sure you've heard there was another terrorist incident last night. This time an entire family was slaughtered, right after we announced that the terrorists were dead and the attacks were over. Well, the terrorists *aren't* dead, at least not all of them, and now we're sitting here looking like assholes with egg on our face."

Though temporarily thrown by Ingram's chaotic mix of images, I knew what he meant. There was nothing more embarrassing in police work—or politics, for that matter—than being caught with your pants down, and the chief was guilty on both counts.

"There has been another development as well," Ingram continued. "That's where you come in, Detective Kane."

"You mean my name being revealed," I said, turning to Snead. "You wouldn't know anything about that, would you?"

"Are you implying that I leaked your name?" Snead blustered.

"That's not an answer."

"I don't know how the press got your name," said Snead, glancing at Chief Ingram. "And I resent your suggesting that I had something to do with it."

I can almost always tell when someone is lying, and I knew that if Snead weren't outright lying, he was at least holding something back. "I'll tell you what I'm suggesting," I said. "I know a call came in on the Bureau hotline threatening the so-called 'mystery hero' and his family. It was probably the same threat your LAPD task force received, but the feds took it seriously. So what I'm suggesting here, Bill, is that if anything happens to a member of my family—if even the slightest hair on any of their heads is harmed—I'm going to find the source of that leak and make certain he never leaks again."

"Are you threatening me?" Snead sputtered, further confirming my suspicions.

"I don't make threats. Consider it a promise."

"We don't have time for this," Ingram interrupted. "I'll say it again. We all need to get on the same page." He scowled at Snead, then returned his gaze to me. "Have you seen their latest video?"

"I've been busy."

"Well, I think it's something you need to watch before we go any further," Ingram said, motioning for me to join him at his desk. As I moved to stand behind him, he brought up a video on his desktop computer. Within seconds the terrorists' new internet posting began playing.

As before, I didn't want to watch. But as before, I had to.

The terrorists started their latest video with the image of a rifle-brandishing intruder standing in front of an ISIS flag. Although the terrorist's face was hidden by a balaclava and dark sunglasses, I could tell it wasn't the same person who had appeared in earlier videos. The terrorist's height was shorter and the build seemed slighter, possibly even that of a woman. The rifle was different as well. Instead of the Chinese AK-47 knockoff from before, this time the intruder was holding what appeared to be a Ruger Mini-14 semiautomatic carbine, or something similar.

My heart fell as two similarly dressed terrorists entered the frame. I thought I recognized one of them—the short, muscular individual I'd seen before. I wasn't certain about the other. The two men were shoving what appeared to be a teenaged boy and girl before them. The teenagers' hands were bound behind their backs. Sacks covered their heads. Roughly, the terrorists forced the teens to their knees and removed the hoods. The girl was weeping. Although silent, the young man appeared to be in shock. I could see fear in his eyes.

None of the terrorists spoke.

The video faded to black. As before, the terrorists' manifesto began scrolling across the screen, opening with the words, "America, be God's curse on you." I forced myself to reread it all, looking for any difference in the script. There was none. Minutes later the text concluded with the words, "All praise be to Allah, and peace and blessings be upon his Prophet Muhammad."

The video returned to the teenagers kneeling before their captors. The terrorist with the rifle stepped out of the frame, returning with a basket containing two dark-handled knives. Each of the men behind the children withdrew a knife.

I thought I could watch, but I couldn't. Shaken, I turned away as the murderers began their grisly executions. Vainly trying to shut out the children's screams, I kept thinking of my own children, imagining how I would feel if that were happening to them.

When it was over, one of the knife-wielding men stepped out of the frame, returning with a second pair of victims—this time a man and woman. Like the children, the man and woman were bound and hooded. Like their children, they were forced to their knees in front of the camera. And like their children, they were executed.

I will never forget the look of horror on the woman's face when her hood was removed and she saw the decapitated bodies of her children. Nor, for as long as I live, will I forget her pitiful, heartrending screams.

When the killers embarked on their second set of clumsy, brutal murders, I again had to look away.

After it was over, the video switched to a close-up of the Arabic word for "infidel" painted in blood on the living room wall. Following that came a final shot of the ISIS flag, and the video faded to black.

None of us spoke. I sat frozen, my heart pounding like a trip-hammer. Although I was shocked and sickened, I also realized that I was trembling with anger. For me, violence assumes a monstrous, unpardonable aspect when children are involved, and what I had just seen shook me to the core. For the killers to behead an entire family was unspeakably cruel, but to make the parents view the bodies of their slaughtered children before their own deaths was hideous beyond measure.

Finally Chief Ingram broke the silence. "Are we all on the same page now?"

I nodded, not trusting myself to speak. Strickland and Snead did the same.

"Good," said Ingram. "And just so there is no misunderstanding about what page that is, let me spell it out for you. We need to take those guys off the street, using *every* means at our disposal."

I wondered what Ingram had meant by that last part. Before I could ask, he posed a question of his own. "Any thoughts on this latest video, Kane?"

I thought a moment. "Yes, sir," I said. "To start, this is the first time we've seen the terrorist with the rifle. I get the impression it might have been a woman."

"Yeah, we thought that, too," said Snead.

"New semiautomatic weapon," I went on. "Looked like a Ruger Mini-14." I turned to Snead. "Speaking of which, ATF came up empty tracing the ownership of the Chinese AK-47 we recovered at Rivas Canyon. You guys have any luck?"

Snead nodded. "Three years back, the AK knockoff was purchased from a private collector at an Arizona gun show. Cash sale to a buyer with phony ID identifying him as David Miller, the same alias used by the man who ordered the magnetic signs. The seller claimed that the Chicom Type 56 rifle was a semiautomatic version, and therefore legal in the U.S. If so, the rifle was subsequently converted to full auto, which isn't that difficult. By the way, we lifted prints from Miller's postal-box registration card and matched them to one of the guys you popped at Rivas Canyon."

"Yeah, I heard that. Anything new on the ISIS flag?"

"Same thing. We located a online manufacturer that shipped it to Miller's box in Flagstaff. The trail ended there."

"Did you notice anything else on the video?" Ingram broke in, looking at me.

"I did recognize one of the terrorists from before," I answered. "Short, muscular guy."

"Yeah, we made that connection as well," said Strickland.

"Something about this latest video seems different," I continued. "Cruder, more amateurish. No camera movement during the murders, for instance. No panning down to the blood puddle or zooming in on the knives, like in the earlier ones."

"So?" said Snead.

"So maybe they didn't have a cameraman this time."

"Meaning maybe there were only three terrorists this time, not four?" Ingram reasoned.

"That's what I'm thinking," I said. "Maybe their killing squad is running out of members."

"From your lips to God's ears," said Ingram. Then he paused, again regarding me closely. "Okay, here's what we're going to do," he said. "Kane, for better or worse, your name is out there now, so we're going to make the most of it."

"By using me as bait?" I said, abruptly realizing what Ingram had meant by his "using *every* means at our disposal" comment earlier. "I don't think so, Chief."

"You don't have much choice in the matter," Snead pointed out with a nasty grin. "As of this morning, you've got a big bull's-eye painted on your back."

I hesitated, realizing Snead was right. My worst nightmare had come true. I had put my family in danger again . . . and there was nothing I could do about it.

"Think of it this way," Snead continued, his tone suggesting that we were getting to the real reason I was there. "As of now, you have nothing to lose. If you cooperate, we'll provide protection. Best-case scenario, we keep you safe and get these pukes off the street, like Chief Ingram said. Are you in?"

All three of them watched me closely, awaiting my response. Despite Snead's assurance that I had nothing to lose, I knew in the worst-case scenario, I had *everything* to lose. I tried to think of another option. Not coming up with any ideas, I finally nodded. "On one condition."

"And that is?" asked Strickland.

"I want round-the-clock protection for my family until this is over." I would have preferred to get them out of town, but I knew they would refuse to leave, so for now twenty-four-hour protection would have to suffice.

Strickland glanced at Snead. "Is that doable?"

"No problem," Snead replied. "I'll set it up with Metro."

"Good. It's settled then," said Ingram. "Kane, Snead will place ironclad protective surveillance on you and your family. In the meantime, you'll go back to your liaison position at the Bureau."

"How exactly is this 'bait' operation going to be run?" I

asked, suspecting there had to be more.

"We'll keep it simple," Ingram answered. "In addition to pursuing other aspects of the case, the feds are currently tracking every current internet search being made on you. With the help of NSA, they're monitoring searches worldwide, but focusing on those with local IP addresses. After this morning there are bound to be thousands, but the Bureau has the resources to sift through them and come up with our killers. We'll continue working our end of the investigation, as well as maintaining a close eye on you—hoping the terrorists try to make good on their threat."

"And this time when the dust settles," Snead added, "it would be helpful to have someone left alive to interview."

I bristled. Contrary to what many people think, including those in the media, when an LAPD officer uses deadly force to protect himself or others, he has been trained to "shoot to stop," not "shoot to kill." Unfortunately, a bullet through an arm or leg may not stop the threat, leaving the torso as the best alternative target. Unfortunately, a torso shot may also result in killing the suspect, but that was not the officer's intent—at least on paper. "I did what was necessary to stop those guys," I said. "After viewing the footage from the terrorists' camera, if you haven't already, you'll know that."

"What I know is this," Snead retorted. "If you had left someone alive in Rivas Canyon, we might have had a chance to roll up their entire organization, in which case we wouldn't be in the position we are now."

"It was a judgment call, and I'll stand by it."

"I agree," said Strickland, surprising me. "Spilt milk and all that." He checked his watch. "Maybe it's time for us to address those reporters downstairs?" he added, glancing at Ingram. "After last night, we need to try to put a good face on things."

Ingram nodded. "I agree. It's time for Detective Kane to meet the media."

"How about adding a few details designed to anger the terrorists, maybe goad them into making a mistake?" suggested Snead. "Build Kane up as some kind of terrorist-killing supercop, for instance."

"That won't be necessary," said Ingram. Then, turning to me. "Kane, we're heading downstairs now to talk with our brothers and sisters in the media. When we get there, I want you to do one simple thing."

"What?"

"Just be yourself."

"No problem," I agreed, feeling trapped but seeing no way out.

Ingram smiled. "Perfect. In one way or another, that should piss off just about everyone . . . including the terrorists."

Chapter 38

Jacob sat at the bar in Neptune's Locker. Alone that evening, he nursed a diet soda and stared into the mirror above the back counter, surveying the crowded tables behind him. For the past hour the room had been steadily filling with customers—couples out on a date, commuters returning home from the city, locals stopping by for a quick one before dinner.

But Jacob wasn't there to drink. Still smarting from the near-fatal mistake he'd made by not keeping current on news developments, he had returned to the Trancas Canyon establishment for one reason, and one reason only: to learn the identity of the LAPD's "mystery hero."

Jacob checked his watch. Then, calling to the bartender, "Could you change the TV station to Channel 2?"

"Hang on, sir," said the bartender. Then, pointing a remote control at the TV, "Channel 2, coming up."

Minutes later *CBS Evening News* came on, opening with the familiar face of the network anchor, Dan Fairly. "Turn up the sound," said Jacob.

Again thumbing the TV remote, the bartender turned up the volume.

". . . lead story, we go to McLean, Virginia, where the president once more addressed the nation from the National Counterterrorism Center," the news anchor was saying, his expression appropriately sober.

Sitting straighter on his stool, Jacob watched as the scene switched to a reporter-filled auditorium. His eyes gleaming like gunsights, he listened as the president delivered a rehash of his NCTC speech of several weeks back, again calling for an end to the violence against Muslims that was ravaging the country. Next, after reminding the nation that by standing together we would overcome any and all extremist threats, the president expressed confidence that the FBI's Joint Terrorism Task Force, working in conjunction with the U.S. Department of Homeland Security and the LAPD's Counter-Terrorism Task Force, would bring to justice those individuals responsible for the beheading murders in Los Angeles.

Following the president's address, the newscast returned to Dan Fairly in New York. "In response to an exclusive CBS revelation made earlier today, LAPD police chief Charlie Ingram called a surprise news conference in Los Angeles," said Fairly, again taking up the reins. "In what appeared to be a hastily scheduled appearance, Chief Ingram introduced the police officer responsible for the Pacific Palisades shooting deaths of three terrorists earlier this month. Here, with more from Los Angeles, is CBS News correspondent Brent Preston."

Following a lead-in by Brent Preston, the scene switched to another reporter-filled auditorium. This time, instead of the president addressing the nation, the TV screen displayed the images of Chief Ingram and a large, tough-looking man whom Jacob didn't recognize. Although Chief Ingram spoke first, it was Ingram's companion who drew Jacob's attention. Tall, hard-edged, and unsmiling, there was something dangerous in this second man's eyes, something disturbing.

After a round of self-serving introductory remarks, Chief Ingram introduced the man standing beside him as Detective Daniel Kane, better known in the press as the LAPD's "mystery hero." Ingram briefly summarized Detective Kane's previous accomplishments on the force, painting the picture of a man who had been pivotal in a number of high-profile homicide cases, including the current task-force investigation led by Captain Snead. Next, following a review of the Pacific Palisades terrorist attack, Ingram described Detective Kane's actions at the scene. Then, in a surprise move, Ingram threw open the briefing for questions from the room.

Reporters immediately jumped to their feet, all directing questions at Kane. "Detective Kane," yelled one of the more persistent correspondents, "this isn't the first time you have shot and killed a suspected criminal. In this recent incident, have you been exonerated by your department for your use of deadly force?"

"Not yet," said Kane. "But I will be."

"How do you know? Is it because you think the LAPD will cover up any improprieties?" yelled another reporter.

"You're suggesting the LAPD will engage in some sort of cover-up? What's your name, pal?" Kane demanded, pinning the questioning reporter in his gaze.

"Callahan, *L.A. Times,*" said the reporter. "And for the record, I'm not suggesting anything. Just asking for clarification."

"Fine, Mr. Callahan. Here's your clarification," said Kane. "I'll be exonerated for shooting those men because I did what I had to, and I'd do it again. And to any bleeding hearts out there who want to second-guess my actions, I'll say this: You shoot at a cop, he's going to shoot back."

"What about the Muslim backlash?" called another reporter. "Do you blame persons of Islamic faith for the beheading murders?"

Kane looked surprised. "Blame Muslims? Why would I do that? This has nothing to do with religion. This is about some murdering scum trying for their fifteen minutes of fame. Well, they may get their fifteen minutes, but they're going to regret it."

Another reporter shouted a question from the rear of the auditorium. "Now that your name is out, are you worried that members of the terrorist cell might retaliate?"

"Against me, you mean?" asked Kane.

"Yes, against you. There's a rumor that they threatened to avenge themselves on the man who executed their members."

Kane scowled. "First of all, I didn't *execute* anyone. They shot at me. I shot back, only better. Second, the terrorists committing these murders are gutless cowards who specialize in butchering defenseless men, women, and now even children. I assure you, I am *far* from being defenseless."

"So you're not concerned that they might come after you?"

Kane lips twisted in a smile, but his eyes held no warmth. "I'm saying if they decide to come for me, it'll be the last thing they ever do."

Following several more questions, the newscast returned to Dan Fairly in New York. "That was Brent Preston reporting on Detective Daniel Kane, now identified as the 'mystery hero' in the Pacific Palisades terrorist shootings," said Fairly, winding up the piece. "Meanwhile, amid ongoing fears, a countrywide Muslim backlash still rages, with people of Islamic faith being targeted by confused, misguided people."

At the conclusion of the newscast, Jacob finished his diet soda, left some change on the bar, and started for the door. Now that he had learned the identity of the LAPD's "mystery hero," he regretted the threat he'd sent to authorities after losing Caleb. He had been angry, and anger led to mistakes. Nevertheless, at least he had taken the precaution of ensuring his threat couldn't be traced, and the resultant harm seemed negligible.

Absently, Jacob wondered why the name Daniel Kane seemed familiar. Suddenly he remembered the young female correspondent from an earlier newscast. Allison Kane. It seemed a bit of a coincidence . . . but possible. As he returned to his car in the parking lot, Jacob decided to do some research on Detective Kane.

Chapter 39

A lthough I repeatedly tried to convince Allison, Travis, and Dorothy to leave town until the terrorist threat was over, they all refused, reiterating a belief that Nate's recovery depended on continued family support. Dorothy and Travis did, however, agree to move in with Allison and Mike in their Pacific Palisades home, and all were willing to cooperate with any protective measures the LAPD could provide. As promised, Snead subsequently stationed twenty-four-hour surveillance at the Palisades house—a measure that included the presence of an LAPD officer inside the residence at all times.

In the hope that the terrorists would try to make good on their threat, I remained living at the beach house, which was also being monitored on a round-the-clock basis by Metro surveillance teams. For the time being, I sent Callie to live with neighbors down the beach, not wanting our family dog in the line of fire if anything happened.

As Allison had predicted, my face wound up plastered on every supermarket tabloid, newspaper, and television in the country. If there were ever any question upon whom the terrorists wanted to extract revenge, my media notoriety cleared things up nicely—painting a great big bull's-eye on my back, as Snead had predicted. It felt strange being targeted that way, but deep down I *wanted* the terrorists to make a try for me. If they got past the Metro surveillance units, I was ready.

On the morning following my press conference, I returned to my nominal position as the LAPD/FBI liaison—attending Bureau briefings, accompanying two-man investigative units on assignments, and reporting regularly to Ingram's office. By then Taylor had been reteamed with Agent Duffy, which seemed to suit Duffy just fine. Taylor and I kept our distance, although I got the impression that she wanted to talk if the opportunity arose.

After Nate's initial seventy-two-hour evaluation, the UCLA psychiatric team decided that he should continue his in-patient stay for an additional period, possibly as long as several weeks.

During a subsequent conference with Dr. Rota, Nate's doctor again made it clear that outpatient treatment was still not an option.

As the UCLA Medical Center lay just blocks from the Federal Building, I visited my son daily. Allison dropped in to see her brother every evening on her way home from work, and Mike, Travis, and Dorothy made the trip to Westwood on a regular basis as well. Although Nate always appeared grateful to see me, we all agreed that something was still deeply wrong with the youngest member of the Kane clan, and often I came away from hospital feeling anxious and discouraged.

Weeks passed with no further terrorist incidents. There were no attempts on my life, or on those of my family, either. During this time, however, I found people staring wherever I went, although not many of them got up the nerve to approach me. I suppose being a terrorist killer wasn't the type of notoriety that made people to want to take a selfie with me.

Predictably, the media spotlight eventually moved on, with the horror of the Westside beheadings gradually fading from memory. On a Friday morning following the second week of my return to liaison duties, Taylor stopped me as I was heading into the FBI briefing. "Hey," she said, placing a hand on my forearm. "I've been meaning to talk with you."

"Morning, Taylor. What's up?"

Taylor glanced into the conference room, then back at me. "I just . . . well, I wanted to apologize again for making an ass of myself the night you drove me home. I hope we can still be friends."

"I told you that was forgotten, Taylor. In fact, I don't even know what you're talking about. And yeah, we're still friends. I'd give you a brotherly hug to prove it, but I don't want your boyfriend Duffy getting jealous."

"I told you, he's not my boyfriend."

"And I told you, you should probably let him know that," I advised with a grin. Then, more seriously, "By the way, I was curious about that kayaking trophy of yours. That metal claw thing? I looked you up online and found a YouTube video on the

North Fork Championship. It blew me away. Damn, Taylor, I had no idea. You're the real deal."

"Thanks," said Taylor, looking embarrassed.

"You didn't mention that you competed against thirty of the world's top kayakers on some of the most dangerous whitewater in the country."

"It's quite an event."

"And you took second place. I'm impressed."

"Thanks," Taylor repeated. She paused, seeming to consider for a moment. "Because I took second last year, I get an automatic placement in this year's race. It's in June, and it's a lot of fun. Maybe you'd like to drive up to the Payette River and cheer me on?"

"I don't know," I said, thinking of Nate. "I have a lot on my plate right now. But . . . maybe."

"You'll think about it?"

"I will."

"Great." Then, again glancing into the briefing room, "We'd better go in. Looks like the meeting's about to start."

"Right," I agreed, sensing that something had just changed between us. As I followed Taylor into the briefing, I also sensed that something in the room had changed as well. I didn't have to wait long to find out what.

"Grab a seat and settle down," said SAC Vaughn, stepping to the front to start the meeting.

As everyone found a place, I detected an almost palpable pall of hopelessness descending over the assembly. Despite ongoing efforts made by the Bureau, each and every trail that might have led to the terrorists had dead-ended. Locating the owner of the AK-47 had fizzled out in an anonymous gun-show purchase. Attempts to identify the owner of the postal box in Flagstaff had hit a brick wall. Investigating known associates of Ethan Hess, the only identified terrorist at the Clark residence, had gone nowhere. A forensic examination of the murder van recovered at the Clark residence, an early source of hope for the team, had dried up with an LAPD 503 stolen-car report filed two years earlier. And despite hundreds of tip-line leads, the other two men

I'd shot in Rivas Canyon had yet to be ID'd.

In the Bureau's defense, Snead's task-force investigation had fared no better.

After everyone had found a seat, Vaughn referred to his notes. "Okay, we have an update on the computer IP search," he said. "It's not good."

A number of agents groaned. Following the media's release of my name, the Bureau's main investigative thrust had been to examine all internet searches performed on me. Not surprisingly, there had been tens of thousands. One of them, a Safari browser inquiry made at a coffee shop in Oxnard, had rung an alarm.

That particular inquiry had been made on the day following my press conference. Notably, it had been performed using the Tor IP masking service, employing the same encrypted channels that had been used to post the terrorists' murder videos. Unfortunately, there had been no webcam surveillance in the coffee shop, nor were there other cameras in the area that might have proved useful. With no other options, the Bureau's CART unit had been attempting to pierce the Tor veil and come up with an IP address.

"Despite early hopes, CART was unable to track the IP address any further back than the Oxnard coffee shop," said Vaughn, confirming everyone's fears. "We've gone as far as we can on that."

"Another dead end," someone commented.

"Unfortunately," Vaughn admitted. "Along those same lines, the tactic of using Detective Kane as terrorist bait has now come to an end, too. LAPD is pulling their surveillance on him later today. We're back to square one."

"Excuse me?" I spoke up. "Did I just hear you right? They're cancelling the surveillance?"

"Sorry, Kane," said Vaughn. "We just got word this morning. I thought you knew."

"First I've heard of it," I said, wondering whether the surveillance was being pulled on Ali and Mike's residence as well.

"After weeks with nothing happening, the feeling at LAPD is

that the threat on your life was a hoax," Vaughn explained.

"This came from Snead?"

Vaughn nodded.

"Is he cancelling surveillance on my family as well?" I demanded, fighting to control my anger.

Again, Vaughn nodded. "I'm sorry, Kane, but that's my understanding. I'm sure you'll be notified."

Angry and disillusioned and sick at heart, I sat through the rest of the briefing, a hollow feeling building inside. I had been betrayed by my own department. I intended to confront Snead and Ingram and anyone else at PAB who might be willing to listen, but I had no illusions about the outcome. I had always known that LAPD had neither the will nor the funding to continue an indefinite surveillance on me and my family, but I hadn't thought the end would come so quickly. Clearly, using me as bait had failed. And following that failure, even if canceling the surveillance had been Snead's decision, approval had undoubtedly come from the top.

I had been left blowing in the wind.

I thought carefully. I didn't have the luxury of giving in to my anger. The LAPD now considered the threat on my life a hoax. My gut told me otherwise, and how I chose to proceed could mean the difference between life and death—both for me, and for my family.

And I didn't have much time to decide what to do.

Chapter 40

R udy slowed as he turned onto Galloway Street. Moments later he accelerated and proceeded north, keeping his speed just below the Pacific Palisades limit. Careful not to turn his head, he noted that a surveillance vehicle was still parked on Bashford. It had been there for the past several weeks, and Rudy knew a police stakeout when he saw one. As a result, he had made a point not to visit the neighborhood more than once every few days, and then always driving a different vehicle.

Still keeping his eyes on the road, Rudy passed Allison Kane's modest, one-story bungalow, its white stucco walls and red tiled roof partially hidden behind a hedge of holly. Satisfied, he smiled and continued on.

Weeks earlier Rudy had followed Kane's daughter from the Channel Two news studios, trailing her from Studio City to her home in the Palisades. Over the intervening weeks Rudy had seen a number of people coming and going from the Palisades residence, including Allison, an older woman, and several men— one of whom looked like a cop. Unfortunately, the surveillance unit on Bashford had always been present as well.

Several blocks farther up Galloway Rudy turned west, deciding to check on Kane's beach house next. Locating Kane's residence had been simple, an online search quickly revealing its location. Rudy still didn't understand how Kane could afford to live in Malibu on a cop's salary, but that didn't matter. What did matter was that like Allison's house, Kane's residence was being guarded as well.

Well, that couldn't go on forever, Rudy thought grimly.

They could put things off a little longer.

But not too long.

Soon.

Chapter 41

F ollowing the FBI briefing, I informed Gibbs that I would be taking a few days off to attend to personal matters. Though he didn't comment, I could tell from Gibbs's expression that he understood, and that he also knew I wouldn't be returning. Moments later, as I exited the conference room, Taylor caught up to voice her opinion that I was getting a raw deal, adding that she would be willing to help in any way she could.

After thanking Taylor, I found a quiet corner in the building and called Chief Ingram, deciding to start at the top.

After placing me on hold, a secretary in the chief's office eventually came back on the line to inform me that Chief Ingram was unavailable, adding that I could leave a message. I described the surveillance situation and requested that Chief Ingram call me as soon as possible, but I knew it wasn't going to happen. A call to Snead was similarly rebuffed. In a moment of frustration, I even tried calling Strickland, with the same results.

As I had concluded earlier, I'd been hung out to dry.

I considered driving to headquarters and confronting Snead, or Strickland, or maybe even Chief Ingram. After taking a deep breath to get my anger in check, I decided against it. Throwing a punch or two at PAB might have made me feel better, but losing my temper was not an option.

Next I made several additional calls—one to Arnie, another to Banowski. After that I phoned Travis, Grandma Dorothy, and Mike Cortese. That done, I retrieved my car from the Federal Building lot and headed to UCLA. Things were about to start happening quickly, and I wanted to check in with Nate while I still had time.

Leaving my Suburban in a hospital parking structure, I entered the medical center. After navigating a maze of hallways, I took an elevator to the Resnick Psychiatric Hospital on the fourth floor, where I registered with a secretary and waited for Nate to be called. Minutes later I met my son in an in-patient psychiatric foyer located deeper in the facility.

"You're early, Dad," said Nate, looking surprised to see me before my customary noon visit. "Couldn't stay away, huh?"

Nate seemed better than he had in some time—calm, rested, maybe even a little happy. "Yep," I replied, glancing around the airy space and admiring its tall windows, expansive skylights, and a pleasing arrangement of modern furniture throughout the room. "I could get used to being here," I added.

"Don't get carried away," Nate advised. "This is a psychiatric facility, remember?"

"Yeah, I remember. How are you doing?"

Nate thought a moment. "Better, I think. I'm enjoying the group sessions, and I've been working through some issues with one of the shrinks. Dr. Berns's friend, Dr. Freimer, has visited a lot, too. She's nice. Dr. Berns dropped by several times, and I like him, too. Plus I think the meds are helping. I don't want to take them forever, but they're fine for now. And I'm finally getting some sleep. At any rate, I haven't tried jumping out of any windows lately," he added with a fleeting smile.

"Glad to hear that," I said, smiling back.

Nate regarded me closely. "Something's on your mind. What's up, Dad?"

I hesitated, wondering where to start. "You know I've been working on the terrorist case, right?"

Nate nodded. "The Bel Air murder story that Ali was so excited about. We get the news in here. I know another family was killed in Holmby Hills, and a third home was attacked in the Palisades, where you saved a woman's life."

"That's the one," I sighed. "Unfortunately, another family has been murdered since then. You know that when I saved that woman's life in the Palisades, I shot three of the terrorists?"

Again, Nate nodded.

"The Bureau received a death threat against the officer who killed the terrorists," I continued. "The Bureau took that threat seriously. So did I. My name was kept quiet for a while, but it finally came out."

"And now the killers are looking for you."

"Right. Don't get me wrong. I'm not worried about those

guys, but until they're off the street, I can't take a chance of them harming any member of our family."

"You're thinking about what happened to Mom."

My heart sank as I saw the pain in Nate's eyes. "I'm sorry, Nate. But yes. I am," I replied, wishing more than anything that I didn't have to say those words. "Right now Arnie is in the Palisades evacuating Mike and Ali. Detective Banowski is there picking up Grandma Dorothy and Travis as well. Banowski is putting Dorothy and Trav on a plane for New York. Arnie is doing the same for Allison and Mike, except they're headed to Canada, where Mike will finish shooting his film."

"And Ali will sit around doing nothing?"

I smiled. "I'm sure that's the way she'll see it. I left it up to Mike to convince her to go. She wouldn't have listened to me."

"Probably not."

"Actually, everyone wanted to stay and continue visiting you. But keeping our family protected is more important than visiting right now, and I didn't give them an option."

"I understand," said Nate. "I imagine I'm fairly safe here," he went on, glancing around the room. "The only thing that might kill me in here is the food."

"Was that a joke?" I chuckled, encouraged by a glimmer of Nate's customary humor. "That's a good sign, kid. Maybe you *are* getting better."

"I am, Dad. Don't give up on me."

"I'll never give up on you. No matter what."

"Good. So what are you going to do?"

"You mean about the terrorists?"

"Uh-huh. Now that they're looking for you, what are you going to do?"

Until that moment, Nate's question was something I had delayed considering. Upon learning that Snead had cancelled the surveillance teams, my initial reaction—aside from anger—had been to ensure the safety of my family. Now that the ball was rolling on that front, I needed to decide how to proceed. I hesitated, the vague outline of a plan beginning to form. It might not work, but it was the only option I had.

"I'm going to do what I always do," I replied, surprised by the simplicity of my answer.

"What's that?"

"I'm going to find them before they find me."

After leaving UCLA, I placed several more phone calls—one to Deluca, another to Taylor—arranging to meet both of them later at the West L.A. station. Next I phoned Charlie Padilla, a surveillance-expert friend at Metro, and requested a favor. After describing what I needed, I arranged to have Padilla meet me at Allison's house. Padilla said he'd be glad to help, adding that he'd be there within the hour.

When I arrived at Ali's house in the Palisades, I noted with satisfaction that Arnie and Banowski had already picked up Mike, Dorothy, and Travis—removing them from danger, at least for the moment. Charlie Padilla arrived forty-five minutes later. Following a quick conference, I watched as he concealed several motion-activated wireless webcams at Ali's front and back entries, along with several more placed inside the house. Next Padilla followed me to Malibu, where he did the same for the beach residence. Along with sending email notifications when the webcams were activated, live camera feeds were available online, and all motion-activated events would be saved in an online archive. Though I had no illusions that Padilla's cameras could match the defense of a Metro surveillance team, they were better than nothing.

Next I visited Lieutenant Long at the West Los Angeles station. Sitting in Long's office, I brought him up-to-date on the terrorist investigation, informing him that Snead had cancelled protective surveillance on me and my family.

"Damn," said Long, rubbing his chin when I'd finished. "When I advised you not to trust the feds, I should have added our own department to the list, too."

I nodded. "At least now my family is out of danger."

"That's the most important thing," Long agreed. "But how long can they stay away?"

"Long enough for me to find those guys."

"What's that supposed to mean? You just told me you were off the investigation."

"I'm putting myself back on. But now I'm going to work the case *my* way."

Long regarded me thoughtfully. "I don't suppose you'll be asking permission from the department."

"Nope."

"You know running a maverick investigation could get you fired."

I shrugged.

Long found my eyes with his. "What can I do to help?"

"Lieutenant, I don't want you to jeopardize your—"

"What can I do to help?"

I met Long's gaze. "You realize that helping me could get *you* fired?"

Ignoring my question, Long asked again. "What can I do to help?"

For the first time since the FBI briefing that morning, I felt I wasn't alone. "Thanks, Lieutenant. I hope you won't regret it."

"Whatever happens, Dan, I won't regret it."

Later that afternoon Deluca, Banowski, Arnie, Long, and I met in the squad room. By then the regular detectives' shift had ended, and we had the space to ourselves. "I noticed everyone was gone at Allison's," I said to Banowski. "You got Travis and Dorothy off to New York?"

Banowski nodded. "Trav said he'd call when they landed."

"Thanks." Then, to Arnie, " How about Ali and Mike?"

Arnie smiled. "Your daughter took some convincing. I'm glad it was Mike and not me doing the convincing. Mike finally had to bring up Ali's pregnancy and the danger to her baby to get her to leave."

"But they're gone?"

"I put 'em on a plane for Toronto. Ali said she'd call when they landed, too."

"Good work, Arnie."

Just then Taylor arrived, her presence lighting up the station like a ray of sunshine. As she topped the stairs to the second floor, I gave the others a moment to stare, then rose to greet her. "I appreciate your being here, Taylor," I said. "When you offered to help, I wasn't certain you meant it."

"I meant it," Taylor replied, glancing around the squad room with obvious distaste. "Your department hung you out to dry, and the Bureau hasn't acted much better. It's not right."

"Well . . . thanks. Did you bring what I asked?"

Taylor opened her purse. After a moment of rummaging, she withdrew a USB thumb drive. Without comment, she handed me the memory device.

After pocketing the thumb drive, I escorted Taylor into the squad room and introduced her to the others. Then, turning to Deluca, "Paul? You have something for me?"

Deluca reached into his jacket, withdrew another flash drive, and placed it on the table.

"What's on that?" asked Banowski as I scooped up the second device.

"It's amazing how much you can pack onto one of those little things," Deluca answered. "For instance, the one I just gave Kane contains the entire LAPD terrorist database that Snead's task force has compiled so far."

Banowski whistled softly. "I don't suppose Snead would be too happy knowing you gave it to Kane."

"Don't imagine so," Deluca agreed.

Banowski turned to Taylor. "What's on yours?"

Taylor hesitated.

"The thumb drive you just handed Kane," Banowski persisted.

"It's okay, Taylor," I said. "You're among friends."

Taylor hesitated a moment longer, then answered. "It contains the FBI's 'Infidel' database—all of it." At a puzzled look from Banowski, she added, "'Infidel' is the Bureau's code name for the case."

"Damn," said Arnie. "There could be a few terminated careers here if any of this ever comes out. Makes me glad I'm already retired and drawing my pension."

"If this gets out, the rest of us will be retired, too—*without* pensions," noted Long.

"So let's make sure it doesn't get out," said Deluca.

"Look, I appreciate that all of you want to help," I broke in. "But now that I have the databases, I'll take it from here. There's no sense in everyone risking—"

"I'm in, partner," said Deluca.

"Me, too," added Banowski. "Whatever you need."

"I think the Crenshaw Mall security team can manage without me for a bit," said Arnie.

"Count me in, too," said Taylor. "I'm available through the weekend. Plus I've accumulated a few sick days, if you need me after that."

"I'll provide investigative authorization and cover for working the case out of West L.A.," offered Long.

"I . . . well, thanks," I repeated, a lump rising in my throat.

"Now that *that's* settled, what's next?" asked Long.

I thought a moment. "Okay, with the Metro surveillance being cancelled, I think we should establish our own two-man presence at Mike and Ali's for the next few days, just in case we have visitors."

"Good idea. I can bunk at Ali's starting tonight," offered Deluca. "My wife will be glad to get rid of me."

"Yeah, me, too," added Banowski. "Except for the wife part."

"Fine," I said, writing Ali's address on a slip of paper and handing it to Deluca. "Here's her house key," I added, removing a key from my key ring and passing it to him as well.

"Two of us should be present at the beach house, too," suggested Arnie. "How about if I move down there for a couple days, starting tomorrow? I'm assuming you'll want us sleeping in shifts, with someone awake at all times?"

I nodded. "If nothing happens soon, we might have to abandon Allison's and move everyone down to the beach. That way we could switch to two-hour shifts and maybe actually get some sleep."

"You think they're going to make a try for you?" asked Long.

"My gut says yeah, but who knows?" I replied.

"And if they don't?" asked Long.

I didn't have an answer for that. "The weekend's coming up," I said, glancing around the table. "After you all finish your Friday shifts, let's meet back here and put our heads together. In the meantime, I'll review the thumb-drive material and see whether anything jumps out."

"Seems like combing through those databases will be a waste of time," said Deluca. "So far nothing on them has brought us any closer to the killers. What are you looking for?"

"I'm not certain, Paul," I replied. "But I still haven't been able to shake the feeling that we're overlooking something."

"What?"

"I don't know. But I think it might be important."

Chapter 42

"Damn, Kane. Don't take this wrong, but you look like hell. You been here all night?"

I glanced up from my workstation, noticing Lieutenant Long entering the squad room. "Yeah, Lieutenant, I have," I said, passing a hand across a rough stubble covering my chin. I took a swig of black coffee, ran my fingers through my hair, and resumed staring at the computer screen.

"Anything turn up?"

I shook my head. "Still working on it." I had spent the night combing through the Bureau and LAPD task-force databases, searching for something we might have missed. So far nothing had turned up.

In summary, the dumpster DNA from the killers' bloody clothing had presented the FBI with their best opportunity to come up with a suspect, and that had fizzled. The identities of two of the suspects I'd shot in Rivas Canyon still remained a mystery, and tracing the activities, known associates, and so on of the third deceased terrorist—Ethan James Hess—had been fruitless as well. As for Snead's task force, the LAPD's main contribution to the investigation had been to locate the postal box of Mr. David Miller, to which the ISIS flag and the fake magnetic signs had been delivered. Frustratingly, the postal-box lead had also dried up. Although forensic analysis on other fronts was still underway, nothing looked hopeful.

On the upside, I had received calls from both Allison and Travis informing me that they had arrived safely, and in Allison's case, demanding to know when she could return. For that I didn't have an answer.

Hearing heavy footfalls in the staircase outside, I looked up again from my desk. A moment later Banowski entered the squad room carrying a large Starbucks coffee. "Morning, Lieutenant," he said, nodding to Long. Then, looking closely at me, "Kane. You, ah, get any sleep?"

"Morning, John," I replied. "I've already been told I look like hell, so don't bother."

"Wouldn't think of it," Banowski chuckled, dropping his considerable bulk onto a chair nearby. "Just don't look in a mirror. At least I got half a night's sleep at Allison's. By the way, Deluca snores." Then, glancing at the pile of notes on my desk, "You getting anywhere?"

"Working on it," I repeated.

"Just so you know, I'll need the rest of the morning to clear up a few things. After that I'm all yours."

"Thanks, John. Whenever you're ready. I still have a few things to clear up myself."

After refilling my coffee cup from a stale pot that had been brewing all night, I returned to my desk, put up my feet, and rocked back in my chair. Closing my eyes, I began working the edges of the case, using a mental technique akin to not looking directly at something in the dark, hoping to tease out whatever it was that had eluded me earlier.

As I reviewed the case in my mind, one item kept popping up—something about the investigation that I had never satisfactorily resolved.

Why had Arleen Welch's 911 calls gone unanswered?

As Vaughn had pointed out, one possible explanation was that Arleen had simply disconnected before an overworked emergency operator had been able to pick up, resulting in the "cancelled call" status shown on Arleen's cellphone. What that didn't explain, however, was the sudden "no service" status of my phone when I'd entered Dr. Clark's residence. Snead had accused me of breaking my cellphone connection with Taylor in order to execute the terrorists without repercussion, but I knew that wasn't true. Also puzzling at the time, and even more difficult to explain, was that later my phone service had been unexpectedly restored—again for no apparent reason.

Since then I'd learned that there had been a fourth terrorist present in the house, and that he had probably escaped out the back door, right around the time my phone service had been reestablished. With a long-due flash of insight, I suddenly realized that the presence of this fourth man changed everything, reviving a theory I had proposed earlier. But before I acted on that theory, there was someone I needed to consult. After informing Long and Banowski that I'd be back later, I retrieved my Suburban from the station parking lot and headed to Santa Monica.

Fifteen minutes later I pulled to a stop in front of an unassuming, one-story building with a storefront window displaying an eclectic selection of televisions, stereos, computers, and ham radio equipment. Above the door, a neon sign read, "Hank's Radio and TV."

Upon entering the shop, I made my way to a brightly lit service area at the rear. There, a balding man with wire-rimmed glasses sat hunched over a workbench inspecting the innards of a flat-screen TV.

"Electricity's dangerous, pal," I said, leaning across the service counter. "You sure you know what you're doing?"

The elderly man looked up, his weathered face creasing in a grin. Setting down a soldering iron, he rose to shake my hand. "Dan, it's been too long. Great to see you."

"You, too, Hank. How's Mitchell doing?"

Earlier in my career I had worked a drive-by shooting in which Hank Dexter's teenaged son, Mitchell, had been present in a crowd indiscriminately sprayed with gunfire. Mitchell had wound up riding a wheelchair. During the course of the investigation, Hank and I had become friends, and we still kept in touch.

"Mitch is fine," Hank answered. "My second grandchild is due this summer," he added proudly.

"That's wonderful, Hank. I'm happy for you. Please give Mitchell and his wife my best."

"I will," said Hank. Then, regarding me curiously, "Not that it isn't good to see you, but I gather this isn't a social call."

"No, it's not, although I've been meaning to drop by for some time. But yeah, there's something I want to run by you."

"I've seen you on the news lately. Those terrorist beheadings. It's unspeakable what happened to those families," said Hank. "I was happy you were able to save that woman in the Palisades, and I was grateful you weren't hurt yourself."

"Thanks, Hank."

"Is this about the terrorist case?"

I glanced around to make certain no one was listening. "It is. But I'd like you to keep quiet about my visit here today, okay?"

"Absolutely," said Hank. "Let's go someplace more private," he suggested, motioning for me to join him at the rear of the service area. I ducked under a counter and followed him to the back.

"Now, how can I help?" he asked, regarding me curiously when we arrived at the rear of the shop.

I paused to collect my thoughts. Then, "Okay, here's my problem," I said. "I have a victim who tried to make several 911 calls. None of them went through. Her phone log lists them as cancelled calls, which could mean she simply hung up before a connection was established."

"But you don't think that's the case?"

"I'm not sure, Hank, but I am suspicious. One of the 911 calls went unanswered for over nine seconds, which seems a bit long for an emergency operator to respond. On the other hand, I suppose it's possible."

Hank nodded. "What makes you think otherwise?"

"Something that happened later. When I entered the Rivas Canyon crime scene, I unexpectedly lost phone service. Later my service was restored, again for no apparent reason."

"Happens all the time in the canyons."

"Yeah, but no one on the street lost service. Just me."

"Still, it happens. Dead spots are common, especially in canyons that can block a cell-tower signal."

"That may be, but there's more," I continued. "What I'm about to tell you wasn't revealed to the press, so keep it under your hat. There was a fourth terrorist present that night. He escaped, right around the time my cell service was restored."

Hank remained silent for a long moment. "I think I see where you're going," he said, looking pensive. "A cellphone jammer."

"Right. Our SWAT teams use tactical jammers at active crime scenes all the time. Jammers are also employed in prison environments, and they're used by military units as well. But in those cases, the units are large and bulky. I'm wondering whether a portable jammer could explain what happened to me."

"What range are we talking?"

During the canvass of Arleen and Gary Welch's neighborhood, investigators had failed to turn up anyone who had experienced a loss of phone service. Agent Taylor hadn't lost service on the street in Rivas Canyon, either. "Relatively short, I think," I replied, trying to gauge the distances involved. "Say, a radius of a couple hundred feet or so."

"That's in the ballpark for a portable unit, depending on the strength and type of cellular system it's blocking," Hank replied. "That said, there are a few caveats."

"Like?"

"For one, under the U.S. Communications Act of 1934, the use of a cellphone jammer by a private party is illegal."

"Actually, I knew that—except for the Communications Act part. Tell me something I don't know, like how do people get one?"

"Online, mostly," said Hank. "Notice that I said the _use_ of a cellphone jammer is illegal. The devices themselves fall into an odd category of items that are legal to own but illegal to use— like radar detectors in many states, along with stun guns and even flamethrowers. By the way, jammer use *is* legal in countries like France and Japan, where they're commonly employed in art galleries, concerts, and movie theaters."

"Flamethrowers?"

Hank nodded. "Crazy, huh? Anyway, the takeaway here is that it's illegal in the U.S. for private citizens to advertise, market, or use a cellphone jammer, so jammers aren't available for purchase from domestic companies. If someone has one, he either brought it into the country illegally, or he purchased it online from an international distributor. The latter is still a gray area, but online distributors usually attempt to sidestep legal restrictions by warning U.S. customers that federal law prohibits interfering with any authorized radio communication. But bottom line, it's still the internet, where you can get just about anything you want."

"International distributors, huh? That narrows things down a bit. What else?

"You know how a jammer works, right?"

"Not really. Does it matter?"

"It does if you're trying to trace the purchase of one, which I assume is your intention."

"Okay, how do jammers work? But keep it simple, okay?"

"Of course," Hank sniffed, looking disappointed. He considered a moment and then continued. "Basically, a cellphone is a two-way radio. In our country most mobile phones operate on a frequency band of 1.9 gigahertz, with a grid of cellular communication towers amplifying and relaying phone signals to a service network. A jammer transmits a noise signal on the same frequencies used by your phone, preventing your device from connecting to a cell tower. It's called a denial-of-service attack. In layman's terms, a jammer simply drowns out your phone signal with a louder one."

"Sounds pretty basic."

"Yes and no. There are several factors that a criminal would want to consider when buying a jammer. For instance, most phones are full-duplex devices, meaning that for simultaneous talking and listening, they operate on two separate frequencies— one for speaking, the other for listening. Although a jammer that blocks only one of those frequencies could be effective, I would select a more sophisticated jammer that blocks both."

I saw where Hank was going. "What else might our hypothetical criminal consider?"

"Well, most phones are designed to add power if they experience interference, so a good jammer should be able to match a cellphone's increase in signal strength. Another consideration would be that when dual-and tri-mode phones can't find an open signal, they automatically switch among different networks to establish a connection. If I were a criminal, I would select a high-end, multiband device that can block all frequencies and digital formats at once."

"Anything else?"

"Battery life would be important. Wouldn't want your portable jammer crapping out at the wrong time," Hank mused. "Size would be a factor, of course, as would the unit's radius of interference and the number of antennae necessary. Price, too, I suppose."

"Are they expensive?"

"Not cheap, but reasonable," Hank answered. "Five hundred to a thousand dollars would be plenty for what you need. Of course, you could always pay more."

"A lot of factors there," I noted, wondering whether I'd headed down the wrong path. "Things are sounding more complicated than I'd hoped."

Noting my look of disappointment, Hank said, "Tell you what. Give me a few hours to do some research and get back to you. There may be a lot of portable jammers out there, but I think I can narrow your search."

"Thanks, Hank." I withdrew a business card and wrote my cellphone number on the back. "I'm working out of West L.A. at the moment, but if you can't get me there, phone me on my cell. And again, thanks," I said, passing him the card.

"No need to thank me. I hope you get those guys, and I'm glad to help in any way I can."

"And I appreciate it." I paused, regarding Hank thoughtfully. "I'm curious, though. How do you happen to know so much about jammers?"

Hank grinned. "I was wondering when you'd ask." Again signaling for me to follow him, he added, "I know a bit about jammers because I happen to own one."

I trailed Hank to a cabinet near his workbench. Mounting a small stepladder, he retrieved a piece of electronic gear from one of the upper shelves. About the size of a wireless router, the glossy black unit had several switches on the front and six stubby antennae protruding from the top. "That's a jammer?" I said.

"Yep. This is a short-range model I used at one time to block cellphone chatter in the store. Haven't turned it on in years, not since the FCC started clamping down. There's a steep fine now for using a jammer, and it's not worth the risk."

"Could you turn it on?" I asked, pulling my cellphone from my jacket.

"As long as you don't arrest me," Hank joked.

"No worries. This is official business. Besides, it'll just be for a minute. I want to see how it works."

"There's not much to see. You have phone service right now?"

I checked my phone. "Four bars."

Hank plugged in the jammer and flipped a switch on the front.

Again, I checked my phone.

No service.

Just to be sure, I dialed Lieutenant Long's number at the station.

Nothing.

I counted to ten, then hung up.

Next I scrolled to a listing of recent calls. My phone log showed Lieutenant Long's telephone number, the time and date, and a call duration of eleven seconds. I felt a chill as I checked the log's final entry.

Like Arleen Welch's 911 attempts, my effort to reach Lieutenant Long was listed as a cancelled call.

Chapter 43

After talking with Hank, I felt more certain than ever that a phone jammer might have played a role in the terrorist attacks. Still, I needed the results of my electronics friend's research before determining my next step. There was another decision I had to make as well, but as I hadn't eaten since yesterday's breakfast, I decided to grab lunch first and think about things later. The Apple Pan, a mom-and-pop restaurant that had been in business for as long as I could recall, was nearby. It was also inexpensive, and it arguably served one of the best burgers in town.

During a short drive down West Pico to The Apple Pan, I received an email alert on my phone informing me that one of Allison's webcams had been activated. Pulling off the road to check, I found that a concealed camera at Ali's back door had been activated by a neighborhood dog. It was the ninth false alarm from Allison's residence since yesterday. By then I had received five other motion-activated notifications from the beach house as well—all useless. With a sigh, I deactivated the email notification feature, deciding that with everyone now gone and both houses vacant during the day, checking archived webcam events would have to suffice.

Once more back on the road, I considered placing a call to Taylor, and another to Deluca. Both were phone calls I had mixed feelings about making. In setting me up as a target and then yanking the rug out from under me, I had been shafted by my own department. The Bureau hadn't been much help, either, and trust was now an issue. Part of me simply wanted to go my own way. Unfortunately, I wasn't the only one involved. There was my family to consider.

With the possibility of a cellphone jammer now back on the table, we had a new lead to pursue, and the more investigators pursuing that lead, the better. In a moment of anger, I had told Lieutenant Long that I intended to work the case on my own, but that simply wasn't being realistic. Much as I hated to admit it, both the Bureau and Snead's task force had resources that I didn't. I needed results, and I needed them quickly.

Minutes later I arrived at The Apple Pan, finding every available parking space filled out front. After leaving my car in a shopping pavilion across the street, I crossed Pico and snagged an empty stool at the diner's U-shaped counter. Not bothering with the menu, I ordered my usual from a grumpy waiter behind the counter—hickory burger with cheese, fries, Coke, and a slice of apple pie. Though my thoughts kept returning to the terrorist investigation, I wolfed down my food in record time, with The Apple Pan's fare proving as delicious as I had remembered.

By the time I finished, a number of people had lined up around the counter, some of them waiting not-so-patiently for a stool. Deciding it was time to let another customer have my spot, I finished a final bite of pie and made my way to an ancient cash register near the door. The Apple Pan was a cash-only establishment, which now seemed the norm for small, off-the-beaten-path restaurants in L.A. As I was withdrawing my wallet, my previously grumpy waiter waved me off, saying that lunch was on him. Although I tried to object, he refused to take my money. Then, leaning across the counter, he shook my hand and thanked me for my service to the city. Feeling slightly better about myself, I headed back to my Suburban, thinking that sometimes being in the media spotlight wasn't *all* bad.

Upon returning to my car, I slid behind the wheel and sat for several minutes, staring at a cement support column and trying to decide what to do next. Finally swallowing my pride, I did what I had always known I would have to do. Withdrawing my phone, I punched in Taylor's number. When she picked up, she sounded slightly out of breath.

"What's up, Kane?" she asked. "We're still meeting at the station later, right?"

"We are," I replied. "But there's something I need you to do first."

I brought Taylor up to date on what I had learned from Hank, reiterating that the terrorists' use of a jammer could explain Arleen Welch's cancelled 911 calls. As a clincher, I added that my losing network service inside the Clark residence could also be explained by the presence of a portable, short-range jammer— a jammer that was later removed by the escaping terrorist, thereby restoring my service.

When I had finished, Taylor remained silent for a long moment. Then, "It may be a bit of a stretch, but a jammer does account for several unexplained details," she said thoughtfully. "Actually, this is the first positive development I've heard in weeks. What do you want me to do about it?"

"Take it to Vaughn. And again, don't mention me. The presence of the fourth terrorist changes things, but Vaughn has already shut me down on the jammer angle more than once. Maybe he'll listen to you."

"Okay," said Taylor, beginning to sound excited. "I'll see you at the station later."

Next I phoned Deluca. I caught him at lunch. He put me on hold, saying he had to step away from his table to take my call. When he came back on the line, I gave him a condensed version of what I had learned from Hank. Again swallowing my pride, I asked him to take that information to Snead. As I had with Taylor, I suggested that Deluca leave my name out of things. Although doubtful that Snead would be receptive, Deluca agreed, promising to let me know how things went when we met later that afternoon.

Upon returning to West L.A., I found Arnie and Banowski already waiting in the squad room. After retiring to the privacy of Lieutenant Long's office, I filled them in on what I'd learned. Arnie was surprised when I mentioned giving the jammer lead to Snead, noting that after Snead's cancelling the surveillance on my family, Arnie would have sooner given his bank-account password to his ex-wife. Although I agreed, I didn't have that luxury. I needed help from wherever I could get it, including Snead . . . if he would give it.

Hank Dexter called thirty minutes later, informing me that he was emailing me the results of his jammer research. His email arrived shortly, turning out to be a reasonably manageable list of portable cellphone jammers with the size, range, battery life, and other capabilities that Hank deemed necessary for the terrorists' needs. Accompanying his list, Hank sent a disconcertingly longer inventory of international online distributors that sold the jammers he had named. In his email Hank also advised me to check other online marketers, as his website directory was merely a preliminary stab at the subject.

Although I hoped that Snead's task force and Shepherd's Bureau agents would agree to investigate the jammer lead, I also intended to work the case myself. Upon conferring with Long and the others, we decided that our best approach lay in developing a database of persons who had purchased one of the jammers on Hank's list, and then proceed from there. Because we needed to establish reasonable parameters for our search, we set a three-year time span on previous sales, concentrating on purchasers in the western United States, especially those in California.

As Hank had pointed out, domestic jammer manufacturers were forbidden to sell to private citizens in the United States. As a result, all the distributors on Hank's list were based in either Europe or Asia. Because distributors in Asia wouldn't be opening until 4:00 p.m. California time, and as the European business day had already ended, we worked on adding names to Hank's distributor list throughout the rest of the afternoon, piling on an alarming number of additional distributors to my friend's original catalog.

During that time, a number of West L.A. detectives dropped by my desk to welcome me back, many of them expressing curiosity about what I was doing. I told them that they didn't want to know, providing plausible deniability if our unauthorized investigation were ever to come to light.

After the detectives' shift ended and we again had the squad room to ourselves, our team started making calls to Asian distributors, to our relief finding that English seemed to be the universal language of business. Without a warrant, procuring a roster of jammer purchasers from international marketers occasionally proved tricky, especially considering that jammer sales in our country were illegal. Nevertheless, upon explaining the general reason for our request and occasionally threatening an official investigation if a distributor didn't cooperate, we usually got what we wanted.

And rapidly, our list of jammer purchasers began to grow.

Later, Taylor and Deluca came up the stairs together, having arrived at the station around the same time. I glanced up from a phone call to Hong Kong, realizing from the expressions on their faces that neither of their respective agencies had agreed to pursue the jammer lead. "Bad news?" I said, covering the mouthpiece with my palm.

"Afraid so," said Deluca.

"Same here," said Taylor.

"Hold on a sec," I said, returning to my call. After requesting an email listing of the distributor's jammer purchasers, I disconnected. "So what happened?" I asked.

Deluca spoke first. "Snead laughed in my face."

"You didn't mention that the jammer lead was my idea?"

"Nope. Told him it was mine."

"And you brought up the fourth terrorist, and that my phone service was restored after the guy escaped?"

"I did. Snead's not buying your jammer theory. He still thinks you turned off your phone so you could dust those guys, no questions asked. Afterward, you simply turned your phone back on. He claims you're pushing the jammer idea to clear yourself in the use-of-force investigation."

"That's bull, and he knows it."

"Maybe so, but he's not going to follow up on the jammer lead. Instead, he now has our entire team running down hot-line leads."

Disgusted, I turned to Taylor. "What did Vaughn say?"

"Same as before," she replied. "He thinks Arleen Welch panicked and hung up before her 911 calls were answered. As for your losing cellphone service in the Clark residence, he reminded me that network connections are spotty in the canyons. Fourth terrorist or not, he says there's no reason to assume the killers were using a jammer. Bureau agents already have their hands full combing through Ethan Hess's background, working assets in the

Muslim community, checking domestic recruitment and radicalization sites, and trying to ID the other two terrorists."

"And how's that going?"

Taylor shrugged. "It's not."

"Okay," I sighed, unable to hide my disappointment. "Looks like it's just us."

Working through the rest of the evening and taking only a short break to grab dinner at a fast-food joint in Westwood, we finished compiling a database containing the names of anyone who had purchased one of Hank's jammers from an Asian distributor. As the evening had worn on, our list showed signs of becoming unmanageably large, and we eventually elected to restrict the remainder of our search to a two-year cutoff, rather than three. Granted, two years was an arbitrary limit, but we hadn't even started contacting European distributors yet, and we had to draw the line somewhere.

Long and Arnie departed around 11:00 p.m. Taylor left shortly afterward. All three promised to return early the next morning. Banowski and Deluca both offered to continue working, but as they'd each had only a few hours sleep at Ali's house the previous evening, I told them to return to Allison's for one more night and get some rest. Forty minutes later I checked Padilla's webcams, noting that the motion-activated cameras at Allison's residence had archived Banowski and Deluca's arrival.

Later I grabbed a catnap on a cot in the back of the station. Afterward, I shaved and cleaned up a bit in the detectives' bathroom. Then, at 1:00 a.m., I prepared to start calling European marketers.

With a growing sense of discouragement, I stumbled back to the squad-room coffee station, poured my ninth cup of the day, and returned to my desk. Although unsure where my efforts would lead, as I glanced at our list of European distributors, I knew one thing for certain.

It was going to be a long night.

Chapter 44

Taylor and Long returned to the squad room early the next morning. Arnie, Banowski, and Deluca showed up shortly afterward, and together we worked straight through until noon, contacting nearly every distributor on our European list.

After a quick lunch at the Brentwood Country Mart, we returned to the squad room and spent several additional hours prioritizing potential suspects. By then we had developed a disconcertingly large database of U.S. private citizens who owned cellphone jammers that had the capabilities our terrorists would have required. Even by limiting our search by concentrating on purchasers in Southern California, then Arizona, and finally the remainder of the western states, we still wound up with an almost unmanageable number of names.

Our first investigative attempt was to compare individuals on our list with every person on the Bureau and LAPD databases, in particular checking for anyone connected with Ethan James Hess, the only identified terrorist to date. Disappointingly, this approach proved a dead end.

It was time to hit the streets.

For that we broke into three teams—Deluca and Banowski, Taylor and me, and Arnie and Long. Our first two teams were tasked with interviewing jammer purchasers within driving range. Arnie and Long would remain at the station calling jammer owners farther out, including those living out-of-state. It would have been optimal to have something definite for which we were searching, but we didn't. Instead, we would have to depend on our intuition and investigative experience, asking questions and looking for anything that didn't seem to fit.

Not the greatest plan, but it was the best we had.

We worked through the remainder of Saturday and all of Sunday, starting with the closest jammer purchasers and progressing outward. By Sunday evening Taylor and I had made it north to Glendale; Deluca and Banowski had covered south to Torrance and east to Whittier. Arnie and Long had completed calls to Northern California and were starting on purchasers in the San Diego area.

So far nothing had turned up.

As time went on, I found that I liked working with Taylor. She had good instincts and a nice touch with the interviews, her more subtle techniques dovetailing well with my direct, in-your-face approach. Nevertheless, despite our best efforts, by week's end we had come up cold.

On Monday Long had to resume his regular duties at the West L.A station, although he continued calling out-of-the-area jammer owners when he had a chance. Deluca, Taylor, and Banowski also returned to their day jobs, leaving Arnie and me to interview jammer purchasers on our own. Each night after finishing their regular shifts, Deluca and Banowski joined me at the beach house, trading off watch and grabbing a few hours sleep in between.

During that time, in the hope that I would receive visitors, I intentionally left my home security system unarmed. As with our jammer interviews and the growing number of false-alarm webcam events that had swelled Padilla's surveillance archive, nothing positive developed, and by the following weekend I was beginning to think our efforts had been for naught. Complicating matters, Mike's work in Canada was coming to an end, and Allison was calling daily demanding to know when she could return. I still didn't have an answer for that. Nor had I decided how to keep Nate safe once he was released from the medical center.

Notably, during that week I heard nothing from Bureau or LAPD authorities questioning my absence, confirming my conviction that both agencies had hung me out to dry. Now they just wanted to forget the issue, and to forget me, too.

And the sooner, the better.

Chapter 45

Early the following Saturday, our small team reconvened at the West L.A. station. With Arnie and Long again working the phone lines, our other two units hit the streets. Later that morning Taylor and I had progressed to interviewing a jammer owner in Sylmar, a residential area in the northern San Fernando Valley. I was driving. Taylor was riding shotgun, checking her cellphone GPS for directions.

At a little after 10:00 a.m., we arrived at a rundown house on the south edge of town. After parking on a seedy street out front, we exited the Suburban and climbed a short flight of stairs to the front door of the one-story residence. By then we had developed a system. I knocked. Taylor did the talking.

Our knock was answered by a tall, thin woman in her early twenties. She opened the door but left her security chain in place. "Yeah?" she said, peering out from behind a straggly fringe of bleached blond hair.

"Ms. Perkins?" said Taylor, referring to her notebook. "Sally Perkins?"

"So?"

"I'm Special Agent Taylor, and this is Detective Kane. We're investigating a series of incidents in the area," Taylor continued pleasantly, flashing her credentials. "May we come in and talk?"

"I didn't do nothing," the woman replied, regarding us suspiciously.

"We didn't say you did," I replied not so pleasantly, also flipping out my ID. "We need a minute of your time. Everyone else in your neighborhood has cooperated," I lied. "No reason you shouldn't, either . . . unless you have something to hide."

"I ain't got nothing to hide," the woman mumbled. "I guess you can come in," she added, unlatching the security chain.

"Thank you, ma'am," said Taylor, easing past her into the house. I followed Taylor in. As I did, Taylor shot me a look that said she sensed something was odd.

As we trailed the woman into a small living room, I smelled

the distinctive reek of pot, possibly explaining the woman's reluctance to invite us inside. The woman lit a cigarette and slumped onto a couch facing a large-screen TV. Taylor sat in a chair across from her. I remained standing.

"What's this about?" Ms. Perkins demanded, exhaling a cloud of smoke. "I swear, if this has anything to do with that piece-of-shit ex-boyfriend of mine—"

"We're checking on an online purchase you made," Taylor broke in, again referring to her notebook. "About a year ago. You bought a cellphone jammer in December, just before Christmas?"

"I knew it!" said the woman. "That goddamn Parker."

"What are you talking about? Who's Parker?" I asked.

"Parker's my ex-boyfriend, the one who used my credit card to buy a bunch of stuff and then stuck me with the bill."

"Where is Parker now, Ms. Perkins?" I asked.

"Haven't seen him in a year. Don't want to, neither."

"But you know where to find him?"

The woman hesitated, then shrugged. "Don't know, don't care."

"Does Parker have a last name?" asked Taylor.

"Parker Dillon."

Reaching into my jacket, I withdrew several morgue shots of the two unidentified intruders at the Clark residence. "Is Parker either of these men?" I asked, passing the photos to Ms. Perkins.

"Jesus, are these guys dead?" she mumbled, staring in shock. Then, stubbing out her cigarette, she grabbed a pair of eyeglasses from the coffee table and looked closer. "Actually, this guy looks a little like Parker," she said, tapping the image on one of the photos. "He had a beard when I knew him. Hard to tell. Maybe."

At this, I felt my pulse quicken.

"Was Parker tall or short?" asked Taylor.

"Tall. And skinny. That prick could eat anything and not gain an ounce."

"Did Parker ever live in Arizona?" I asked, taking a shot in the dark.

The woman nodded. "Before I met him. Flagstaff, I think. How'd you know that?"

"Does Parker have any Muslim friends or affiliations?" I asked, ignoring her question.

The woman looked puzzled. "Not that I know of."

"Do you have any pictures of Parker?" Taylor jumped in. Although she kept her tone neutral, I could tell she was getting excited, too.

The woman shook her head. "I threw out all his stuff. Didn't want to be reminded."

"You didn't keep anything?" I asked. "Nothing?"

"Well . . . I did save a couple things. He owed me money."

"What did you keep?"

"Parker was a gun nut," the woman answered. "I stashed a couple of his pistols before he moved out. Like I said, he owed me money."

"We're going to need those items," I said. When the woman looked doubtful, I added, "Don't worry, you'll get them back when we're done."

"Okay. Long as I get 'em back. They're in my closet."

The woman rose and headed deeper into the house. Taylor and I followed her back to a cluttered bedroom. Standing on her toes, the woman pulled a shoebox from the top shelf of a closet. Without opening the box, she set it on a bedside stand. "You promise I'll get this back?" she asked.

"When we're done," I assured her. Using a pen and touching only the edges, I flipped open the box. Inside, along with several cleaning rags, were two handguns—a Smith & Wesson .357 magnum revolver, and a Kimber .45 caliber semiautomatic pistol. "Have you touched either of those weapons?" I asked.

The woman shook her head. "Don't like guns."

"You never handled them, even when you put them in the box?" asked Taylor, realizing where I was going.

"Parker put 'em in there."

"That's good, Ms. Perkins," I said, using my pen to close the box. "I'm also going to need to borrow one of your pillowcases," I added, stripping one from a pillow on her bed and using it to enclose the shoebox.

"You'll get that back, too," said Taylor.

"Whatever," the woman grumbled. Then, regarding us curiously, "All this because Parker bought a cellphone blocker? Seems like you're going to a lot of trouble for nothing."

"You've been helpful, Ms. Perkins," said Taylor. "We'll be in touch."

"I have one more question," I said, turning in the doorway to block the woman's exit. "And before you answer, Ms. Perkins, I'd advise you to think real hard. Your boyfriend Parker may be in serious trouble, and not just because of a cellphone jammer. If there's anything you're not telling us, you could be considered an accomplice."

The woman shifted uncomfortably. "I told you everything."

"I don't think so," I said. Ignoring a curious look from Taylor, I stepped closer to the woman and held her eyes with mine. "I can tell when someone's lying. Earlier, when I asked whether you knew where to find Parker, you lied. Or at least you held something back. What was it?"

The woman looked away. "Nothing. I mean, nothing for sure," she corrected. "Parker was involved with some cult he kept trying to get me to join. They have a compound where they raise their own food and such—an intentional community, Parker called it. He said we could move out there and live for nothing."

"And?"

"And I think he went there after I kicked him out."

"Where is this 'intentional community' compound of Parker's?"

The woman thought a moment. "I don't know for sure . . . but I think he said it was somewhere in Trancas Canyon."

Chapter 46

From their concealed position on the hillside, Rudy peered down at the beach house below. "I'm tired of waiting. You think someone is still inside?"

Jacob lowered a pair of high-powered binoculars with which he had been studying the beach residence. "Patience, Rudy. We'll wait as long as it takes to be certain no one is present."

"Who were the men who left with Kane?"

"Police officers, most likely," Jacob answered, again raising his binoculars. "Because surveillance vehicles are no longer present on the street, it appears the authorities have now stationed men *inside* Kane's home."

Patiently, Jacob studied the residence for another minute. Then, "I think everyone is gone," he said. "Are you sure you'll be able to disable the security system?"

"Positive," Rudy replied. "It's a wireless system with no landline, so no problem."

"Are you certain?"

Rudy shrugged. "I didn't work at a security company for nothing, Jacob."

Satisfied, Jacob returned with Rudy to their vehicle, a nondescript van displaying magnetic door panels and a roof cap that read: "Onkin Pest Control." Minutes later, after following a narrow, winding road down to Pacific Coast Highway, they pulled to a stop, parking several houses down from Kane's residence. Then, wearing workmen's coveralls, they quickly walked to Kane's front door.

"Is the jammer on?" Rudy asked when they arrived.

After checking a small device clipped to his tool belt, Jacob nodded.

Rudy rang the buzzer and banged on the door.

No answer.

At a nod from Jacob, Rudy opened a leather satchel he had carried with him. After snapping on a pair of latex gloves, he rummaged inside the bag. Finding what he wanted, he removed an electric pick gun, an oddly shaped device that resembled a flashlight with a strip of metal jutting from the front. Using the pick gun and another metal tool called a torsion wrench, Rudy opened Kane's six-cylinder mortise lock in exactly eight seconds. It took even less time for the buzzing device to breach Kane's doorknob lock.

Jacob put a hand behind his back, curling his fingers around the grip of the Charter Arms snub-nosed .38 Special revolver tucked in his coveralls. "Hello?" he called into the house, opening the door a crack. "Pest control. Anyone home?"

Both men paused, listening.

"Here, boy," Jacob called into the house again, hoping Kane didn't have a dog. "Here, boy," he repeated, whistling softly.

Nothing.

Donning a pair of latex gloves of his own, Jacob followed Rudy inside. As they entered, Jacob noticed a light blinking on an alarm panel by the door. Forcing himself to remain calm, he glanced at his watch. "Thirty seconds."

With a nod, Rudy inspected a Vivint wireless alarm panel mounted in the entry, then punched in the numerals 2580, entering a factory-preset duress code to disarm the system. In addition to deactivating the alarm, the Vivint "secret" duress code, designed for use by someone being forced to deactivate his or her alarm, was also programmed to notify the police. The panel's emergency call, however, was being blocked by Jacob's jammer, preventing the internal radio circuit from linking to a nearby cell tower.

With the system now deactivated, Rudy entered another factory-preset default sequence, this time punching in the installer code 2203. Moments later he had access to the entire system.

"No one ever changes the defaults," said Rudy, making note of Kane's master code. Then, pressing another series of buttons, "What code do you want to add?"

Jacob thought for a moment. "6666," he said, deciding to pick an easy sequence to remember.

Rudy paused, concentrating on programming in Jacob's new code. "Okay, done."

"Excellent." Jacob again checked his watch. "We have five minutes to reconnoiter the residence. And if possible, to find a key."

"Right," said Rudy.

"Five minutes," Jacob repeated. "No more."

Chapter 47

The weather took a turn for the worse on our drive back from Sylmar, with the wind picking up and storm clouds gathering over the ocean to the west. Fighting freeway traffic on our way in, I phoned the other members of our team, bringing them up to date on our visit with Sally Perkins. After asking them all to meet us in the West L.A. squad room, I next called Jimmy Wú, a friend who worked in the LAPD's latent prints unit. Although Jimmy was off-duty for the weekend, he agreed to join us in West L.A. as well—no questions asked.

In recent years, staffing shortages and LAPD budget cuts had created a backlog in the department's fingerprint analysis unit, with thousands of theft, burglary, and other property crimes going unprosecuted as a result. The situation had deteriorated to the point where detectives and sometimes even patrol officers were being trained to collect latent-print evidence at selected crime scenes, allowing analysts more time to work on other cases. As such, I had received basic fingerprint training myself, and I briefly considered attempting to lift latent prints from Parker's weapons. In the end I decided against it. Given the situation, any evidence we recovered was simply too important to risk screwing things up.

We found Jimmy Wú waiting for us at the station when we arrived. As requested, he had brought a fingerprint kit with him. After describing what we needed, I set Jimmy up at an empty desk in the back and gave him the pillowcase-wrapped shoebox. Next, Taylor and I met with the rest of our team in Long's office. As we waited for Jimmy's results, I reviewed what Taylor and I had learned in Sylmar, stressing that confirmation of our suspicions would depend on matching any latent prints recovered from Parker's guns to one of the unidentified terrorists at the Clark residence.

"Damn, amigo," said Arnie when I'd finished. "This could be it."

"Maybe," I said. Then, glancing around at the others. "So

305

where do we go from here?"

Taylor spoke up. "Assuming we get a print match, we don't have a choice. We turn everything over to the Bureau."

"Or to Snead's task force," said Deluca.

"Or both," said Long.

"I'm not saying I disagree, but let's think about this for a minute," I suggested, not willing to turn things over just yet. "Snead and the Bureau have both discounted the cellphone-jammer theory, so no one at either agency is going to be particularly receptive. Without authorization, we followed up on the jammer lead ourselves and came up with a name—Parker Dillon. If Parker turns out to be one of the dead guys at the Clark house, maybe our unauthorized investigation gets forgiven. But then what?"

"Then it's out of our hands," said Taylor. "We have to—"

"I hate to point this out, but we still don't have enough for an arrest, or even a search warrant," I interrupted. "Before we do anything, I think we should check out Parker's so-called intentional community. His affiliation with some Trancas Canyon cult may have nothing to do with the terrorist killings."

"But if Snead or the Bureau stomp out there in the meantime, we lose the element of surprise," reasoned Deluca, picking up on my train of thought. "Or worse, like Kane said, maybe Parker's cult has nothing to do with the terrorists, in which case we all look like idiots. We should at least check things out first."

"Makes sense to me," said Banowski.

"I'm in," added Arnie.

Everyone glanced at Lieutenant Long, who as the ranking member present had the final say.

"Well, we've gone this far," Long sighed. "Assuming the prints match and we can locate this intentional community compound of Parker's, surveillance would normally be the next step to confirm we're on the right track. How about this: Let's head out there tomorrow and check things out. If it looks like we're on the right track, we give everything to Snead and the Bureau first thing Monday morning. That work for you, Taylor?"

Reluctantly, Taylor nodded. "I suppose waiting one more day

won't make any difference. Unfortunately, I'm not certain how to explain things when we do finally reveal the results of our, uh . . . independent investigation."

"Simple. You came up with this on your own," I suggested. Then, to Deluca, "You, too, Paul. Figure a way to leave the rest of us out of it."

"I could say I checked on some jammer purchases in my spare time and got lucky," said Deluca.

I looked at Taylor. "How about you?"

"I guess I could do the same," she said. "Anyway, if our information pans out, it's possible no one is going to be looking too hard at the source."

I thought a moment. "Okay, next step. Does anyone have an idea on how to locate this commune of Parker's?"

"I saw something on TV last week about intentional communities," offered Arnie. "It's the politically correct term now for communes."

"I saw that, too," Deluca chimed in. "A lot of hippy collectives are still in operation, not to mention a bunch of new ones—over a thousand in the U.S. alone. I think the show mentioned a registry. Want me to check it out?"

"Yeah, do that."

"I'll help," said Arnie.

"Me, too," added Banowski.

"Fine," I said. Then, to Taylor, "Let's see how Jimmy is doing."

Working with different fingerprint powders and a special LED light, my latent-prints friend had raised a number of fingerprints on Parker's pistols, and a few on the shoebox as well. When Taylor and I joined him, Jimmy had just finished lifting a print with clear tape. "Raised a few good, clear latents," he said, attaching the tape to a white "lift card" for preservation.

"Can you do a comparison for us?" I asked.

"Sure, if you have comparison prints handy. Tenprint cards, JPEG photos, something like that?"

I glanced at Taylor.

"I have access to the IAFIS fingerprint files," she said.

"Perfect," said Jimmy. "Can you email them to me?"

"No problem."

Using her phone, Taylor transmitted the IAFIS files in question to Jimmy's email address. Within minutes my friend had the prints from Parker's guns displayed on his laptop, arranged side-by-side with those of the unidentified terrorists from the Clark residence. By then the rest of our team had joined us.

"Anything?" I asked, peering over Jimmy's shoulder.

"Just a sec," said Jimmy, scanning through the IAFIS files. Then, leaning closer, he said, "Bingo."

I felt an electric current pass through our group.

"A match?" I asked.

"One hundred percent," Jimmy answered, lining up an IAFIS thumbprint with a latent he'd lifted from one of Parker's guns. "Right down to the scar," he added, using the computer cursor to point out a V-shaped notch in the whorls and ridges on two adjacent prints.

We all stared at the screen. Even to a layman, the match was unmistakable.

"Damn," Deluca said softly.

I glanced at my print-analyst friend. "Thanks, Jimmy. I appreciate your help, but I don't want to take up any more of your time."

"What do you want me to do with this stuff?" Jimmy asked, indicating at his stack of latent print cards. "You have a case number?"

"Leave the cards with me for now," I said. "Email me the latent-print photos, too."

"I get it," said Jimmy. "I wasn't here, right?"

"You were never here. Not unless I need you to suddenly remember."

"Understood. You owe me one, Dan."

"Anytime, Jimmy."

After Jimmy had departed, I turned to Arnie. "Any success locating the Trancas Canyon site?"

"Yep. I was right about the commune thing," Arnie replied. "As I thought, they're now being called intentional communities, and there are thousands of them—241 in California alone. Many are religious, with different levels of membership and so on, but some fulfill secular purposes as well. I located a registry listing all those in Southern California. One name jumped out—The Christian Apostolic Community Foundation, located in Trancas Canyon."

"Christian?" I said. "Not Muslim?"

"Christian," said Arnie.

"Some old hippy communes were nonprofits, so I checked the California Secretary of State database," Long jumped in, referring to his notes. "The Christian Apostolic Community Foundation is an active nonprofit corporation that was registered with the State of California about five years ago. The corporate officers are Jacob Lee Wallace, president; Caleb Wallace, secretary; and Zoe Yoder, treasurer. I ran those names through the DOJ and NCIC computers. No hits."

"I checked the commune's IRS status," added Banowski. "The Christian Apostolic Community Foundation is listed as a tax-exempt 501(c)3 religious organization. The registered contact name is Jacob Wallace."

"Any mention of Parker Dillon?"

"No."

"Anything else?"

"I located the compound on Google Earth," said Deluca. "Check it out."

We trailed Deluca to his workstation, where he had a satellite view of a heavily wooded area displayed on his computer. Winding up the center of the screen was a narrow street labeled Trancas Canyon Road. After passing the outskirts of a more developed area near the coast, the road continued up the canyon, eventually dead-ending in the trees. Near its terminus lay The Christian Apostolic Foundation.

"Can you zoom in?" I asked.

"Sure." Deluca expanded the image, bringing the Christian Foundation grounds into closer view. A large building sat in a meadow in the center of the compound, with a number of smaller structures scattered around it. A significant portion of the surrounding grounds appeared to be under cultivation, with a stream and irrigation ditches traversing the canyon to the west and livestock pens bordering a wooded area to the north.

I stared at the screen, wondering whether this pastoral setting could harbor a terrorist enclave. The prospect seemed to be growing less likely by the minute.

As Arnie and the others began discussing the best position from which to run our surveillance the following morning, I stepped away to check my security webcams—something I hadn't done since visiting Sally Perkins in Sylmar. After returning to my squad-room workstation, something else I hadn't done in quite some time, I booted up my computer. After logging into Padilla's surveillance archive, I found I had four new motion-activated incidents from Allison's house, along with seven more from the beach. The first three from Ali's residence were the neighborhood dog again. The fourth was a kid selling Girl Scout cookies.

With a sigh, I checked the motion-activated incidents at the beach. Like Allison's, the first two were useless—a bird on our back deck, and another dog. The next one sent a shiver up my spine.

The third archived video showed two men outside my front door. One was tall and lean, with rawboned hands and a hard, deeply lined face. The shorter of the two was built like a block of granite and looked vaguely familiar. Both were wearing workmen's coveralls. As I watched, the shorter one pulled on latex gloves and went to work with an electric pick gun. Within seconds he'd unlocked my front door.

The camera picked up their entry, losing them as they stepped inside. Two additional incidents were recorded when the men activated concealed webcams in the house. A final shot from the front-door camera showed them as they exited. Scrolling back, I checked the timestamps. The men had been in my house for under six minutes, and they had been gone for almost an hour.

What had they been doing inside?

I had been arming my home security system each day upon leaving, and I was sure I'd set the alarm that morning. I considered calling the Malibu Sheriffs and sending them out. After a moment's thought, I decided against it. Maybe I *had* left the alarm off. And anyway, the intruders were gone. Nevertheless, the presence of those men in my house shocked me more than I wanted to admit.

I replayed the video from the beach house one more time, pausing on a frame that showed the intruders' faces. As I listened to Deluca and Banowski going over details of tomorrow's surveillance operation, I stared at the screen. Although balaclavas had concealed the terrorists' features on their murder videos, I thought I recognized the short, muscular one—almost certain he was the killer who had stared into the camera lens while butchering Gary Welch.

Taylor was the first to notice that something was wrong. "You okay, Kane?" she called across the room.

"Yeah, why so glum, *paisano*?" added Deluca. "I've got a good feeling about this. I think we found our guys. In fact, I'm sure of it."

I nodded, a sick feeling growing inside. Things were moving quickly, and I realized we were approaching an end I couldn't foresee.

"Yeah," I said, still staring at the computer screen. "And they found me."

Chapter 48

The following morning, the El Niño-fueled storm that had been gathering over the ocean the previous afternoon struck full force, with sheets of rain sweeping the Southland and a fierce southerly wind whipping the Santa Monica Bay into an angry cauldron of white. From the looks of the downpour, I knew it was only a matter of time until flooded culverts and rain-triggered mudslides made life miserable for coastal residents, not to mention every commuter passing through. As usual, February in Malibu was shaping up to be a wet, miserable month.

Upon returning home the previous evening, I had found my security system armed, just as I had thought I'd left it. Although I still hadn't figured out how the intruders avoided tripping the alarm, I knew it was possible, and at my first opportunity I intended to call Charlie Padilla and find out. On the upside, the presence of the two prowlers now gave me reason to request a resumption of Metro's protective surveillance. For the moment, however, as my family was safely out of the picture, I decided to postpone a decision on that. Nevertheless, in the hope that the intruders might return, Deluca, Banowski, Arnie, and I again spent the night at the beach, alternating watch every two hours.

We had no visitors.

The next morning our team assembled well before dawn, meeting at a Malibu café that opened early. Taylor, who had insisted on being included on the surveillance, and Lieutenant Long, who also had to drive up from Santa Monica, arrived after the rest of us had ordered coffee and taken a table near the rear. Long looked tired. With a nod in our direction, he stepped to the counter and ordered a large coffee. Arriving a few minutes later, Taylor ordered tea. Paper cups in hand, they both joined us at our booth.

"Any luck with your facial recognition attempt?" I asked Taylor as she slid into the booth beside me. She had taken screenshot photos of the intruders from my computer, suggesting that feeding the images through the Bureau's Criminal Justice

Information Service's facial-recognition system was worth a try.

Taylor shook her head. "Facial recognition takes time, if it works at all. Duffy's working on it."

"Duffy? What did you tell him?"

"I emailed him the files and asked him to see whether any names popped up."

"That's it? You didn't tell him anything else?"

Taylor hesitated. "I, uh, did give him the names of the corporate officers listed on the State of California filing. I thought it might help with the facial recognition search."

"Damn, Taylor," said Banowski. "Now the feds are in on this?"

"Don't worry, I told Duffy to keep quiet," Taylor replied. "Besides, tomorrow we're turning everything over to the Bureau anyway, right?"

"Right," I said, unable to hide my irritation. "Depending on what we find. This still may turn into a wild goose chase."

"Maybe, but I have a feeling about this," said Deluca. "Speaking of which, what are we looking for out there? Guys wearing balaclavas waving ISIS flags?"

"That would be great," I said with a brief smile. "Barring that, spotting either of the men who broke into my house would be grounds for a search warrant. A vehicle with phony magnetic signs or stolen license plates would be another."

"The presence of an automatic weapon would be cause for a search warrant, too," Arnie pointed out. "Let's keep our eyes peeled and see what turns up."

"Right," Long agreed. "Everyone bring binoculars, raingear, and vests?"

"I forgot my raincoat," Banowski mumbled. "We're not gonna be in the cars?"

Yesterday, after studying a satellite view of Trancas Canyon, we had selected several possible surveillance positions, including a fire road that overlooked the compound. Unfortunately, we were still unsure whether any of those sites would offer vehicle concealment. "Maybe, maybe not," I answered. "We might have to leave our cars and head up there on foot. If that's the case, we'll break into teams and take turns in the rain. Don't worry, Banowski. If it comes to that, you and I can alternate using my raingear."

"Assuming John can squeeze his fat ass into your stuff," noted Deluca.

"Hey, I just started a new diet," said Banowski, patting his stomach. "Gonna lose twenty pounds by this summer."

"Only thirty left to go," laughed Deluca. "Face it, Banowski. Your idea of a balanced diet is a beer in each hand."

"Screw you, Paul."

"Enough, you two," I said, checking my watch. "We need to get moving if we want to be in position by first light."

"I agree," said Long, rising to his feet. "Let's do this."

In the interest of maintaining a low profile, we decided to drive two of our vehicles to Trancas Canyon and to leave the others at the Malibu coffee shop. As we began loading our weapons, ballistic vests, and raingear into my Suburban and Long's Chrysler sedan, I noticed that in addition to her other gear, Taylor had brought what appeared to be a scoped rifle in a gun case.

At my questioning look at this, Taylor shrugged. "You never know," she said, piling into the Suburban beside me. "Pays to be prepared."

The drive up the coast to Trancas Canyon took about twenty minutes. Deluca had printed several Google satellite maps of the area, and with one of them for reference, Taylor acted as my navigator. Upon proceeding several miles up the canyon, we stopped short of the road's dead-end terminus, ensuring we wouldn't be visible from the compound. After donning raingear, Taylor and I abandoned the Suburban and continued on foot, leaving Long and the others to conceal the vehicles.

Taylor and I arrived at the compound perimeter about a quarter-mile farther on. Stepping off the dirt road, we took a washed-out fire trail to the right, climbing the canyon's southern ridge to a point where we could make out most of the intentional community grounds. The trees bordering the fire trail were sparse, barely offering adequate cover for someone on foot, and I was glad we had left the cars farther back.

After a brief inspection of the compound, Taylor and I made our way back down, rejoining Long and the others at the cars. By then they had concealed our vehicles well off the road, and minutes later the eastern sky began lightening to a somber gray. With the coming of dawn, the rain, which earlier had eased to a steady drizzle, again increased to a downpour. Following a short conference, Taylor, Arnie, and I decided to take the first watch. Long and Banowski stayed with the cars, agreeing to relieve us in two hours.

The original plan had been for our teams to stay in touch via cellphone, but upon arriving we'd found there was no phone service in the canyon, and unfortunately we had neglected to bring radios. Hoping a lack of communication wouldn't be an issue, Arnie, Taylor, and I returned to the fire trail and spread out, each taking a vantage position that covered a different portion of the compound.

Hours passed. We were relieved by Long's team. Two hours later, we again relieved them. Banowski and I repeatedly traded off raingear, with the result that both of us wound up getting soaked. During that time the enclave slowly came to life, with more than thirty men, women, and children going about their morning activities.

At around 9:30 a.m., compound members began drifting into a large central structure. There they remained for over an hour, eventually coming out to resume their daily routines. Disappointingly, at no time did we see any sign of the men who had broken into my house. Nor did we note the presence of automatic weapons, stolen vehicles, phony magnetic signs, or any other basis for a search warrant.

Chapter 49

From his perch high in the canyon, sheltered from the storm by the walls of his rocky outcrop, Jacob gazed down upon his compound. With a feeling of satisfaction, he decided that his morning service had gone well. Extremely well, in fact. Even the storm seemed to have enhanced his sermon as he spoke the gospel of God, an occasional stroke of lightning and the subsequent rumble of thunder adding both power and authority to his words.

Although recent setbacks had skewed Jacob's timetable, he had faith that his holy mission would continue unabated once certain obstacles had been removed, obstacles that included the troublesome Detective Kane. The decision to remove Kane before others were taken was a necessary delay, as Kane's death would serve as a warning to all.

Besides, it was God's will.

It had been days since God had spoken to Jacob. Although puzzled by his Creator's silence, Jacob sat patiently beneath his outcrop, hoping to hear the sound of God's voice once more.

And as he waited, Jacob noticed something puzzling.

A quarter-mile down the canyon, hidden from the compound grounds but easily visible from his elevated position, Jacob noticed that two vehicles had been parked off the road, partially concealed beneath the branches of a large oak. One of the vehicles, a dark sedan, was occupied by several men, although Jacob couldn't make out their faces. The other, a large SUV, looked empty.

Alarmed, Jacob eased back beneath the rocky ledge, focusing his attention on the surrounding hillsides. Within minutes he saw the first of them, the watcher's position betrayed by the brief flash of a binocular lens. Moments later Jacob discovered two more.

They had found him.

Jacob didn't know how, but of that he was certain. They had found him.

Where had he gone wrong? The stolen van? The magnetic signs? The murder videos? His visit to Kane's house?

Think!

Forcing himself not to panic, Jacob pondered the situation, his mind racing. The authorities couldn't be sure. Not yet, anyway. Otherwise they would have come for him, instead of lurking out there in the woods.

They couldn't be certain, Jacob assured himself. Besides, God wouldn't allow him to be discovered like this. It had to be a mistake.

No, they know, Jacob realized, finally accepting the horrible truth.

They might not be able to prove it, but they know.

Think!

Although it didn't matter how he had been discovered, Jacob suspected that Kane had somehow played a part. Kane had ruined their operation in Rivas Canyon. Kane had demeaned their holy cause during his insulting news conference. Worst of all, Kane had killed Caleb and Parker and Ethan. God had told him that Kane was the Devil, and Jacob berated himself for not acting sooner on that knowledge.

Nevertheless, what mattered now was what happened next.

For almost every situation in life, Jacob had made contingency plans, should something go wrong. He needed to continue doing the will of God. Everything else was secondary, as was everyone else. Evidence could be destroyed, witnesses eliminated, and escape was still possible. Thanks to funds amassed from his intentional community donors, Jacob had the resources to begin again . . . but only if he were free to do so.

Shaken, Jacob rose to his feet. Following an almost invisible trail down the hillside, his mouth set in a grim line of determination, Jacob descended to the compound. God, in His wisdom, had helped Jacob prepare a plan for just such an occasion.

The time had come to set that plan in motion.

Chapter 50

Toward the end of my second watch, people in the compound again began flocking into the central building. This time things were different. The earlier assembly had been a casual, unhurried affair. This one smacked of panic.

Taylor glanced over at me from her position thirty yards to my left. Hoping our presence hadn't been detected, I shrugged, letting her know I wasn't sure what was going on. I looked over at Arnie, who was hunkered down behind a clump of bushes to my right. Arnie shook his head, indicating he didn't know what was happening, either.

Shortly afterward, Long's team arrived to relieve us. I decided to stay, hoping to learn what had sparked the compound's sudden activity. Taylor and Arnie stayed, too. Minutes later, although we still hadn't determined the cause of the rush to the central building, something else happened that none of us had anticipated.

Plowing up the muddy road, a dark SUV fishtailed into the compound, skidding to a stop inside the compound grounds. Badge in hand, Agent Duffy stepped from the vehicle. A second man I didn't recognize exited the other side of the SUV, also waving his credentials.

"What the hell?" said Long.

"Jesus, Duffy," said Taylor, staring down at the compound. "What are you doing?"

"Damn, Taylor," I said, getting a bad feeling as I watched Duffy and his partner exit their car. "Looks like Agent Duffy took your facial-recognition request and ran with it."

A door to the central building swung open. A short, muscular man stepped out. He was holding a newspaper over his head to shield him from the rain. I trained my binoculars on him, feeling a surge of excitement. "That's one of the guys who broke into my house."

"Are you certain?" asked Long, raising his own binoculars. "My eyes aren't as sharp as yours, Kane. A warrant requires a positive ID."

"I'm sure," I said.

"Me, too," said Taylor. "And my eyes are just fine. That's one of the guys on Kane's security video."

Newspaper overhead, the muscular man approached Duffy. The two exchanged words. Then, with a glance at the sky, the muscular man began walking back toward the central building, indicating for Duffy and his partner to follow.

"Oh, God, Duffy," said Taylor softly. "Don't go in there."

Seconds later Duffy and his partner disappeared into the compound building.

"Now what?" said Arnie. "Call for backup, or just bust in?"

"Too many people down there," I said. "We're going to need backup."

An instant later we heard the bark of a gunshot. The sharp report came from the direction of the central building. Moments later we heard the sound of a second shot, followed in rapid succession by two more. Then silence.

"God damn it, Duffy," said Taylor, tears starting in her eyes. "What the hell were you thinking?"

"It may not be . . . what you think," I said. "There could be another explanation."

"Yeah, maybe," Taylor mumbled.

I could tell she didn't believe it. Neither did I.

I glanced at Long. "The keys are still in our cars, right?"

Long nodded. "Driver's side floor."

I turned to Taylor. "Go back to our vehicles. Take my Suburban down the canyon," I said, hoping that giving her something to do would take her mind off Duffy. "As soon as you get into cellphone range, call LAPD for reinforcements. Tell them we need SWAT out here ASAP. Have them send a hostage negotiator, too. And call the Bureau. We're going to need all the help we can get."

Her face pale with shock, Taylor turned and started down the canyon.

Lowering my head against a gust of rain, I watched as Taylor's slim figure disappeared into the downpour. Then I returned my attention to the compound, worried that I couldn't tell what was happening inside.

I remembered reading somewhere that in war, even the best battle plans rarely survived first contact with the enemy. Our situation seemed proof of that. Despite efforts to the contrary, our surveillance had probably been spotted, explaining the sudden rush into the central building. And now Duffy and his partner were inside the enemy camp, being held hostage . . . or worse. We all wanted to do something, anything, to help them. But we couldn't.

There was nothing to do but wait.

*****

With a nightmarish sense of déjà vu, Jacob ran, thorny undergrowth tearing at his arms and legs as he climbed higher into the canyon. Slipping on the muddy path, he raced past his rocky overlook without looking back. Though his muscles ached and his lungs burned, he forced himself to keep going. When the time came, the more distance he had put between himself and the compound, the better.

Earlier Jacob had heard gunshots, followed by silence. Wondering whether authorities had finally decided to attack, he kept moving, forcing himself not to panic. He had tasked Rudy with covering his escape, which might explain the gunfire. If nothing else, Rudy was dependable when it came to violence.

A half-mile higher on the ridge, his breath now coming in ragged sobs, Jacob began descending into an adjacent drainage. Picking his way down a steep incline to the west, he made his way toward Encinal Canyon Road, a parallel byway that accessed other roads to the north.

And those roads led to freedom.

Several miles down Encinal Canyon Road, Jacob had hidden a pickup truck in an abandoned shack. The nondescript vehicle concealed there contained weapons, money, bank passbooks, and new ID. It was for the shelter of that shack that Jacob now headed. Once there he would have everything he needed to start over. Careful not to slip as he descended, Jacob smiled grimly, recalling his vow in Rivas Canyon. Before starting over, despite the danger it would entail, he knew there was still one thing left to do.

Lowering his head against the stinging rain, Jacob continued on, certain that the Lord would provide for his safety.

Chapter 51

Twenty minutes later, when nothing new had developed, Arnie and I decided to return to where we'd hidden the cars, leaving Long, Deluca, and Banowski to watch the compound. Just as we reached Long's vehicle, I noticed my Suburban side-slipping toward us through the downpour—windshield wipers flapping, a thick layer of mud caking all four tires. Arnie and I stepped to the shelter of a nearby oak, watching as Taylor careened to a stop.

"Backup's on the way," Taylor announced as she piled out of the Suburban. "LAPD is dispatching a SWAT unit and a hostage negotiator, like you asked. The Bureau is sending an HRT squad, and every available officer from both agencies is on the way out here. Before long, this place is going to look like a police convention."

"In that case, let's move our vehicles up to the fire road," I suggested. "I don't want my car getting shot up, and I'm sure Long doesn't, either—but they could provide cover if things go south."

"Good idea," said Arnie. "Not to mention that it would be nice to get out of this goddamn miserable rain."

"That, too," I agreed.

We drove the cars up to the compound, positioning them to block any cult members attempting to leave. Next we donned our ballistic vests, deciding to err on the side of caution. As Taylor had pointed out, the area would soon be swarming with men carrying guns. When that happened, compound members might start shooting, and a vest might come in handy. Also, although not often mentioned, in similar situations it wasn't inconceivable for someone to catch a friendly bullet, in which case a vest could come in handy as well.

While waiting for backup, we decided to have two of our team guard the compound while the others stayed dry inside the vehicles, alternating watch every twenty minutes. Banowski, who was still sharing my raincoat, had just relieved me at my surveillance post when I heard the crack of a high-powered rifle. I turned in time to see Banowski's right leg buckle. A red spray jetted from the back of his thigh.

Banowski collapsed, screaming in agony.

Heart in my throat, I raced back. A clump of ground exploded near Banowski's head. An instant later I heard the crack of a second shot. I had thought we were out of gunfire range from the compound. Clearly, I was wrong.

"Hang on, John," I said, grabbing Banowski beneath his shoulders. Digging in my heels, I began dragging him toward the cars.

A bullet thumped into a nearby tree, followed by another report from the opposite ridge. "I have to get you out of here," I said, slipping in the mud as I hauled Banowski backward.

Banowski moaned, clutching his thigh. By then blood had soaked through his pants. From the angle of his twisted leg, it looked like the rifle slug had shattered his femur.

Another shot struck wide to the left. I looked over my shoulder in time to see a muzzle flash high on the canyon wall, accompanied by another bullet zinging over our heads. Gritting my teeth, I kept dragging, hoping to make it to safety before the gunman dialed in our range.

Somehow we made it. Once at the shelter of our vehicles, I stripped off my belt. Arnie found a tree branch, and together we fashioned a crude tourniquet to stem Banowski's bleeding—at least temporarily. Then, leaving a sweaty, cursing Banowski in Arnie's care, I rejoined the rest of our team behind Long's Chrysler.

Although there were no further shots from the sniper, I knew the man on the ridge wasn't done. And when our reinforcements began arriving, he would have a lot more targets. I thought a moment. "We need someone down the road," I said. "Our guys need to know there's a shooter up there with a rifle."

"I'll go," said Deluca.

"Thanks, Paul," I said. "And when our forces get here, make sure Banowski receives medical treatment ASAP. And inform SWAT there's a friendly up on the ridge."

Steve Gannon

"You're going up there?" said Long.

"Someone has to. Otherwise, we're all sitting ducks."

"Be careful, *paisano*," said Deluca. "I'm too old to be breaking in a new partner."

"Don't worry, I'll be fine," I said, wishing I was as sure of myself as I sounded.

From the muzzle flash I had noticed earlier, I knew the approximate position of the rifleman. Assuming he hadn't moved, my plan was to ascend the eastern ridge of the canyon, staying out of sight of the sniper. After reaching higher ground, I would drop down on his position. What happened then would be up to him.

Not much of a plan, but sometimes simple was best.

I withdrew my Glock and confirmed the presence of a chambered round, with thirteen more in the magazine. Along with a pair of fully loaded spare magazines, I figured I was ready.

After returning the pistol to my shoulder rig, I started up the slope, following a gully that shielded me from the western ridge. Lowering my head against the downpour, I scrambled up through low bushes and loose rocks, clawing my way up the steep incline. Twenty minutes of hard climbing brought me to a promontory with a commanding view of the valley. By then I was muddy, cold, and soaked to the skin.

Careful to stay out of view of the western canyon wall, I noted that police reinforcements had started to arrive. A SWAT van was parked several hundred yards down the road from the compound, flanked by a swarm of black-and-whites and several unmarked Bureau vehicles. Among the men gathered near the SWAT van, I thought I recognized Captain Snead, SAC Gibbs, and ASAC Vaughn, although at that distance I couldn't be certain. I also thought I detected a flash of movement lower down on the opposite ridge, but I couldn't be certain of that, either.

Hoping someone else might be attempting to flank the sniper's position from the other side, I took a few seconds to catch my breath. Staying under cover, I watched as a SWAT team moved into position closer to the compound. An officer with a bullhorn accompanied them. A moment later I heard his amplified voice echoing up from below.

"Jacob Wallace, this is Officer Bruce Moore of the Los Angeles Police Department," the voice said. "Your compound is surrounded. You and your followers have no chance of escape. We can end this peacefully, but first you must release Special Agents Duffy and Gutierrez."

No response.

"Mr. Wallace, please allow Special Agents Duffy and Gutierrez to leave the building. You must let them leave so we can end this peacefully."

This time there was a response, but it didn't come from the compound. A shot rang out from the western ridge, striking a SWAT team operator. The officer fell to the ground, blood gushing from his throat. Staying low, several team members began dragging him back toward the SWAT van.

I wasn't sure whether the sniper's bullet had been the work of a master marksman, or merely a lucky shot. Given the number of police personnel present, I hoped for the latter. Either way, the SWAT retreat seemed a signal for those inside the compound to begin shooting as well. Within seconds the area sounded like a war zone.

In response, additional police units moved in, firing at the compound. Tear gas canisters were lobbed as well—at that distance most of them coming up short.

Again, the rifleman on the opposite ridge resumed firing. I took a moment to memorize his location. From my elevated location, I could see that he was shooting from beneath an overhanging ledge, high on the far side of the canyon. I estimated it would take me ten to fifteen minutes to get into position to drop down on him from above.

Maybe less, if I hurried.

I set out again, topping the gully minutes later. From there I moved left, traversing to a position above the gunman. Breathing hard from the climb, I then began working my way down, taking care not to dislodge anything that might alert the shooter of my presence. By then the sniper had again stopped firing, making his position difficult to pinpoint. Worse, during my traverse I had lost sight of the overhang, and for a moment I thought I'd descended too far.

There!

Just below me, I saw the rock ledge.

I withdrew my Glock.

What now?

The overhang was more massive than I'd first estimated, the space beneath it easily large enough for a man to stand within.

Bushes blocked my view. I didn't have a shot from my position. I considered retreating and approaching from the other side. Either that, or rushing the overhang and trying to take out the sniper before he could react.

"Don't move, cop."

The voice came from behind me.

I knew I'd made a fatal mistake.

"Don't turn around."

Sweat trickled down my back.

"You're Kane, aren't you?" the voice demanded.

I didn't bother responding.

"It's you. I recognize you from TV."

Again I didn't respond, preparing to make my move. Unless he had a handgun, the shooter probably had his rifle zeroed on my spine, or maybe pointed at the back of my head. I also knew that at close range my ballistic vest would prove worthless against a high-powered rifle.

But if he missed with his first rifle shot, the gunman would have to chamber another cartridge for a second attempt. That might give me time to fire back . . . if I was still alive.

I'd only have one chance, and it was a slim one.

"Drop the gun," the voice commanded.

Without my weapon, I had no chance at all.

"Drop the gun and I'll make this easy on you. If you don't, I promise you'll be thankful to finally die."

I took a deep breath. Regretting all the things I had left unsaid, all the times I had wasted, and all the loved ones I had disappointed, I extended my gun hand out to my side. Slowly, I eased to one knee, as if preparing to place the Glock on the loose shale at my feet. An instant later I dropped to the ground and tumbled to the right, hoping to get off a shot.

I was too late.

I heard the crack of a rifle.

Strangely, I felt no pain.

How could he have missed?

Heart pounding, I rolled onto my back and quickly brought up my Glock. The fire-plug intruder I had seen in my house stood several yards away. A puzzled expression twisted his features. A widening patch of red bloomed on his chest. His rifle slipped from his grip, clattering to the rocks at his feet.

The man stared at me with a look of surprise. He sank to his knees. Moments later he fell forward and slid down the slope, coming to rest with his face in the mud.

Keeping my Glock trained on him, I rose to my feet. Moving closer, I kicked away his rifle. Then, carefully, I leaned down and searched him for other weapons. He had a sheathed knife, which I removed. Finally I checked for a pulse.

There was none.

"Is he dead?"

Turning, I saw Taylor. She was carrying her scoped rifle.

"Yeah," I answered. "He's dead."

Her face pale, Taylor made her way to the outcrop, never taking her eyes from the gunman. I remembered the first man I had killed, and I knew how she felt. It wasn't good.

"I . . . I was too far away to give warning," Taylor stammered. " I thought he was going to shoot you, and . . ."

"He *was* going to shoot me, Taylor. I owe you my life. Thank you."

"Thank my dad," Taylor replied shakily. "Along with kayaking, he taught me to hunt."

"I'm glad he did." Then, noticing the look on Taylor's face, I searched for something to say that might ease the feelings I knew she was experiencing. I searched, and came up short.

Echoing from the compound below, the sound of gunfire reminded me there was still a police action taking place down there. I took a deep breath, then let it out. "Maybe we should head back and—"

A gigantic explosion suddenly rocked the valley.

Taylor and I both ducked—a reflex cringe triggered by the blast. Then, turning, we stared in disbelief at the valley below.

The meeting hall into which Duffy and his partner had disappeared no longer existed. Instead, building materials, roofing shingles, and body parts were now raining from the sky, littering the meadow in an expanding ring of absolute and utter destruction. Fire was rapidly consuming what little was left of the central structure, with billows of smoke and ash rising on a twisting pillar of flame. Of the men, women, and children who had been inside, clearly there were no survivors.

"Oh, my God," said Taylor. "All those people . . ."

Fortunately, most of our forces had been far enough away to escape injury. Nevertheless, having been in a similar situation, I knew that every officer close by wouldn't be hearing well for the next several weeks. Many of them, especially the nearest SWAT units, were still lying flat on the ground where they had been knocked by the explosion. As Bureau agents and LAPD officers began slowly rising to their feet, I turned to Taylor. "I'm sorry about Duffy," I said. "His partner, too."

"They were probably already dead," Taylor said quietly.

"Either way, I'm sorry."

"Me, too."

With an expression of utter desolation, Taylor turned and again regarded the man she had killed. The terrorist she'd shot had deserved to die. There was no arguing that. But having been there myself, I knew that for Taylor, nothing would ever again be the same. And with that realization, I finally knew what I wanted to say.

It wasn't much, but it was all I had.

"You did good, Sara," I said.

Standing in the steadily falling rain, Taylor raised her eyes to mine.

"So did you, Kane," she said. "So did you."

Chapter 52

S ilent as a shadow, Jacob stood outside the darkened house. Careful not to make a sound, he used the key stolen on his earlier visit to unlock the front door. Repocketing the key, he withdrew his pistol, eased into the entry, and closed the door behind him.

Inside, the security panel began blinking.

Heart hammering in his chest, Jacob thumbed in a number: 6666.

The blinking stopped. An LED display above the keypad read, "Good evening. Everything looks good. Your system is ready to arm."

He was in.

He paused, hands sweaty inside the latex gloves.

He listened.

Nothing.

He relaxed his grip on the silenced Beretta. Holding his breath, he continued to listen, his other hand fingering the black-handled knife at his waist.

Give it a few minutes. Better safe than sorry.

Still nothing.

Satisfied, Jacob breathed a sigh of relief. Still, he waited several additional minutes before moving, letting his eyes adjust to the darkness.

It was time.

Crabbing down a hallway to the left—pistol out front, back pressed against the wall—he made his way to the master bedroom.

After his escape from the compound, Jacob had watched the beach residence for the past several nights. He knew that only one other person was present in the house, and that person was about to pay for his transgressions.

Jacob had elected to wear a balaclava for tonight's holy mission. When the moment came, he wanted his victim to know what was about to happen, and the mask said it all.

Stealthily, Jacob edged into the Kane's bedroom.

From his earlier visit, Jacob remembered the layout. In patches of moonlight filtering in from a window, he could make out shadowy images in the room—desk, handgun safe, door to an adjacent bathroom. And against the back wall, Kane's king-sized bed.

Kane's bulky form lay outlined beneath the covers, silent and sleeping. The cop was larger than Jacob had first thought, definitely bigger than he would have been able to handle without Rudy.

Taking no chances, Jacob raised his silenced pistol and put a bullet into Kane's lower back, careful not to hit anything too vital. Jacob wanted to cripple Kane, not kill him . . . yet.

Kane had to be alive and conscious when the time came for the knife.

The Beretta's sound suppressor muffled the shot. The blast was nowhere near the "Hollywood quiet" often depicted in films, but quiet enough. Trusting that the noise had been adequately reduced so as not to alert neighbors, Jacob fired two more rounds, putting a bullet into each of Kane's shoulders.

Strangely, although the muzzle flashes temporarily impaired his vision, Jacob sensed that Kane hadn't moved.

Nor had he made a sound.

Something was wrong . . .

"Don't move," a harsh voice commanded.

*****

The intruder froze.

"What happens now is up to you," I warned, the Glock in my hands rock-steady, the muzzle centered on the intruder's back. "Drop your gun, or die."

"You won't shoot me in the back, Detective Kane," the intruder said, not moving. Still gripping his pistol, he raised both arms, extending them outward. "Wouldn't look good on your record, would it?"

"Drop the weapon, Jacob."

The intruder stiffened, telling me I had guessed correctly. "Of course, Detective," he said. "But first, how did you know?"

"Guys like you always leave someone else holding the bag," I replied, my finger tightening on the trigger.

Jacob Lee Wallace's remains hadn't been found in the aftermath of the explosion, opening the possibility that the cult leader might have escaped. It was a possibility I couldn't afford to ignore. I had suspected all along that the commune's unexplained rush to their central building had been the result of our surveillance being discovered. And for our concealed position to have been spotted, someone *outside* the compound must have spotted us. As such, I'd had a hunch I would be getting a visit from that particular someone.

Following our botched surveillance in Trancas Canyon, I had called my Metro friend, Charlie Padilla, hoping to learn how the intruders had breached my security system. Upon examining my alarm panel, Padilla had discovered that someone had added a new entry code, confirming my suspicions. I had instructed Padilla leave in the new code. I had also asked him to leave my webcam surveillance in place, and then to forget he had ever visited.

"Last chance, Jacob," I said. "Drop the gun."

"You're Satan. I don't take orders from the Devil."

The intruder still hadn't moved. He also hadn't dropped his pistol, despite my warning.

"I know what you're thinking," I said, attempting to delay the moment I knew was coming. "I know, because not long ago I was in the exact same position that you are now. You're thinking if you're fast enough, maybe you can get off a shot and take me down. Believe me, that won't happen. You'll be dead the moment you move."

"God put me on this path. He will protect me."

"Like He protected the rest of your followers?"

Upon interviewing the scant few surviving cult members— several fortunate women and a few children who hadn't been in the central building when it exploded—we had learned of Jacob

Lee Wallace's fanatical hatred of Muslims, and of his determination to expel them from our country. From there it hadn't taken much imagination to figure out the rest.

"My followers were a necessary sacrifice. They died so I could continue God's holy work."

"Don't count on God's help this time, Jacob. Live or die. Your choice."

"God will protect me," Jacob repeated.

I tensed.

An instant later he made his decision.

He chose to die.

After kicking away the intruder's weapon and confirming that he was dead, I gazed down at the body, my ears still ringing from the gun blasts. I decided to leave the balaclava mask in place. It seemed appropriate. Besides, I didn't really want to look at his face. I already knew who he was. In my opinion, Jacob Lee Wallace was just another zealot who thought he could do anything in the name of religion, and who had paid the ultimate price for his actions.

Withdrawing my cellphone to report the shooting, I realized once more that killing a man is something you never get over, something you never forget. But if I had things to do over, I wouldn't have done anything differently. Recalling the butchered bodies of Gary and Arleen Welsh, and the Davenports, and the entire Nichols family, and Dr. Clark, and all those who had died at the compound because of the man at my feet, I was again struck by the thought that some people didn't deserve to live.

Jacob Lee Wallace was one of them.

Epilogue

With the coming of spring, weather in Southern California again turned pleasant, the rainsqualls and storm surf and mudslides of winter gradually fading to a distant memory. Days were lengthening, temperatures were rising, and fields of wildflowers, native grasses, and sage were once more blanketing the coastal mountains. Best of all, with the coming of spring, Allison's delivery date was fast approaching as well.

On a sunny Sunday morning in May, Nate and I were eating breakfast outside on our redwood deck. Grandma Dorothy, who for the past several weeks had been staying in Allison's old bedroom upstairs, had recently moved into Ali's guest room in the Palisades, leaving Nate and me to fend for ourselves.

Earlier that morning, Nate and I had attended 8:00 a.m. Mass at Our Lady of Malibu Catholic Church. It was the first time I had been to church in quite a while. After Catheryn's death, I hadn't felt much like going. Actually, I wasn't sure how I felt about God or religion or any of that anymore, as following recent events it had seemed to me that, on balance, the religions of the world may have done more harm than good.

On the other hand, I knew that my admittedly prejudicial opinion wasn't completely fair. It wasn't religion per se that had caused the faith-based suffering of the world. It wasn't Islam, or Christianity, or any of the other sacred philosophies that were at fault. It was the malevolence of men who had perverted those beliefs, twisting them to their own hateful uses. And that perversion was still going on.

Nevertheless, I had driven Nate to church that morning anyway, which I suppose said something. Bottom line, I guess I hoped a spiritual approach might benefit my son, and I wanted to hit his problem from all angles.

Upon returning home, I had prepared us a huge breakfast of pancakes, scrambled eggs, bacon, sausage, fresh-squeezed orange juice, and roasted red potatoes. Although I have always liked spending time in the kitchen, I also realized there was more to my preparing a meal for my son that morning than simply cooking breakfast.

Being male, my natural reaction upon confronting something broken has always been to fix it. Although I understood Nate's problem, both intellectually and emotionally, I also knew that "fixing" my son was utterly beyond my ability. Nevertheless, I guess I thought that if nothing else, I could at least cook for him. Food was something that gave comfort, something I understood. As a result, I spent a lot of time in the kitchen following Nate's return home.

A few days after the windup of the Infidel Case, Nate had been released from the UCLA psychiatric hospital, and for the most part he seemed back to his old self. Although I was still driving him to Westwood on a weekly basis for outpatient counseling, and he was still taking prescription meds, Nate had returned to classes at Santa Monica High and had quickly caught up on his studies. He had even resumed his former position on the Vikings' baseball team. Everything seemed to be back to normal, but I knew from experience that it was impossible to know what was actually going on in someone else's head.

That morning, as we were partway through breakfast, Nate gazed out at the beach. "Know what the ocean said to the shore, Dad?" he asked.

"What?"

Nate grinned. "Nothing. It just waved."

"Good one," I chuckled. "I recall hearing that one in first grade. Brings back memories."

Nate laughed and continued eating, working on a huge portion of scrambled eggs and potatoes piled high on his plate. Then he paused, seeming to sense my thoughts. "Dad, I still miss Mom," he said. "But I'm going to be okay. Stop worrying."

"I know you're going to be okay," I replied, again wishing that Catheryn were there to help. "I can't help worrying, though, at least a little. That's my job. I'm your father."

"As long as it's only a little."

I nodded. "Deal."

"And I'm sorry I caused everyone so much trouble," Nate went on. "I wish I could do a few things over."

"You're no trouble, kid," I said. "Well, maybe a little," I admitted with a smile. "As for doing things over, the world doesn't work that way."

"I know. Nobody ever said life was easy." Nate paused again. Then, changing the subject, "So what do you think about our driving to Idaho to check out Agent Taylor's kayak race?"

Nate had viewed several North Fork Championship videos with me on YouTube, and he'd been as blown away as I had. "Idaho's a long way," I said. "Are you sure you want to go?"

"Oh, yeah. I want to go. Sara promised that after the race, she'd get me into a hard-shell kayak and take me down the Main Fork of the Payette."

"Sara? That's Agent Taylor to you, kid."

"Right. Agent Taylor," Nate corrected. "Anyway, she also said we could camp on the South Fork at a really cool spot where kayakers hang out. It sounds like fun. I like her."

"Yeah. Me, too."

Nate regarded me closely.

"She's a *friend*, Nate," I said, anticipating his question. "I'm not looking for anything more."

Nate remained silent.

"I'm not looking," I repeated, realizing that Nate was being protective of the memory of his mother, and feeling the same way myself. "No one is going to replace your mom. Not now, not ever."

"Well, I still think Agent Taylor is nice," Nate said finally. "And I think we should go."

As this was the first thing in which Nate had shown a real interest in quite a while, I decided to consider it. "A road trip," I mused. "Just you and me? I'll tell you what. I still have a few vacation days left. No guarantees, but I'll see whether I can set things up."

"All right!" said Nate, his face lighting with enthusiasm.

Our conversation had drifted into an area I hadn't anticipated. Given the situation, I wasn't certain whether driving to Idaho for

Taylor's race was a good idea. On the other hand, Nate really wanted to go. Fortunately, my cellphone buzzed before I had to think any further on the subject. The call turned out to be from Mike. As I listened to his message, I felt a grin spreading across my face. "We're on our way," I said.

"What?" asked Nate as soon as I had disconnected.

"Mike, Grandma Dorothy, and your sister are all on their way to Saint John's," I replied, still smiling. "Ali's baby is coming."

"Awesome!" Nate exclaimed, pumping a fist. "I'm going to be an uncle!"

Food forgotten, Nate and I piled into the Suburban, leaving our plates on the table for the birds. We made the drive to Saint John's Health Center in record time, arriving at the Santa Monica hospital where Allison would be delivering her baby.

After leaving our car in a hospital lot, Nate and I wandered a maze of unfamiliar health-center corridors for several minutes. At Nate's insistence, I finally asked directions from a friendly receptionist. With a smile, the woman directed us to the obstetrics department. There, in a comfortable reception room in the McAlister Women's Health Center, we found Grandma Dorothy talking excitedly with Travis and McKenzie, who had flown in earlier that week for the birth.

Christy White, who had been my son Tommy's girlfriend before his accident, arrived minutes later, looking as beautiful as ever. Christy had been pregnant with Tom's baby before his death, and even though she had later lost her child to miscarriage—a devastating blow that had robbed our family of an ongoing connection with Tommy—Christy would always be a member of the Kane family, and I was delighted to see her.

Last of those present, Mike was spending most of his time with Allison in the maternity room, but he occasionally popped in to let us know how things were progressing . . . which turned out to be slowly.

Very slowly.

Arnie arrived later that morning, grinning like he was going to be the new grandfather instead of me. Shortly after that, Deluca, Lieutenant Long, and Banowski showed up as well, also having received calls from Mike. As my thick-necked police friends joined us in the waiting room, I noted that Banowski was still limping. Although he had received emergency medical treatment at Trancas Canyon from a SWAT team doctor, Banowski had come close to losing his leg—something he still jokingly blamed on the tourniquet that Arnie and I had placed. Nevertheless, Banowski was now up and around, and back to work in West L.A.

And so was I.

As for the Infidel Case, credit for bringing the investigation to a successful conclusion had been shared by Mayor Fitzpatrick, Chief Ingram, Assistant Director Shepherd, and Captain Snead's LAPD task force. By then my unauthorized investigation had been retroactively approved by Chief Ingram, and to my surprise, I learned I had been working under the direction of Captain Snead the entire time.

For their work on the case, Lieutenant Long, John Banowski, and Paul Deluca all received commendations. As Arnie had retired from the department years earlier, his presence at the compound that morning was conveniently forgotten. Following a private and somewhat contentious meeting with Chief Ingram, I had also received a commendation letter in my personnel jacket. Later I was even offered back my former position in West L.A.— once more working under Lieutenant Long.

And after discussing the offer with my children, I had accepted, with their blessing.

Special Agent Sara Taylor had experienced a similar situation at the Bureau. As the FBI considered any and all noncompliance with Bureau regulations absolutely unacceptable, the "empty suits at headquarters," as Taylor referred to them, were forced to decide whether to dismiss Taylor for disobeying orders, or to promote her for showing initiative. There could be no in between. After some debate, Bureau HQ informed Taylor that although she had been hired for meeting FBI expectations, she was now being rewarded for exceeding them. As a result of initiative demonstrated on the Infidel Case, Taylor received the FBI's Medal for Meritorious Achievement, along with a bump in pay.

At the time of her commendation, Taylor had requested a temporary leave-of-absence to prepare for the North Fork Championship kayak competition in June. Surprisingly, her request had been granted. Taylor later told me that despite her commendation, she was certain the suits at HQ had granted her a leave-of-absence so they wouldn't have to see her around for a while. Before her departure for Idaho, I had spent some time with Taylor, including having her out to the beach for dinner. While there she had met Nate, and to my surprise, the two of them had hit it off.

Regarding the media, there had been a wave of revived interest in the terrorist story following the Waco-style siege in Trancas Canyon, and in a renewed news blitz, both the Bureau and the LAPD had been blamed for the staggering loss of life at the compound.

Eventually, however, the truth had come out.

With the revelation that members of a Christian organization were responsible for the Los Angeles beheading murders, another media firestorm had again divided the country, quickly spreading to Europe and the Middle East as well. Christian Churches were burned and lives were lost, especially in France, where angry Muslim youths once more set fire to the countryside. Not surprisingly, the media again fanned the flames, adding to the problem. Notably, at no time did any major news organization offer an apology, or accept one iota of responsibility, for the violence over the past months that had been at least partly inspired by sensationalized, inflammatory reporting—reporting that had ultimately proved wrong.

Nevertheless, I did my part to bring out the truth. Asking not to be identified as the source, I had given Allison an early, exclusive interview following Jacob Lee Wallace's midnight visit to the beach house. The facts were going to come out anyway, and I saw no reason Ali shouldn't have them first. Allison had filed her news report from Canada and booked a flight home.

There were many in Chief Ingram's office, especially Assistant Chief Strickland, who would have liked to put a different spin on things. Allison's version of events ended that possibility. Assistant Chief Strickland subsequently accused me of leaking to the press—which, of course, I had. I shrugged at Strickland's accusation and, for the second time in as many months, suggested that he go pound sand.

Based on her coverage of the story, Allison had been offered a network position in New York. After discussing the offer with Mike, she had declined. As I had already lost Travis to the east coast, I was overjoyed with her decision. Although I knew Ali's news broadcasting career in Los Angeles would undoubtedly cause future friction between us, I could deal with that, and having her and Mike and my new granddaughter close by would be worth it.

Later that afternoon at the hospital, as I was about to invite everyone to join me in the cafeteria downstairs for a quick bite to eat, Mike stuck his head into the reception room. From the look on his face, it was obvious that Allison had finally given birth.

"A perfect baby girl," Mike said with a grin. "The doctor said it would be okay for all of us to go back for a few minutes, if we don't stay too long."

"All of us?" asked Arnie.

Mike nodded. "It's a huge room. Ali's exhausted, but she wants to see everyone."

With Mike leading the way, our entire group trooped down a hallway to Ali's maternity room. When we arrived, Allison smiled up from her bed, a sleeping infant cradled in her arms. My daughter looked tired. Tired, but happy.

"Hey, everyone," said Allison, gently rocking her red-faced, sleeping baby. "Meet Catheryn Cortese."

I had known that Mike and Allison intended to name their baby Catheryn. Months earlier Ali had asked whether that would be okay with me. Of course I had told her that I was pleased beyond words, but I hadn't really thought about it much since then. But now, when I heard Allison first speak her child's name, something broke inside me. I felt a sudden rush of emotion, a surge of feeling welling up from deep within that I hadn't experienced since Catheryn's memorial. Surprised by my reaction, I fought a stinging in my eyes, unable for a moment to speak.

Christy was first to hold Baby Catheryn. "Meet your Aunt Christy," said Allison, placing her child in Christy's arms. As she did, I sensed something pass between the two. It was a moment of both happiness and sorrow—a joyful looking toward the future and a sad glancing back. And as I witnessed the circle of life beginning anew, I wished with all my heart that Catheryn could have been there to see it.

Catheryn, and Tommy, too.

Next, as the others watched spellbound, Baby Catheryn went to Uncle Travis.

And then to Uncle Nate.

And then to me.

Holding Baby Catheryn in my arms, I again felt an unaccustomed flood of emotion. I recalled the toast I had made at Mike and Ali's wedding, not so long ago. Bitter and disillusioned and reeling from Catheryn's death, I had reminded everyone there that although life could be beautiful and filled with love, it could also be unimaginably cruel as well. I had noted that all of us were going to experience heartbreak and loss before we exited this world, adding that we were *all* going to be hurt, and get sick, and experience pain, and lose people we loved.

And all of that was true. But that unfortunate reality, I reminded myself again, was exactly what made cherishing moments like Baby Catheryn's birth so important, for it was just such moments that made life worth living.

As I cradled Baby Catheryn in my arms, surrounded by those I loved and who loved me, I wondered what the future would bring for her, what the future would bring for us all. When I had pondered that same question at Allison's wedding, I hadn't held much hope. Now, to my surprise, I found that something profound had shifted within me. Over the past months, when confronting the ache of Catheryn's loss and the heartbreak of Nate's illness and even the possibility of my own death, I had been forced to consider what was truly important in my life. And in doing so, I had come to accept that despite its tragedy and loss, life still continued . . . and that maybe the world was unfolding as it was meant to, even if I didn't understand each turn of the journey.

I knew there would be more ahead in life for all of us—beautiful, unpredictable, heartrending, joyous, meaningful events to come. But no matter what life might bring, I found that I once more had the will to face that future, for I now held a kernel of hope that in the end, everything would turn out as it should.

And if at times I didn't completely embrace that belief, at least I wanted to.

And that was a start.

Acknowledgments

I would like to express my appreciation to a number of people who provided their assistance while I was writing *Infidel*. Any errors, exaggerations, or just plain bending of facts to suit the story are attributable to me alone.

To Detective Lee Kingsford (LAPD, retired), I again owe a debt of gratitude. His gift of time, knowledge, and friendship once more proved invaluable during the preparation of the manuscript. To Susan Gannon, my wife and trusted muse with a sharp eye for detail, to friends and family for their encouragement and support, to my eBook editor Karen Oswalt, to Karen Waters for her help on the cover, and especially to my core group of readers—many of whom made suggestions for improvements—my sincere thanks.

If you enjoyed *Infidel*, please leave a reader review on Amazon or your favorite retail site. A word-of-mouth recommendation is the best endorsement possible, and your review would be truly appreciated and will help others like you look for books. Again, thanks for reading! ~ Steve Gannon

About the Author

STEVE GANNON is the author of the bestselling "Kane Novel" series, which includes *A Song for the Asking*, first published by Bantam Books. Gannon divides his time between Italy and Idaho, living in two of the most beautiful places on earth. In Idaho he spends his days skiing, whitewater kayaking, and writing. In Italy Gannon also continues to write, while enjoying the Italian people, food, history, and culture, and learning the Italian language. He is married to concert pianist Susan Spelius Gannon.

To contact Steve Gannon, purchase books, check out his blog, or to receive updates on new releases, please visit Steve's website at: stevegannonauthor.com

Printed in Great Britain
by Amazon

28873139R00195